Hannibal: Fields of Blood

Also by Ben Kane

Hannibal: Fields of Blood

BEN KANE

preface

Published by Preface 2013

2 4 6 8 10 9 7 5 3 1

Maps by John Gilkes

First published in Great Britain in 2013 by Preface Publishing
20 Vauxhall Bridge Road
London, SW1V 2SA

An imprint of The Random House Group Limited

www.randomhouse.co.uk
www.prefacepublishing.co.uk

Addresses for companies within The Random House Group Limited
can be found at www.randomhouse.co.uk

The Random House Group Limited Reg. No. 954009

A CIP catalogue record for this book is available from the British Library

ISBN 978 1 84809 235 8

The Random House Group Limited supports the Forest Stewardship
Council® (FSC®), the leading international forest-certification organisation.
Our books carrying the FSC label are printed on FSC®-certified paper. FSC
is the only forest-certification scheme supported by the leading environmental
organisations, including Greenpeace. Our paper procurement policy can be found at
www.randomhouse.co.uk/environment

Typeset in Fournier MT by Palimpsest Book Production Limited,
Falkirk, Stirlingshire

Printed and bound in Great Britain by Clays Ltd, St Ives plc

For Arthur, Carol, Joey, Killian and Tom: veterinary classmates
half a lifetime ago, and good friends still

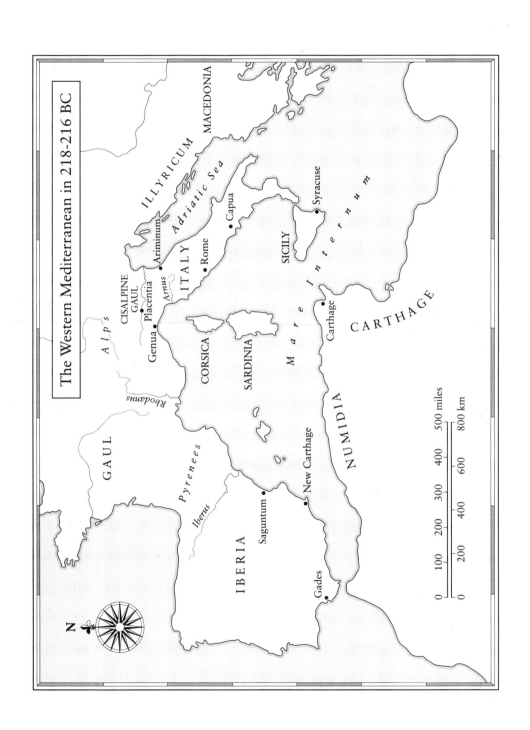

The Western Mediterranean in 218–216 BC

Hannibal's campaign in Italy, 218-216 BC

→ Hannibal's route

N

A l p s

CISALPINE GAUL

Placentia

Trebia

Padus

Genua

LIGURIA   ITALY

Pisae

Arnus

A p e n n i n e s

ETRURIA

Lake
Trasimene

Ariminum

ILLYRICUM

A d r i a t i c   S e a

Rome   LATIUM

CAMPANIA   SAMNIUM

Larinum   Gerunium

Cannae

Capua   *Aufidius*   Canusium

Venusia

Brundisium

Tarentum

CORSICA

SARDINIA

*T y r r h e n i a n
S e a*

*M
a
r
e*

*I
n
t
e
r
n
u
m*

Rhegium

*I o n i a n
S e a*

SICILY

Syracuse

Carthage

CARTHAGE

0	50	100	150	200 miles
0	100	200	300 km	

Chapter I

Cisalpine Gaul, winter

For the most part, the ground was flat, agricultural land that supplied grain for the nearby town. Green shoots of wheat a handsbreadth high were the only flash of colour in the frozen fields. Everything else had been turned silver-white by a heavy frost. The lowering clouds provided little contrast. Nor did the walls of Victumulae, which reared up, grey and imposing, in the distance. By the side of the road that ran to the gates lay a small, unremarkable copse.

Standing in the trees was a tall, rangy figure in a wool cloak. He had a thin face with a crooked nose and startlingly green eyes. Black curls escaped from the felt liner covering his head. His gaze darted restlessly over the terrain, but he saw nothing. It had been the same since he'd sent the sentry off to get some food. Hanno hadn't been watching for long, but already his feet were numb. He mouthed a curse. The cold wasn't going to go away. The ice was showing no signs of melting; nor had it for several days. A pang of homesickness. It was a different world from his childhood home on the north African coast, which he hadn't seen for almost two years. He could still picture the massive sandstone walls of Carthage, painted with whitewash so that the sunlight bounced off them. The magnificent Agora and, beyond it, the elaborate twin harbours. He sighed. Even in winter, his city was quite warm. And the sun shone most days, whereas here the only sign he had seen of it for a week was an occasional glimpse of a pale yellow disc through gaps in the murk overhead.

Peee-ay. Peee-ay. The characteristic cry made Hanno's head lift. Against the dull grey-white of the cloud, a couple of jackdaws jinked and turned, pursuing a hungry, and angry, buzzard. The familiar sight — the small birds harassing the larger one — felt ironic. Our task is far harder than theirs, he thought grimly. To learn that Carthage is its master, Rome has to bleed as it never has before. Once, Hanno would have doubted that could ever happen. His people had been decisively beaten by the Republic before in a bitter, drawn-out war that had ended a generation previously. The conflict had left a hatred of Rome in every Carthaginian's heart, but there had seemed no way of winning redress from the enemy. In the last month, however, the world had been turned on its head.

Only a madman would have believed that an army could be led hundreds of miles from Iberia to Cisalpine Gaul, crossing the Alps as winter began. Yet, driven by his desire to defeat Rome, Hannibal Barca had done just that. Strengthened by an alliance with local tribes, Hanno's general had smashed the large Roman force that had been sent to meet him. As a result, the whole of northern Italy lay open to attack, and against all probability Hanno, who had been enslaved near Capua, had escaped to join Hannibal. In doing so, he had been reunited with his father and brothers, who had thought him long since dead.

Now anything seemed possible.

Hanno's belly rumbled, reminding him of his mission to find food and gather intelligence. He wasn't here to watch the local fauna or to ponder the future. His phalanx of Libyan spearmen, hidden to his rear where the undergrowth afforded better concealment, needed supplies as much as he did. He had another purpose too. His eyes traced the line of the empty, muddy track that ran past his hiding place, arrowing through the fragile young wheat, straight to the town's front gate. There were fresh holes in the nearest icy puddles, evidence that some time that morning, a horse had been ridden hard towards the town. The sentry had told him about it. Hanno felt sure that it would have been a messenger carrying word to Victumulae of the Carthaginian army's approach.

A thin smile traced his lips at the thought of the alarm that would have caused.

Since Hannibal's stunning victory at the River Trebia, every Roman for a hundred miles had been living in fear of his life. Farms, villages and even smaller towns had been abandoned; terrified citizens had fled to anywhere that had thick walls and a garrison to defend them. The widespread panic had worked to the Carthaginians' advantage. Exhausted first by their harrowing crossing of the Alps and then by the savage battle with a double consular army, they had badly needed to rest and recuperate. Even so, hundreds of men – injured and whole – had died in the harsh weather that had followed the fighting. All but seven of the thirty-odd elephants had succumbed too. Ever the canny general, Hannibal had ordered his weakened forces to stay put. All non-essential military duties had ceased for a week. The deserted homesteads and farms had been a blessing, needing nothing more than men with accompanying mules to empty them of food and supplies.

These provisions soon ran out, however. So too did the foodstuffs offered by their new Gaulish allies. Thirty thousand men consumed a vast amount of grain daily, which was why the Carthaginians had broken camp the week before. At that very moment, they were marching on Victumulae. Word had it that the wheat stored behind its walls would feed them for weeks. Hanno's patrol was one of a number that had been sent out to reconnoitre the terrain in advance. He only had to return if he found evidence of an enemy ambush; otherwise, he could wait in the vicinity until the main force reached the town, which would be in the next day or two.

To his satisfaction, the countryside had been bare of nearly all human life. Apart from one clash with the enemy, from which they had emerged victorious, and a night spent in a friendly Gaulish village, it had been like travelling through a land inhabited by ghosts. Hannibal's cavalry, which was ranging far ahead of the infantry units, had brought more interesting news. Most of the survivors of the recent battle were holed up in Placentia, which lay some fifty miles to the southeast. Others had fled south, beyond the Carthaginians' reach, while an unknown number had sought refuge in places such as Victumulae. Despite the inevitability that the town would fall to Hannibal's superior forces, Hanno had taken the risk of moving closer to it than any of the cavalry units. He wanted to discover how many defenders they would face when the attack came, perhaps even strike a blow at an enemy patrol. Thus armed, he might be able to win his general's favour again.

3

It was unfortunate how things currently stood, he brooded. Ever since Hannibal had assembled a vast army and used it to take Saguntum, reopening hostilities with Rome, Hanno had longed for nothing more than to join the general in his struggle. What hot-blooded Carthaginian wouldn't have wanted to take revenge upon Rome for what it had done to their people? After being reunited with his family, things had started well. Hannibal had honoured Hanno with the command of a phalanx. Yet it had all gone wrong soon after that. Hanno's pulse quickened as he remembered recounting to Hannibal what he had done during an ambush on a Roman patrol a few days before the battle at the Trebia. Hannibal's fury at the news had been terrifying. Hanno had come within a whisker of being crucified. So too had Bostar and Sapho, his brothers, for not intervening. Since then, his general's disapproval would have been patent to a blind man.

In that ambush he had let two Roman cavalrymen – Quintus, his former friend, and Fabricius, Quintus' father – go free. Perhaps it had been foolish, Hanno mused. If he had just killed them and had done, life would have been far simpler. Instead, in an effort to wash away the stain on his good name, he had volunteered for every subsequent patrol, every dangerous duty going. So far, none of it had made the slightest difference. Hannibal had given no sign that he'd even noticed. Full of resentment, Hanno wriggled his toes inside his leather boots, trying to restore some sensation to them. His effort failed, irritating him further. Here he was, freezing not just his extremities but his balls off, on a mission that was doomed to failure. What chance had he of determining the enemy's strength in Victumulae? Of ambushing an enemy unit? With Hannibal's army closing in, the chances that any legionaries would be sent beyond the town's walls were slim to none.

Hanno checked his disgruntlement. He'd had good reason for acting as he had. Despite the fact that he was the son of Hanno's owner, Quintus had become a friend. It would have been wrong to have slain him, not least because he had owed Quintus his life twice over. A debt is a debt, Hanno thought. When the time is right, it has to be repaid, whatever the risk of punishment. He had survived Hannibal's subsequent wrath, and then the battle, had he not? That in itself was proof that he had done the right thing – that for the moment he held the gods' goodwill. Afterwards, Hanno had been careful to make generous sacrifices to Tanit, Melqart, Baal Saphon and Baal Hammon, the most important Carthaginian deities, thanking them for their protection. His chin lifted. With luck, he held their favour still. Something might yet come of his plan to gather intelligence.

He studied Victumulae with renewed interest. Thin trails of smoke drifted aloft from the inhabitants' chimneys, the only sign at this distance that the town had not been abandoned. The defences were impressive: behind a deep ditch, high stone walls with regular towers had been built. Hanno had little doubt that there would be catapults on the battlements as well. He and his men had no chance of success there. Along the eastern side of Victumulae wound the sinuous bends of the Padus, the great river that made the region so fertile. To the west lay more agricultural land; Hanno could see the shape of a large villa with its attendant cluster of outbuildings. Hope flared in his breast. Could someone be left within? It wasn't unreasonable to think that there might. So close to the walls, a stubborn landowner might still feel protected, might have emptied his house of valuables but chosen to remain until the enemy came into sight. Hanno made a snap decision. It was worth a try. They would advance under the cover of darkness, and if it came to nothing, they might at least find some food. If that strategy failed, he would have exhausted all possible avenues.

He hesitated. His plan meant the possibility of revealing his presence to the defenders. If they realised that his depleted phalanx was on its own, they might attack. In all likelihood, that would end with his and his soldiers' deaths. That won't happen, he told himself. Would they find anything of use, however? He fought the disappointment that met his lack of inspiration. More opportunities would come his way. He might win some glory in the taking of the town. If not then, perhaps in another battle. Hannibal would again come to see that he was worthy of trust.

The hours until darkness dragged by. Hanno's soldiers, who numbered fewer than two hundred, grew disgruntled as time went on. They had been cold and miserable for days, but until now they had been able to light fires each evening. Today, Hanno had banned them from doing so. His men had to make do with wearing their blankets as extra cloaks, and stamping up and down within the copse. Gambling that they would find supplies at the villa, he placated the soldiers by allowing them to eat the last of their rations. He spent the afternoon moving among them as Malchus, his father, had taught him. Making jokes, sharing pieces of his ration of dried meat, calling out dozens of names that he'd been careful to memorise.

The spearmen – in red tunics and conical bronze helmets such as those he had been used to seeing around Carthage since he was a small child – were nearly all veterans, old enough to have been his father. They had served in more campaigns than Hanno could imagine; had followed Hannibal from Iberia, over the Alps to the enemy's heartland, losing more than half their number in the process. Just a few weeks before, Hanno would have found commanding such troops daunting in the extreme. He had had some military training in Carthage but had never led an army unit. He'd had to learn fast, however, when appointed as these men's commander by Hannibal. That had happened after Hanno's near-miraculous escape from slavery, and journey north with Quintus. Since then, he had led the Libyans in an ambush and then through the savagery of the battle at the Trebia. There were still a few who threw him scornful glances when they thought he wasn't looking, but he seemed to have won the acceptance, even respect, of the majority. In a fortunate twist of fate, he had saved the life of Muttumbaal, his second-in-command, during their recent clash with the enemy. Mutt now regarded him with considerable respect, which no doubt aided Hanno's cause. As the light leached from the sky, he felt that these were the reasons that their grumbling had not developed into anything more threatening.

He waited until his hand was nothing but a blurred outline in front of his face before he gave the order to move. Most people went to bed soon after night fell. If there was anyone in the villa, they would be no different. With audible grunts of satisfaction, his soldiers tramped out of the trees. They raised and lowered their massive round shields, or thrust their spears up and down to loosen muscles that had stiffened in the cold. The mail shirts that many had taken from the fallen at the Trebia jingled. Sandals crunched across the frozen mud. Here and there, a muted cough. Growled orders from the officers had the men form up, twenty wide, ten deep. It wasn't long before they were ready. The air, thick with the soldiers' exhaled breath, grew tense. In the distance, Hanno could see red pinpricks moving slowly along the ramparts: the legionaries unfortunate enough to have drawn sentry duty. He grinned. The Romans on the wall had no idea that he and his phalanx were out there in the darkness, watching them. That their torches gave him sufficient light to plot a course towards the villa.

'Ready?' he hissed.

'Ready and willing, sir,' replied Mutt, a slight man with a perpetually doleful mien. It was inevitable that his cumbersome name had been shortened to 'Mutt'.

'We advance at the walk. Make as little sound as possible. No talking!' Hanno waited until his orders had been passed on and then, gripping his own shield and thrusting spear, he paced forward into the darkness.

It was hard to be sure, but Hanno stopped at what he estimated was three hundred paces from the town's walls. He indicated to Mutt that the men were to halt. Peering up at the battlements, he pricked his ears. Beyond catapult range, and out of sight, there was little chance that they would be discovered. When he heard the sentries talking to each other, his hope that they would pass unnoticed became certainty. Even still, the knot of tension in his belly tightened as he drew near to the darkened villa. It didn't help when he heard an owl calling. Hanno felt the hairs on his neck prickle, but he shoved the disquiet away. The sound did not signify bad luck to Carthaginians. He only knew of it because of his time in Quintus' household. All the same, he was glad that his men didn't know of the Roman superstition.

He crept on. The villa loomed out of the black, as silent as a vast tomb. Hanno's stomach clenched further, but he kept moving. Every damn household in Italy was the same at this time of night, he told himself. There were no dogs barking because they had all gone inside with the inhabitants. If that's the case, his inner demon shouted, you're not going to find out anything. You're a fool to think that they'll have left any food behind either. Every last morsel will be needed inside Victumulae.

Reminded of the pompous lectures that his oldest brother Sapho was so fond of giving him, Hanno set his jaw. In his search for intelligence, what he was doing made sense. There was no going back now, and they would be in and out in no time. His plan was for Mutt and most of his men to remain on guard outside, their job to listen out for any indication of troops approaching from the town. If that happened, Mutt was to give a prearranged whistle to alert Hanno so they could all withdraw in secret. While his second-in-command stood watch, four parties, ten strong each, were to move on to the property. One, under Hanno's command, would steal into the house itself while the others, each led by a dependable spearman, would search the farm buildings for supplies.

Hanno padded up to one of the small windows on the villa's south-facing wall and stared between the gaps in the closely spaced wooden slats. It was pitch black inside. He laid his ear against the cold shutters. He listened for a long time, but heard nothing. Reassured, he had the four files of men fall out.

'Be careful, sir,' whispered Mutt.

'I will. Remember, if there's any sign of Roman troops, you're to pull back. I don't want to lose men in a pointless clash.'

'And you, sir?'

'I'll be right behind you.' Hanno threw him a confident grin. 'To your position.'

Mutt saluted and withdrew. Hanno watched as most of the phalanx moved out of sight before he led his party forward. The three other files moved alongside his, the spearmen leading them parallel with Hanno. They paced along the length of the eastern wall, coming to a halt by the corner of the building that would open on to the courtyard. Before he exposed himself, Hanno took a couple of quick looks around the angle of the brickwork. The gloom afforded him little detail, but he discerned the outline of paved paths and manicured plants and trees: the household garden. A short distance away, towards the town, lay what looked like sheds, stables and a large barn. There was no sign of life. Feeling calmer, he eyed the three leading spearmen. 'Search every building. Take only food. Stay alert. If you meet any serious resistance, pull back. I want no heroics in the dark. Clear?'

'Yes, sir,' they whispered.

Hanno stepped around the corner; behind him, he sensed his soldiers following. There was a metallic *tap* as someone's spear knocked off the helmet of the man in front. Hanno shot a furious glare over his shoulder, but didn't pause. With luck, the sound wouldn't have been loud enough to wake anyone who might be inside the villa. He traced his way along the wall, searching for the main entrance. It was twenty paces further on. It was a typical heavy wooden door, its surface studded with metal, and it was closed. Hanno pressed his fingers against the timbers and pushed. Nothing happened, so he pushed a little harder. His efforts made no difference. His heart began to race. Could someone be within, or had the door just been locked when the residents left?

Hanno could feel the weight of his men's stares on his back. He ignored it as best he could. He was on the horns of a dilemma now. Anyone inside would be woken if he tried to force an entrance, but Hanno didn't want to walk away. If the house turned out to be empty, then he would have given up without even trying. He moved away from the door and looked up, gauging the height of the roof. Laying his shield and spear to one side, he beckoned to the three nearest soldiers. 'Bogu, you're to come with me.' As the shortest of the trio scurried over, Hanno pointed to the others. 'You two can give us a boost up.'

They gave him a blank look.

'Bogu and I will climb up, drop down the other side, and open the gate from within.'

'Shall I go in your stead, sir?' asked the older of the pair. 'Save you the trouble.'

Hanno didn't even consider the suggestion. His blood was up. 'No. It won't take us more than a few moments.'

Obediently, they shuffled in and made a bridge with their hands.

Hanno placed one foot on to their interlinked fingers. At once they swept him upwards. Throwing his arms forward to balance himself, he swung his free leg over and scrambled up on to the roof. The bottom of his bronze cuirass made a heavy, clunking sound as it connected with the tiles. *Shit!* Half kneeling, half upright, Hanno froze. For several heart-stopping moments, he heard nothing. Then the sound of someone moving into the courtyard. A cough, a snort. *Hoyc-thth* as the man spat. 'Fucking cats,' Hanno heard him mutter in Latin. 'Always wandering around on the roof.'

Hanno waited, his pulse racing, as the man slouched back to his post, right under his very position. It had to be a doorman, he thought. Which possibly meant that the master of the house was at home. What should he do? It only took an instant to decide. If he left without proceeding further, he would have to live with the regret that he might have discovered something useful to Hannibal. What risk could there be anyway? He and Bogu were more than a match for some old, unfit slave. The fool had probably gone back to sleep already.

He leaned over and indicated that Bogu should join him.

Hanno hissed a warning about Bogu's mail, and the soldier joined him on the roof with hardly a sound. 'I heard one man below,' Hanno whispered. 'I'll go first. You come down after.'

Taking great care not to let his cuirass or the tip of his scabbard touch the clay tiles, Hanno shuffled forward with bent knees. Reaching the apex of the roof, he stared downward. The courtyard within was typical, and resembled that in Quintus' house. Covered walkways ran around the rectangular space. Ornamental shrubs and statues dotted the fringes. Fruit trees and short rows of vines filled most of the rest of the area, which was dominated by a central fountain, now frozen into silence. Not a soul was to be seen.

Content, Hanno eased himself on to the inward-sloping face of the roof. He realised at once that to descend safely, he needed to sit down. That meant his cuirass would clash off the tiles again, alerting the doorman. There was only one thing for it. Stand up, start to walk down the roof. Pick up speed. Reach the roof's edge and jump. He filled Bogu in on his plan, ordering him to follow at once. Hanno expected to fall about his own height, landing on a mosaic floor. To roll and jump up, drag out his sword and kill the doorman before opening the portal to admit his soldiers.

He didn't expect to land on top of the doorman, who had wandered back outside.

Nor in fact was he a doorman. He was a veteran legionary, a *triarius*, in full armour.

Hanno realised there was something wrong as they fell in a tumble of flailing limbs. Unfortunately, he was the one who cracked his head on the ground. His helmet took much of the impact, but it couldn't prevent him from being momentarily stunned. In considerable pain, Hanno struggled to get his bearings. A punch from the enraged triarius didn't help either, snapping his chin back and knocking his helmet against the floor again. Somehow he managed to wriggle free of the other's grasping hands and clamber to his feet. The triarius did the same. In the flickering light cast by a lamp in a wall alcove, the pair studied one another, both equally stunned by what they saw.

What in Baal Hammon's name is a legionary doing here? thought Hanno, fighting panic. He won't be alone. 'Bogu! Get down here!'

'Gods above, you're one of Hannibal's men! Awake! Awake! We're under attack!' bellowed the Roman.

Hanno threw a glance at the door. His heart sank. It wasn't just bolted; there was a large lock as well. His gaze shot back to the triarius. A bunch of keys hung from his gilded belt. Cursing, Hanno ripped out his sword. Their only chance was to kill the Roman as fast as possible and let the rest of his men in.

Shouting again for his comrades, the triarius pulled out his *gladius*. 'Gugga filth!'

Hanno had been called a 'little rat' before, but the insult still stung. By way of answer, he aimed a savage thrust at the other's belly. He laughed as the triarius dodged to the side, unable to block it. 'Filth? You stink worse than a sow.'

A series of loud thumps on the roof presaged Bogu's arrival. The spearman had the sense to jump down on the far side of the triarius, who spat a loud curse. He couldn't fight with an enemy on each side. Rather than run, however, he bravely backed into the archway that framed the entrance, thereby stopping either Carthaginian from getting to the door.

The sound of raised voices in the courtyard told Hanno that time was of the essence. 'On him, Bogu!' he shouted. As the spearman advanced, Hanno feinted for the triarius' left foot but as the Roman tried to move out of range, Hanno brought his right hand up, smashing the hilt of his weapon into his opponent's face. With an audible *crunch*, the man's nose broke. There was a cry of agony and the triarius staggered back, blood pouring from his nostrils. Hanno followed him as a viper does a mouse. Deadly quick. With all his strength, he rammed his blade into the Roman's flesh just above the top of his mail shirt. Grating off the vertebrae in the man's spinal column, it sank in nearly to the crossguard. The triarius' eyes bulged; his mouth worked; bloody froth left his lips; he died.

Grunting with effort, Hanno pulled the sword out. He closed his eyes against the shower of blood that followed. The corpse sagged to the floor, and he stooped, frantically ripping the bunch of keys free. Hanno glanced to his rear and wished he hadn't. At least a dozen *triarii*, in various states of undress, were charging across the courtyard. 'Keep them back!' he screamed at Bogu. He spun to the door. Fists were pounding on it from the other side. 'Sir! Are you all right? Sir!' clamoured his men. Hanno didn't waste his breath answering. First, he slid open the bolt. Selecting a key, he shoved it into the massive lock and tried to twist it to the left. It wouldn't move. He moved it in the opposite direction. Nothing happened.

Frantically, he selected another key. Sandals slapped off the mosaic. Angry yells as the body was seen. Bogu screamed a battle cry. Then, the clash of arms not half a dozen steps behind him. Close. They were so close. Hanno fumbled with the key, unable to fit its bulky end into the hole. It took all of his effort not to scream. Forcing himself to slow down, he managed to insert it into the lock. It fitted better than the previous two, and his hopes rose. A turn to the left didn't work. Undaunted, Hanno had begun wrenching it to the right when he heard someone emit a strangled gasp of pain. 'I'm hurt, sir!' hissed Bogu.

Hanno made the fatal mistake of twisting his head to look. As he did, two triarii charged at the same time. Bogu shoved his spear at the one without a *scutum*, but that allowed the other to close with him. Driving his shield into the spearman, the triarius rammed Bogu against the wall. As Hanno realised, it wasn't to kill the spearman. It was to allow the Roman's comrades to barge past – towards him. Too late, he turned. Too late, he tried to engage the key in the lock's mechanism. An instant later, something smashed into the back of his head. Stars burst across his vision. His world narrowed to a tunnel before him. All he could see was his hand, which was slowly letting go of the key. A key that had not turned enough to open the lock. In the distance, he could hear his soldiers' shouts mingling with those of the triarii. He wanted to shout, 'I'm coming,' but his voice wouldn't work. His strength had gone too, and there was nothing Hanno could do to stop his knees from buckling.

Then everything went black.

Hanno woke, coughing and spluttering, as a tide of icy water was emptied over his head. Fear and rage surged through him as he tried to get his bearings. He was lying on the flat of his back on a cold stone floor – where, he had no idea. He struggled to rise, but his arms and legs were bound. Trying to ignore the worst headache he could remember, Hanno blinked to clear his eyes of water. Two men – triarii from the look of them – were studying him, sneers twisting their faces. Above them, the low roof of a cell. Panic made his heart flutter. Where in hell's name was he?

'Enjoyed your little sleep?' asked the man on his left, a shifty-looking type with a wall eye.

'You've been out for long enough,' added his companion in a falsely solicitous tone. 'But now it's time for a little chat.'

Hanno sensed that would involve a lot of pain. He strained his ears. There was no sound of fighting. No clash of arms. His heart sank. Mutt and his men were gone – if he was even still in the villa.

A scornful laugh from the first man, who saw what he was doing. 'You'll get no help here. We're safe inside Victumulae.'

A moan. Hanno's gaze shot to his left. Bogu was lying a few paces away. A large bloodstain on the tunic over his belly and a wound to his lower right leg didn't bode well.

It's just me and Bogu. Hanno spat several ripe curses in Carthaginian.

Another snort of amusement. 'Wondering why your men didn't break down the door, eh?'

That *was* what Hanno was thinking, but he kept his face blank. They would have no idea that he could speak Latin.

'They pissed off as soon as we sounded the alarm,' said the second soldier to his comrade. 'We couldn't believe our luck. They must have thought reinforcements would be sent out from the town. Stupid bastards.'

A tide of weariness washed over Hanno. They were just following my orders, he thought.

The second man leered. 'If only they'd known that the sound of the trumpets was all the back-up we were going to get!'

Hanno felt sick at the very thought. He closed his eyes, but the kick to his ribs that followed made them shoot open again with pain. He tried to roll away from the next kick, and it caught him in the back instead. He steeled himself for the next.

'Enough,' snapped a voice. 'I'll decide how and when he and the other maggot are to be punished.'

The sound of men snapping to attention. 'Yes, sir. Sorry, sir.'

'Get him up.'

Hanno felt hands grabbing him under his armpits; he was lifted to a standing position. His surroundings were grim: a square, stone-flagged chamber with no windows. Three small lamps shed enough light to see the damp running down the walls and the table to one side upon which sat a frightening array of metal instruments, every one of them barbed or sporting a cruel blade. A glowing brazier promised more varieties of pain. Watched in impassive silence by the officer who had entered, Hanno's arms were raised and the rope around his wrists was looped over a hook that dangled from the ceiling. As his shoulder sockets took his entire body weight, Hanno's agony reached new heights. Desperate, he reached down with his feet. The floor was agonisingly close – he could brush it with the tips of his sandals, but couldn't support himself for more than a few moments. Gasping with frustration and pain, he looked up.

To Hanno's utter shock, he recognised the stocky officer – square-chinned, clean-shaven, about thirty-five – before him. It was the man who'd been beneath his blade during the fight with a Roman patrol a week or more earlier. The enemy he had let live, so that he could save Mutt's life. *I should have killed him.* Hanno felt terrible for even thinking such a thing. Doing that would have ensured this man's death, but also that of Mutt. *He* would still be a prisoner, and merely faced with a different torturer. Hanno noted that the man did not appear to have recognised him. There was a tiny chance that that might work to his advantage. He held fiercely on to that hope.

The officer gave him a mirthless smile. 'Excruciating, isn't it? Count yourself lucky that I didn't tell them to tie your hands behind your back first. That would have dislocated your shoulders the moment they hauled you aloft.' A scowl when Hanno didn't answer. 'You can't understand a word I say, can you?'

Hanno said nothing.

'Hang the other one up too,' commanded the officer.

Hanno watched with helpless rage as Bogu was dragged up, moaning, and suspended beside him. Eventually, the spearman's eyes came into focus; he tried to smile, but grimaced instead. 'We'll be fine,' Hanno whispered.

''S'll right, sir. You don't need to lie to me.'

Hanno's next words died in his throat. Fresh blood had already soaked through Bogu's tunic from his belly wound. They were both going to die in this room. Bogu knew it. He knew it. There was no point pretending. 'May the gods give us a safe passage.'

'Silence!' cried the officer. He clicked his fingers. 'Find me that gugga slave who was mentioned earlier.'

'Yes, sir.' The wall-eyed soldier moved towards the door.

'There's no need for the slave. I speak Latin well enough,' said Hanno.

The officer mastered his shock well. 'How do you know my tongue?' he barked.

'I had a Greek tutor as a boy.'

The officer's eyebrows rose. 'A civilised gugga, eh?'

'Plenty of us are well educated,' replied Hanno stiffly.

A surprised look. 'Does your man also speak Latin?'

'Bogu? No.'

'There are differences between the classes then, as there are here,' mused the officer, with a scornful glance at his soldiers. 'Your Latin accent is not that of a Greek-speaker, though. It sounds more as if you come from Campania.'

It was Hanno's turn to feel startled. Yet it wasn't surprising that he spoke like Quintus and his family. 'I have lived in southern Italy,' he admitted.

The Roman prowled closer. He pushed Hanno between the shoulders so that he swung forward, off the tips of his toes. His arms wrenched back in their sockets, and Hanno bawled with pain. 'Don't lie to me!' shouted the officer.

Desperate to relieve the pressure on his shoulders, Hanno pushed downwards with all the power in his legs and managed – just – to stop himself from swinging back and having the agony rip through him again. 'I–It's true. I was captured at sea between Carthage and Sicily with a friend of mine. We were sold into slavery. A Campanian family bought me. I lived near Capua for over a year.'

'What's your owner's name?' demanded the officer, quick as a flash.

Hanno's pride reared up. 'I don't have an owner.'

A punch in the solar plexus knocked the air from his lungs; more pain as his shoulders took the strain of his body weight. An involuntary retch brought up a little fluid from his stomach.

The officer waited a moment before shoving his face into Hanno's purple, wheezing one. 'I doubt very much whether your master granted you manumission so that you could fuck off and join Hannibal's army. If he didn't, that means that you're still his slave. Understand?'

Arguing was futile, but Hanno was furious. 'Being captured by pirates doesn't turn me into a damn slave. I'm a free man. A Carthaginian!'

His reward was another powerful punch. Hanno vomited what liquid remained in his belly. He was sorry that it didn't hit the officer's feet, but the Roman had stepped well back. He waited patiently until Hanno had finished. Then he muttered in Hanno's ear, 'If you've been sold to a Roman citizen, you're his slave whether you like it or not. I'm not going to argue about it, and if you've any sense, neither are you. What's your master's name?'

'Gaius Fabricius.'

'Never heard of him.'

Hanno waited for another punch, but it didn't land. 'His wife's called Atia. They have two children, called Quintus and Aurelia. Their farm is about half a day's walk from Capua.'

'Continue.'

Hanno described the details of his life in Quintus' household, including his relationships with Quintus and Aurelia, and the visit of Caius Minucius Flaccus – an extremely high-ranking nobleman – to their house. He didn't mention Agesandros, the overseer who had made his life a misery, or his search for Suniaton, his friend.

'All right, that's enough. Maybe you were a slave in Capua.' The officer's gaze became calculating. 'So you ran away when you heard Hannibal had entered Cisalpine Gaul?'

Hanno was damned if he was going to pretend that he had skulked off like a wolf in the night. 'No. Quintus, my master's son, let me go.'

Disbelief twisted the officer's face. 'You expect me to believe that?'

'It's true.'

An incredulous hiss. 'Where was his father while this was going on? And his mother?'

'Fabricius was away with the army. Atia had no idea what Quintus was up to.'

'What a little viper! Not a son I'd wish to have.' The officer shook his head. 'This is all neither here nor there, however. What's far more import- ant is discovering why you and your men were prowling around that villa at night.'

It didn't matter if the officer knew, thought Hanno. 'I hoped to find someone who knew how many defenders there are in the town.'

'And you did! Me!' crowed the officer. 'But I'm not going to tell you.'

You prick.

'So you were scouting for Hannibal?'

Hanno nodded.

'They say his army is heading here. Is that correct?'

'Yes.'

A heartbeat's pause. 'How many soldiers has he?'

'Fifty thousand or so,' lied Hanno.

The officer's face grew thunderous, and Hanno felt a dark joy. 'More Gauls arrive to join him every day.' The instant the truthful words had left his mouth, Hanno knew that he'd pushed the officer too far. The next punch was the hardest yet. Hanno felt pain so intense that he blacked out. He came to with the officer slapping him across the face.

'You think that's bad? It's nothing compared to the suffering to come. You'll be nothing but a shell when my men have finished with you.'

Hanno's eyes followed the officer's to the tools on the table. He felt his gorge rise. How long before he was begging for mercy? Pissing himself?

Would he be granted a quick end if he mentioned sparing the Roman's life? Shame filled him. *Have some pride!*

'Roman scum,' croaked Bogu in poor Latin. 'Wait. For . . . pain . . . Hannibal's army inflict . . . you. Hannibal . . . better general than any . . . you have.'

Hanno shot a warning look at Bogu, but it was too late.

'Heat me an iron!' cried the officer. He stalked over and drove a balled fist right into the middle of the bloodstain on Bogu's belly.

Bogu roared in agony, and the officer laughed.

'Leave him alone. He's injured!' shouted Hanno.

'Which means he'll talk more easily. When the dog dies, I'll still have you.'

Hanno felt instant relief, but guilt tore at him because Bogu would suffer first. Perhaps that had been the spearman's motive, though.

'Fetch that gugga slave! I need to understand what this injured piece of shit says, and I can't trust the other to translate.'

The wall-eyed soldier beat a hasty exit.

The officer stood over the brazier, tapping his foot with impatience until the second legionary declared that the iron was hot enough. Using a thick piece of blanket, the Roman seized the cool end of the instrument and held it aloft. Hanno's skin crawled. The tip was a bright orange-red colour. He struggled to free his wrists, but all he did was hurt himself even more.

'This might stop the bleeding,' mused the officer.

Bogu's eyes bulged with horror as the Roman casually approached but, to Hanno's admiration, he did not utter a word.

Hissss. The officer scowled with concentration, twisting the iron around in the spearman's belly wound.

Bogu let out a long, ear-splitting shriek.

'You cruel bastard!' roared Hanno, forgetting his own pain.

The officer whirled around, thrusting the still-glowing end at Hanno's face. Terrified, he shoved backward with the tips of his toes until he could go no further. Grinning, the Roman brought it within a finger's width of his right eye. 'Do you want a piece of this as well?'

Hanno couldn't answer. He was still aware of Bogu's screams, but it was taking all of his strength to hold himself still. He could already feel the muscles in his legs protesting, could feel cramp developing in his toes. A few heartbeats, and his eyeball would rupture on the red-hot iron. Great Baal Saphon, he prayed. Help me!

The door opened, and the wall-eyed soldier entered. He was followed by a brown-skinned man in a threadbare tunic. With his tight, curly black hair and dark complexion, he could have been any one of thousands of Hanno's fellow Carthaginians. The officer turned, lowering his iron. 'Finally.' He gave the slave a hard look. 'You speak Latin?'

'Yes, sir.' The slave glanced at Hanno and Bogu. A flicker of emotion flared in his brown eyes, but it was instantly masked.

'Good. I want you to interpret every word that this wretch says.' The iron stabbed towards Bogu before the officer replaced it in the brazier and selected another. 'How big is Hannibal's host?'

The slave translated.

Bogu mumbled something.

'What did he say?' demanded the officer.

'It's greater than any army that Rome can raise,' said the slave warily.

'Gods above, this one is also too stupid to give me the truth!' The officer leaned down and laid the iron on to the shallow cut on Bogu's left thigh. More hissing. More roars of pain. Bogu moved his leg away, but he was too weak to stop the Roman from following it with the hot metal. 'It's fifty thousand strong,' he shouted.

The slave repeated his words in Latin.

The officer's eyes swivelled to Hanno, who would have shrugged if he could. 'That's what I told you.' He thought that the Roman had swallowed the bait, but the scowl that followed soon told him otherwise.

The officer went searching through the instruments on the table. There was an exclamation of delight as he lifted a length of iron the end of which had been fashioned into the shape of a letter 'F'. He brandished it at Hanno in triumph. 'See this? F stands for *fugitivus*. You won't survive our little session here, but with this mark on you, there'll be no way of forgetting what you are during whatever time is left to you.'

Hanno watched with rising dismay as the length of metal was pushed into the brazier's heart. He had seen a runaway slave who'd been branded in a similar way once before. The puckered F on the man's forehead had filled him with revulsion. Now he was to endure the same fate. He writhed in his bonds, trying to free his wrists. All he did was to send waves of fresh torment through his arms and shoulders.

The officer seized another hot iron and approached Bogu again.

'Who are these men, sir?' ventured the slave.

The officer paused. 'They're soldiers who answer to Hannibal. We captured them outside the walls.'

'Hannibal?' repeated the slave slowly.

'That's right, you idiot!' The officer raised his iron in threat and the man cowered away.

I'd wager that your heart is singing at the idea, thought Hanno. As mine is. Let the gods bring our army to the gates soon. Give this monster and his henchmen a lingering death. But he knew that his family and his comrades would come too late for Bogu – and for him.

It was time to prepare for death as best he could.

Chapter II

Outside Placentia

In the initial panic after the defeat at the Trebia, Quintus and his father had been but two of the hordes who had fled to the safety granted by the town's walls. Sempronius Longus, the consul who had led the Roman army into battle and who had brought ten thousand legionaries clear of the slaughter, had arrived not long after. So too had Publius Cornelius Scipio, the second consul, whose ability to command in the field had ended after he sustained an injury in an earlier clash at the River Ticinus. Placentia had rapidly been filled to bursting point. After only two days and amid much consternation, Longus had ordered the gates to be opened. The consul had held his nerve. Nearly all of the men within had been marched outside. Under Longus' personal direction, half his men had stood guard while the remainder constructed a large marching camp. As one of the few cavalrymen who had made it back, Quintus had promptly been sent on patrol. His job had been to warn his comrades about any Carthaginian troops in the vicinity.

The first day had been the worst by far. He, his father Fabricius and about two score riders – stragglers from many units – had scouted five miles and more to the west of Placentia, territory that was now under enemy control. His mind still full of the carnage caused by Hannibal's army, Quintus had been jittery; some in the patrol had been terrified. Fabricius had been the exception: calm, alert, measured. His example had been an inspiration to Quintus and, after a while, it had rubbed off on the others too. The fact that they'd seen no enemy cavalry had helped. Word of Fabricius' leadership spread, and in the days that followed, every Roman rider to reach Placentia placed themselves under his command. He had been tough with them, insisting on twice-daily patrols as well as hours of training. Quintus had received no special favours. If anything, Fabricius had been harder on him than the others. Extra duty details had become Quintus' norm. He assumed that it stemmed from his father's disapproval of his release of Hanno and his own unapproved journey north to join the army, so he gritted his teeth, did what he was told and said nothing. This morning, Fabricius had unexpectedly been called to meet with the consuls, which meant a welcome break from Quintus' and his comrades' daily drudgery. They would have to go on patrol, but not until the afternoon. Quintus decided to make the most of it.

Together with Calatinus, a sturdily built man and the only one of his friends to have survived the Trebia, he ambled into Placentia. They soon lost their good humour, however, and their appetite for adventure wasn't long following. The majority of the troops might now be living outwith the walls, but the narrow streets were as packed as ever. From the ordinary citizens to the officers and soldiers who shoved their way through the throng, everyone they saw looked miserable, starved or angry. The shop-keepers' cries had a sour, demanding note that jarred on the ear, as did the incessant bawling of hungry babies. The beggars' numbers appeared to have doubled since the last time Quintus had been within the walls. Even the half-clad whores who leered at them from the rickety steps up to their wretched apartments were charging double their normal rates. Despite the cold, the smell of piss and shit was all pervading. Some food-stuffs had run out; what remained was being sold at extortionate prices. Wine had become the preserve of the rich. Rumour had it that supplies would soon start arriving up the River Padus from the coast, but that hadn't happened yet. Chilled, ravenous and irritable, the pair abandoned the town. Avoiding their tent lines in case Fabricius had returned, they made for the southern edge of the encampment that now housed Longus' battered army. If nothing else, they would stretch their legs crossing the huge area.

They took the shortest route, the *via principalis*, or central track that bisected the camp. Every so often, they had to move out of the way as a century of legionaries marched out from their tent lines and headed south. Calatinus grumbled, yet Quintus cast sly but admiring looks at the foot soldiers. He had always looked down on infantry before. Not now. They weren't just the earth-digging, foot-slogging fools that cavalrymen referred to. The legionaries were the only section of the army that had given a good account of themselves against Hannibal, while the cavalry had much to do in order to regain the honour that had been lost at the Trebia.

The central area that housed the consuls' headquarters faced on to the via principalis and was marked by a *vexillum*, a red flag on a pole. The ground before the group of sprawling tents was a hive of activity. In addition to the normal guards, there were messengers on horseback arriving and leaving, small groups of centurions deep in conversation and a party of trumpeters awaiting orders. A couple of enterprising traders had even managed to set up stalls selling fresh bread and fried sausages, the price of their entry no doubt a decent contribution of their stock to the officer in charge of the gate.

'No sign of your father.' Calatinus gave him a broad wink. 'He'll be deep in conversation with Longus and the other senior officers, eh? Plotting our best course of action.'

'Probably.' Quintus' humour soured even more. 'Which I'll hear nothing about until the time comes to implement it.'

'Same as the rest of us!' Calatinus gave him a reassuring thump on the arm. 'Things could be worse. Hannibal's left us alone for weeks now. Our position here is strong, and the ships will start arriving up the Padus soon. Before you know it, we'll have reinforcements as well.'

Quintus made an effort to smile.

'What is it?' Calatinus cocked his head. 'Still worried about your father forcing you to return home?'

A nearby soldier gave them an inquisitive glance.

'Not so loud!' muttered Quintus, increasing his pace. 'Yes, I am.' When he'd been reunited with Calatinus after the Trebia, their friendship had reached a new level. They had talked a great deal, and he had revealed everything about Hanno, and Fabricius' anger at Quintus' unexpected arrival not long before the first clash at the Ticinus.

'He's not going to make you leave. He can't. We need every man we can get!' Calatinus saw Quintus flush. 'You know what I mean by that. You're a trained cavalryman, and they're like hen's teeth right now. Whatever crime you might have committed in your father's eyes is irrelevant at this moment in time.' Calatinus blew out his chest. 'You and I are valuable material!'

'I suppose.' Quintus wished he felt so sure. Yet, lifted by Calatinus' good humour, he managed to put the matter from his mind.

Reaching the camp's southern edge, they clambered up a ladder to the top of the earthen ramparts, which were ten paces high and half a dozen deep. The wall's outer face had been lined with sharpened branches; a deep defensive ditch lay beyond that. The fortifications were robust, but Quintus had no desire to see them put to the test. The memory of their defeat at Hannibal's hands was yet raw. Morale was fragile, not least his own. Brooding again, he studied the horizon with great intensity. No enemy forces had been sighted for days, but that didn't mean today would be the same. To his relief, Quintus could see no life on the broken ground that ran from the town down to the thick silver band that was the River Padus. On the road that snaked off to Genua and beyond, a few boys were herding sheep and goats to pasture, and an old man with a mule and a cart full of firewood limped towards the main gate. The flatter area to his left was full of legionaries being drilled. Their officers roared, blew whistles and waved their vine canes. Part of Quintus would have liked to study the foot soldiers. But mostly he wanted to forget about fighting and war, for a few hours at least. He glanced at Calatinus. 'See anything?'

Calatinus shrugged his broad shoulders. 'I'm glad to say "no".'

All was as it should be. Satisfied, Quintus studied the mounds of ominous-looking clouds that were scudding overhead. A biting wind from the Alps was speeding them southwards, and more were following in their wake. He shivered. 'There'll be snow before nightfall.'

'You're not wrong there,' Calatinus said irritably. 'And if it's as bad as it was the other day, we'll be stuck in the damn camp for a couple of days afterwards.'

A sudden devilment took Quintus. 'Let's go hunting then, while we have the chance.'

'Have you lost your wits?'

Quintus poked him. 'I don't just mean you and me! We'll gather up ten men or so. Enough of us to make it safe.'

'Safe?' Calatinus' voice was disbelieving, but he punched Quintus back. 'I'm not sure that there is any such thing as "safe" any more, but a man can't live in fear forever. What are you thinking – a deer, maybe?'

'If Diana aids us, yes. Who knows? We might even spot a boar.'

'Now you're talking.' Calatinus was already halfway down the ladder that they'd used to climb up to the rampart. 'With enough meat, we can barter for wine.'

Quintus followed, his spirits rising at that thought.

Some time later, Quintus was wondering if his idea had been rash. He and his companions, ten men in all, had ridden several miles through the woods to the east of Placentia. Finding a fresh game trail had proved far harder than he had anticipated. Despite the cover granted by the mixed beech and oak trees, the harsh weather had frozen the ground to one great block of ice. There were old tracks aplenty, but in many places it was impossible to see any newer marks made by passing wild animals. They'd had one sighting: a couple of deer, but the startled creatures had fled long before any of the men with bows could let off an accurate shot.

'We're going to have to turn around soon,' Quintus muttered.

'Aye,' said Calatinus. 'Your father will have our heads on a plate if we're not back in time for our patrol.'

Quintus grimaced. He tugged on his mount's reins. 'We might as well go now. Diana isn't in a good mood. I don't think that's about to change.'

There were grunts of agreement from those who were within earshot; shouts rang out, calling in those who had been riding further away. No one disagreed with Quintus' suggestion that they return to Placentia. Everyone was chilled to the bone, and eager not to miss the hot meal that would be served before their afternoon patrol.

The narrow paths meant that they had to ride in single file. Quintus took the lead; Calatinus came next. The idle banter that had filled the early part of the hunt had died away to an occasional lament about how cold and hungry a particular man was, or about how much he wanted to spend a night in an inn by a fire, drinking until dawn. If there was an attractive whore to take him upstairs as well, all the better. Quintus had heard such talk a hundred times, so it went in one ear and out the other. His horse seemed to know the route to take, allowing his mind to wander. He thought of the letter that Fabricius had written, to which he had added a footnote, and hoped that it had reached his mother. His sister Aurelia might grieve the death of Caius Minucius Flaccus, her betrothed, but at least she'd know that he and their father were alive. That they would return one day.

Feeling happier, he lapsed into a pleasant daydream about home, near Capua. He and his father were there with Atia, his mother; so too was Aurelia. The family were reclining on couches around a table piled high with dishes of succulent fare. A side of roast pork. Mullet fried with herbs, and bream that had been baked in the oven. Sausages. Olives. Freshly baked bread. Greens. He could almost reach out and touch the food. Quintus felt saliva pooling in his mouth. An image of Hanno walking into the room with a platter of fowl in a rich nut sauce popped into his mind, and he blinked. Was his mind playing tricks? With the gods' help, he would dine with his family again, but Hanno would not be present. The Carthaginian had honoured his debt, but he was now one of the enemy. Quintus had little doubt that Hanno would kill him if he got the chance. He, Quintus, would have to do the same if it came to it. He sent up a prayer that that day never arrived. It wasn't too much to ask that he never met Hanno again.

These dark thoughts made his brief good mood vanish. A sour squint to either side, and Quintus judged that they were about halfway back to the camp. The time will go by fast, he told himself, but his ploy wasn't convincing. There was a good distance to go yet. His feet were frozen in his sandals. The brazier in his tent at which he might thaw them out before the patrol seemed half a world away.

The dim sound of a whistle didn't register for a couple of heartbeats.

Then it was repeated, and the staccato hammering of a woodpecker some distance away came to a halt. There was a shriek of alarm from a blackbird, and another. Quintus felt sweat breaking out on his forehead. There were men nearby. Diana had not forsaken them after all, because the wind was blowing into his face, so he had heard whoever had whistled rather than the other way around. He turned and raised the flat of his hand towards Calatinus, the signal to halt.

His friend, who was twenty paces to his rear, peered to the front. 'Deer?' he asked in a hopeful voice.

'No. We've got company! Tell the others to shut the hell up!'

Calatinus' mouth worked in surprise, but then Quintus' words sank in. He twisted around on his horse. 'Quiet! Someone's out there. Quiet!'

More whistles. Quintus scanned the trees in front of him, looking for movement of any kind. He was grateful for the wide gaps between the leafless trunks and the lack of undergrowth, which made it hard to hide. The ground before him dropped away gradually, leading down to a small, pattering stream some distance away. They had crossed it a short way into the woods. Instinct told him that whoever was calling had no idea of his or his comrades' presence. The tone of the whistle wasn't urgent. It felt more like a message to let one hunter know where another one was. It wouldn't be other Romans – or at least that was doubtful. Since the Trebia, few men were inclined to go far from Placentia unless they were part of a strong force. That meant the men he'd heard were Carthaginian, or more likely Gaulish tribesmen. His guts churned.

He had vivid memories of what some Gauls – so-called Roman allies – were capable of. Both he and Calatinus had been fortunate to survive a night attack soon after their arrival in which scores of their fellows had been decapitated. The scarlet tracks left in the snow as the Gauls fled with their trophies still haunted him. At the Trebia, Quintus had been attacked and nearly slain by Gauls who'd had heads hanging from their mounts' harnesses. That memory made red rage coat his vision for an instant. He had a bone to pick with any, and every, tribesman who fought for Hannibal. Blinking away his fury, Quintus took a deep breath. Caution was vital here. He and his comrades could have been followed into the woods. They could be outnumbered. There might even be an ambush set.

An odd calm descended over him. Maybe he was to die here. If that were the case, he would die like a man. Like a Roman. Taking plenty of the enemy with him.

Letting the reins drop to the ground, Quintus slipped off his horse and padded back to Calatinus. 'Let's go and take a look.'

'And the rest?'

'They can wait here. If we don't return soon, they're to make their own way back.'

Calatinus nodded. Quickly, they conferred with the eight other riders, who looked most unhappy. When the whistle rang out again, any trace of their earlier good mood disappeared completely.

'Gods know how many warriors that could be. We won't wait for long,' warned the oldest, a taciturn man called Villius.

'Give us enough time to see who's out there,' snapped Quintus. 'Otherwise you could ride into a trap. They could be all around us.'

Villius gauged his companions' mood. 'All right. But on the count of a thousand, we're riding away.'

'That might not be sufficient,' protested Quintus.

'I don't care.' Villius' tone was snide. 'I'm not hanging around here to be butchered by Gaulish savages.'

There was a chorus of agreement.

Quintus shot a furious glance at Calatinus, who shrugged. He swallowed his anger. Their comrades' reaction wasn't surprising, and this was no time to hesitate. 'Start counting.' He turned his back on Villius' sour smile. With his spear at the ready and Calatinus two steps behind, Quintus loped off. 'You keep count as well,' he growled.

'Fine. One. Two. Three . . .' answered Calatinus.

Quintus silently matched his friend's speed. They came first to Calatinus' horse, and then his own, muttering calming words to both beasts as they passed. Quintus' gaze roved from left to right at speed, taking in every detail. *Thirty-eight. Thirty-nine.* An old forked beech, taller than a block of flats in Capua. A spider web on a bush, its radiate patterns picked out by the frost. Leaves frozen to the ground singly, in piles, on the surface of puddles. Above them, bare branches rose up in a meshwork of layers to the grey sky. A dead oak, its gnarled trunk blackened and cracked by a lightning strike, leaning against the tree next to it, as if drunk. A flash of colour in the branches as a woodpecker – the one he'd heard? – flitted off in alarm. Quintus paused, but he could see nothing ahead. He hadn't heard any fresh whistles either. The bird must have taken fright at their arrival. His pulse rate didn't decrease, however, and he had to keep wiping the sweat from his eyes. He glanced around, saw his friend's knuckles white on the haft of his spear, but Calatinus gave him a determined grin. Reassured, Quintus kept moving. *Two hundred and fifty-five. Two hundred and fifty-six.*

They had had a couple of glimpses through the trees, but as the slope bottomed out, Quintus had his first decent view of the stream. He peered at it from the concealment of a chunky beech. Calatinus tumbled in beside him. It was as he'd remembered, with a narrow grassy bank on this side, and trees right down to the edge on the other. The watercourse was mostly shallow, but with a deeper, rocky section in the middle. Spray rose into the air as the water struck the boulders. The stream was easy enough to ford on a horse, but slippery and cold for a man on foot.

'Where the hell are they?' whispered Calatinus. 'Were we imagining the whistling?'

'You know we weren't.' *Four hundred. Four hundred and one.* Quintus considered going down the slope, but this was as far as they could go without the risk of the others leaving. Calatinus knew it too.

They watched in silence.

Flakes of snow began twirling down from above. They came almost dreamily at first, but it wasn't long before they were falling in earnest. The visibility began to deteriorate. It might have been Quintus' imagination, but the temperature dropped as well.

'My count is four hundred and seventy-five,' Calatinus announced. 'What's yours?'

Quintus sighed. His breath plumed before him. 'Four hundred and sixty.'

'You know that that piece of shit Villius will ride off the moment he reaches a thousand?'

'We can run all the way back. That will shave a hundred, a hundred and fifty off the total.'

Calatinus scowled, but to Quintus' pleasure, he didn't move.

They gazed down at the stream, their muscles stiffening in the cold. Quintus reached five hundred and eighty without seeing anything untoward. He decided that whoever he had heard must have moved off in another direction. It had all been nothing to worry about. He turned. 'Time to go, then.'

There was no immediate answer.

Quintus was about to nudge his friend when he saw the look in Calatinus' eyes. His head swivelled. It took all his self-control not to gasp out loud. There was a man – a warrior – halfway across the stream. Bulky in his wool cloak, he wore the patterned trousers and boots of a Gaul. He carried a long hunting spear. Behind him, two more men, similarly dressed, had emerged on the far side and were wading into the water. Both had arrows fitted to the strings of their bows. As the first warrior reached the near bank, he hailed a fourth figure, who had come out of the trees opposite.

'Are they looking for us?' Calatinus' lips were by Quintus' ear.

'No. They're hunting. D'you agree?'

'Aye. The whoresons are relaxed.'

Quintus studied the hunters with care. No more had appeared, but that didn't mean there weren't more coming through the trees on the far bank. Already the first man was climbing towards them. His nerves jangled. 'We can't stay.'

'I know.' Calatinus' lips twitched. 'The count must be nearing six hundred by now.'

Walking backwards until they could no longer see the stream, they stole away for perhaps a hundred paces. Then, after a look back towards where the warriors would emerge, they began to run. Hard.

'What in Hades should we do?' asked Calatinus. 'They're blocking the way back to the camp. That was the only ford we found.'

'We could try to go around them.'

'Easier said than done.'

'It's that, or we ride straight at the bastards. And pray that there aren't twenty others taking up the rear.'

Frost crackled beneath their feet as they ran.

An attack was risky, thought Quintus, but it was the best option. Trying to avoid the Gauls seemed cowardly, especially when they were so few. 'I say that we attack,' he said, willing his heart to slow down.

'Me too,' muttered Calatinus. 'I want revenge for what happened at the Trebia.'

Quintus gave his friend a fierce grin. United, they had a better chance of convincing their comrades.

They made it back just as the others were riding away. Quintus' low, urgent cry caught their attention, and they wheeled their horses about as the pair charged up. A few looked ashamed that they'd not waited, but Villius' lip curled. 'Can't you count?'

Quintus gave him a withering stare. 'We've just seen a party of Gauls.'

Villius' next comment died in his throat. Everyone's gaze focused on the trees behind the friends. 'Gods above! How many?' demanded one man.

'We saw only four,' replied Calatinus.

'Are they tracking us?' asked Villius, shifting on his horse's back.

'I don't think so. They seem to be hunting,' said Quintus.

Relieved glances all round.

'There could be more, though, eh?' suggested Villius.

'Of course, but we didn't have time to wait and see,' retorted Quintus acidly.

Villius scowled. 'I say we give them a wide berth. Ride around them.'

A few riders nodded, but Quintus was having none of it. 'We could get lost by doing that. What if there isn't another ford across the stream? We'll end up riding through terrain that we know even less than this. And if the snow gets worse, we'll run the risk of getting lost.'

'What he's suggesting' – Calatinus butted in – 'is that we attack the sheep-fuckers.'

'Even if there are more than four, they won't be expecting us,' urged Quintus. 'If we ride down there hard and fast, the dogs will get the surprise of their miserable lives. We'll be gone before the ones that aren't dead even know what's happened.' His eyes roved from man to man. 'Who's with me?'

'I'm not,' snarled Villius.

'Let's have a show of hands,' said Quintus before Villius could say any more. He raised his arm. Calatinus did likewise.

Ignoring Villius' foul expression, two men copied them. With a shrug, another rider lifted his right hand. He was quickly joined by a sixth. The instant that happened, three of the remaining men followed suit. Quintus clenched his fist in triumph.

Villius shot him a poisonous glare. 'Fine. I'm in.'

Quintus was already halfway to his horse. 'Let's move. They'll all be on our side by now. We go five men wide, two deep. Those with bows are to ride at the back.

'Cut down anyone you meet. Stop long enough to retrieve your spears, but that's all. It's every man for himself. Cross the stream and ride like the wind. Regroup where we entered the woods.'

Men nodded, made grunts of assent. Looped their reins around their left hands. Gripped their spears tightly with their right. Two of the more confident men even nocked shafts to their bowstrings. Villius wasn't one of them. They moved off, urging their mounts into an immediate trot. Quintus took the centre; Calatinus rode to his right. Villius was directly to his rear. No one had brought a shield. Quintus felt naked without his. The Gauls had spears and arrows and would be good shots. He'd have to trust in the gods that their charge panicked the warriors, that any missiles they launched would miss. He shoved the thought from his mind. *Stay focused.* They had covered half the distance to the stream now. Through the trees, he caught sight of a cloaked figure. A heartbeat later, the warrior stiffened as he saw Quintus. Perhaps a hundred paces separated them.

'Charge!' Quintus shouted, urging his mount on. 'Remember our comrades who died at the Trebia!'

A swelling cry of anger from the other riders. Calatinus was swearing and throwing insults at the tribesmen. 'Roma! Roma!' roared a voice.

As the air filled with the thunder of hooves, the Gaul vanished behind a beech. Blood pounded in Quintus' ears. He readied his spear and prayed that at least one warrior came within his reach. This was the third occasion that he had charged an enemy and, for the first time, he felt no fear. Just a mad exhilaration that he had engineered the attack and that, in some small way, retribution might be gained for what they had suffered at the Trebia.

Quintus caught a glimpse of the stream. Then another. His heart leaped. One, two, three, four figures were sprinting down the slope towards the water. 'They're running!' he yelled. 'Charge!' Low branches whipped past his head as his horse reached a full gallop. At the edges of his vision, Quintus could see two other riders, one of whom was Calatinus; the noise to his rear told him that someone – Villius? – was still there.

In his excitement, Quintus forgot that there might have been more than four Gauls. The next thing he knew, a figure was darting in from the protection of a tree to his left. He glanced down in horror, saw the spear heading straight for him. It was pure luck that the blade rammed into his horse's flesh rather than his own. It struck the beast high in the shoulder, just in front of Quintus' thigh. The horse's near foreleg dropped, and its charge came to a convulsive halt. Quintus was unable to prevent himself being thrown off. Air whistled past his ears. There was a jarring impact as his left side hit the hard ground. The pain was intense; he suspected that a couple of his ribs had broken, but he kept rolling, managing to come to his feet with his spear still clutched in his fist. The world was spinning. Shaking his head, Quintus hissed in dismay. His horse – maybe his only way out of here – was staggering down the slope. He had no time to dwell on his misfortune. The Gaul was on him already, a big bear of a man, snarling in his guttural tongue and sweeping an unpleasant-looking dagger at Quintus' belly. He rammed his spear at the warrior's face, forcing him to back off.

A torrent of abuse followed.

Quintus went on the attack, and the Gaul had to retreat. He did not seem scared, which Quintus found odd. A man with a knife had no chance against an enemy with a spear. An instant later, he almost missed the flash of triumph in the other's eyes. Almost. Quintus threw himself the only way he could. Down, and to his left, on to his bad side. As the pain from his ribs surged through him, he heard a familiar sound. *Hiss.* An arrow shot through the space he'd just vacated, and the Gaul cursed. Quintus clambered up, shooting a glance to his rear. Thirty paces away, among the trees, stood a warrior with a bow. He was already fitting another shaft to his string.

Hooves hammered the ground, and Villius arrived. He took in Quintus, and the warrior with the knife, and slowed his horse. Quintus felt a surge of relief, but it vanished almost at once. Seeing the bowman, Villius changed his mind. Without as much as a second look, he drove his mount down the slope to safety.

The warrior with the knife let out an ugly laugh.

Hiss. The barbed shaft ripped a hole in Quintus' tunic, tearing an agonising trail through his skin before it thumped into a tree a few paces away.

'You're bastards, all of you!' cried Quintus. Eyes swivelling from one Gaul to the other, he jabbed his spear at the knifeman, putting him on the back foot. If he wasn't to be slain by the bowman, he had to down his opponent. Fast. Quintus' skin crawled. He could almost feel the next arrow sinking into his back. Or his side. Inspiration struck, and he darted off to his left before turning to face the Gaul again. His enemy roared with anger as he realised what Quintus had done.

Protected from the arrows by the other's body, Quintus stabbed his spear forward again. The warrior dodged, but Quintus anticipated the move. With a mighty shove, he slid the spear point deep into the Gaul's belly. An ear-splitting shriek rent the air, and he twisted the blade for good measure, before wrenching it free. The warrior staggered. His dagger fell to the ground unnoticed. He clutched at his stomach, but he couldn't stop a couple of loops of bowel from slithering out of the hole in his tunic. His knees buckled, but he fought himself upright.

Quintus remembered the bear that he'd fought near home, a lifetime ago it seemed. It had taken an injury as severe as this, but had still nearly killed him. As his father was fond of saying, a man was dangerous until he was dead. He stepped in and thrust his spear deep into the Gaul's chest. The man's expression grew startled; his lips worked; a deep groan issued forth and then the light went from his eyes. He sagged down, a dead weight on the spear, but Quintus did not let him fall. Protected by the corpse, he peered over its shoulder. He was just in time to see an arrow punch into the Gaul's back.

That was enough. With a great heave, he pushed the body off his blade. Blood drenched his arms, chest and face, but Quintus paid it no heed. Spinning on his heel, he sprinted for the stream, biting back the nausea that swelled in his throat. Everything now was about speed and tactics. How far he could get from the bowman before the next shaft was loosed. How difficult a target he could make of himself. After fifteen paces, he turned to his right. Ten steps further on, he zigzagged to his left. *Hiss.* An arrow struck the ground close to his foot. Quintus gasped with a mixture of relief and terror but didn't dare to look back. On the count of ten, he changed direction once more. The Gaul missed again, and Quintus risked running straight down the slope for a bit before darting off to the right. The following shaft missed him by a good distance, and his heart leaped. He had to be more than a hundred steps from the treeline. The stream was drawing near. If he reached it without being hit, the bowman's chances of success would be slim indeed.

One of his companions was halfway across the ford. Hope filled him until he saw it was Villius. The cur had a bow, but he wasn't even looking back. Quintus' order that each man was to save himself seemed stupid now. *Bastard. He could be distracting the Gaul.* Of the rest, Quintus saw no sign. He turned and sprinted left, heading in a diagonal direction to the watercourse. Twenty steps, then a jink to the right. Five steps and an about-turn. The lapse since the last arrow was longer than before, and Quintus' guts churned. He risked a look at the warrior, and wished he hadn't. The man was tracking his every move, and had an arrow aimed straight at him.

For the first time, panic ripped at Quintus. He couldn't stop or slow down. His only choice was to keep going, to continue changing direction and hope that the Gaul didn't second-guess his move. Given the number of times he'd evaded being struck, however, his luck had to be wearing thin. The bank was less than twenty paces away now. Eighteen. Sixteen. On impulse, Quintus decided to make a break for it. At full speed, he'd reach it in four heartbeats, maybe five. He would dive into the water and swim across. See if the whoreson could hit him then.

He ducked his head and sprinted forward.

Quintus had only gone a few steps when he felt a tremendous blow hit his upper left arm. The tiniest delay, and then pain such as he'd never felt before. Looking down, he saw a bloody arrow tip protruding from his left bicep. *Moving, I have to keep moving,* he thought. *Otherwise the bastard will get me in the back with the next one.* To his relief, the bank was now very close. He lunged into the water, gasping at the biting chill. Swimming wasn't an option, so Quintus began wading across, praying that the Gaul had not been emboldened enough to come out of the safety of the trees to take another shot. On the other side, he'd be at the very limit of most bows' range. A splash off to his right – another arrow

– provided a little relief, but it wasn't long before the extreme cold of the water began to sap his strength. His legs seemed to have lead weights attached; waves of agony from his arm were washing over him. Desperate for a rest, Quintus ground to a halt. He could taste acid in his mouth. The Gaul would keep releasing as long as he could. A glance over his shoulder confirmed his fears. The warrior was aiming high in the air to give his arrow more distance. Quintus had no desire to drown in the stream, choking on his own blood, so he ducked down until the water met his chin. Walking like a crab, he battled on.

The sight of Calatinus, on foot but with a bow, and one of the others, armed similarly, on the far bank was as welcome as any he could remember. In unison, they released arrows in a massive arc that took them high over-head. Quintus couldn't stop himself from looking again. The shafts landed within twenty steps of the Gaul, who turned and fled back into the safety of the trees. The slope opposite was empty now. Drained, relieved, Quintus waded ashore. He staggered as he clambered up the bank, but strong arms stopped him from falling.

Quintus shoved them away. 'I'm all right.'

'No, you're not! How bad is it?' Calatinus' voice was concerned.

'I'm not sure. I didn't exactly have time to examine it,' he replied with a flash of humour.

'Come on. Get under cover. We can look at it there.'

With the other rider covering them, they entered the shelter of the trees. A few steps in, Quintus saw three more of his companions. They greeted him with real relief.

'Seen any Gauls on this bank?' he asked.

'Not a sign, thank the gods,' came the answer. 'They're probably still running.'

Quintus yelped as Calatinus' fingers probed at the point where the arrow entered his arm.

'Sorry.'

'What can you see?'

'You're lucky. It looks to have missed the bone. Once it's been removed and cleaned up, the wound should heal all right.'

'Take it out now!' demanded Quintus. 'Get it over with.'

Calatinus' forehead creased. 'That's not a good idea. It's not bleeding that much now, and I have no saw to cut the shaft. If I try to remove the arrow by breaking it in two, I'm bound to set it haemorrhaging again. We haven't got time to hang around trying to stem the flow of blood. We killed at least three warriors—'

'Four,' interrupted Quintus.

Calatinus grinned. 'But only the gods know how many others might be out there.'

There were loud murmurs of agreement.

Quintus scowled, but he knew his friend was right. 'Very well.'

'You can ride behind me,' said Quintus. 'We'll be back in the camp before you know it.'

Gritting his teeth against the pain, Quintus followed Calatinus through the trees. It was only then that he began to wonder how his father would react. Surely he'd be pleased? They had slain most of the Gauls and put to flight the rest – without any apparent losses. That had to be a good thing. Deep in his belly, however, Quintus wasn't so sure.

Get back to the camp first, he told himself savagely. You can worry about it then.

By unhappy chance, Fabricius happened to be near the camp's southern gate when the exhausted party got back. Snow was falling thickly, coating the ramparts, the ground and the soldiers' cloaks and helmets, but that didn't stop him from focusing on the nine riders as they passed through the entrance. His face twisted in disbelief as he recognised first Calatinus, and then Quintus. 'Stop right there!' he bellowed.

Their relief at reaching the camp dissipated a little, but they reined in. Quintus, numb with cold and half-conscious, mumbled a curse.

'Curb your tongue, you insolent brat!' roared Fabricius, approaching. He came in from their right, so he did not see the arrow in his son's arm.

Quintus coloured. He made to speak again, but the combination of his father's glare and his weakness held him silent.

Fabricius pinned Calatinus with his eyes. 'What is the meaning of this? Where have you been?'

'We, er, went hunting, sir.'

'Hunting?' Fabricius' voice rose in disbelief. 'In this weather? When you had a patrol to go on?'

'The conditions weren't too bad when we left, sir' – here Calatinus looked to his companions for support – 'and I think we're still in time for the patrol.'

'I'll be the judge of that.' Fabricius' gaze moved along the line of horses, searching for bodies slung over their backs. Seeing nothing, his lips thinned. 'Did you manage to bring down anything then?'

'No game, sir, no.' Calatinus couldn't stop himself from grinning. 'But we did kill four Gauls.'

'Eh? What happened?'

Quintus' mouth opened, but his father silenced him with a look.

Calatinus quickly told the story of the clash by the stream. As he mentioned Quintus being struck by an arrow, Fabricius rushed to his son's side. 'Where were you hit?'

'I'm f-f-fine.' Vaguely aware that he was slurring his words, Quintus tried to lift his left arm, but was unable to.

'Hades below! You must go to the hospital at once.' Fabricius took the horse's reins. 'Was anyone else injured?'

'Our tenth companion didn't appear at the appointed meeting place, sir,' admitted Calatinus. 'We waited for a little while, but the weather was worsening, so we carved the word "camp" on a tree trunk before we left, and hoped he would see that.'

'One man lost, and another injured, for what – four measly Gauls?' cried Fabricius. 'Whose idea was this hare-brained expedition?'

'It was mine, sir,' replied Calatinus.

Quintus tried to protest, but his tongue wouldn't move.

'You're a damn fool! We will speak later of this,' snapped Fabricius. 'Get back to your tents. You've got just enough time to fill your bellies and warm up before we ride out on patrol. I will leave my son in the care of the surgeon, and join you shortly.'

Quintus heard Calatinus mutter his good wishes. He was too tired to do more than nod.

'Get off then,' barked his father.

All at once, the world came rushing in on Quintus. He felt his thighs' grip on his mount weaken; he began to lose his balance, could do nothing about it. 'Father, I—'

'Don't talk. Conserve your strength.' His father's voice was surprisingly gentle.

Quintus didn't hear it. In a dead faint, he slid off Calatinus' horse to the ground.

Chapter III

Near Capua, Campania

'Aurelia!'

She ignored her mother's voice, which had carried all the way from the house to where she was standing, at the edge of their property. She'd been thinking about Quintus and Hanno, and her feet had carried her here of their own volition. This was the way the three of them used to come when they sneaked up into the woods. There Quintus had trained her to use a wooden, and then a real, sword. Atia called again, and Aurelia's lips twitched with brief amusement. What would she, or her father, make of the fact that she could use a weapon? Ride a horse? Both activities were forbidden to women, but that hadn't stopped Aurelia badgering Quintus to teach her. Eventually, he'd given in. How glad she was that he had; how she treasured the memories of those carefree times. But the world was different now, a harsher, darker place.

Rome was at war with Carthage, and her father and brother were possibly among its casualties.

Stop thinking like that! They're still alive.

Fabricius had been the first to leave, riding away to fight a people whom he'd fought before, a generation ago. Quintus had gone a few months later, and he had taken Hanno too. Sadness filled Aurelia as she recalled saying goodbye to her brother, and to the slave who had become a friend. If she admitted it, Hanno had perhaps meant something more. Yet he was one of the enemy now, and she would never see him again. That hurt more than she cared to concede. Sometimes she dreamed about running away, to Carthage, to be reunited with him. Aurelia knew it for a crazy fantasy.

Yet there was more hope of achieving that than seeing Hanno's friend Suniaton – Suni – again, she thought sadly.

'Aurelia? Can you hear me?'

Remembering the horror, she walked a few steps further. Against all wise judgement, but with little other choice, Aurelia had brought an injured Suni from the shepherd's hut where he'd been hiding back to the family house. Runaway slaves weren't uncommon, and he had pretended to be mute. The ruse had pulled the wool over everyone's eyes for a time, but then she had made the worst mistake of her life, calling him by his real name instead of his assumed one. It wouldn't have mattered if Agesandros, the farm's overseer, hadn't overheard her and put two and two together. Embittered by the murder of his entire family by the Carthaginians during the previous war, he had slain Suni before her very eyes. Aurelia could still see the knife slipping between Suni's ribs, the blood soaking through his tunic and the odd tenderness with which Agesandros had lowered him to the floor. She could still hear Suni's last shuddering gasp.

'Where are you, child?' Atia was beginning to sound annoyed.

Aurelia didn't care. In fact, she was glad. Relations with her mother had been cool – to say the least – since Suni's death. This was because despite some initial misgivings, Atia had accepted Agesandros' explanation that Suni had been a Carthaginian and, worse still, a fugitive gladiator who had joined the household by subterfuge. He had been a danger to everyone in the household; all the overseer had done was to rid them of a lethal threat. 'I know you thought of the boy as harmless, dear,' Atia had sighed. 'With his maimed leg, so did I. But Agesandros saw through him, thank the gods. Remember, the injured viper can still deliver a fatal bite.' Aurelia had protested vociferously, but her mother had put her foot down. Mindful of her need to protect Quintus' involvement in Hanno's escape, Aurelia hadn't been able to reveal more.

'Gaius is here! He has come all the way from Capua. Don't you want to see him?'

Aurelia's head snapped around. Gaius Martialis was Quintus' oldest and closest friend; she had known him since she was tiny. He was steady, brave and funny, and she had a lot of time for him. Yet at their last meeting, a few weeks previously, he'd brought news that had rocked her world.

Hundreds of Romans had been lost in the cavalry clash against Hannibal at the Ticinus; there had been no word of her father and Quintus, or of Flaccus, the high-ranking noble to whom she had been betrothed. She and her mother had lived in painful uncertainty since. Since hearing of the subsequent and unexpected defeat at the Trebia – the Senate had called it a 'setback', but everyone knew that for a lie – their anguish had known no bounds. In all likelihood, at least one of the three men had died, probably more. How could they have survived when more than twenty thousand others had not? Aurelia felt sick at the thought of it, but something in her mother's voice gave her hope.

It didn't sound strained or unhappy. Maybe Gaius' visit was *not* ominous. A flicker of hope lit in her heart. It would be good to have some normal social interaction. Lately, she had had nothing but fractious exchanges with her mother, or frosty silences when she came across Agesandros. There was time for a swift, silent prayer, asking that those she loved be granted protection, especially her father, Quintus and Hanno. At the last moment, Aurelia added Flaccus, and then she turned and ran back down the path.

She found Atia and Gaius in the courtyard that lay adjacent to the main house, a cobbled affair that was bordered by storerooms, a hay barn, grain and wine stores, and slave quarters. In the warmer months, it was the busiest place on the farm. During the winter, it became a route between the buildings, which housed livestock, tools and a wide variety of preserved foodstuffs from fish to hams and herbs. Tracks crisscrossed the once-white snow in dizzying patterns. They had been made by men and women's sandals, children's bare feet, dogs, cats, poultry, horses and mules. Aurelia walked with care, avoiding the regular piles of manure. It was time to have the yard swept again, she thought absently.

'At last you grace us with your presence. Where have you been?' demanded Atia.

Elation filled Aurelia. Gaius couldn't be the harbinger of bad news today – not when her mother greeted her in that way.

Gaius gave her a broad grin.

Aurelia bobbed her head in reply. Was she imagining it, or had he looked her up and down for the first time? Suddenly self-conscious, she tossed back her thick black hair and wished that she wasn't wearing her everyday wool dress and old cloak. 'I was walking. I came as soon as I heard you call.'

Her mother's eyebrows rose in evident disbelief, but she did not push further.

'It is good to see you again, Aurelia.' Gaius inclined his head.

'And you, Gaius.' She gave him a demure smile.

'You're becoming quite the young woman.' Again the fleeting appraisal. 'You'll be fifteen before long, won't you?'

'In the autumn, yes.' She fought the instant blush that warmed her cheeks, and failed. 'You bring no bad news, I hope?'

'None, I am happy to say.' He turned to Atia. 'Have you had any word of Fabricius, or Quintus?'

'No. Nothing regarding Flaccus either. I spend enough time on my knees in the *lararium* to mean that no news is good news.' Atia's tone was brittle, and brooked no argument.

'Your husband and Quintus are ever in my prayers, and in those of my father,' said Gaius quickly. 'So too is Flaccus. The day that they all return will be one of great celebration.'

'It will,' declared Atia.

An awkward silence fell.

Aurelia felt guilty that she hadn't been praying for Flaccus as much as her father and brother. I only met him once, she thought defensively.

'You'll stay for the night?' asked Atia.

'That's very kind of you, but—' demurred Gaius.

'You have to,' cried Aurelia. She clasped his hand in hers. 'We haven't seen you for weeks. You must tell us what you and your father have been up to, and what's happening in Capua.' She stuck out her bottom lip. 'We get no news here, in the middle of nowhere.'

At least Fabricius' creditors leave us alone in this weather, thought Atia sourly. Come the spring, it will be a different matter. 'Stay. Otherwise you'll have to set out on your return journey within the hour. The low clouds and the snow mean it gets dark so early these days.'

'How can I refuse?' declared Gaius with a gracious half-bow. 'I would be delighted to stay. Thank you.'

Aurelia clapped her hands with happiness.

'Entertain our guest, Aurelia. The *tablinum* is the warmest room.' Atia made for the house. 'I shall speak to Julius about the dinner for tonight.'

'Shall we?' Gaius indicated the path back to the front door.

'Can't we walk for a little while? It's dark so much at this time of year. It's good just to be outside, to breathe the fresh air.'

'Whatever you wish,' Gaius acceded. 'Where do you want to go?'

Delighted by the idea of his company, Aurelia pointed. 'The only path away from the house that isn't covered in snow is the one that leads up to the woods.'

'Let's go that way then.'

The hours that followed were Aurelia's happiest in many weeks. Her walk with Gaius had lasted until the light had dimmed in the western sky. With chilled faces and feet, they had stamped back into the house. Ignoring the empty tablinum, they had retired to the warmth of the kitchen, where they had got under the slaves' feet and stolen tasty morsels of the food that was being prepared. Julius, the main cook, would normally have driven her out of his domain. Instead, he had offered her a bowl of the best olives and muttered something about how good it was to see her mood lift. When Atia came in to check on the meal's progress, she too had looked pleased. Aurelia had pretended not to notice.

Gaius had been full of small talk from Capua. Isolated on the farm, and locked in by grief, Aurelia took interest in stories that would have been of little appeal before. Her favourite was about one of the sewers in Capua, which had blocked a week before. Gaius went into great detail about the resulting overflow, which had swamped part of the city, filling homes and businesses with liquid ordure. A vicious frost two nights afterwards – usually a most unwelcome event – had proved to be the salvation of those trying to remove the vast quantities of sewage. 'You have to see it to believe it,' Gaius had said with a chuckle. 'When shit and piss freeze solid, the result can be chopped up with spades into manageable chunks, tossed on to a cart and carried away.'

'You're making it up!' Aurelia had said in delighted horror.

'I'm not! On my honour. There was so much work that carters were coming in from every village for miles.'

She had given him a wicked nudge. 'Mother would love that story.' Despite Gaius' protests, she had persuaded him to tell the tale again – but before they dined.

Despite herself, Atia had laughed her way through his account. 'That must have been quite a sight,' she said when he'd finished. 'I imagine that the smell must have been far less severe than in summer.'

Gaius had grimaced. 'It was still bad enough – the affected area was only a few streets away from our house. Father had the slaves burning lavender and incense night and day to combat the odour.'

'None of your household got sick then?'

'No, thank the gods. Surprisingly few people in the city did; whether it was because of the cold or the amount of offerings they left at the temples, I don't know.'

'How is your father?'

'He is well, thank you. He sends you his best wishes. I am to tell you that if there is anything he can do, you have only to mention it.'

'My thanks. He is a good man, Martialis. I will remember his kind offer.' Atia's smile was warm, but the gesture had made her worries resurface. Fabricius had always refused to countenance asking his oldest friend for help with his debts. Martialis wasn't wealthy, but his loyalty knew no bounds. Anything he had, he'd lend to them if they asked. Atia hoped never to be forced into such a situation, but if Fabricius didn't return, the possibility was there – whether she liked it or not. She resolved to make an offering to Mercury, the god of war, and also of messengers. *Bring me good news of my husband, please.* She gestured to the nearest slave, who made swiftly for the kitchen. Soon a procession of dishes was carried through to the dining room, where the three were reclining on couches. The conversation died away for a time. Gaius fell on the food as if he'd been starved for a week. Atia looked on in approval as she took small portions from various platters. Despite her rumbling stomach, Aurelia nibbled only at a piece of baked fish. She didn't want to appear greedy in front of Gaius.

'How is Martialis' bad leg?' asked Atia. 'This weather can't be good for it.'

'A good rub-down by his body slave once a day keeps him moving.

That, and the produce of Bacchus.' Gaius' wink set Aurelia giggling. Martialis had always been fond of his drink. Since trying it on the sly, she'd developed a taste for it herself. Atia's firm grasp of the jug was the only thing that had stopped her from trying to fill her own cup. Throwing a resentful look at her mother, Aurelia hung on Gaius' every word. How had she not noticed before? He was intriguing – funny and clever. As a friend of Quintus, she had never really thought of him in a romantic way, but that had just changed. She studied him sidelong, drinking in his broad shoulders, muscular physique and open, pleasant face. He caught her eye on occasion, and smiled.

His next story concerned a Capuan official who had been discovered stealing money from the city's coffers. He had only been caught because of his taste in expensive mosaics. The alarm had been raised by a colleague who had seen the new flooring in his home and known that it would have cost more than the man's yearly income. An investigation revealed that all of the embezzled money had been spent. The enraged Capuan leaders had ordered the floors to be taken up. The resultant debris was to be used as filler when local roads were being repaired. The zealous workmen sent to complete the job had mistakenly dug up every room in the house, causing the hysterical official to collapse at the scene.

Aurelia gasped. 'Did he die?'

'No, he recovered well enough to appear at his trial the next day. Ironically, half the crowd had stolen pieces of his own tesserae to pelt him with. They were showering in from all sides as the court convened. The lawyers got hit; so too did the magistrate.' Gaius mimed ducking down, wincing as he was struck. 'The city guards had to be sent in to restore order.'

Aurelia snorted with laughter. 'You're so funny, Gaius.'

Atia raised a hand to stifle a yawn. 'Excuse me.'

'I'm sorry. I've been carrying on all night, boring you stupid,' said Gaius, looking a little embarrassed.

'No, no. It's interesting to hear what's going on in Capua. I think it's time for bed, though. It has been a long day.' Atia cast a meaningful glance at Aurelia. 'You too, young lady.'

'But, Mother—' she began.

'Bed. Now.'

Aurelia flushed with anger, but before she could protest, Gaius had risen from his couch. 'The ride from Capua has tired me more than I would have thought. A night's sleep, and I'll be as good as new.'

Atia smiled. 'One of the slaves will show you to your room. There are extra blankets in the chest at the foot of the bed should you need them.'

'My thanks. Until the morning, then.' Gaius bid them both good night.

Aurelia rose. 'I'm not a child, Mother,' she whispered the instant he was at the door. 'I don't need to be told when to go to bed.'

Atia turned on her in a fury. 'When you are mistress of Flaccus' household, you can do as you please. While you're under this roof, however, you'll do exactly as I say!'

Gaius checked at Atia's raised voice. He half turned, but then thought better of it, and left the room. Aurelia's cheeks burned with embarrassment and shame that he had heard her mother's words. She sensed her mother get up, felt a hand close on her arm.

'Do you understand me?' Atia demanded.

'Yes, Mother,' she muttered from between clenched teeth.

'I want no more casting soulful eyes at Gaius either. He's a good man, and will make someone a fine husband, but you are betrothed to another. There must be no suggestion of impropriety. Caius Minucius Flaccus would not approve.' *And the alliance with his family cannot be jeopardised. It will be vital in the restoration of our fortunes.*

'I don't care about him,' spat Aurelia, forgetting that she had found Flaccus quite attractive. 'Or you! I want to marry whom I choose, like you and Father did.'

Slap! Atia's hand connected with her left cheek.

Complete shock filled Aurelia. Tears of humiliation welled in her eyes. It had been years since her mother had struck her.

'You forget yourself!' Atia hissed. 'What your father and I did is none of your concern. None! You will marry whomever we decide upon, whenever we tell you to. Do I make myself clear?'

'It's not fair! You and Father are hypocrites.'

Slap! 'Keep this insolence up, and I will have a whip brought to me.'

Aurelia's guts knotted with fear. Her mother's threat was real. She bit her lip and stared at the floor.

'Look at me!'

Aurelia raised her unwilling eyes to Atia's.

'So you will do as I say?'

'Yes, Mother,' Aurelia said, hating herself for being weak.

'Good. On that we are agreed at least.' Atia waved a hand in dismissal. 'Go to bed. I will see you in the morning.'

Aurelia left the room, ignoring the curious stares of the less discreet slaves. Damn Mother to Hades, she thought. It was no more than ten steps to her bedchamber, but in the only act of defiance left to her, she made them last an age. She flung a murderous glance back at the dining room. I hate her. I hate her. Her mother had read far too much into the situation, she thought angrily. She had been enjoying Gaius' company, that was all. Deep in her heart, though, Aurelia knew that Atia's instinct had been correct. A stab of remorse. How could she find a man attractive when she was promised to another? Instinctively she knew why. *I have met Flaccus once, whereas I've known Gaius for many years. Gaius is young, not old. Kind, not arrogant. It's not a crime to have feelings for someone.* An unexpected image of Hanno popped into Aurelia's mind, filling her with even more guilt. She blanked him out at once. They had never even shared a kiss. He had left, his aim to join Hannibal's army, and she would never see him again. For all she knew, he was dead.

'Into your room!' Atia had come out to check on her.

Aurelia's resentment towards her mother resurged with a vengeance, but she kept quiet as she opened her door and slipped inside. A plan was hatching in her mind. Everyone in the house would go to bed soon. If she waited, she could creep to Gaius' chamber and let herself in. Intense satisfaction swept through her. How angry her mother would be if she ever found out! Not that she would. I'll be quieter than a mouse, she thought with glee. And then I can be alone with Gaius.

Perhaps an hour later, all sounds outside her door had ceased. There had been soft talking among the slaves who were clearing up the remains of their dinner. Plates clattering off one another. From the kitchen, the sound of Julius chiding his minions, telling them to be quiet. Atia's voice, thanking Julius for his efforts. Her feet pausing by Aurelia's door; a faint creak as she opened it and peered inside. Aurelia hadn't moved a muscle, had kept her breathing deep and regular, and her eyes closed. Her efforts had seemed to work. Atia had gently shut the door and gone on her way. The last noises Aurelia had heard were a dog barking from the outbuildings and the subsequent yelps as one of the farm slaves kicked it into silence. She had lain in the darkness since, her blankets pulled up to her chin, listening hard.

All she could hear was her own heart, which was thumping hard off her ribs. Aurelia realised that her previous behaviour had been nothing more than bravado. Sadly, it had worn off. Was going to see Gaius worth the risk? If her mother were ever to realise, a whipping would surely follow. Aurelia had seen Atia punish a slave that way once when her father and Agesandros hadn't been to hand. The slave had screamed throughout the entire procedure. Don't be a coward, she thought. What she was about to do could not even compare to the dangers faced daily by Quintus.

With renewed resolve, she threw back the covers and climbed out of bed. Lighting her oil lamp was too risky. Besides, she knew the layout of her room like the back of her hand. Shrugging a blanket over her shoulders to guard against the chill, she tiptoed to the door and placed her ear against the timbers. Not a sound. Aurelia had long since perfected the knack of lifting the latch without making any noise. Pulling the horizontal bar towards her, she raised it while with her other hand she firmly pulled the door ajar. A glance outside. Nothing moved. No one stirred.

Aurelia slipped into the covered passageway that bordered the courtyard. Everything had been turned a beautiful shade of silver by the moon. The cold was piercing, and she clutched the blanket to her. Her exhaled breath formed instant clouds before her face, so she was careful to remain in the shadows as she scanned the square for any sign of life. The only creature in sight was the cat that hung around the kitchen, and it ignored her. Content, Aurelia slid her feet across the mosaic floor, counting each step. To reach Gaius' chamber, she had to go past her parents' room, which lay fifteen paces from hers. By the time she'd reached ten, she could feel sweat running down her back. Eleven. Twelve. Somnus, she prayed to the god of sleep, keep my mother firmly in your grasp, I beg you.

Aurelia was right outside Atia's door when there was a cough from within. It took all of her self-control not to turn and bolt. She froze. Time stood still as she waited to be discovered. Blood rushed in her ears. She saw her mother before her in a towering fury, a whip in her right hand. She blinked. The horrific image disappeared. Aurelia forced herself to breathe slowly. By the count of twenty, there had been no further sounds. Knees weak from trembling, she crept on. Outside Gaius' room, she paused. There was still time to return to her bed unnoticed. That notion vanished in a heartbeat. After the fear, she wanted some reward. She shocked herself by visualising a lingering kiss with Gaius. That picture bright in her mind, she lifted the latch with a practised hand and padded inside, closing the door behind her.

The momentousness of her actions hit home like a hammer blow. If she were caught, her mother would be incandescent. The very *least* she could expect was a whipping. Aurelia's resolve weakened. Her arm reached back to the latch.

'Who's there?' It was Gaius' voice.

Her courage returned. 'It is I, Aurelia.' She rushed to his bedside.

'Aurelia?' He sounded confused. 'Is something wrong? A fire?'

'Don't be alarmed. Nothing's wrong. I wanted to talk to you.'

'I see.' He sat up. It was so dark that she could see only the outline of his face. 'Your mother would kill us both if she found us like this.'

'She won't. She's asleep.'

'I hope so. What was it that couldn't wait until the morning?'

Aurelia's self-confidence vanished. She was here as much to defy her mother as she was to see Gaius. Admitting to either would involve losing face, though. 'I'm so worried about Quintus and Father,' she whispered in a rush. 'I pray to the gods all the time, but I never hear anything back.'

He reached out and touched her cheek. 'It's bad enough for me not knowing about Quintus. It must be far worse for you.'

Unexpected tears began to flow. In the weeks since hearing about the disaster at the Trebia, Aurelia had buried her fears deep inside. Because of the arguments with her mother, she had no one to turn to. So she had battled on alone. One human touch, and her defences came tumbling down. 'Oh, Gaius! W-what will I do if they're both dead?' she whispered jerkily.

He moved along the bed so that he could put his arms around her. 'You poor thing.'

Aurelia began to sob.

'Shhhh,' murmured Gaius, rubbing her back. 'Shhhh. Your mother will wake.'

She gulped and managed to rein her emotions in a little. Burying her face in his shoulder, she clutched him as if she were drowning. Gaius didn't speak. He just held her tightly. Aurelia began to cry in earnest. She cried, silently, for a long time. For Quintus, for her father, for Suni, but most of all, for herself. Never in her whole life had she felt so alone as she had in the previous few months. It was as if Gaius understood that. His grip on her strengthened. It gave Aurelia the most incredible sense of reassurance. She relaxed into his embrace and let herself take comfort from his presence, his acceptance, his lack of questions. Here, she was safe. No one could hurt her. Her fears gradually abated, and a little while after that, her tears dried up.

Aurelia did not want to move from the circle of Gaius' arms for a long time. His flesh was warm; his breath warmed her neck as he exhaled. She could feel his heart beating beneath her ear. He smelled very *male*. He was so strong. Her original purpose in entering his room returned to her mind. It was almost as if he noticed the change in her.

'Feel better?'

She looked up at him. The curve of his lips was so tempting. 'Yes, thank you.'

His grip eased. 'Once it takes hold, despair is damn near impossible to shake off. It's easy to become so mired in it that nothing makes sense.'

'That's how I've been feeling.'

'The news from Cisalpine Gaul has all been bad, but your father's a shrewd man. He fought Carthage for ten years before, and survived, remember. He will look out for Quintus. There's every chance that they're still alive. Flaccus too. Don't give up on them just yet.'

'You're right,' she whispered. 'I'm sorry.'

'There's no need to apologise. I saw how strained you were with your mother. You have no one to confide in, do you?'

She shook her head miserably.

'Well, you've got me,' he said, giving her a squeeze. 'You're my best friend's little sister. You can tell me anything.'

Not anything, thought Aurelia. 'Thank you.'

'I will make it my business to come out here every week or two. How's that?'

'That would be wonderful.'

Another squeeze, conspiratorial this time, before his arms fell away. 'Now, away with you, before Atia wakes up and hears us.'

Aurelia didn't really hear him. His face was so close. So inviting. If she leaned in a little, she could kiss him. It might have been her imagination, but she thought that he began to move towards her lips. Her head swam.

'Aurelia.'

She returned to reality with a start. 'Yes?'

He had pulled back a fraction. 'You must go.'

'Yes, yes. Thank you, Gaius.'

'It's all right.' His whisper was a little gruff. 'In future, though, it'd be best if you didn't come into my bedroom at this hour.'

'I won't. I promise.' Her heart sank. *He doesn't find me attractive. He's only comforting me because I'm Quintus' sister.*

'We'll go for walks instead, eh?'

Her spirits rallied. There would be opportunities to be alone with him again. 'I look forward to that.'

'As do I. Now, good night.'

Aurelia returned to her room without incident. She lay in bed, listening to her own breathing. Thoughts of Quintus and her father came and went, but her worries about them had lost their sharp intensity. Flaccus didn't even enter her mind. All she could think about was Gaius.

Gaius.

Despite the fact that she had had little sleep, Aurelia's mood was buoyant when she awoke the following morning. She'd had a vivid dream about Gaius. Just remembering it made her blush. From the strip of light under her door, she knew that it was full light outside: time to rise before her mother came knocking. Today, she was careful to put on her best dress, a dark green, loosely cut garment given to her by Atia as a birthday present.

Aurelia brushed her hair with more care than she'd taken in weeks. She wanted to put on her garnet earrings, but her mother's eagle eyes would spot them long before Gaius did. Contenting herself with a dab of rose-water at the base of her throat and on her wrists, she stepped out into the covered walkway that ran around the courtyard. Gaius emerged at the same moment; he gave her a sly wink, which she returned with a little grin.

At breakfast she acted subdued, even penitent, before Atia. To her relief, her mother gave no sign of being suspicious. Relief filled Aurelia. Their secret appeared to be safe.

'When will you leave?' asked Atia.

'With your permission, as soon as I have finished this.' Gaius indicated his plate, upon which lay half a small flat loaf, some olives and a thick wedge of cheese. 'It's delicious bread.'

'Julius has a real talent. He could make his living as a baker,' said Atia with a smile. 'You must take some for your father.'

'Thank you. He'd like that very much.'

'Maybe you can persuade him to come along next time.'

Gaius grinned. 'He would jump at the chance of your company.'

The pleasantries went over Aurelia's head. Gaius was going to leave so soon. Her happiness was overtaken by disappointment. 'Do you have to go?'

Atia gave her a sharp look. 'Gaius isn't free to stay here at your beck and call, you know. He serves in the *socii* cavalry. He has duties to fulfil.'

Aurelia glowered but said nothing.

'I would like nothing better than to stay, but your mother is right. I'm supposed to report to my unit by midday.' Gaius gave a rueful shrug. 'Weapons drill first, and practice at riding in formation later.'

Aurelia pulled an understanding smile. 'I see.'

'I can come back in ten days or so, if your mother will allow it.' He glanced at Atia.

'You'd be most welcome.'

Aurelia did her best to look pleased. It was better than nothing.

The slap of sandal leather off the floor in the atrium stopped any further conversation.

Aurelia's lips thinned when the bandy-legged figure of Agesandros appeared in the doorway. She had come to loathe him. Besides, what business had he here?

Atia frowned. 'We are at breakfast, in case you can't see.'

'My apologies, mistress.' Agesandros bowed his head, but stayed put.

'What is it?'

'A messenger has arrived. He's military, from the look of him.'

Aurelia thought her heart would stop. Across from her, Gaius' face was the picture of shock. Even her mother struggled to speak.

'A messenger?' barked Atia after a moment, regaining her self-control. 'From where?'

'I don't know. He wouldn't say. He wants to see the mistress of the house.'

'Bring him in. At once!' cried Atia. 'We shall meet him in the tablinum.'

'Yes, mistress.' Agesandros spun on his heel and trotted off.

'Do you think he's carrying a message from Father?' Aurelia's voice faltered. 'O-or *about* Father?'

'Let us pray to the gods that it's the former,' replied her mother, standing up and smoothing down her dress. 'Follow me.'

Aurelia shot to her mother's side like a child in need of a hug.

Gaius stayed where he was.

Atia threw him a look. 'You come too.'

'I don't want to intrude.'

'You're practically family.'

Aurelia was grateful for Gaius' presence by her side as they hurried to the tablinum. There was no time for a prayer at the lararium – she could hear the clash of hobnails in the atrium – but she threw up the most fervent of prayers to her ancestors, that their protection of her father and Quintus had worked. Had kept them alive.

Her mother took up a position before the household shrine, back upright, a stern expression on her face. Aurelia stood to her right, with Gaius on the other side. Despite herself, Atia's face worked as Agesandros reappeared with a weary-looking man in a thick wool cloak a step behind him. Within a heartbeat, her mien became more welcoming. Aurelia didn't know how her mother could remain so calm. She had to clench her fists by her sides to stop herself from instantly screaming questions.

Agesandros stepped to one side. 'The mistress of the house, Atia, wife of Gaius Fabricius.'

The man approached. Snow fell from the broad brim of his Boeotian helmet as he walked, and his calf-high boots left wet impressions on the mosaic floor. Aurelia studied the messenger's face as he drew near. He was unshaven, gaunt-cheeked, exhausted-looking. She wanted to be sick. Was he carrying bad news?

'My lady.' A crisp salute.

'You are welcome . . .'

'Marcus Lucilius, my lady. I serve with the cavalry that's attached to Longus' legions.'

Aurelia's world stood still. She could see every detail of Marcus' face. The marks that had been left on his cheeks by the pox. A spot on his chin. A scar, possibly caused by a blade, running along the left side of his stubbled chin.

'What brings you here?' Atia's voice was serene, while Aurelia could taste bile in her mouth. Gaius didn't look too happy either.

A weary smile. 'I bear a message from your husband.'

'He lives?' cried Atia.

'When I left the camp near Placentia, he was in good health.'

'And his son?' blurted Aurelia.

'He was also well.'

'Oh, thank the gods!' cried Aurelia, her hands rising to her mouth. Her mother was more composed, but her expression had softened further. They even exchanged a tentative smile. Gaius was grinning like a fool.

The messenger rummaged inside his off-white tunic and produced a rolled parchment. 'Pardon the state of it, my lady,' he said, proffering it. 'Fabricius bade me guard it with my life. It's been against my skin for the whole journey.'

'It's of no matter,' said Atia, practically snatching it from his hand. Silence fell as she slit the wax seal with a thumbnail and unrolled the letter. Her eyes drank in the words; her lips moved in silent synchrony.

The tension was too much for Aurelia. 'What does it say, Mother?'

'Your father is alive and unhurt.' There was a slight shake in Atia's voice. 'So too is Quintus.'

Tears of joy rolled down Aurelia's cheeks. She shot a glance at the lararium and the death masks on the walls to either side of it. *Thank you, household spirits. Thank you, my ancestors. I will make offerings in your honour.* 'Does he send other news?'

'The fighting at the Ticinus was bitter. The cavalry gave a good account of themselves, but they were substantially outnumbered. That was when Publius Scipio was injured.'

Gaius and Aurelia nodded at one another. Naturally, the news that a consul had been wounded had reached Capua soon after the clash.

'Shortly afterwards, he was sent on a patrol with Quintus, over a river into enemy territory. Flaccus went with them. It seems to have been his idea.'

Aurelia felt a trace of unease.

'They were ambushed not just once, but twice. Only a handful of riders made it back to the ford where they'd crossed. Your father, Quintus and Flaccus were among them.' A little gasp. 'Hanno was among the enemy soldiers!'

A pause.

Atia's eyes shot to Aurelia's. 'I'm sorry.'

Aurelia struggled to understand for an instant. If her father and Quintus were all right, then . . . 'Flaccus?' she asked in a small voice.

'He's dead. Apparently, one of Hanno's brothers killed him.'

Her husband-to-be, slain? Aurelia felt neither sadness nor relief. She felt numb. Detached. 'I don't understand. How did Father and Quintus survive?'

'Apparently, Hanno said he owed Quintus his life twice over. Two lives for two debts. Quintus and your father were allowed to go, but they killed the others.'

'Savages!' growled Gaius. Lucilius rumbled in agreement.

Our troops would do the same, thought Aurelia angrily. At least Hanno honoured his obligations. That's more than many Romans would do. Still she felt nothing for Flaccus.

'They managed to retrieve Flaccus' body the next day so that he could be given a proper burial,' Atia went on. 'That will be of some consolation to his family.'

'Does he say ought of the battle at the Trebia?' asked Gaius.

Atia read on. 'A little. The fighting there was even more intense than at the Ticinus. The weather was appalling. To reach the battle, our troops had to cross several streams. By the time the battle began, they were soaking wet and freezing cold. Hannibal's troops, his cavalry in particular, fought very well. He also sprang an ambush on the rear of our army. Both flanks broke under the pressure.' She closed her eyes for a moment. 'Your father and Quintus were lucky to escape the slaughter. With a band of others, they made for the safety of Placentia. Longus arrived a few hours later with around ten thousand legionaries.'

Aurelia tried to imagine the scene. She shuddered. 'It must have been carnage.'

'It was terrible,' agreed Lucilius. 'Or so my comrades say.'

'You weren't at the Trebia?'

A grimace. 'To my shame, I was not, my lady. As a messenger, I am often away from the army. It was my bad luck not to be present at the battle.'

'Or your good fortune,' said Atia.

A lopsided smile. 'You might think so, but I would have wished to have been there with my comrades.'

'There is no shame in doing your duty,' said Atia. 'You can take pride today in what you have done as well. Our lives have been a complete torment since hearing of the events in Cisalpine Gaul. Although the war is still going on, we can take great consolation from the fact that our men are alive.'

Lucilius half bowed.

'Will you stay for a little while, to rest and eat?'

'Thank you, my lady. Some hot food would be welcome, but then I must be on my way again. I have to return to Rome. The Senate will have messages for me to carry to Longus and Scipio.'

'Agesandros, take Lucilius to the dining room,' ordered Atia. 'Tell Julius to bring him the best food in the kitchen.'

Aurelia watched the pair go. Her heart was singing. Quintus and her father were alive! She thought of Flaccus, and her feelings crystallised. It was sad that he was dead, but she wasn't especially sorry. Their betrothal was over now: she was promised to no one. Lifting her head, she found Gaius watching her. Colour flooded her cheeks as her desire for him returned. At that, she felt a little shame. But only a little.

'It's sad that Flaccus is gone,' said her mother. 'We must travel to Capua soon, to offer a sacrifice in his memory at the temple of Mars.'

Aurelia nodded, pretending that she cared. All her attention was on Gaius, though. A daring idea entered her mind. Perhaps she could win his affections?

Atia's next words shattered her fantasy. 'After a suitable period, the search for a suitable match for you will need to be renewed.'

Aurelia shot her mother a poisonous glance. Fortunately, it wasn't noticed. Atia had gone to the lararium, there to give thanks for Lucilius' news.

'Don't worry,' said Gaius. 'She'll find you a good man.'

'Really? All they're looking for is a man who's rich and important,' Aurelia shot back. What she didn't dare to add was: 'I want someone like you.'

Chapter IV

Victumulae, Cisalpine Gaul

Hanno's admiration for Bogu had risen considerably. The spearman had been tougher than he could ever have imagined. He had soaked up the officer's punishment, answering questions only when he could take the pain no more. Somehow Bogu had managed to give only snippets of information, which meant that the officer had to keep probing him for more. He had done so with great zeal, using sharp pliers to remove Bogu's fingernails. Now reddish serum oozed from the letter 'F' on the spearman's forehead. There were burns all over his body. He'd had glowing pokers shoved into both of his wounds. After a few hours, his great strength had ebbed away. Weakened by blood loss and the unremitting agony of his injuries, he had lapsed into unconsciousness. Two buckets of water roused him a little, but not enough to face further interrogation. Now Bogu hung like a discarded puppet from the rope, his head lolling on to his chest. It would be a miracle if he survived to see the morning, thought Hanno bitterly. Whenever that would be. In the windowless cell, time meant nothing.

Before Bogu died, however, Hanno would face the same treatment. The irons were ready; the legionaries watching; the slave waiting to interpret. The officer had left, promising to be back soon. Hanno's fate was sealed. His guts roiled in fear. The stabbing pain in his belly took his mind off the throbbing ache in his shoulder joints, for a moment at least. He could no longer feel his hands below the wrists. Not that that mattered. He would be dead soon, and his last few hours would be excruciating. Shameful too, because he feared his ability to take pain would be as nothing compared to Bogu's. Why could he not have died in battle, fighting for Hannibal? That death he could have borne.

Steps outside. A loud creak as the door opened inwards to reveal the smiling officer.

Sweat slicked down Hanno's back.

'That's better.' The Roman slapped his stomach. 'I had a hunger on me like a wild beast. Now I'm ready to start work again.'

Work? You're a damn monster, thought Hanno.

The triarii shared an envious glance. There had been no mention of food for them.

'Rations might be tight, but for the right price, there's still meat and cheese to be found.' He leered at Hanno. 'Fancy that?'

'I'm not hungry.'

A dirty chuckle; a gesture at Bogu. 'I'm not surprised. He'd put anyone off their dinner. Bet you're thirsty, eh?'

Hanno's mouth was as dry as a riverbed in high summer, but he didn't utter a word.

The officer picked up a red clay jug from the table, and placed it to Hanno's lips. 'Drink.'

It's piss, thought Hanno, keeping his mouth firmly shut.

The officer tipped the jug up. A little fluid poured out. To Hanno's surprise, it didn't smell bad. His thirst got the better of him. He tasted it and was amazed. The liquid was stale, warm, but it was water. Opening his mouth, he let the officer pour more down his throat. Unable to swallow it fast enough, some went into his windpipe. He jerked his head away, coughing. The movement made fresh pain radiate from his shoulders.

The officer laughed. 'Had enough?'

He was only being offered it so that he'd be able to endure more torture, but Hanno was so thirsty that he didn't care. 'More.' He managed to swallow three mouthfuls before the officer took away the jug.

'Right. Back to business.' Using a piece of cloth to protect his hand from the heat, the officer trailed his fingers over the irons that jutted from the brazier. 'Which one shall we start with?' He pulled out the length of metal with the 'F' on the end of it, and the triarii sniggered. Hanno thought he would lose control of his sphincter. *Not that, please.*

'It's too soon for that one.' He selected another, a simple poker. Its end glowed white hot as it emerged from the fire. The officer studied it with a bemused look.

Eshmoun, Hanno prayed. Lend me some of your strength, for I am weak. He tensed as the officer stalked over. Bogu had revealed a substantial amount about Hannibal's army. What else would the Roman want to know?

Without a word, the officer reached up and placed the poker against his left armpit.

Shock that there hadn't even been a question filled Hanno, but the burning agony from the hot metal was far worse. A bellow ripped free of his lips, and he was unable to stop himself from jerking away to try and escape his tormentor. This in turn nearly wrenched his arms from their sockets. He sagged back down, straight on to the poker. 'AAAAAHHHHH!' Hanno screamed, pushing backwards with his toes.

With a sneer, the officer moved his hand a fraction, bringing the poker back into contact with Hanno's flesh. This time, he could not move away from it. There was a sizzling sound, and his nostrils filled with the smell of cooking flesh. He shrieked again. To his shame, his bladder voided itself. Warm urine soaked through his garments and ran down his legs.

'Look! The gugga has pissed himself!' crowed the officer. He stepped back to study his handiwork.

Hanno mustered his strength, and what was left of his pride. 'Come closer. I was trying to piss on you,' he croaked.

'You filth. Still got a bit of spirit, eh?'

Hanno glowered at him.

'So you're this maggot's commander?'

'I am.'

'You're young to lead a phalanx. Hannibal must have few choices if he selects a child to command some of his best men.'

'There were many casualties crossing the Alps.' Hanno said nothing about his father having Hannibal's ear.

A *phhhh* of contempt. 'There must have been junior officers who had survived, or veterans who had proved themselves.'

Hanno didn't reply.

The officer's face grew crafty. 'In the Roman army, it's often about whom you know. I doubt it's any different among the guggas. Who's your father? Or your brother?' Hanno didn't answer, so he brought the poker towards his face.

Hanno's fear swelled. What's in a name? he thought. 'My father is called Malchus.'

'What rank does he hold?'

'He's just a phalanx commander, like me.'

'You're lying, I can tell!'

'I'm not.'

'We'll see about that later,' retorted the officer, eyeing Bogu. 'Was your man telling the truth about the size of Hannibal's army? Thirty-odd thousand soldiers?'

Answering truthfully wouldn't tell the Roman anything more than a good scout would find out. 'That'd be about right, but it's growing in size. More Gauls and Ligurians are joining every day.'

'Tribal scum! Most of them would turn on their own mothers if they thought there was any gain to it.' The officer paced up and down, brooding. 'Hannibal wants our grain, I take it?'

'Yes.'

'And if we give it to him?'

Hanno doubted the officer had the authority to open the gates. He was asking because he was scared. That gave him a little satisfaction. Hanno had no idea how many of the inhabitants of Victumulae were citizens. Most, he supposed. Non-citizens had no need to live behind the protection of high walls. Did they know what lay in store for them when the town fell? Hannibal had begun using a clever new tactic, exploiting the fact that Cisalpine Gaul was not fully under the Republic's control. All non-Romans who surrendered to his forces were being spared. They were told that Carthage had no quarrel with them, and sent on their way. Captured Romans, on the other hand, were executed or enslaved. The policy was designed to foment unrest among Rome's allies. The strategy was in its early stages, but Hannibal had high hopes for its success.

The officer would know, or at least suspect, what might happen when Hannibal's army stormed in, Hanno decided. That knowledge alone would ensure him an agonising death. He might as well put the fear of Hades into the whoreson. 'Most of the citizens here will be enslaved; some will be executed. Their properties will be confiscated or destroyed.'

His tormentor's lips pinched white; behind him, the triarii growled with anger. 'And the non-citizens?' asked the officer.

'They will not be harmed. Carthage wishes them no ill.' Hannibal's concept was a bloody clever one, Hanno thought.

'D'you hear this whoreson?' cried the officer. 'He's got some nerve, eh?'

'Let me have a turn with him, sir,' pleaded the wall-eyed soldier.

'And me!' added his companion.

The officer studied Hanno's face. Although his fear was rising to new heights, Hanno managed to glare back. A long moment passed, but neither would look down first.

'I know a better way of making the dog suffer,' said the officer. 'What made him most angry was when I called him a slave.'

Sheer terror convulsed Hanno as the Roman pulled the iron with the 'F' on the end of it from the fire. *Not that, Eshmoun, please! Baal Hammon, save me! Melqart, do something!*

His pleas were in vain.

'This is what stings your gugga pride, isn't it?' The officer brandished the iron as he approached. 'The fact that you'll be marked as a slave for the rest of your miserable life!'

More than anything, Hanno longed to have a sword in his hand, so he could run his tormentor through. But his reality could not have been more different. Gritting his teeth, he steeled himself for the worst pain of all.

The officer glanced at the triarii. 'Of course he'll be halfway to Hades in a few hours, but who's counting?'

The soldiers' roars of laughter rang in Hanno's ears as the 'F' moved up towards his face.

His fear got the better of him. 'Don't do it. I spared your life.'

'What are you talking about? Have you gone mad?' cried the officer, but he stayed his arm.

'About a week ago, you and your men were ambushed in your camp. The fighting was vicious and many of your men were slain. You were retreating when I got the better of you. I let you go, when I could have killed you.' As shock filled the officer's face, Hanno prayed that he didn't know the real reason that he yet lived. All he, Hanno, had been trying to do was save Mutt's life.

His prayer seemed to have been answered, as the officer smiled. 'By Jupiter, you *were* there! How else could you know those details?'

'I ask for a quick end, that's all,' said Hanno quickly.

Silence fell.

Let him just kill me. Please.

'You should have slain me. It's what I would have done to you,' said the officer with a cruel smile. 'It changes nothing. For invading our land, you guggas deserve everything that comes your way. Hold him,' he ordered. 'He'll buck like a mule.'

Hanno bit down on his disappointment and terror, and gambled all on something utterly crazy. 'There's no need,' he said. 'I can take the pain.'

The officer's eyebrows rose. 'The gugga reconciles himself to his fate.'

His tormentor took great care to aim the iron right at the centre of Hanno's forehead. The heat radiating from it was unbearable, but Hanno waited until the last moment before he jerked his head up and to the left. The officer swore, but was unable to stop himself planting the 'F' on the right side of Hanno's neck, just below the angle of his jaw.

Hiss. Stars of white-hot agony burst across Hanno's vision. Waves of it tore from his neck and down into his chest. They shot up into his very brain. He screeched at the top of his voice. He cursed. His bladder emptied itself again. As his legs gave way beneath him, his shoulders took all of his body weight. Yet the pain of that was as nothing compared to the excruciating hurt where the iron had met his flesh. The smell of burned meat filled his nostrils, caught in the back of his throat. He retched; up came a few mouthfuls of bile. And then he was falling, falling, down a bottomless well. At the mouth of the well, he could dimly make out the officer's face, which was twisted with fury. The Roman was shouting something, but Hanno could not make out the words. He wanted to reply, to say, 'I'm no slave,' but his throat wouldn't work. A door slammed; other voices were raised. They too were unintelligible.

Confusion filled Hanno as he slipped away into the blackness.

* * *

Bostar burned with anger as he gazed at Victumulae, which lay a quarter of a mile distant. It was entirely surrounded by the antlike figures of thousands of men. The air was filled with the tramp of feet on the hard ground and shouted orders as the units designated for the attack marched into position. There were regular twangs from the light *ballistae* as they shot at the ramparts. The stones landed with dull thumps, which were often followed by screams. Bands of Balearic slingers in light tunics whirled and spun before the walls, adding their slingshots to the showers of missiles. Large formations of Gauls advanced, chanting war songs and blowing their carnyxes in a deafening crescendo of sound. Ringed by his senior officers and a group of *scutarii*, his best Iberian infantry, Hannibal watched the operation from the back of his horse, some two hundred paces away. The remaining elephants stood nearby, their mere presence designed to intimidate the defenders.

After the rousing speech that Hannibal had just given, Bostar longed to be with the Gauls who were advancing with ladders to the foot of the walls, or with those who were already battering at the main gate with a ram fashioned from the trunk of a massive oak. Hannibal had praised every man in his army. Told them that he was proud of how they had overcome all obstacles in their path. He was impressed by their discipline, their bravery and fortitude. He'd said that their loyalty to him could be repaid in only one way – with a deep loyalty of his own. 'I will do anything for you, my men,' Hannibal had cried. 'I will endure the same hardships. Sleep on the same rough ground. Fight the same enemies. Shed my blood. And if I have to, I will lay down my life for you!' Those last words had stirred Bostar's passions deeply, and from the mighty roar that had followed, he judged it to have had the same effect on every soldier within earshot. All he'd wanted to do after that was to attack. Yet he and his spearmen had been ordered to stay put. As at the Trebia, Hannibal was conserving his veterans. They had seen some action during a vicious mêlée on the road the previous day, but that was it. Bostar's fist clenched on the hilt of his sword. *There had better be some Romans for me to kill when we get into the town.* His desire to shed blood wasn't just because of Hannibal's rallying call. Hanno's presumed death by drowning had been hard enough to bear. The grief of it had scourged Bostar for many months. Why couldn't the gods have taken Sapho, his other brother, with whom he had a fractious relationship? To have been reunited with Hanno out of the blue had seemed the most incredible of divine gifts, but to lose him again so soon was too cruel. It wasn't as if he could even blame Hanno's second-in-command. Mutt had asked to be punished, but, as Hannibal had said, it was clear that, misguided or not, Hanno had brought his own fate down on his head. Why did he act so rashly? wondered Bostar yet again.

'A shekel for your thoughts,' said a deep, gravelly voice.

Bostar's head turned. A short but distinguished-looking officer in a *pilos* helmet with a scarlet horsehair crest stood before him. An iron cuirass decorated with gold and silver inlay protected his midriff; layered *pteryges* concealed his groin. Under his armour, he wore a red short-sleeved tunic and a padded jerkin, and he was armed with a stabbing sword that hung in its sheath from a baldric over his right shoulder. To either side, Bostar's men were grinning and saluting. 'Father,' he said, dipping his head in respect.

'You were a world away as I walked up,' declared Malchus. 'Thinking about Hanno, I'd wager.'

'Of course.'

'My thoughts are full of him too.' Malchus scratched at a tight grey curl that had escaped from under his felt liner. 'The best we can hope for is that he died bravely.'

That's not much consolation, thought Bostar sadly, but he didn't say it. Instead, he nodded. 'It would be good to discover what happened to him.'

A grimace. 'With the mood the Gauls are in after Hannibal's speech, I wouldn't bank on finding many Romans alive after the town falls.'

'That was partly why I wanted to take part in the initial assault,' whispered Bostar.

Malchus sighed. 'You know why Hannibal sent in the Gauls first. Disobeying his orders again would not be advisable, however good your reason. The needs of the army come before our own.'

Although the sentiment was true, it was hard to accept. Bostar did his best. He was sure now that Hanno had been attempting to discover information of potential use to Hannibal. If he'd succeeded, it would have been a first step in restoring himself to favour. Instead, it was a move that had ended with his death. Now Bostar was about to lose the only chance of finding out what had happened to his younger brother. He swallowed his anger. Hannibal was their leader. He knew best. 'Yes, Father.'

'The gods give, and the gods take away. But at least we will have our vengeance this day.' Malchus' lips peeled into a snarl, and he raised his voice. 'In order that the surrounding towns understand that resistance is futile, Hannibal has ordered that the Romans' attempt to surrender this morning is to be ignored. Every citizen within the walls is to be killed.'

That set Bostar's spearmen to cheering.

It wasn't Bostar's way to find commands of this type appealing – as Sapho did – but the thought of what Hanno might have been put through made his blood boil. He spun to regard his men. 'The Gauls had best leave some alive for us, eh?'

'Yes!' They bellowed their enthusiasm. 'Kill! Kill! Kill!'

The chant was taken up from the phalanx that stood a short distance to their right. Bostar raised a hand to the figure who stood at its head. Mutt returned the gesture. With Hanno gone, he had been given temporary command of the unit.

'Those lads will fight you for a position on the ladders,' said Malchus. 'The Romans have to learn the harshest of lessons for there to be any chance of us succeeding in our mission. They won't be won over by lenient treatment of their towns and of the prisoners we take.'

Malchus took no joy in killing civilians. Nor did Bostar, yet it had to be done. Why did Sapho have to enjoy it? he wondered.

'That's why Hannibal is sending in a man like Sapho in the first wave,' said Malchus, as if reading his mind.

Bostar said nothing.

Malchus gave him a sharp look. 'You two, eh? Always quarrelling. Hannibal knows that your skills lie elsewhere. Nor will he have forgotten how you saved his life at Saguntum. He will call on you again in the future. That doesn't mean he doesn't need Sapho too.'

'I understand.' Secretly, Bostar wished that things were different. That Sapho had been the one to have been captured and killed, not Hanno. He'd thought it at other times, but never so strongly and with so little guilt.

'Maybe you two can see this as a way to move on. To come together a little.'

Their father had no idea of the depth of bitterness between him and Sapho, thought Bostar. Their feud had been going on since they had left Hannibal's base in southern Iberia more than a year and a half previously. It had alleviated somewhat during the elation after the victory at the Trebia, but it had soon returned. Sapho would stop at nothing to become one of Hannibal's favoured officers. His desire for Roman blood seemed unquenchable. But Bostar's conscience nagged at him. Sapho was still his brother. His only living brother, who had saved his life in the Alps – despite not really wanting to. Bostar had sworn to repay the debt. Until that had been achieved, he'd have to make a pretence for his father's sake. Maybe their relationship would improve as a consequence. He pulled a weary smile. 'I'll talk to him, Father, I promise.'

'Hanno would approve.'

'He'd also like to know that we sent him on his way with a fitting sacrifice,' said Bostar, giving the walls of Victumulae a pitiless stare.

'I think we can guarantee him that,' growled Malchus.

Hanno woke, lying on the floor, screaming. The pain was even worse than before. A constant thrumming sensation centred in his neck. It made all his other hurts disappear. It consumed Hanno as flames eat away at dry tinder. All he wanted was for it to end. 'Help,' he mumbled. 'Help.'

A soft voice answered.

Hanno didn't recognise it. He opened his eyes, puzzled. Instead of the Roman officer, he saw a dark-skinned figure crouched over him, a man he vaguely recognised. He licked dry lips. 'W-who are you?'

'I'm called Bomilcar.'

'Bomilcar?' As confusion filled Hanno, the darkness took him again.

When he awoke, he could feel something cool trickling into his mouth. Water. His eyes blinked open. Bomilcar was leaning over him, holding a cup to his lips. Hanno's thirst was overwhelming, but terror consumed him at the thought of the agony that swallowing would cause.

'You must drink,' urged Bomilcar.

Hanno had seen men drop from lack of water during the summers in Carthage. Since his capture, all he'd had was the few mouthfuls the officer had given him. He forced himself to take a tiny sip. The pain in his throat was extreme, but the pleasure as the liquid hit his stomach was worth it. He kept swallowing until he could take no more. The effort used up a lot of his strength. Hanno lay back on the cold stone, wondering where the officer and his two men were, but feeling too tired to care. His eyelids fluttered and closed.

'Wake up! You can't sleep. Not now.'

Hanno felt a hand take his arm. The movement set off a fresh wave of pain in his neck. 'Gods, that hurts! Leave me alone,' he snarled.

'If you want to live, you need to get up.'

Bomilcar's urgent tone sank in. Hanno eyed him askance. 'You have a Carthaginian name.'

'That's right. I was brought here to translate what your comrade said, remember?'

Slowly, it came back to Hanno. 'You're the slave?'

A flicker of emotion. 'Yes.'

Suspicion filled Hanno. 'Have they sent you to see what you can find out from me on your own?'

Sounds from beyond the cell. A man shouting.

Bomilcar's gaze shot to the door. After a few heartbeats, the noise died away and he relaxed a fraction. 'No. I'm here to get you out.'

'I-I don't understand.'

'Can you sit up?' Bomilcar extended both his hands.

Struggling to understand, Hanno let the other help him to a sitting position. The first thing he saw was Bogu, hanging limp from his bonds. A fool could tell he was dead. Go well, thought Hanno dully. I will see you in the afterlife. His eyes flickered to the brazier, which had gone cold. Hours, maybe more must have passed. 'Where are the Romans?'

'Gone to defend the town.'

Shock filled Hanno before a stab of hope struck home. 'Hannibal's army has arrived?'

'Yes. The Romans marched out to meet him, but he routed them on the road. Hundreds of legionaries were killed, many of them within sight of the town. Hannibal's troops are attacking from all sides as we speak. The garrison is massively outnumbered. It won't be long before our men get a foothold on the ramparts.'

Our men. Hanno's head swirled. He had no doubt that Bostar and Sapho, his brothers, would be among those in the assault's vanguard. 'How long have I been here?'

'A day and two nights. We need to move. Pera swore to come back and kill you once the end was near.'

'Pera?'

'The officer who tortured you.'

'You're really here to free me?' whispered Hanno.

'Of course. You're a Carthaginian, like me. But if we don't move fast, it won't happen at all.'

Hanno's heart filled. 'Thank you.'

'It's nothing.' Bomilcar offered his hand. 'Can you stand?'

Hanno was lightheaded with pain, but his desire to live was still strong. He took the grip and let the other haul him upright. That was when he saw the gladius in Bomilcar's other fist. 'Where did you get that?'

A conspiratorial wink. 'I took it from the guard outside – after I'd smashed an amphora over his head and cut his throat with his own dagger.' He proffered the sword. 'The knife's enough of a weapon for me. Can you use this?'

Hanno reached out eagerly. His fingers closed on the hilt. He hefted the blade, which was heavier than his own sword. Gods, but it felt good to be armed again, although he knew in his bones that he was no real match for a legionary right now. Hanno was about to hand it back when he saw the admiration in Bomilcar's eyes. To him, Hannibal's arrival outside the town must seem like an intervention by the gods. Hanno's protest died in his throat. Despite his weakened condition, he had more chance in a fight than Bomilcar, who had probably never handled an edged weapon until a few moments before. 'Just show me a bastard Roman,' he muttered.

Bomilcar grinned. 'With Baal Hammon's help, that won't be necessary.'

'What's your plan?'

'I brought you a cloak like mine. Once it's on, most people won't give either of us a second look.' Bomilcar eased it over Hanno's shoulders, taking care not to touch his wound. He lifted the hood, which concealed Hanno's neck. 'We'll head for the main gate. That's where Hannibal's attack is concentrated. They're using a battering ram on the doors, and catapults have wreaked havoc on the defenders atop the wall.'

'We can't just stand around in the street waiting for them to break in.'

'No. There's a stable belonging to an inn close to the gate. It's not far. We can hide in the adjacent hay barn. Once our men get inside the town, we'll go out and you can make yourself known.'

'That will be easier said than done,' replied Hanno, remembering Bostar's tales of the madness that had descended on Hannibal's soldiers when Saguntum, in Iberia, had fallen. It would be all too easy for them to be slain in the confusion. He saw Bomilcar's incomprehension but thought it better not to elaborate. 'But it's the best we can do. Lead on.'

'I'll take it as slow as I can. Stay close.' Bomilcar padded to the door, which lay ajar, and peered into the passage beyond. 'All clear.'

Scarcely believing that his legs would carry him, Hanno followed. The acute pain in his neck had lessened a little. Was it thanks to his level of excitement and fear? Hanno didn't know, but he prayed that his newfound strength lasted – and that if it came to it, he would have the energy to fight.

Outside the cell, a flickering oil lamp in an alcove shed a dim light on a scene of carnage. A dead legionary lay in an ever-widening puddle of blood. Hanno felt a grim satisfaction at the rictus of dismay twisting the corpse's face. It was the wall-eyed soldier. He hoped that the opportunity to kill Pera and the other legionary also arose. Don't be rash, his more prudent side shot back. You couldn't best a child, let alone a hale legionary. Everything now was about survival. Swallowing his desire for vengeance, Hanno shuffled around the crimson pool.

The dank corridor led from his cell past a number of other doors. Hanno stopped by one and listened. After a moment, he heard a faint moan. What wretch lay on the other side? he wondered.

'We don't have time to help anyone else,' hissed Bomilcar.

Numbing himself to the fate of the anonymous prisoner, Hanno did as he was told. Every step was sheer agony, but he forced his legs to keep moving. Trying to keep up with Bomilcar's slow pace was difficult, however, and Hanno had to ask him to pause before the end of the passage. The gladius felt as if it were made of lead, but he kept a deathlike grip on it.

At last Bomilcar turned left. Motioning Hanno to stay put, he crept up a stone staircase. He soon returned, looking pleased. 'It's the same as when

I came in. There's only one guard on duty. The rest have been sent to man the defences.'

'Why did he let you through?'

'I told him that Pera had given me a message for the guard on your door.' Another wink. 'He won't suspect a thing until my dagger has cut him a new smile.'

'I'll come too,' Hanno protested.

'No. Our best chance is if I go alone. Wait here until I call you.'

Hanno's wound was throbbing with a new intensity. He could do little but nod.

Padding as silently as a cat, Bomilcar vanished up the staircase.

Trying to ignore his racing heart, Hanno listened with all his might. The murmur of voices, both friendly. A low laugh. The sound of studded sandals moving fast. A question, followed by a cry, cut short. The sound of something heavy hitting the floor. Silence.

Who had died? Unsure, Hanno raised the gladius and prepared to meet his end fighting. When Bomilcar appeared, he let out a relieved sigh. 'You did it.'

'The dog didn't know what hit him.' Bomilcar's tone was wondering. 'I wish I'd done this a long time ago.'

Hanno managed an encouraging smile. 'You'll have plenty of opportunities to hone your skills in Hannibal's army. A man like you will be most welcome.'

Bomilcar gave him a pleased look. 'Best keep moving.'

At the top of the staircase was a small, square guard chamber. A pair of empty bunk beds lined one wall; chunky logs smouldered in a fireplace. Oil lamps guttered from a few spots around the room. Bronze pots and cooking implements lay to one side of the fire, along with loaves of flat bread and a joint of meat. The man who'd been left to watch over the cells was sprawled on his back before the fire, his three-legged stool lying between his legs. A deep wound in the side of his neck still oozed blood.

They skirted the body, making for the only door. Hanno's stomach twisted as Bomilcar opened it. Who knew what lay beyond it? The Carthaginian saw his uncertainty. 'We go up another set of stairs, and then out into the courtyard of the garrison buildings. It's virtually deserted. Every man who can fight is on the walls.'

'There'll be guards on the gate, surely?'

'Only one.'

'We'll have to kill him.'

'That's too risky. Lots of people are going by on the street beyond. There's a storeroom to one side of the prison, though. If we each take an amphora of *acetum* from there, I can say that we've been ordered to take them to the soldiers on the frontline.'

'I'll have to take down my hood. What if he sees my neck?'

Bomilcar frowned in concentration. 'I think he's standing to the right of the entrance. He won't see it.'

Knowing that they had no other option, Hanno nodded in acceptance. May the gods be with us, he prayed. They would need all the help they could get.

After his incarceration, stepping outside felt odd. The chill air stung his wound, but it provided a little relief from the pain. Hanno scanned the cobbled courtyard, which was bordered by barrack buildings. Not a soul was in sight. Overhead, the sky was a dramatic mix of dark reds and pinks. It was early morning and the sun had returned at last, with the promise of blood. Bomilcar led the way to the store, where they both picked up a small amphora. Hanno staggered as he raised his to his left shoulder, sending jagged waves of pain through his body. 'He won't see it now.'

Bomilcar gave him an encouraging look. 'Good idea. Can you make it to the first corner? You can rest there.'

'I have to.' Hanno locked his knees to stop his legs from buckling. *I have to make it that far.*

There was no more discussion. They crossed the courtyard in a diagonal, straight to the main gate. Bomilcar didn't pause as he reached it. Hanno stayed on his heels, keeping his gaze on the ground before him. The gladius, which he'd tucked into his right armpit, threatened to slip from his grip with every step. All he could do was to clench his arm even tighter against his body and pray.

'Where are you going?' barked a voice.

'Taking some acetum to the men on the ramparts, sir,' replied Bomilcar.

'On whose say so?'

'One of the centurions, sir. I don't know his name.'

Silence for a moment. Then, 'Be off with you! My comrades' tongues will be hanging out with thirst.'

Muttering his thanks, Bomilcar headed off to the left. Hanno followed, taking in only the sentry's lower legs and *caligae*. Bomilcar's speed was such that he could barely keep up. Despite his anguish, Hanno dared not slow down. He could feel the soldier's eyes boring into his back. Flutters of panic rose from his stomach, but he shoved them away.

'Hey!'

Hanno almost dropped his amphora.

'Keep moving. Pretend you didn't hear!' hissed Bomilcar without turning his head. 'He can't desert his post.'

'You! Slave!'

They kept walking. Ten paces, then twenty. The sentry spat an oath, but he did not follow them. When Bomilcar turned to his right, on to a wider way, Hanno cried out with relief. His wound and the muscles of his neck were screaming in protest. He could feel fluid oozing down on to his tunic. The moment he was around the corner, he let the amphora slip from his shoulder.

Bomilcar grabbed the bottom before it hit the ground. 'Careful! If it breaks, you'll draw attention. The same if anyone sees that damn sword.' He shoved the gladius, which had slipped down, back up under Hanno's cloak.

'Sorry.' Hanno sagged against the wall, uncaring. It took all of his strength not to fall in a heap.

Bomilcar glanced around the corner. 'We're in luck. The sentry hasn't moved.'

'Just as well. I couldn't run anywhere.' Despite the cold, sweat was pouring down Hanno's face.

'You'll never reach the inn like this. I'll get rid of the amphorae. Pull your hood up and wait here.'

Hanno obeyed. He didn't even see Bomilcar go. Eyes closed, he tried to manage the alternating waves of nausea and stabbing torment that consumed his very being. Around him, he was dimly aware of panicked voices moving past. He heard the name 'Hannibal' being repeated again and again. That's right, you bastards, Hanno thought. Be scared. He's coming.

'Ready?'

Bomilcar's voice made him jump. 'What did you do with the amphorae?'

'I left them down an alleyway.' Bomilcar's face was concerned. 'Can you keep going?'

Hanno rallied what was left of his strength and shoved himself upright. 'I'm not staying here.'

'Good.' Bomilcar's teeth flashed. 'It's about two hundred and fifty paces to the inn. We'll take it slowly. Pretend you're a slave. Don't look at anyone.'

Gritting his teeth, Hanno followed his rescuer. The walk seemed to last an eternity. Most of the traffic was heading away from the gate as men led their wives and families from the fighting. Slaves tottered behind, carrying valuables or leading mules weighed down with food and blankets. Where were they going? Hanno wondered vaguely. There was no escape. The town had to be surrounded. A few soldiers were hurrying the same way that they were, but, locked in discussion about what was happening, they paid the pair no attention. Hanno was glad. He was incapable of fighting. The amphora's weight had distracted him from his neck, but now his wound was sending stabs of pain into every part of his body. They even reached his toes. Lights flashed in front of his eyes and he struggled not to retch constantly. Lightheaded, Hanno had trouble keeping Bomilcar in focus. With a supreme effort, he kept his gaze locked on the Carthaginian's back. By counting his steps in groups of ten, he gave himself tiny goals to reach. Each time he succeeded felt as if he'd run a mile, and by the time Bomilcar halted, Hanno was ready to collapse.

'Nearly there. Another fifty paces and we've made it.'

Hanno's eyes moved down the street. A painted sign depicting a man with a bow and arrows jutted out from a building on the left. 'The Hunter's Rest?'

'That's the one.'

The din of fighting was clearly audible now. Hanno's heart lifted to hear it. The dull booming sound had to be the battering ram smashing into the main gate. The noise of lighter impacts would be stones from Hannibal's catapults. Men were shouting, screaming, crying out. Best of all, he could hear the clash of weapons off each other. *Hannibal is here!* 'D'you hear that?'

Bomilcar frowned. 'What?'

'The sound of metal on metal. It means that Carthaginian soldiers have reached the ramparts! We need to hurry. Best to be out of sight until they've cleared the streets near the gate.'

Bomilcar cast a glance up and down the street before taking Hanno's right arm and placing it over his shoulder, holding it in place with his own right hand. 'I can make it,' Hanno protested, but the Carthaginian was having none of it.

'There's almost no one about. You're weak, and it will be quicker this way.'

Grateful for the assistance, Hanno did not protest further. He remembered little of the rest of their journey. A pair of wounded soldiers limping past on their way to the surgeon. A glance from a curious child. The suspicious stare of the ostler at the stables. His expression changing to a welcoming smile as Bomilcar slipped him a couple of coins. A barn full of hay. The nicker of a nearby horse. And then nothing.

The men of Sapho's phalanx cheered as the main gate cracked and fell inwards, its timbers shattered and riven. Clouds of dust rose. Cries of dismay could be heard from within the walls. The Gauls at the entrance dropped their battering ram and swarmed into the gap, screaming like men possessed. Hundreds of their fellows, prepared for this moment, were hot on their heels. Bare-chested, or clad in tunics or mail shirts, the heavily armed warriors tore into the breach, striking the waiting Romans with an almighty crash. Sapho and his men roared with approval. The Gauls would smash apart the shocked legionaries, clearing the way for them to advance.

Sapho's chest swelled with pride. A stocky man with curly black hair and a broad nose, he took after their father. He was here because Hannibal had not lost his trust in him. His unit would be the first of the regular Carthaginian forces to enter Victumulae. The danger might not be extreme, but there would be ample opportunity to slay Romans. Hannibal's order had deprived them of their right to live. The more that died, the merrier. His general had given the order, and he would follow it to the letter. Like his brothers, Sapho had grown up on tales of the wrongs done to Carthage by Rome. This war, this battle provided the chance for revenge. If he was lucky, there might be opportunity to secure the grain stores, which would surely raise him in Hannibal's regard. Sapho didn't suppose that anyone would happen upon Hanno, but that was possible too. The garrison buildings would need to be searched. It would please their father if his body were found. Despite Sapho's jealousy of Hanno, who had always seemed Malchus' favourite, his youngest brother deserved a decent burial.

He shot a spiteful glance in the direction of Bostar's phalanx. At last he was receiving more recognition than his younger brother. It was unfortunate that he was out of sight. Sapho would have loved to see Bostar's unhappy expression before he entered the town. Behind him, Sapho suddenly became aware of his men's eagerness. Their ranks were swaying forward and back several steps. To their rear, a large group of Iberian infantry were shouting and calling for him to advance. It was time to move. Hannibal was watching.

'Form up, six men wide. Close order. Those at the front and sides, raise shields. Expect missiles, and have your spears at the ready.' Placing himself in the centre of the first rank, Sapho led his spearmen forward at a slow walk. His eyes carefully scanned the ramparts, searching for any indication of an attack. To his satisfaction, the defenders he could see were concentrating on their attempts to repel the Gauls who were ascending more than half a dozen ladders. Sapho kept his guard up until they had reached the wall. Even then, he did not relax. A single legionary with a javelin could be dangerous.

They passed under the arched gateway, stepping over the cracked planking of the gate. Just a few steps further, the carnage began. The street was strewn with the dead, almost all of them Roman. Gaping hack wounds to the neck, chest or limbs decorated many of the corpses. More than one had been decapitated. The entire area had been stained a shocking red colour. Discarded equipment was strewn here and there, left by the men who had run. Sapho felt a new respect for the Gauls. This was proof of the effectiveness of their charge on a disorganised enemy.

'Let's hope they've left some for us, eh?' he shouted.

His men bellowed their bloodlust back at him.

They moved down the main street, while behind them the Iberians spread out into every side alley. Sapho had no idea that Hanno, still living, was so close. Or that his fate hung by the slimmest of threads.

*   *   *

Hanno was woken by shouting. Cursing. Grunts of pain. As his eyes opened, the agony from his neck wound returned with new force. What he saw instantly made him forget his own discomfort, however. Bomilcar had been strung by his neck from an overhead beam by a length of rope. A strip of cloth was tied round his head, gagging him. A trio of Iberian infantrymen stood in a circle, taking it in turns to boot him from one to another. With each blow, Bomilcar struggled not to fall over. If he did, he would choke to death. The Iberians were passing a cracked amphora around, and their flushed cheeks told Hanno that they'd already consumed plenty of its contents. That was probably the reason that Bomilcar was still alive. How much longer he would survive was debatable, though. One man had drawn his *falcata* and was whetting its blade with an oilstone.

Why haven't they done the same to me? Hanno moved a hand, disturbing a pile of hay. Understanding hit home. Only his head was visible. Bomilcar had scattered hay over him as a blanket and the Iberians hadn't noticed him. Heart pounding, Hanno lay back down. If he didn't move, chances were that they would never discover his hiding place, which was fifteen paces deeper into the barn. By the next morning, it would be safe to go out on the streets again. He would be reunited with his family.

His pleasure at that thought was washed away by a surging guilt. To do that, he would have to watch Bomilcar die, tortured to death as he would have been by Pera. Hanno could no more do that than he could have slain Quintus after the ambush. He had to act, and fast. What was his best tactic? The rigid length by his side had to be the gladius, but standing up with that in his fist would guarantee a quick death. Better to be unarmed. Less of a threat. New fear caressed his spine. What if the Iberians didn't speak enough Carthaginian to understand him? Many of the lower ranking troops in Hannibal's army knew little to none of their General's tongue. There was no need because their officers could.

The man with the falcata tested the edge of his blade with his thumb and grimaced in approval. His gaze moved to Bomilcar.

He would have to take the chance, decided Hanno. Otherwise, it would be too late. Brushing the hay from his body, he sat up, careful not to touch the gladius.

No one noticed him, so he stood up and coughed.

Three startled faces spun to regard him. There was an instant's delay, and then the Iberians were drawing their weapons and swarming towards him.

'HANNIBAL!' shouted Hanno as loudly as he could.

That brought them to a screeching stop.

'Hannibal is my leader too,' he said in Carthaginian. 'You understand?'

Blank looks from two of the men, but the third scowled. He spat a question in Iberian.

Hanno didn't understand a word. He repeated Hannibal's name over and over, but the Iberians didn't look impressed. Raising their swords, they padded towards him, reminding him of how deadly they were in battle. It hasn't worked. I'm dead, he thought wearily.

That was when one of them pointed at him and asked another question.

Hanno looked down in confusion. He glanced at their crimson-edged tunics and then at his own red one. Understanding, he tugged at the fabric like a maniac. 'Yes! I am the commander of a phalanx! Libyan spearmen! Libyans!'

'Pha-lanx?' demanded one of the Iberians, adding in accented Carthaginian, 'You from Carthage?'

'Yes! Yes!' cried Hanno. 'I am from Carthage! The other man is Carthaginian too.'

The tension vanished as the smell of a dead carcase is carried off by the wind. Suddenly, the Iberians were all smiles. 'Carthaginians!' they roared. 'Hannibal!' Bomilcar was ungagged and cut down with many apologies; both of them were given some wine. When Hanno's wound was spotted, there were hisses of dismay. One Iberian produced a clean strip of cloth, which he insisted on wrapping around Hanno's neck. 'Surgeon,' he kept repeating. 'You need . . . surgeon.'

'I know,' said Hanno. 'But first I need to find my father, or my brothers.'

The Iberian didn't understand, but he heard the urgency in Hanno's voice. 'Wait,' he ordered.

Hanno was happy to obey. Sitting beside Bomilcar, with the first warm flush of the wine coursing through his veins, he felt vaguely human. 'We made it,' he said. 'Thanks to you.'

Bomilcar grinned. 'I can't believe it. For the first time in five years, I'm free.'

'You'll be well rewarded for what you've done,' swore Hanno. 'And I'll always be in your debt.'

They gripped hands to seal a new bond of friendship.

The Iberian soon returned with one of his officers, who spoke better Carthaginian. Hearing Hanno's story, he arranged for a stretcher to be brought and for a messenger to find Malchus.

'I need to see my father first,' Hanno insisted.

'You're as pale as a ghost. He can find you in the field hospital,' replied the officer.

'No.' Hanno tried to stand, but his legs gave way beneath him.

It was the last thing he remembered.

Hanno woke to the sound of raised voices. His mind filled with an image of the Iberians who had attacked Bomilcar and his eyes jerked open. To his confusion, the first face he saw was Bostar's. His brother looked angry; he was gesticulating at someone beyond Hanno's range of vision. Overhead, there was tent fabric. He was in a bed, not the hay barn. 'Where am I?'

'Praise all the gods! He's come back to us,' cried Bostar, his expression softening. 'How are you feeling?'

'A-all right, I suppose.' Without thinking, Hanno's hand rose to his neck. He had enough time to feel the thick bandage before Bostar's hand closed over his.

'Don't touch. The surgeon says it's just starting to heal.'

Hanno felt a dull throbbing from the area. 'It doesn't hurt like it did.'

'That will be thanks to the poppy juice. The surgeon has been dosing you with it three to four times a day.'

A series of fractured images flashed past Hanno's vision. He did have a vague recollection of bitter-tasting liquid being forced down his throat.

'Bomilcar has told us a lot of what went on,' said Sapho in an enquiring tone.

Hanno managed to sit up, wincing at a jag of pain from his wound. 'After I was taken prisoner?'

'Yes,' said Bostar gently. 'And Mutt told us the first part of the story.' Hanno saw his favourite brother's eyes travel to his neck. 'It's bad, eh?'

Bostar didn't answer.

'What has the surgeon said?' demanded Hanno.

'At first, that you wouldn't survive. But you made it through the first night and day, and then the next. It was a surprise to all of us.' Bostar cast his eyes at Sapho, who nodded to acknowledge the truth of his words. 'If prayer can help, then the gods had a hand in your recovery. We spent most of the time on our knees. Even Father joined in!'

Hanno began to appreciate the relief in his brothers' faces, especially that of Bostar. 'How long have I been asleep?'

'Six days so far,' replied Bostar. 'You seemed to turn a corner yesterday, though, when the fever broke. The surgeon said that the wound was weeping less and starting to close over.'

'It's not a wound. It's a Latin letter "F",' said Hanno bitterly. '"F" for fugitivus.'

'You're no slave!' cried Sapho angrily. Bostar echoed his words.

'I had told the officer who was interrogating me about my enslavement,' Hanno explained. 'He wanted to mark me out as a runaway for the last few hours of my life. It was supposed to be in the centre of my forehead, but I managed to move at the last moment. Better to have the brand on my neck, eh?' He pulled a grim smile.

Neither brother laughed. 'Where did the filthy son of a whore go?' spat Sapho.

'To defend the walls, I think. That's the only reason I'm still alive. Bomilcar must have told you how he then came in and killed my guard. If it hadn't been for him . . .' Hanno's voice trailed away.

'Yes. He's a good man. His actions won't be forgotten,' said Bostar. 'A shame we didn't know what had happened as we entered Victumulae. Although seeking you would have been like looking for a needle in a haystack.'

'Did many get away?' asked Hanno resignedly. He didn't doubt that a cur like Pera would find a way to escape even the sacking of a town.

'Only the non-citizens, and there were precious few of them,' Sapho replied with a savage leer. 'Our men won't have known who your officer was, but he's still deader than a fly-blown corpse that's been on a crucifix for a week.'

'I'd have liked to slay him myself, though,' said Hanno. It felt fortunate

– and odd – that Pera had refused to grant him an easy death. If the Roman had granted his request, he wouldn't be lying where he was. That didn't stop Hanno from wishing that Pera had died screaming.

'There will be plenty more opportunities to kill men like him,' said Sapho. 'New Roman armies will come to meet us.'

'Good!' Hanno couldn't wait to be part of it. He wanted some tangible revenge for what had been done to him. He would have preferred Pera, but any Roman would do.

'Soon we march south. Hannibal wants all of us ready for the journey, including you,' added Bostar.

'He has asked for me?' asked Hanno, surprised.

'Asked for you? He has visited twice,' declared Sapho.

'He said that you have more lives than a cat!' Bostar winked. 'Even he has heard how all of our spearmen think of you as something of a talisman. "Let him bring us good luck as we march," he said.'

Hanno's heart leaped. It seemed that he was returning to Hannibal's good books, which was most unexpected. Something good had come of his rash behaviour after all.

Chapter V

Outside Placentia

Quintus scowled as he caught sight of his father approaching. A lot had happened in the month since his hunting trip, but one thing had been constant: Fabricius' towering anger at what he had done. It hadn't been as evident during the week he'd spent in the camp hospital, having his wound cleaned and monitored, and poultices applied to it twice a day. Once the surgeon had discharged Quintus, however, things had changed. Fabricius had subjected him to a long lecture about his stupidity. Leaving the camp without permission. Taking so few men with him. Attacking the Gauls instead of trying to avoid them. He had gone on and on until Quintus thought his head would explode. He'd tried to justify his actions, tried to explain how their casualties had been light compared to those suffered by the warriors. It had been like banging his head on a wall. As his father, Fabricius could say and do what he wished. It was even permissible for the head of a Roman family to strike his children dead if they displeased him. That wasn't likely, but Fabricius swore that Quintus was to return home the moment he'd sufficiently recovered. His father had also declared that, if needs be, he had enough friends in high places to ensure that Quintus didn't serve in the military again. That didn't bear thinking about.

The worst thing about his convalescence was that he couldn't train with Calatinus and his comrades, or go on patrol, during these, the last opportunities he would have for a long time, possibly ever. His ribs had healed and the strength was returning to his left arm, but Quintus still couldn't hold a shield for long. He spent a couple of hours every day riding his horse, but his interest in that had palled long since. Fabricius kept him busy running errands around the camp, but that felt demeaning. Quintus had taken to avoiding his father. He would lurk in his tent after his comrades had left for the morning, playing endless games of Three in a Line on Calatinus' small clay board. In between, he'd lift his shield to strengthen his left arm. Of course Fabricius knew where to find him, which was no doubt why he was here now. Quintus thought about retreating further into the tent, but there was no point. He threw his shoulders back and stepped outside instead. 'Father.'

'I find you here, again.'

Quintus gave a careless shrug. 'I was lifting weights with my arm.'

Fabricius' lips thinned. 'You were supposed to come to my quarters first thing.'

'I forgot.'

Slap! Fabricius' palm struck his cheek, and Quintus yelped.

'You're not too big yet for me to take a whip to your back. Is that what you want?'

'Do what you wish,' said Quintus with a curl of his lip. 'I can't stop you.'

Fury flared in Fabricius' eyes. 'Lucky for you, I need an important message taken somewhere. Otherwise, I would tan your hide right now!'

Quintus felt a sour delight at his father's frustration. He waited.

Fabricius produced a tightly rolled parchment. 'You're to find a centurion by the name of Marcus Junius Corax. He serves in Longus' first legion, and commands a maniple of *hastati*.'

'What does it say?' Fabricius rarely told him anything, but Quintus was curious. Cavalry and infantry didn't often have much to do with each other.

'None of your business!' snapped Fabricius. 'Just deliver the damn message.'

'Yes, Father.' Biting his lip, Quintus took the parchment.

'Wait for a reply, and then find me on the open ground beyond the camp.' Fabricius was already half a dozen paces away.

Quintus threw a poisonous stare after him. Upon his return, he'd have to traipse around after Fabricius, acting as his unofficial messenger for the rest of the day. He rubbed at the purple scar on the front of his bicep, willing it to recover. It was time for another offering to Aesculapius, the god of healing. He could do that this evening. Donning his cloak, Quintus set out for the legionaries' tent lines. Taking his horse didn't appeal; holding the reins quickly tired out his weak arm.

Despite the losses at the Trebia, the camp had still been erected as a double consular one, albeit smaller than usual. The fact that Corax was in one of Longus' legions meant a long walk indeed. The consuls' quarters were placed back to back and the legionary tent lines extended to the furthest rampart.

Quintus' spirits rose a little as he walked. His interest in legionaries and what made them the men they were had persisted, but he never got to spend any time with them. Cavalrymen were a social class above infantry, and the two rarely mixed. Quintus longed to push through that barrier, if only for a while. He wanted to know what it had felt like to drive through the Carthaginian centre. Perhaps Corax wouldn't give him an immediate reply, which would give him time to talk to some of his men.

His search took a long time, but Quintus finally came upon Corax's maniple's tent lines. They lay not far from Longus' headquarters, but the centurion wasn't there. As a cynical-looking *hastatus* told him, Corax liked to get out and about. He was drilling his men, 'Somewhere on the training ground.' Trying not to feel frustrated, Quintus headed for the *porta praetoria*, the entrance that lay furthest from his own tent.

Beyond the walls and the deep defensive ditch lay the area designated for the soldiers' training. As usual, it was filled with thousands of men. The four types of legionary were for the most part easy to differentiate one from another, which made Quintus' task a little easier. Many of the *velites*, or skirmishers, had been on sentry duty at each of the gates, but the rest were hurling javelins while junior officers looked on. These were the youngest and poorest members of the army. Some could be distinguished by the strips of wolf skin adorning their helmets. In another section, the triarii, the most experienced legionaries who formed the third rank in battle, stood out thanks to their mail shirts and long thrusting spears. The hastati and *principes*, who made up the first and second ranks respectively, were harder to differentiate. Both these types of soldier wore simple bronze helmets, although some had triple feather crests; square breastplates protected their chests. Only the wealthiest men wore mail shirts similar to those seen on the veteran triarii. Their weapons and shields were similar too. There were thousands of them marching, halting, presenting arms and assuming battle formation in maniples, or double centuries. Volleys of javelins followed, and then a charge, before the whole procedure was repeated. Centurions and *optiones* looked on, roaring orders and reprimands in equal measure. The maniples' standards were present, but the writing on each was so small that Quintus would have to approach each one. With a sigh, he walked to the nearest.

By the tenth maniple, he was getting angry. From the occasional snickers that followed him, Quintus felt sure that he was deliberately being sent astray. The eleventh unit he approached was some distance from the rest. The two centurions had separated their soldiers into their individual centuries. Each man carried a wooden shield and sword. Over and over, they charged each other, slowing at the last moment before smashing together in a loud crash that wasn't dissimilar to what Quintus had heard in battle. The thrusts he saw being delivered were as savage as the real thing too. It was so very different to fighting from the back of a horse, which, thanks to its mobile nature, rarely involved more than an exchange of one or two blows. Engrossed by the scene, Quintus drew quite near to the centurions without realising.

'It's tough work,' said a voice.

Quintus looked around, startled. One of the centurions, a man in early middle age with deep-set eyes and a narrow face, was staring straight at him. 'It looks it, sir.'

'You're here on business.' He pointed at the parchment in Quintus' fist.

'Yes, sir.' Quintus wasn't sure why, but he didn't want to be taken as the spoilt son of a cavalry officer. He adopted a rougher accent than his usual one. 'Have you any idea where I'd find Marcus Junius Corax, centurion of hastati in Longus' First Legion?'

A sardonic smile. 'Look no further. Why do you want me?'

'This, sir.' Quintus hurried forward. 'It's from Gaius Fabricius, cavalry commander.'

'I've heard of him.' Taking the parchment, Corax slit the wax seal and unrolled it. His lips moved silently as he read. 'Interesting,' he said after a moment.

Quintus didn't hear. All his attention was on the nearest hastati, who were striving to knock one another over with great shoves of their *scuta*.

'It's filthy, dirty work,' said Corax. 'Not like the glory stuff the cavalry boys get to take part in.'

'There isn't too much glory being in the cavalry these days,' Quintus replied bitterly.

'No, I don't suppose there is. I've heard good things about Fabricius, though.'

'I'm sure you have, sir.' Quintus failed to keep all the sarcasm from his voice.

He was relieved when Corax didn't comment.

'When does he want a reply?'

'He just told me to wait, sir.'

'Fine. I won't be long.' Corax barked an order, and his men pulled apart, their chests heaving. He stalked over to them and issued new orders. This time, his soldiers formed into two lines and began trotting up and down, at speed.

Quintus watched, fascinated. This was fitness training as he'd never seen it. The wooden training equipment was twice as heavy as the real thing, and soon the hastati were sweating heavily. That was when Corax had them sprint back and forth ten times. His father never had his men train this hard, thought Quintus critically. Just because they rode horses didn't mean that it wasn't a good idea. He wondered again what it would be like to fight on foot, surrounded by dozens of comrades. Would it feel better than being a cavalryman?

'You're interested.'

'Yes, sir.'

'Ever thought of joining the infantry?'

Quintus struggled for an answer. His assumed accent, simple cloak and plain tunic had made Corax think he was nothing more than Fabricius' servant. 'As it happens, I have, sir.'

'Well, we need velites as much as any type of soldier.'

Quintus tried to look pleased. His fantasy had been that of becoming a heavy infantryman, but Corax's words had put a madcap plan into his head. For it ever to have any chance of becoming reality, he had to continue the charade. 'Yes, sir.'

'Your master might not be too happy, but we'd be pleased to have you. If you make it through the initial training, of course. Some officers don't bother making the new recruits do too much, but not me.'

'Thank you, sir. I'd be honoured.' Would I? Quintus wondered. He'd heard it said before that the velites were the dregs at the bottom of the amphora. Yet joining their number would be better than the shame of being sent home. Of never serving in the army again.

'Don't be honoured. Give some serious thought to it. Rome needs men like you in its legions. After a year or two's service, you could be promoted. Become a hastatus.'

Excitement gripped Quintus at that idea, but a twinge from his left arm put paid to any sudden decisions. Even if he were to start training with the velites, his injury would soon be discovered. Explaining away a wound that had been caused by an arrow would be nigh-on impossible. Besides, he needed time to consider his options. 'I'll think about it, sir.'

Corax studied him for a moment, but then his *optio* shouted a question and he was gone.

Yet by the time that Corax had scribbled a reply at the bottom of Fabricius' message, Quintus' mind was racing. With his father's threats to send him home about to be realised, what better way was there of remaining in the army? Moving to another cavalry unit wouldn't work – Fabricius certainly wouldn't allow that, and every officer knew who he was anyway. But this, this might work. If he fought well, he'd be promoted to serve as a hastatus. It seemed a good plan, and Quintus' stride was light as he made his way back to the cavalry lines. All he needed to implement it was for his left arm to regain its strength.

A few hours later, he wasn't so sure. Calatinus' initial reaction had been one of disbelief. 'Your father won't send you home, surely!' he had cried. But when he'd seen that Quintus was convinced that that *would* happen, he had done his best to dissuade him from the idea of enlisting in the infantry. Quintus' identity would be revealed in no time; thanks to his accent, his new comrades would never accept him; that was without considering the high casualty rates suffered by the velites in battle. ('Remember the number of men we lost at the Trebia?' Quintus had protested.) Yet it was Calatinus' final shot which had hit home the hardest. 'What about me?' he'd asked. 'You would leave me with no friends. Don't do that to me, please.'

'All right,' Quintus had muttered, trying not to think of his father. 'I'll stay.'

Inside, however, he wasn't sure how long he could stick it.

Etruria, spring

Feeling a tickle, Hanno brushed at the scar on his neck for the hundredth time. The flesh where the brand had burned him had healed, but for some reason, it attracted flies like a fresh cowpat. He swatted the air in frustration. 'Piss off!'

'There aren't that many flies around, sir,' said Mutt in a mild tone. 'Count yourself lucky it's not later in the year.'

'They say the air is black with them then,' added Sapho.

Hanno threw them both an irritable look, but they were right. He'd seen the midsummer clouds of midges over the marshy ground near Quintus' home, knew what it was like to have every visible piece of flesh covered in bites. It was easy to find something else to be irritated about, however. There was a loud sucking sound as he pulled his left foot out of the calf-deep mud and tried to find a drier spot to step on to next. He failed. 'This place is a hellhole,' Hanno grumbled.

'That it is, sir. And you're going to find the way out of it, aren't you?'

Hanno wondered if he was being mocked, but Mutt's dirty face was as serene as a baby's. 'Yes. I am. Me, or Sapho here.' His brother grinned at him. Not for the first time, Hanno wondered if his offer to Hannibal had been rash. A day earlier, he had gone to his general and asked to lead a reconnaissance party, his purpose to find a more rapid way through the marshes in which the army found itself. To his surprise and pleasure, Sapho had offered to come with him, 'as moral support', he'd put it.

Hanno had been grateful when Hannibal had acceded to his request. 'One more set of scouts won't do any harm. If anyone can find a way, you can. Being the lucky one that you are, eh?' he'd growled, wiping at the reddish fluid that ran from under the bandage over his right eye. Despite being pleased at the praise, Hanno had had to force himself not to look away. Men said that Hannibal was going to go blind, that they were going to lose as many soldiers as they had during the crossing of the Alps. Hanno came down hard on anyone he heard spreading the rumours. Hannibal had brought his army over the Alps, in winter. His general would find a way through this, with or without him, Hanno had told himself. Yet here, in this godforsaken wilderness, without Hannibal, he didn't feel quite so certain.

'Maybe the army should have taken a different path,' he muttered.

'It's not as simple as that,' retorted Sapho.

Hanno sighed. 'I know. There was little else we could do without a fight.' With the arrival of spring, word had come that Gaius Flaminius, one of the new consuls, had moved his legions to Arretium, in the Apennines. Hannibal's response was to avoid Flaminius by crossing the floodplain of the River Arnus, which ran westwards to the sea through the heart of Etruria.

'It's been difficult, but the ploy has worked,' said Sapho. 'There's been no sign of Roman troops for several days.'

'Course not! Why would they even think of marching in here?' Hanno gestured angrily at the water all around them.

'It will soon be over,' declared Sapho jovially.

Hanno let out an irritable grunt by way of reply. Things had been getting steadily worse since they had entered the delta. Thanks to heavy spring rains, the Arnus was running a lot higher than normal. With much of the land covered in water, often the only method of finding a way through was to choose a path and start walking. This proved hazardous in the extreme, with scores of men drowning in deep pools, or being swept away by powerful, unseen currents. The pack animals were no less susceptible. Some panicked and swam away from their handlers to a certain death. Others sank to their bellies in the mire and could not be extricated. The more fortunate of these beasts were slaughtered, but many were just stripped of everything that could be carried and abandoned. As things deteriorated, the same had happened to men. A careless step off the path taken by those in front could be fatal. Trapped in glutinous mud up to their chests or chins, the trapped soldiers had begged to be saved. At first, men tried to help their comrades but as lives were lost in repeated unsuccessful attempts, they gave up. Hanno's phalanx had been lucky to lose only three men. The unit Bomilcar had been assigned to had had many times that number of casualties. Unwilling to leave his soldiers to suffocate in the mud, Hanno had ended their suffering himself with a bow.

The Gauls had been most badly affected by the savage conditions. After a number had deserted, Hannibal had ordered the undisciplined warriors into the middle of the column. The Iberian and Libyan infantry had taken the van, while the heavy cavalry made up the rear. The Numidian horsemen under Mago, Hannibal's brother, had prevented any escape on the flanks. The move had prevented mass desertion, thought Hanno bleakly, but it had not stopped men's spirits from being sucked ever downwards, like the poor bastards who'd suffocated in the mud. He had been grateful for Bostar's and his father's ability to remain steadfast in the face of difficulty. Even Sapho had been a help, making macabre jokes about the worst things he'd seen. Yet despite his family's support, the horror had continued.

The temperatures had risen just enough for any fresh provisions to rot, meaning hunger became a new enemy. Stocks of water and wine had run low, forcing men to drink from the river. Inevitably, many who did so went down with vomiting and diarrhoea. Most were able to continue the march but some became too weak to go on. Like the trapped mules, they were left behind. Night-time, a usual source of respite, had been no better. Conditions had been so damp that fires had proved impossible to light. Cold, ravenous and with nowhere dry to lie down, soldiers had tried to sleep on top of their equipment. Hanno had even seen men dozing on the corpses of dead mules.

Going to Hannibal hadn't just been about regaining his general's approval, therefore. Anything had to be better than trudging through a mire without end, in a world that consisted of only sky and water. Hanno hadn't been surprised when almost every spearman in his phalanx had volunteered to go with him. In the end, he'd taken twenty of the strongest soldiers. He would have preferred to leave Mutt in charge, but the dour officer would not be left behind. 'I lost you once before, and I'm not having it happen again,' he'd muttered. 'And I owe you one.'

Hanno glanced at Mutt again, deciding that his comment a moment before had been genuine, not sardonic. During a clash with a Roman patrol before reaching Victumulae, he had saved his second-in-command's life. He hadn't done it to ensure Mutt's loyalty, but the fact that that had been one of the results felt good. Hanno determined to live up to Mutt's devotion. He had to prove himself to Sapho too.

They had left the column behind at dawn, taking only their spears, some water and food. Hanno judged that it was now some time after midday. They'd been gone for more than five hours and, in that time, hadn't found any dry ground that persisted for more than a few score paces. Everywhere he looked, there was still endless water. Grateful that the clouds had parted, Hanno checked the position of the sun. At least he could use that to maintain a rough course to the south. They would keep moving in that direction and, with the gods' help, find a path that the army could take.

He trudged on, each step feeling more difficult than the last.

Time passed, and the sun fell towards the western horizon. The midges continued to focus on Hanno's neck. The scar ached, his belly grumbled and his throat was parched. The clods of mud on his feet grew so heavy that he was forced to stop and scrape them off from time to time. He didn't know why he bothered. The relief granted lasted on average all of twenty steps before the operation needed to be repeated. Hanno began to think that a fight against a Roman force far stronger than his own would be preferable. Anything to stop the torment.

His gaze roamed from left to right, taking in the usual clumps of rushes. Beyond them, far away, a line of trees. And something else. 'What's that?'

'What, sir?' Using his spear as a crutch, Mutt squelched to his side.

'That.' Hanno pointed slightly off to their left.

Mutt squinted for a moment, and then his dour expression cracked. 'It's a small boat, sir.'

'By all the gods, so it is,' said Sapho.

Hanno fought his excitement. They'd seen hardly a soul since entering the floodplain. It wasn't surprising that the local inhabitants had fled, but it had meant there had been no chance to hire guides. 'It'll be someone fishing.'

'Could be, sir,' said Mutt.

'What shall we do?' asked Sapho, making no attempt to take charge.

'If they see twenty of us, they'll vanish.'

'You're not going on your own, sir,' said Mutt at once.

'I'll come,' offered Sapho.

Hanno's lips tugged into a smile. 'You're like two old women. But I suppose I'd better not go alone, or I'll never hear the end of it.'

Even though there was precious little dry ground to sit on, the spearmen were content at the idea of a break. Ordering them to keep out of sight, Hanno set off with Sapho. They left their helmets and shields behind, taking just their spears. A peasant would be terrified by the sight of soldiers – any soldiers – so Hanno wanted to pose as little threat as possible.

They crept along quietly. Hanno was so busy watching the boat through the breaks in the rushes and shrubby bushes that he paid less heed to where he was going than before. Suddenly, the ground underfoot vanished. He lurched forward into a deep pool, remembering somehow not to cry out, for fear of alerting their quarry. As the water closed over his head, Hanno struck out with one arm, trying to right himself. The other arm was useless to swim with thanks to his spear, yet he instinctively clung on to it. He reached down with tiptoes, trying to find the bottom.

After what felt like eternity, he felt something solid. Relief turned to horror as his right sandal sank deep into mud. His arms splashed the surface as he struggled to free it. He thrashed about with his other leg, but it made no difference. Water sloshed into Hanno's open mouth, and he began to cough, in the process swallowing some more. It was difficult to keep his chin above the surface. His eyes were blurred, full of water. Panic tore at him. I could easily drown here, he thought. His head spun frantically, looking for Sapho. If he reached out with his spear, his brother might be able to drag him out.

It might have been Hanno's imagination, but as he focused on Sapho's face, he could have sworn it bore a curious, satisfied look, like that on a cat's when it has trapped a mouse. Hanno blinked, and it was gone. 'Help!' he hissed. 'My foot is stuck in the mud.'

'I thought you were enjoying a swim.'

It was an odd time to make a joke, thought Hanno. He was so desperate, however, that the thought vanished. 'Can you reach this?' He shoved his spear in Sapho's direction.

Using his own weapon to probe for secure footing, Sapho moved a few steps towards him. Before long, he was able to grab the spear's tip. 'Hold on!'

Hanno had rarely felt so relieved as he did when he felt his sandal suck free of the mud at the bottom. Drowning was not the way he wanted to die. The damp soggy ground beneath his feet felt wonderful. 'Thanks.'

'Anything for a brother. You all right?'

'Just wet, but that's nothing new.'

Sapho clapped him on the shoulder, and they moved on, using their spears to assess the water's depth with even more care than before. Fortunately, the ground became a little drier for some distance, allowing them to close in on the boat. At about two hundred paces, Hanno reckoned that its occupant hadn't been disturbed by the noise of his immersion. The craft had not moved at all. The figure within was busy leaning over the side, adjusting what looked like a fishing net. Hanno's pace picked up. Perhaps another thirty paces later, his foot came out of the mud with an extra loud sucking noise. He cursed and ducked down, but it was too late. The figure stiffened, stared in their direction and straightaway began pulling his net out of the water.

Shit, thought Hanno. This was what he'd worried would happen.

'He'll be long gone before we can get close,' observed Sapho dourly.

'I know.' Hanno cupped a hand to his mouth. 'Help!' he shouted in Latin.

The fisherman's urgency did not waver.

'Come on,' said Hanno. 'The instant that he's taken in that net, he'll be gone.'

Half walking, half swimming, they managed to narrow the gap by half before the last strands of the net had been heaved aboard. The fisherman seized his oars and set them in the rowlocks. Leaning forward, he began to row.

Utter frustration took Hanno. 'Please,' he roared. 'Help us, please! We mean you no harm.'

The figure stared at them, hesitated and then renewed his efforts at the oars.

'We can pay you! Silver. Gold. Weapons!'

A glance over his shoulder. The oars went still in the water.

Hanno shot a look at Sapho and pushed a dozen steps closer. 'We need a guide. Can you help?'

'A guide?'

'Yes, that's right.' He made it another ten paces. 'To lead us through the floodplain to the south. Do you know the way?'

A short laugh. 'Of course.'

Now Hanno could see that the fisherman was in fact a boy of about ten years. Scrawny, with lank hair, he looked wary and ill fed. A tunic full of holes was his only garment. 'Can you take us? You will be well rewarded, I swear it. How does a bag of silver sound?'

'What need have I of silver?' retorted the boy. 'It's of no use to me here.'

'How about a spear like this?' asked Hanno. With a flash of inspiration, he raised his weapon in the air. 'It's good for hunting.'

The boy scowled. 'Maybe. Arrows are more useful, though.'

'I can give you arrows,' promised Hanno. 'As many as you want!'

For the first time, there was a hint of warmth. 'Really?'

'I swear it to you on my mother's grave.'

There was no immediate answer. Hanno let the boy think. Then he said, 'Can I come closer?'

'Just you. Not the cruel-looking one.'

Sapho, who didn't speak much Latin, was oblivious. Hanno hid his surprise at the comment. 'Wait here,' he said to his brother. He moved towards the boat. At about twenty paces, the boy signalled him to halt. 'No nearer.'

He did as he was told. 'My name is Hanno. What's yours?'

'Sentius. Mostly, though, I'm just called "Boy".'

Hanno sensed that however hard his life in Quintus' household had been, it had been nothing compared to this boy's existence. 'I'll call you Sentius, if that's all right?'

A nod. 'Show me the spear.'

Hanno held it out with both hands. 'It's for thrusting. You could use it for fishing, or maybe hunting deer.'

Sentius' eyes studied the spear greedily. 'Give it to me. Butt first.'

Ignoring Sapho's hiss of dismay, Hanno waded to the side of the boat and handed it over. He wasn't remotely surprised when Sentius whirled it around and aimed the tip at his face. All the same, he couldn't stop his stomach from clenching with nerves.

'I could kill you now.' The spear jabbed forward. 'Your friend wouldn't be able to do a thing. I'd be gone before he ever got close to me.'

'True,' said Hanno, forcing himself to stay where he was, forcing himself to think of Hannibal's reaction when he returned with a guide. 'But if you did, you wouldn't get the arrows you want.'

'I want two hundred at least.'

'Fine.'

'And a dozen spears,' added Sentius quickly.

'If you can lead my general's army out of this place, you'll have them, I guarantee.'

A short pause.

Sentius had not agreed yet, which bothered Hanno. 'Is there anything else you want?'

'They say that great beasts accompany your soldiers. Creatures taller than a hut, with long noses and long white teeth. They can crush men underfoot like beetles.'

'Elephants,' said Hanno.

'El-e-phants,' Sentius repeated, his voice full of awe.

Joy filled Hanno. *This* was what would finally win the boy over. He knew it in his gut. 'That's right. Sadly, we only have one left. Would you like to see him, up close? His name is Sura.'

A dubious glance. 'Is it not dangerous?'

'Only when his rider orders him to attack. Otherwise, he is quite gentle.'

'You can show me the el-e-phant?'

'I can do better than that. You can even feed Sura if you wish. He especially likes fruit.'

Sentius looked amazed.

'Have we a bargain?' Hanno shoved out his right hand.

Sentius didn't take it. 'You will stay with me?'

'I won't leave your side the whole time you are with us,' Hanno promised. 'May the gods strike me down if I prove false.'

Sentius' eyes flashed. 'I will strike you down. With your own spear!'

Hanno pulled open his tunic, exposing his chest. 'You can drive it in right here.'

At last Sentius seemed satisfied. He stuck out a grubby paw. 'It's a deal.'

Hanno smiled as they shook hands. Sentius hadn't guided them to dry ground yet, but he would. Their suffering would soon be at an end. The price of ten score arrows, a dozen spears and a chance to feed Sura was cheaper than Hanno could have imagined. Surely, neither Sapho nor Hannibal could fail to be impressed.

'Did you hear about the ox that escaped from the Forum Boarium the other day?' asked Calatinus. It was evening, and they had finished their duties. Their comrades had gone in search of some wine, leaving the two friends alone in the tent.

'No. They get out of the pens all the time. A slave forgets to push home the bolt and the gate opens,' said Quintus dismissively. 'I've seen it happen in Capua.'

'It doesn't matter how the beast got out. It's what it did afterwards. For some reason, it ran up a set of stairs on the outside of a three-storey *cenacula*.'

Quintus sat up on his blankets. 'What?'

'You heard,' said Calatinus, pleased that he had Quintus' attention at last.

'Who told you?'

'A lad I know in another troop was talking to one of the messengers from Rome who arrived yesterday. Apparently, the crazy brute went all the way to the top of the building! The residents were terrified, and their screams sent it even madder. It jumped over the bannisters and fell to the street, where it crushed a child to death.'

'Gods,' muttered Quintus, picturing the gory scene.

'I wouldn't mind if that's all that had happened,' Calatinus went on gloomily, 'but it's just one of a litany of things. A shrine in the vegetable market was struck by lightning the same day. Among the thunderclouds overhead, men saw the ghostly shapes of ships. A damn crow even flew down to the temple of Juno and perched on the sacred couch.'

'Did the messenger see any of these things?' demanded Quintus, thinking of how his father rubbished such tales. 'Or was it someone's aunt's cousin who did?'

Calatinus gave him a withering look. 'So many people witnessed the ox throw itself off the balcony that it cannot be anything but true. The messenger saw the lightning bolt strike the temple with his own eyes, and the ships in the sky.'

Quintus didn't like that, but he wasn't going to admit it. 'And the crow?'

'He didn't see that,' Calatinus admitted.

'Well, then. Even if it did land on the couch, it was probably just sheltering from the rain.'

Calatinus half smiled. 'Maybe so. You know I wouldn't pay these things much notice, but they're happening all over. It rained rocks in Picenum a little while back.'

'Come on! Rocks?'

It was as if Calatinus hadn't heard him. 'The priests at Hercules' spring saw flecks of blood in the water last week. That can mean but one thing.'

Despite himself, Quintus felt uneasy. People were superstitious – they would easily assume divine hands directing the most ordinary events, but priests were less gullible. They knew whether the gods were involved or not, at least that was what most believed. His father was a little more cynical; Quintus remembered the comments Fabricius had made about the priests after his son had killed a bear to celebrate reaching manhood, and again before the Trebia, when ominous signs had occurred thick and fast. It had been easier then to dismiss the stories as mere rumours, thought Quintus unhappily. But the defeat by Hannibal had almost been a fulfilment of the bad omens. If they were recurring aplenty, did that not mean the gods were still unhappy? That the Carthaginians were about to win another victory? *Stop it!* 'I'd wager that Gaius Flaminius doesn't worry too much about such nonsense,' he said as confidently as he could.

Calatinus risked a glance outside. 'That's as may be. But what new consul leaves Rome before he's been officially elected to office?'

'He was just doing that to piss off the Senate. Flaminius has a grudge against many of the senators because of the way they treated him six years ago over his triumph celebrating his victory over the Insubres.'

'Who cares?' cried Calatinus. 'This is no time to risk angering the gods.

And that's what he surely did by leaving the capital before the proper ceremonies have been carried out.'

Quintus didn't reply. He felt the same way. If that had been the only thing that Flaminius had done, it wouldn't have felt so bad. Ignoring the Senate's demands that he return to Rome wasn't the end of the world, but Quintus had not liked hearing the story of the calf chosen to be sacrificed when Flaminius arrived at Arretium. To everyone's horror, it had slipped out of the priest's grasp after just one, non-fatal strike of the knife. Even when it had been recaptured, no one had had the courage to kill it. The second calf chosen had died without protest, but the whole experience had left a bad taste in men's mouths.

'No doubt that's why his horse threw him when we were about to move out the other day,' said Calatinus. 'And why that standard stuck in the ground.'

'I think that telling the *signifer* to dig up the damn standard if he was too weak to pull it out was the right thing to say,' said Quintus, forcibly rallying his spirits. 'Flaminius is a brave man and a good leader. The soldiers love him. It's not as if we're sitting around on our hands. We're trailing Hannibal until the right opportunity presents itself. We're lucky that we were posted to Flaminius' cavalry. Imagine still being stuck in Ariminum. Surely you'd rather be following a general who wants to fight?'

'Gnaeus Servilius Geminus is no coward!' barked a familiar voice.

Both men looked around, surprised and embarrassed. Calatinus jumped up and saluted, while Quintus glowered.

'I don't think that's what Quintus meant, sir,' protested Calatinus.

Fabricius' gimlet stare turned. 'Well?'

'I wasn't saying that Servilius is a coward,' muttered Quintus.

'I'm glad to hear it!' Fabricius' tone was sarcastic. 'It's not down to you, a stripling cavalryman, to stand in judgement on a consul. Servilius is doing what he was ordered to by the Senate, and that is to guard the east coast in case Hannibal should march that way. Just as Flaminius has been chosen to protect the west coast in the event that the gugga does the opposite.'

'It feels wrong just to let Hannibal and his army ravage the country-side. I'm sick of seeing farms that have been burned to the ground and had all of their inhabitants butchered,' said Quintus, letting his anger against his father flare alongside his outrage at what the Carthaginians were doing.

'So am I.' Calatinus' tone was heartfelt.

'Oh, for the eagerness of youth! Fear not,' said Fabricius with a wink, 'for Flaminius hopes to catch Hannibal between his army and that of Servilius. If he succeeds with that, we shall carve up the guggas like the Gauls at Telamon.'

Quintus' spirits rose at that idea, but his father's next words struck him like a punch in the solar plexus.

'If it works, Calatinus, you should see action as well.'

Quintus gaped at Fabricius. No, not now, he thought. Please! Beside him, Calatinus' surprise was also palpable. 'I don't understand. My arm is better. I'm ready to fight.'

'It's nothing to do with your wound. You're to return home at once. Calatinus and seven others are to be posted back to serve with Servilius' horsemen.'

Quintus was stunned into silence.

'In Ariminum? Why, sir?' asked Calatinus, looking confused.

'Flaminius has had word from Servilius. He wants men who have fought Hannibal's cavalry before. Too many of us were assigned to Flaminius' units. Servilius has been left short, and he needs riders who can instruct his men in Carthaginian tactics. We agreed on a figure of eight men. I suggested the candidates.'

'Why can I not go as well?' demanded Quintus hotly. 'I am old enough now! Besides, I have taken the oath.'

'Hades, will you never learn to curb your tongue? I see your mother in you more and more,' snapped Fabricius. 'I've spoken to Flaminius. You're going home, and that's an end to it.' He saw something in Quintus' eyes and pointed a stern finger. 'Technically, you will still be in the cavalry. You could be called up again – but only if you have demonstrably matured. If I hear otherwise, I'll be sure to have your military oath annulled.'

In that moment, Quintus absolutely hated his father.

Fabricius rounded on Calatinus. 'Are you going to protest too?'

'No, sir. I'd rather not leave, but if those are your orders, then I shall follow them.'

'Fine. As you were.' Fabricius ducked out of the tent without another word.

Furious, Quintus watched him go. *Curse him to Hades!*

'By all the gods, that was unexpected,' muttered Calatinus.

'For you maybe, but not for me,' said Quintus bitterly. 'At least you have a chance of getting to close with Hannibal. I'll be stuck at home, with the women.'

'Being around your father isn't good for you. All you do is clash off one another. Maybe a period away from him will do you some good. Who's to say that the war will end soon anyway? Hannibal seems to be a shrewd leader. I'd wager that we'll still be fighting him in twelve months. Your father won't be able to deny you a place in the cavalry forever. Just keep your nose clean at home. Make sure your mother is happy.'

Quintus didn't bother arguing. In his mind, his father would prevent him from ever serving again. That had made up his mind for once and for all. If ever there had been a perfect opportunity to approach Corax about joining the velites, it was now. That way, he could stay in Flaminius' army, close to Hannibal. His father would never know. *He won't send me home,* Quintus thought furiously. *I'll be my own master. Learn to fight as an infantryman.*

It was a good feeling.

Capua

Aurelia's spirits lifted as they left the temple of Mars. She hadn't begrudged visiting to pray for Flaccus' soul the first time, but it seemed a bit much to have to do it again and again. Her mother said that it was important, however, and Aurelia was playing it safe by not arguing. To be fair, she was sorry he was dead. The one and only time that she had met Flaccus, he had seemed personable. She had even fallen a little for his looks, and his air of confidence and power. But then he had gone to Rome, taking her father, and she had not seen him again. There had been one letter, and then nothing. Aurelia felt a twinge of remorse. There would have been more communications, but the war had been more important than writing to her, a mere child. Soon after, Flaccus had been killed. It was sad, but she wasn't going to spend her life grieving over a man she had not known at all.

Their duties done, they could soon visit Gaius and Martialis, his father. Her heart leaped. Gaius had been away, training with his unit, on the previous occasion they had been to Capua. Aurelia loved Martialis, but seeing him instead of his son was not the same. How she hoped he would see past her status as Quintus' sister today. She was wearing her best dress, all of her jewellery, and even a hint of perfume filched from a vial belonging to her mother. With a little luck, it would go unnoticed, but Aurelia was careful not to go too near Atia, whose sense of smell was impressive. So too was her ability to see through Aurelia's actions.

'That went well, I thought,' said Atia.

'Yes,' mumbled Aurelia. How could one judge? she wondered. It wasn't as if the statue of Mars responded in any way, to anyone. It just stood there, imperious and regal, glaring down at the long, narrow room that formed the centrepiece of the temple.

Atia turned with a frown. 'I hope that your prayers for Flaccus were sincere?'

Aurelia caught the first warning sign fast. Best not to start an argument before they had even seen Gaius. 'They were heartfelt, Mother,' she lied, using her most sincere voice.

Atia's face relaxed. 'His soul will rest easier knowing that he is still remembered. You remembered to ask the gods to watch over Father and Quintus?'

'Of course!' This time, Aurelia's reaction was entirely unfeigned.

'Good. To the market, then. There are things I forgot to tell Agesandros to get.'

Aurelia's eyes darted towards the crowd at the mention of the overseer, but, to her relief, there was no sign of him. With luck, they wouldn't see Agesandros until later, at Martialis' house. Buying everything on Atia's list would take time. Not as long as it normally would, however. She had noticed on their last visit that her mother had not ordered as much food as usual; today it had been the same. Aurelia didn't ponder the thought for long; already her head was full of images of Gaius. Smiling as he saw her. Resplendent in his uniform. Offering her his arm so that they might go for a walk. Complimenting her on her appearance. Stooping to brush his lips against hers . . .

'Spare a coin, young lady!'

Aurelia blinked, and flinched in horror. A beggar clad in rags stood before her. His leathery palm and the shiny nubs where his fingers should have been waggled under her nose. The disfigurement didn't end there. The man had almost no nose, just two gaping holes under his inflamed, weeping eyes. His skin was scaly like that of a snake and lay in odd, disturbing angles. Round swellings peppered his face, small things no bigger than a fingernail to lumps the size of a peach stone. Aurelia had seen lepers on countless occasions, but at a distance. They were normally kept outside Capua by the guards at the gate. She had never been this close to one. She recoiled, fear twisting her guts that the disease might transfer to her. 'I have no money.'

'A wealthy young lady like you?' The leper's tone was unctuous but disbelieving. The stump of a hand waved at her again. 'Even the smallest coin would help, if it please you.'

'Get away from my daughter!'

The leper shrank back from Atia, fawning.

'Aesculapius keep us from such a fate.' Atia's hand beckoned. 'Step around him.'

Aurelia couldn't help but look at the leper again. Although she was repulsed by his appearance, she felt a deep pity for him too. To be condemned to a slow, living death – she could think of few things that were worse. 'Please, Mother. Give him something.'

Atia studied her for a moment; then she sighed and reached for her purse. *What difference will a single coin make to our problems?* 'Here.' A hemidrachm flashed in the air. The leper reached up for it, but was unable to catch it with his ruined hands. The small piece of silver dropped to the dirt, and he scrabbled after it, calling down the blessings of the gods on both of them.

Looking down, Aurelia gaped. He had no toes left on his left foot. Where his right foot had been, there was just a scarred bump of flesh loosely covered with a rag.

'Come on, child. That will see him fed for a few days at least.' Atia's voice was kind.

They walked away, fast. The leper vanished into the crowd.

'I won't get his disease, will I?' Aurelia's initial fear had returned.

'With the blessings of the gods, no. He didn't touch you, and you weren't close to him for long enough.' Atia cast a look over her shoulder. 'The men on the gate must have been half asleep this morning to let a creature like that inside the walls.' Her nose twitched; fearing that her mother had smelled her perfume, Aurelia took a step away. A moment later, Atia glided on, and Aurelia thanked the gods for a lucky escape.

They stopped first at a potter's and then at a wine merchant's premises. There Atia began haggling with the owner over the quality of the most recent wine she had ordered. Aurelia soon grew bored. The earrings and necklaces displayed in the entrance to a jeweller's shop opposite caught her eye, and she stepped outside to take a closer look. As she did, a short, balding man in a fine Greek chiton brushed against her. He muttered an apology; her mind on the array of trinkets, she took little notice.

The jeweller, a beady-eyed Egyptian, was quick to see Aurelia's interest. 'Can I be of service?'

She gave him a smile. 'I'm just looking.'

'Please, my shop is yours. Try on anything you like.'

Aurelia sighed. She had no money of her own. She threw a wistful glance at Atia, but there was no point in asking. Her answer would be that the jewellery Aurelia was wearing – a pair of gold pendants decorated with beads of blue glass, and a simple gold ring decorated with a red garnet – was more than adequate. Until her wedding day, her mother would not be purchasing her any more. Sudden mischief took her. The shopkeeper didn't have to know that she wouldn't be buying. 'I like this,' she announced, pointing to a necklace hung with dozens of small tubular red and black stones.

'Carnelian and jet, that is,' said the jeweller. 'From Parthia. Beautiful, isn't it?'

'Yes.'

'Want to try it on?' His hands were already undoing the clasp. 'It will suit your complexion. Your husband will love it, and it won't cost him the sun and moon.'

Aurelia didn't disabuse him. Gaius might like it, she thought. She was about to allow him to place it around her neck when she heard raised voices. Her head turned. Inside the wine merchant's, she could see the short man who'd bumped into her facing her mother, who looked furious. Her curiosity was roused. 'Thank you. Maybe another time.' She walked out, ignoring the protests of the perplexed jeweller.

She crossed the street, weaving her way through the passers-by. A pair of burly men loitering close to the vintner's eyed her up as she went by. One made a smacking noise with his lips. Used to such attention, Aurelia ignored them.

The wine merchant's was a typical, open-fronted shop. A long, rectangular room led in from the arched entrance. Oil lamps flickered from alcoves. A painted statue of Bacchus and his maenads watched from a shelf. On either side, lines of amphorae were propped against the wall or nestled in beds of straw, and a low counter where customers could stand to taste the shop's wines was situated at the back of the room. Atia was ten steps from the doorway, a cup in her hand. The wine merchant stood alongside, looking decidedly embarrassed. The short man stood close to her, his hands raised in apparent placation.

'All I am saying, my good lady, is that these things need to be talked about,' he said as Aurelia drew near.

'This is no place to discuss such matters,' snapped Atia. 'How dare you approach me here?'

A shrug. 'Would you rather I had come to Martialis' house?'

Atia's lips pinched white.

'What's going on, Mother?' asked Aurelia.

'It's nothing important.'

The short man turned. His brown eyes moved up and down, appraising her lasciviously. Her skin crawled. 'Ah. This must be your daughter. Aurelia, if I am not mistaken?'

'Yes. And you are?'

His oiled ringlets moved as he inclined his head. 'Phanes, moneylender, at your service.'

Aurelia was no less confused, but before she could enquire further, her mother was moving towards the door. 'Come on,' said Atia. 'We're leaving.' Aurelia knew better than to argue, and followed.

Phanes moved fast for one so small. In the blink of an eye, he had placed himself in front of Atia. 'There is still the matter of your husband's debt. We haven't discussed it.'

'Nor shall we!' snapped Atia. She tried to move past Phanes, but he blocked her way.

Aurelia could not believe her eyes, or her ears.

'Get out of my way, you low-down piece of Greek filth!' Atia ordered.

Phanes didn't move. 'Lowly I might be, and Greek I certainly am. That doesn't make the forty thousand drachms that your husband owes me disappear.'

'You will have your money! You know he is good for it, damn your eyes.'

'With his breeding and yours, one would think so, but I haven't seen as much as a drachm for more than a year. A man can't live on silence and missed payments. He'd starve.'

'Fabricius is not here. There's a war on, in case you hadn't noticed!'

'No doubt Fabricius is doing us and the Republic proud, but that doesn't mean he can renege on what he owes. For the first few months last year, I gave him the benefit of the doubt. He had been sent to Iberia with Scipio after all. After my enquiries revealed that he had returned and been ordered to Cisalpine Gaul, I sent him a letter. There was no reply.'

'He probably never received it. Everything is chaos up there. The damn Gauls kill most of the messengers.'

A sly smile. 'I sent my message by ship.'

Atia's composure slipped for a heartbeat. 'That still doesn't mean he received it.'

'True. But when the second and then the third letters went unanswered, I decided it was time to take things up with you. I would have paid you a visit soon, but my sources told me that you were to visit the city this very day. What a perfect opportunity to chat. To find out if you had had word from your husband concerning this matter.'

Atia did not so much as acknowledge Phanes' comment. She looked at him as if he were a snake. 'Who told you I was coming to Capua? Martialis would not say a word to anyone that wasn't a friend.'

Nor would Gaius, thought Aurelia.

Phanes' smile widened.

'A slave,' spat Atia. 'One of Martialis' slaves is in your employ.'

'I have ears all over Capua.' Phanes' hands fluttered. 'I'm a moneylender. Men such as I need to know what people are talking about. Who is worried, who wants to try a new business venture and other titbits like that.'

'You're a blood-sucking leech,' Atia retorted.

Phanes made a *tutting* noise. 'Your husband was always far more polite. Especially when he wanted an extension to his loan. It must be the Roman breeding.'

Atia did not deign to answer. 'Aurelia!' This time, Phanes made no move to stop her. His head half turned. 'Achilles! Smiler!'

The two men whom Aurelia had spotted filled the doorway. They were unarmed, but their expressions were far from friendly. 'Boss?' asked the first one, a thug with curving scars that ran from the corners of his lips across both his cheeks.

Aurelia felt sick. That one had to be Smiler. She knew his type; had seen them before. The pair were ex-gladiators, now the Greek's paid heavies.

'No one is to leave the shop until I say so,' announced Phanes.

'Yes, boss.' The pair moved to stand shoulder to shoulder, blocking the way to the street. There was a muted squawk from the wine merchant about damage to his goods being a crime before he vanished into the back of the shop.

Atia drew herself up to her full height. 'What are you going to do? Order these creatures to lay hands on us?'

'I hope it won't come to that,' replied Phanes mildly.

'You dog! If I scream, people will come in here.'

'They might, and they might not. If anyone is foolish enough to try, Achilles and Smiler will soon make them see the error of their ways.'

Phanes was right. From her mother's silence, Aurelia knew that too. Even in daylight, few of Capua's residents would intervene in a quarrel or a brawl. If blood was shed, the city guards might be called, but otherwise it was a case of dealing with one's own problems. In a change of heart, she would have given anything for Agesandros to appear, but even he would have had his hands full dealing with two such large, determined-looking men.

'As they can with anyone, should I give the order.'

'You dare to threaten us?' cried Atia.

'Threat? What threat?' Phanes' smile did not reach his eyes. 'I would merely like to talk about the money owed to me, a considerable sum that I would wager you are fully aware of.'

Atia's lips tightened, but she did not reply, which told Aurelia that her mother *had* known of the money owed to Phanes. She must have been avoiding him, Aurelia thought. They had to get out of here, however. She scanned the room for anything that would serve as a weapon, but could see nothing. Panic flared in her chest. They won't dare harm us, she told herself. Inside, though, she wasn't so sure. She moved closer to her mother. It was time for solidarity. 'Why are you detaining us? What do you want?' Aurelia hoped that he heard the loathing in her words.

If he did, the Greek did not react. 'The wolf cub speaks at last, and with a more civil tongue than its mother! I ask for an agreement, that's all.'

'What kind of agreement?' demanded Atia.

'Why, nothing more than I am entitled to. Regular payments towards the monies I am owed.'

'And if I refuse?' Atia's eyes flickered over the heavies. 'These two get sent in?'

'Come now. You are a woman of high station. Despite your opinion, I am a civilised man,' protested Phanes. 'The courts would have to become involved.' He locked eyes with Atia.

After a long moment, Atia sighed, and Aurelia knew that the Greek had won. She longed to throw herself at him, nails clawing at his face, but her fear of his men froze her feet to the spot. She listened as her mother said, 'How often do you wish to be paid?'

'Every month.'

'Impossible!'

A predatory look. 'Two-, or even three-monthly would also be acceptable, but I would have to increase the interest from two drachms in every hundred to four. That of course is in addition to the amounts that have accrued due to the lack of payments over the last year.'

'You have the paperwork to prove what you say?'

'Indeed. It is in my office, should you care to see it. Your husband's signature was witnessed not just by me, but by my clerk.'

Aurelia could feel the helpless rage radiating from her mother. She felt it in her own belly, but if Phanes wasn't lying – and her gut told her that he wasn't – then he had them over a barrel. She would have given anything for her father to appear, to make everything right, but there was no hope of that. He was far away, fighting a war, and the gods only knew if he would ever return. Hopelessness mixed with her fear, drowning her anger.

'Very well.' Atia sounded older than Aurelia had ever heard her. 'Where is your office?'

'In the street that runs behind the courthouse, adjacent to a lawyer's. You'll see the sign.'

'I will visit you there tomorrow morning to discuss . . . terms.'

'It will be my pleasure.' Phanes bowed deeply. 'Achilles, Smiler. Outside, both of you. The lady doesn't need your ugly faces marring her view of the world any more.'

The knot in Aurelia's belly eased as the two withdrew. Determined to act as if nothing untoward had happened, as if she were their master instead of the other way around, she followed them. Her breath caught in her throat, however, when Smiler saw her purpose. He cupped a hand over his groin and licked his lips. Achilles snickered. Aurelia acted as if she hadn't seen – *Show them no weakness! They will not dare touch me* – and stepped past them into the street. She walked straight into a passer-by. Balance lost, the heavies' laughter ringing in her ears, Aurelia stumbled backwards with flailing arms.

Strong hands prevented her from falling, brought her back up to a standing position. 'In a hurry, young lady?'

Aurelia looked into a pair of amused blue eyes. They belonged to a young man with an open face and short hair, dressed in a crisp white toga. He was perhaps a few years older than Quintus, and quite handsome. 'No. Yes. No,' she said, feeling a rush of heat as her cheeks coloured.

'You're not quite sure.' He chuckled, but then his gaze fell on Achilles and Smiler. His eyes turned hard. 'Have these brutes been troubling you?'

Joy filled Aurelia as she saw the trio of strongly built slaves behind him. There was no doubt in her mind that if she said a single word, her rescuer would set his men upon Phanes'. She glanced into the shop. The Greek was watching her, his face closed. The tiny shake of Atia's head spoke volumes, however. Don't make things worse than they already are, it said. 'No. I wasn't looking where I was going, that's all. My apologies.'

'A beautiful young lady has no need to make apologies.' Finally, he released her arms, and Aurelia coloured even more. 'My name is Lucius Vibius Melito.'

Atia was by Aurelia's side before she'd even realised. 'Atia, wife of Gaius Fabricius. This is my daughter, Aurelia.'

'Honoured to make your acquaintance.' He bowed. 'My compliments on your daughter. She is without doubt the fairest young woman I have seen in Capua. The scent of jasmine she uses is quite . . . captivating.'

Aurelia's eyes dropped. She was doubly embarrassed: firstly by his compliment, and secondly because there was only one place that she could have obtained the perfume. She would pay for it later.

'You are too kind,' Atia purred. 'I have heard your name before. Doesn't your family live to the south of Capua?'

'Yes. My father and I are here visiting friends.' Lucius' gaze slid back to Aurelia, causing her to look away again.

'As we are. Will you be here long?'

'A couple of weeks at least.'

'How nice. Perhaps we shall meet again, in the forum?'

'It would be a pleasure,' replied Lucius. His smile fell mostly on Aurelia.

'Until then,' said Atia. She tapped Aurelia lightly on the arm. 'Come, daughter. We still have much to do.'

'Goodbye,' said Lucius.

'Goodbye, and thank you,' Aurelia managed before Atia led her away. She had a last glimpse of Achilles' and Smiler's scowls, Phanes' slight frown and Lucius' admiring look before the crowd swallowed them up. As she turned back, she found her mother watching her. She cringed inside, expecting a lecture about taking things that weren't hers. But Atia didn't mention the jasmine.

'What a pleasant young man. He's from a good family. I think one of his grandfathers might have been an aedile. He's handsome, polite too, and not scared of helping someone in trouble. Didn't you think?'

'Yes, I suppose so,' said Aurelia, hating the colour that gave the lie to her vague answer.

'There's no need to play coy with me. Did you like him or not?'

Aurelia looked around, self-conscious. Yet in the throng, no one would hear, or care. 'He was nice, yes.'

'So you wouldn't object to meeting him again?'

Does nothing put her off? Aurelia thought of Gaius, but couldn't mention him. The last time she had, her mother had said that Martialis wasn't wealthy enough. It was so unfair! Why could she never do what she wished?

'Well?'

'Does Father really owe Phanes forty thousand drachms?'

'Lower your voice, child.'

Atia looked most discomfited, and Aurelia grew daring. 'Well, does he?'

'Yes.'

'Why?'

'The crops have been poor several times in the last few years, you know that. The money from the sale of the grain provides most of our income. If Father hadn't borrowed from Phanes and . . .' Atia hesitated for a heartbeat, before continuing, '. . . from Phanes—'

Aurelia interrupted, 'He owes money to more than one moneylender?'

Shame flitted across Atia's face. 'It's none of your concern.'

'It is if we are to lose the estate. Our house. That's what will happen if you can't meet Phanes' and the others' demands, isn't it?'

'Gods grant me patience. Where do you get this attitude? If we weren't in public, I would give you a good whipping!'

They glared at each other for a moment.

'We are in some financial trouble, yes. But it's nothing that your father and I cannot see through.'

Something in Atia's tone gave Aurelia insight. 'That's it,' she murmured in shock and anger. 'That's why you've been so keen to find me a husband, isn't it? If I marry into a rich, powerful family, then the moneylenders will leave you and Father alone. Melito is just the latest candidate.'

Unusually, Atia could not meet her gaze.

Aurelia's anger gave her courage. 'Is that all I am to you? A belonging, to be sold to the highest bidder?'

Atia struck her across the face. 'How dare you speak to me in that manner?'

'I hate you!' Aurelia turned and fled the way they had come.

Her mother's cries followed her, but she paid them no heed.

Chapter VI

Near Arretium, north-central Italy

Unsurprisingly, Calatinus wasn't too happy about Quintus' plan. They'd had their first real argument over it, but Quintus would not back down. As a placatory gesture, he'd asked Calatinus to come with him, but his friend had laughed. 'If you think I'm going to give up being a cavalryman to become a *veles*, you're insane.' Calatinus had thought for a moment. 'Clearly, you are insane, or you wouldn't be doing this. Desertion is a serious crime. The oath you swore when you enlisted in the cavalry hasn't been set aside yet, remember?'

'I'll still be serving,' Quintus had shot back.

'Your father won't know that. No one will, except me, and I won't be able to say. You'll be called a traitor, and worse. All that risk, when you might well be back serving within the year?'

'What if Hannibal is defeated in the next few months? I would forever be known in Capua as the man-child sent home by his father, who missed all the fighting. Could you live with that?'

Calatinus had seen the resolve in his eyes and thrown his hands in the air. 'You're going on your own. I'm having nothing to do with it.'

'Fine,' Quintus had said, more determined than ever. The draw of fighting with men who hadn't run away from the Carthaginians was too great, especially when compared to helping run the family farm, which is what his mother would have him do. His fear that he would be known as someone who had not quite done his duty was very real. More than once, he had heard of the guilt suffered by soldiers who had missed a critical battle through injury.

They had got drunk together afterwards, and the following morning, when they'd had to leave, there had been no hard feelings. Calatinus had sworn not to say a word to anyone. Two days out from Flaminius' camp – Quintus had ridden with his friend ostensibly to spend a last period of time together – he stopped to answer a call of nature and casually told the others not to wait for him. Calatinus had whispered a blessing and then ridden off with a cheery wave, saying he didn't want to be around to smell the results of Quintus' efforts.

Quintus waited for a short while before he headed back the way they had come. He rode hard but with care, moving off the road if he saw any Roman troops. Until he got close to the camp, it was imperative that he avoid being seen by anyone in Flaminius' forces. After the comradeship of the previous months, it was odd sleeping out in the open and alone, but solitude, a little fire and the sound of wolves howling from the nearby mountains soon won him over. The following day, he rode to within five miles of Flaminius' camp before reluctantly setting free his mount. There was little else he could do with it. He had to appear as poor as possible. With a little luck, the animal would be caught by a patrol. His few personal possessions were with Calatinus, and in the shelter of a thicket, he dumped his helmet, spear and shield, retaining only a simple dagger. Quintus stripped naked and donned his oldest clothes: a worn *licium*, or undergarment, and a roughly spun, off-white wool tunic. He even threw away his beloved calf-high leather boots in favour of a pair of caligae that he'd bought a few days earlier.

The magnitude of what he was about to do began to sink in as he set out on the road once more. The first patrol that passed by, a troop of Numidians, almost rode him down when Quintus didn't move out of the way in time. A group of hastati were next, tramping by without so much as a second glance. Quintus doubted that many of them even saw him. His determination faltered a little. The things that he had thought about – dreaded – were about to become reality. He was starting life at the bottom of the social ladder. Apart from the few slaves in camp, everyone would regard him as inferior. It would take months, if not years, to achieve any kind of recognition. That was if he wasn't killed in the first battle he took part in. Casualty rates among velites were often high. Quintus rallied his courage. I should have died at the Trebia, he told himself, but I didn't. There's no reason to suppose I'll do so any quicker as a skirmisher. By doing this, I get to stay and fight Hannibal instead of being stuck at home. The certainty that he was doing the right thing solidified.

Quintus couldn't help but think of his father, incandescent with fury, hearing the news that he hadn't arrived home. It was very satisfying and brought a smile to his face. Seeing the gates of the camp, his pace increased. When he reached the velites on the gate, his pretence would begin. Quintus' nerves jangled, but he had his story ready. They would ask what his business was, and he'd tell them that he was one of Fabricius' servants. That would be enough to get him inside, to gain an audience with an officer. Then he'd find a section of velites. He wanted to approach the skirmishers who were attached to a maniple of triarii or principes, but there was no way that would work. As a 'raw' recruit with no officer to sponsor him, he would have to join the velites who served with a unit of hastati. On the upside, that meant he could seek out Corax, who had seemed a decent sort.

He found the centurion easily enough this time. As was standard, the tents of the maniple's two centuries faced each other across a rectangular space perhaps a hundred paces in width. The side nearest the camp avenue lay open. Opposite it were the maniple's wagons and mule pens. Corax was sitting by a table outside his large tent, spooning stew into his mouth. The other manipular centurion sat alongside, hacking a small loaf into pieces with a dagger. A servant was pouring wine. No one noticed Quintus, which made him even more nervous. He kept moving, until eventually the second centurion, a blocky man with receding black hair, looked up with a frown. 'What do you want?'

'I came to have a word with Centurion Corax, sir, if I may.'

Corax threw him a casual glance. 'Do I know you?'

'I met you once before, sir, during the winter,' said Quintus, keeping his accent coarse. 'I brought a message. You mentioned that there were places for men like me in the velites.'

Corax put down his spoon and eyed him up and down. 'Ah, yes. You're the servant of that cavalry commander.'

'Yes, sir.' Please don't ask me about him, thought Quintus, his heart racing. With any luck, Corax would have forgotten his father's name.

'So you've changed your mind, eh?'

Quintus had his story ready. 'It's time for me to do my bit, sir. Hannibal has to be stopped, or the whole of the Republic could go up in flames.'

A nod of approval. 'Has your master given his consent?'

'Yes, sir.' Quintus threw up another prayer that there were no more questions.

'You have no farm, no land?'

'My father works a tiny patch, sir, but it's not worth much. He has to work on the local estate to make ends meet,' lied Quintus, humbly. He couldn't make any pretence of being richer, in case Corax asked him to prove his status.

'As I thought. What's your name? Where are you from?'

'Quintus Crespo, sir,' said Quintus. He couldn't use his real family name just in case his father ever heard it. 'I'm from near Capua.'

'What age are you?'

'Eighteen, sir.' There was a short pause, and Quintus began to feel sick.

'Clearly, there's no chance of taking your oath in Rome, so you can enlist right now.'

'Thank you, sir!' Quintus couldn't stop himself from grinning.

'Sixteen years you'll be signing up for.' Corax's deep-set eyes regarded him unwaveringly.

'Maybe twenty – if we don't defeat Hannibal soon,' added the other centurion with a laugh.

'It won't take that long to beat the gugga, sir,' Quintus declared.

'Not with you in our army, eh?' The centurion chuckled, and Quintus flushed.

'He's eager, Pullo. Nothing wrong with that.' Corax stood up and approached Quintus. 'Ready?'

Quintus swallowed. 'Yes, sir.'

'Repeat after me: I, a citizen of the Republic . . .'

'I, a citizen of the Republic . . .' said Quintus.

'. . . swear to bear allegiance to the Republic, and to defend it against its enemies.' Corax paused to let Quintus echo his words. 'I will obey my officers, and execute their orders as far as is in my power. This I swear before the sacred triad of Jupiter, Juno and Minerva.'

Worrying about how his new promise might affect the vow he'd made when first enlisting, Quintus repeated the last words. With luck, he thought, the gods would see his desire to fight for Rome as more important than the fact that he had disobeyed his father's orders, thereby effectively deserting from the cavalry. Acid roiled in his belly. He had to hope that they didn't disapprove, or he'd be a dead man in the first action he saw.

'Excellent.' Corax clapped him on the shoulder. 'Welcome to the velites, Crespo, and to my maniple!'

'Thank you, sir,' replied Quintus, feeling his nerves settle a little.

'First things first. You need to be assigned to a tent unit. Then a trip to the quartermaster to get your equipment and weapons. Your training starts tomorrow.'

'Very good, sir.'

Corax pointed. 'Do you see the mule pens on this side?'

Quintus peered. 'I do, sir.'

'The velites' tents are down there, beside them.'

Where the smell of piss and manure will be strongest, thought Quintus. 'I see them, sir.'

'The second last tent is one man down. Go and make yourself known. One of the others will tell you where to find the stores. I will see you at dawn tomorrow. Dismissed.'

'Thank you, sir!' Quintus saluted, turned about face and walked off. 'The lad is still wet behind the ears,' he heard Pullo say. His anger flared, but he kept walking.

'Maybe so, but he's eager. I think he'll do all right,' replied Corax.

Quintus' fury subsided. Corax saw something in him. It was up to him to prove it to the centurion, and to the gods, so that they let him get away with breaking his cavalry oath.

A few hastati nodded as he passed, or muttered a greeting, but most gave him nothing more than a hard stare. Quintus stopped smiling, and set a scowl to his face. Life here wasn't going to be easy.

Outside the second last tent, half a dozen young men in dirty tunics sat in a circle, finishing off the last of their meal. No stew, as Corax and Pullo had had. It looked to be bread and cheese. A couple of them looked up.

'Centurion Corax sent me,' said Quintus.

'Oh yes?' sneered a tall soldier with vivid blond hair. 'To kiss my arse?'

'I've just joined. Crespo is the name.'

'What do I care?'

'I'm to sleep in this tent.'

There were universal groans. 'Bloody typical. Just as we're getting used to a little more space, Corax has to ruin it,' complained a short man with ears like jug handles.

Quintus was confused.

The short man explained. 'There are eight hastati to a *contubernium*, but not when it comes to the velites. Your arrival brings us back to full strength, so ten of us have to sleep in that.' He jabbed a thumb at the tent behind him. 'Someone like Rutilus here' – and he indicated an effeminate-looking man – 'doesn't mind, but the rest of us find it a tight fit.'

There were loud chortles, and Rutilus shrugged. 'What can I say? I love it.'

'Arse-lover,' snarled the tall soldier.

'Don't worry, Macerio, I don't find you attractive,' retorted Rutilus. 'You won't ever find me crawling into your blankets. Unless you ask, of course.'

'Watch your mouth!' Macerio lunged forward, but Rutilus danced out of range.

More laughter, and Quintus smiled.

'You think it's funny, do you?' Macerio's attention was on him like that of a hawk.

A first test. Although Macerio was bigger than him, it was vital that he wasn't seen as a pushover. 'It was amusing, yes,' Quintus replied calmly.

Macerio came at Quintus with swinging fists. 'Time you learned a lesson in manners then, new boy!'

'This is stupid.' Quintus backed away from the first punches, but Macerio followed, scorn twisting his face.

'Look, lads! We've got ourselves a coward as a tent mate.'

Quintus thought of the ambush he'd survived, and of the Trebia, where he'd stood his ground until his father had led him away. His blood boiled. For all he knew, Macerio hadn't even been in the velites then. 'I'm no coward!'

'No?' Macerio jabbed at his face, one-two. The second half connected with Quintus' cheek, sending stars shooting across his vision. He dodged backwards. 'No!' he growled. Worry clawed at him. If he lost, his life in the velites would be even more of a struggle. He had to win. Anger makes a man lose his cool, he thought. 'You know what? Rutilus was being kind. You're the ugliest son of a whore I've seen in many a day. Who'd want to fuck you?'

'Cocksucker!' Spittle flew from Macerio's lips.

'Get him, Macerio!' a man called out.

Quintus heard at least two others voicing their support. Other than the fact that it wouldn't have been Rutilus, he had no time to dwell on who the tall man's allies might be. His reach was less than Macerio's, so he was going to have to close to make contact. Protecting his face with his fists and hunching his shoulders, Quintus went on the attack. He moved so fast that Macerio was caught off guard. A punch whistled over his head, and then he was through. *Thump, thump.* He landed two solid blows on Macerio's belly. There was a squawk of pain. Quintus delivered another punch for good measure before bobbing away on dancing feet. Hopefully, that would teach Macerio to leave him alone.

'You bastard!' wheezed Macerio, his eyes bulging with anger.

'You started it,' Quintus replied, rubbing his bruised cheek.

'Aye, and I'm going to finish it.' Enraged, Macerio came on again.

Quintus cursed silently. He should have put Macerio on the floor. He wouldn't make the same mistake again. They traded blows for a time, neither able to gain an advantage over the other. Macerio's right fist was lethally fast. He caught Quintus a couple of times with it in the side of the head, leaving a ringing in his ears. A few more of those, Quintus thought, and the fight would be over. Concerned that his new life would be made infinitely harder if Macerio won, he resolved to win by whatever means necessary. It wasn't as if the blond-haired man wouldn't act in the same way. Quintus had narrowly avoided a kick in the balls a moment before, and he'd seen Macerio throwing meaningful looks at his watching comrades. If I'm not careful, thought Quintus, a shove in the back from one of them will give the prick all the advantage he needs.

Quintus never usually fought dirty, but being outnumbered so greatly really made him want to hurt Macerio. He scooped up a short, bent nail from the ground, the likes of which were used to scratch an owner's initials on his equipment.

Macerio's expression turned evil. 'Going to try and blind me with a handful of dirt, are you?' His gaze shifted. 'Knock the fucker over if you get a chance, lads!'

Several men cheered, and Quintus' stomach twisted. Macerio hadn't seen the nail, but he had still just made things worse for himself. There was nothing for it. Using the nail was imperative now. He launched a ferocious attack on Macerio, throwing punch after punch with his left fist, but saving his right, which held the nail. Surprised, the blond-haired man fell back before his assault, and Quintus managed to thump him hard in the belly several times. Macerio's mouth opened and closed as he gasped for air, and Quintus took his chance. With the nail protruding between his second and third fingers, he raked a blow across Macerio's cheek. A shriek of pain tore the air as the iron ripped a deep furrow in his opponent's flesh. Quintus didn't let up. With all of his strength, he threw a left uppercut at Macerio's chin. There was a loud crack; Quintus felt an intense pain in his left fist, and Macerio went down on to the flat of his back.

Quintus stood back, chest heaving, nursing his left hand. Macerio lay unmoving before him. The fight was over. The gods be thanked, Quintus thought. I've won. Rutilus and the jug-eared man were cheering, while Macerio's comrades had rushed to his side. Casually, Quintus let the nail drop. In the chaos, no one would see. He scanned the watching faces and was relieved to see respect in a few. More scowled at him, however, and Quintus knew that he might well have to fight them later. An already-enlisted man being beaten by a new recruit would not be popular.

'You piece of filth! No one pulls a trick like that on me!' Macerio's voice came out of the blue.

Quintus turned in shock. The blond-haired man had been helped up by his friends. Runnels of blood were flowing down his left cheek, and there was murder in his eyes. 'Let's finish this. Properly,' he snarled, hooking his fingers into claws. 'Be interesting to see how you fare as a veles when missing an eyeball.'

Astonished that Macerio was on his feet again and genuinely worried how the fight might now end, Quintus stepped forward. Intent on second-guessing the other's next move, he didn't see the foot that had been stuck in his path. Quintus tripped over it and went sprawling forward on to his face. Even as he tried to roll away and get up, Macerio was on him as fast as a hunting dog on a hare. A kick to his belly drove the air from Quintus' lungs in a *whoosh* of agony. As he struggled to catch his breath, Macerio dropped to his knees alongside him. He began raining punches on to Quintus' torso and head. 'Think you can just strut in here like you own the place, do you?'

'That's enough, Macerio,' said a voice.

'Piss off, Rutilus, or I'll do the same to you!' Macerio shot back.

Quintus tried weakly to protect himself, but Macerio just swatted his arms aside and landed another flurry of blows to his face. The pain was intense. Quintus was unable to retaliate, even less to stop his opponent. His vision was already blurred and he could taste blood in his mouth. A faraway voice was telling him to get up, to fight back, but his strength was gone. He's going to beat me into unconsciousness, he thought dimly. Then blind me.

In the same instant, he felt fingers gouging into his eye sockets. It was agonising. Crying out, Quintus raised his arms, but he was too weak to stop Macerio.

Someone spoke. Quintus couldn't make out who it was, or what had been said, but the effect was immediate. The fingers dropped away from his face. He sensed Macerio stand up. Relieved his ordeal seemed to have ended, Quintus half rolled over; he coughed and spat out a tooth. Tears of pain spilled from his eyes. He wiped them away, and was intensely grateful that he could still see.

'What's going on here?'

This time, Quintus recognised Corax's voice.

'Nothing, sir,' said Macerio. 'Crespo and I were just getting to know each other. A little welcome to our contubernium. You know how it is.'

'Is that what happened?'

A chorus of 'Yes, sir' filled the air.

'Hmmm.' Corax walked to stand over Quintus. His lips twitched with distaste; whether it was at what Macerio had done or how he had failed to defend himself, Quintus wasn't sure. Corax tapped the vine cane in his right fist off the palm of his other hand. 'What have you got to say for yourself?'

Sitting up, Quintus' gaze flashed to Macerio, whose eyes were bright with malice and the expectation that he would tell Corax what had really happened. He would have liked nothing more than to have seen Macerio punished, but something told him to keep the centurion out of it. 'It's as Macerio says, sir,' he mumbled. 'Just a bit of horseplay.'

Corax scrutinised him with barely concealed disbelief. 'Horseplay?'

'That's right, sir,' said Quintus.

'In that case, Hannibal had best look out.'

The men guffawed, half amused, half nervous.

'Macerio!'

'Yes, sir!'

'In future, keep your aggression for the guggas. Clear?' Corax's voice was iron hard.

'Yes, sir.'

'Both of you, clean yourselves up. The instant you've done that, Crespo, go to the quartermaster's.' With that, Corax walked off, tapping his vine cane off his leg.

Quintus got to his feet, wincing as his bruised abdominal muscles protested. He glanced around. The eyes of every man in the contubernium were on him. A few steps away, the other velites were watching too. Many hastati had clearly seen the fight too, but now that Corax had sorted it out, they turned away. Quintus scanned his tent mates' faces again. Their reactions were far more important. Rutilus looked sympathetic; the jug-eared man did too. A couple of men threw him a filthy scowl; Macerio spat and muttered an obscenity. The others' expressions were, if not friendly, on the verge of accepting. As the pain from his face began to take hold, Quintus took some satisfaction from the situation. He had not ratted out on his contubernium, and the majority of his new comrades recognised that. His good feeling did not last for more than a few heartbeats. A quick glance at Macerio told him that he had made a real enemy.

Quintus sighed. He hadn't anticipated problems like this when he'd decided to join the velites. At least in the cavalry he had not had to worry about one of his own comrades wanting to do him harm.

He did now.

I've made my bed, he thought. I will have to lie in it.

The shore of Lake Trasimene, north-central Italy, summer

Hanno had nearly finished his rounds for the evening. In warm weather, and in such a beautiful location, it was a real pleasure to wander among the tents, chatting with his men, sharing a cup of wine and assessing their mood. The temperature was balmy and warm, light still filled the western sky, and overhead, hundreds of swifts darted to and fro, their high-pitched cries reminding him of Carthage. Beyond the last of the tents and the rushes that lined the shore, he could see the surface of the lake. Earlier, it had been a vivid azure colour. Now, it had become a mysterious and inviting dark blue. Not for the first time, Hanno wondered about having a swim. Even though his phalanx hadn't been involved in the sacking and pillaging of the previous weeks, the day's march had been long and hot. Their duties done, thousands of the soldiers had already been sporting in the shallows. It had gone quiet by the shore of late; not many men would choose to enter the water as night fell, but Hanno wasn't that superstitious. He and Suni had spent many an evening fishing from the Choma, the man-made quay at the southeastern edge of Carthage. Taking a dip at night held immense appeal. Gods, it would be wonderful if Suni were here, he thought. He offered up a prayer to safeguard his friend.

A frown creased his brow as he recognised Sapho's stocky shape. Hanno was still a little pissed off with his oldest brother. His return to the column with Sentius in tow had been a proud moment for him. Hannibal had been pleased with the boy, which had thrilled Hanno. As long as Sentius performed as asked, his reputation would grow. That was when Sapho, for whatever reason, had turned around the situation by mentioning how he'd had to save Hanno from drowning in a puddle. Everyone present had laughed, especially Hannibal. 'That's another one of your lives lost,' he'd said, smiling. Hanno had been mortified, and he wondered after the army had marched out of the floodplain if Hannibal would remember who it was that had secured them the guide. When he remonstrated with his brother, Sapho had laughed it off, saying he had merely been trying to lift men's spirits.

'Hanno?'

Of course that's all Sapho was doing, thought Hanno loyally, dismissing the memory. He would have preferred Bostar to have appeared, but his other brother would do. Perhaps he would find a swimming companion after all. He might even get his own back and shove Sapho's head under the water when he wasn't expecting it. 'I'm here.'

'At last I find you.' Sapho strode over. Like Hanno, he had shed his bronze cuirass and pteryges and was clad in just his tunic. A baldric slung from one shoulder held a knife in a leather sheath. They gripped hands in greeting.

'Fancy a swim?' asked Hanno.

'Eh?'

'The water's lovely and warm.'

'Maybe. There's something I need to talk to you about first, though.'

Hanno felt a tickle of unease. 'Walk with me.' He led the way towards the shore; Sapho followed. Hanno moved fast, dreading what his brother might have to say.

Since leaving the Arnus behind, every soldier's task, on Hannibal's express orders, had been to cause as much destruction as possible. At first, only the skirmishers and cavalry had been deployed, but then the infantry had been put to use too. Thus far, Hanno and his phalanx had escaped being part of the raiding parties who daily ranged far and wide to either side of the army. By now, much of Etruria had been laid waste. What couldn't be taken away was burned or despoiled. The population had suffered too. Slaves were not to be harmed, but Roman citizens of all ages were fair game. Each time that Hanno had spoken with Sapho, his oldest brother had taken particular delight in describing what his soldiers had done. By contrast, Bostar and his father, who had been allotted the same duties, had said nothing. Since his torture, Hanno didn't much care what happened to enemy civilians, but he didn't wish to hear the gory details. It reminded him too much of what might happen to Aurelia – if their army ever made it that far south.

A week earlier, he had been surprised when the chance to approach Flaminius' legions at Arretium had been discarded in favour of sacking yet more farms and villages. By veering east along the lake, they were now threatening to do the same to Umbria. As Hanno had realised, Hannibal's intention all along had been to force Flaminius' hand, and in that he had succeeded. The consul had been tailing their forces for some days, albeit at a decent distance. A battle was inevitable, but Hanno worried if it would come soon enough. Flaminius had to want to catch Hannibal between his legions and those of Servilius, who no doubt had been advised of the enemy's march towards him. The further they marched east, the more risk there was of being caught between two Roman armies.

Hannibal had decided to act, brooded Hanno. Sapho had come to tell him that Flaminius was to be goaded into a more hasty response. An entire village needed to butchered out of hand, or worse. Thus far, it had been Hanno's good fortune not to have to commit such acts of brutality. For his general to order him to do so would be something that he could not refuse, no matter how objectionable he found it. Yet it would ensure his return to the fold, Hanno told himself. What were the lives of a few civilians compared to that? 'What does he want me to do?' he asked, without looking at his brother.

'Who?'

'Hannibal, of course.'

'What makes you think I've come to tell you something like that?' Sapho's tone was curious.

'Is that not it?' replied Hanno, trying to cover his confusion.

'It might be. You're not supposed to know yet, but I thought you might like to hear it early.'

Despite his desire to win Hannibal's approval once more, a leaden feeling settled in his belly. 'What will I have to do?'

'Is my little brother reluctant to fight?' Sapho's fingers brushed at the scar on his neck. 'Did your time in Roman hands break your spirit?'

'Don't touch me!' Hanno spun on his brother, eyes blazing, wishing he'd left on the scarf that protected his still sensitive flesh from the unforgiving metal of his cuirass. 'Show me a line of Roman soldiers, and see how long it takes me to butcher every last one!'

'I'm glad to see that you're still angry,' said Sapho. 'I would love a few hours alone with the whoreson who mistreated you.'

His anger at Sapho for touching his scar lessened. 'Thank you, but that's to be my privilege. May the gods grant that I meet Pera again one day, if he yet lives. He will have an end that even he couldn't imagine.'

'I'll drink to that.' Sapho raised the little amphora that he'd been carrying, unseen, by his side. 'Like some?'

Suddenly, Hanno really wanted a drink. 'Yes.'

They found a parting in the rushes, a small sandy area where the lake came right in to the solid ground, and sat down side by side. Sapho cracked the seal, prised out the cork with his knife and took a long slug. He smacked his lips. 'That's very tasty. Try it.'

Hanno hooked a forefinger into one of the amphora's handles. Balancing it against his forearm, he took a sip. The wine had a deep, earthy taste, and a smooth feel quite unlike most he had drunk before. He swallowed a mouthful, and then another. He was about to drink again, when Sapho gave him a nudge. 'Don't finish it!'

Hanno swigged again before handing it back. 'Sorry. It's delicious.'

'As I thought it would be,' said Sapho triumphantly. 'I took it from a large villa, one of the grandest I've ever seen. The man who owns it must be incredibly wealthy.'

'Is he dead now?'

'No, the prick wasn't there, more's the pity. We had to make do with killing his family.'

Hanno closed his eyes. *Aurelia*. 'Is it just the one amphora you've got?'

Sapho snorted with laughter. 'Of course not! There are another twenty where this one came from. Stick with me, little brother, and you can get pissed every night for the foreseeable future.'

That prospect appealed, especially if he was going to have to supervise his men slaughtering women and children. 'Give it here,' he growled.

'My brother, the oenophile! Best not drink too much tonight, though,' Sapho advised.

Hanno paused, the amphora at his lips. 'Why the hell not?'

'You might need a clear head tomorrow.'

I knew it. 'Why tomorrow?' he repeated stupidly.

'It could be the next day.' Sapho squinted at him. 'Aren't you going to ask what Hannibal wants us to do?'

'Tell me,' said Hanno in a monotone.

'Be more enthusiastic, can't you?' Sapho waited, but Hanno did not reply. 'Hannibal is the best leader we have by a long shot. He's smart, and he's a great tactician. And the soldiers love him.'

'I know that. I love him too, you know.' *Even if he orders us to do terrible things.* Hanno steeled himself. Once they'd slain a few families, it wouldn't be that bad, surely? 'Where's the village, or the estate he wants me to pillage?'

'Eh?'

Hanno felt as confused as Sapho looked. 'Is that not what he wants me to do?'

Sapho's eyes narrowed. 'Ah. I see why you were being funny. You thought I'd come to order you out with the patrols which attack the local farms?'

'Yes,' muttered Hanno awkwardly.

'You might find things like that distasteful, little brother, but the day will come when you have to do them,' warned Sapho. 'And when it arrives—'

'I'll do it,' retorted Hanno savagely. 'I follow Hannibal, to whatever end, like you.'

Sapho studied him for a moment. 'Good.'

'So what is it then?' asked Hanno, keen to change the subject.

'It's something far better than burning down some hay barns and killing a few civilians.' Sapho's manner grew conspiratorial. Although there was no one nearby, he leaned in close. 'Remember Zamar?'

'Of course.' The Numidian officer had led the patrol that had come upon Hanno as he made his way towards Hannibal's army more than six months before. They had fought together since as well.

'Today he and his men were scouting to the front of the column when they found a good ambush site. When Hannibal heard about it, he rode out to see it for himself. Upon his return, he called his senior officers together, and then a few others. Bostar and I were among those.'

A stranger would have missed the change in Sapho's inflection as he mentioned Bostar, but not Hanno. *The pair of them are still fighting,* he thought wearily.

A night bird called as it skimmed over the waves, some distance out into the lake. The sound was eerie. The hairs on Hanno's neck prickled. 'What did Hannibal say?'

'You're interested now, eh?' Sapho's teeth flashed in the darkness.

'Damn right. Are we going to fight?'

'About two miles from here, a high ridge comes down to within a mile of the shore. It forms a narrow kind of "entrance" to the land beyond. If you continue eastwards, it opens out again, in a hemi-lunate shape. The area isn't large, though, and it's fringed to the north by the hills. The road follows the shoreline until it comes to another pinch point in a defile some miles further on. There's ample space to deploy our army on the reverse slopes of the elevated ground. We will all be hidden from view except the Gauls, in the centre. Hannibal wants them to be visible to the Romans if they march through the entrance. A decoy, to draw them further in.'

'My gods,' breathed Hanno. 'If this succeeds, they'll be caught like fish in a trap.'

'I like the analogy. And there will be nowhere for the fish to go, except into the lake, where they belong!' Sapho laughed.

'What's the plan?' asked Hanno eagerly.

'The entire army will march through the entrance in the morning. Each section will take up their allotted position as fast as possible, in case the Romans decide to try and catch up.'

'That's unlikely, surely? They're at least a day behind.'

'I know. The Romans might well not march in until the day after tomorrow, but Hannibal wants nothing left to chance.'

It made sense. Hanno nodded. 'If the Gauls are in the centre, where will we be standing?'

'On the left flank, with the slingers. Every last man in the cavalry will be on the right, ready to sweep down and cut off the Romans' route of retreat.'

'It's bloody brilliant. Hannibal is a genius!'

'Let's drink to him, and to a great victory,' said Sapho with true feeling.

Taking turns with the amphora, they toasted each other solemnly. Hanno forgot all about swimming. He hadn't been this excited since before the Trebia. If Hannibal's plan worked, Rome would receive its second severe beating in a period of six months. That augured well for the future. He also felt a new kinship with his oldest brother. In normal circumstances, he would have expected Bostar to seek him out with the news, but instead it had been Sapho. Their relationship had always been awkward, but Hanno determined to try harder. There was no reason that he couldn't be friends with Sapho as well as Bostar. Perhaps he could even bring them together.

But first, there was a battle to win.

An image of Quintus came, bringing with it a sense of melancholy. Hanno shoved it away, more easily than he had before. He wouldn't meet his former friend during the fighting. If he did, he would do what was necessary.

Quintus stood up a little, but he was careful to keep his body hidden. He peered down the slope, which was covered in a mixture of holm oak, strawberry trees and juniper bushes. The strong, resinous scent of turpentine trees laced the air. It was the middle of the afternoon, and the temperature was stifling. In the still air, the *churring* of the cicadas was deafening. Quintus liked hearing it. The sound reminded him of home, but it also meant that the section of road below was empty of life. Only madmen and Carthaginians travelled at this hour. And velites, he thought with a trace of sarcasm.

His gaze moved to the estate that lay on the flat ground to the west. He would have expected to see slaves working the fields, but the thin columns of smoke that rose from the huddle of buildings just visible in the distance told their own story. Like all the other dwellings in the surrounding area, they had been attacked and burned by the enemy in the previous couple of days. More than once, Quintus had seen what the Carthaginians had done. Men, women, children: no one was being spared. Even the dogs and poultry were slaughtered. He wondered if Hanno had taken part in any of the atrocities. *Of course not.* Whether he had or hadn't was immaterial. Plenty of his fellows had. Angered, Quintus ducked back down.

Rutilus and the short man with jug ears, who was universally known as 'Urceus', meaning 'jar', were squatting on their haunches to his left. On his other side were two more of his comrades. All four had strips of wolf skin tied around their simple bowl helmets. It was a proud tradition among the velites and purportedly helped the officers to make out who was fighting well. Quintus hadn't earned the right to sport one yet – that would come after his first battle.

'See anything?' asked Urceus.

'No,' Quintus replied, annoyed that his hopes for the day – a clash with some Carthaginian scouts – had been soured. 'Same as usual. They're long gone.' He spoke with certainty. They were never ordered to range more than a few miles in front of Flaminius' army. It did make some sort of sense – to follow the enemy, all they had to do was to move towards the trails of smoke that marked burning properties – but it frustrated the hell out of Quintus.

'We'll find the damn guggas eventually. They'll run out of places to hide,' said Rutilus in a mock-placatory tone. 'Be grateful for the times that we don't encounter them, however. Each one of those days is an extra one to have lived. Being dead goes on for eternity, you know.'

Quintus had grown to appreciate Rutilus' droll sense of humour. 'Speak for yourself. I intend to survive this war.'

'Me too,' growled Urceus. 'I've got fields that need tending back home, and a woman that needs ploughing.'

'Sure you haven't got that the wrong way round?' Rutilus snickered, and had to dodge out of the way as Urceus' ham-like fist swept through the air at him.

Quintus grinned. Life in the velites was harder than he'd imagined, but there was a camaraderie and a freedom that he hadn't expected. Corax and his junior officers were in charge of half of the maniple's forty skirmishers, while Pullo and his subordinates looked after the other half. Yet the officers didn't direct them in battle, except from a distance. Nor did they accompany the velites out here, on patrol. Instead, the most experienced men took charge. Whether it was because their positions were unranked or because the velites came from the poorest section of society, Quintus did not know, but there was an appealing lack of formality between those who led and those who followed.

Fortunately, Macerio had no superiority over him. He too was an ordinary rank-and-filer. Their relationship had degenerated even further in the weeks since their brawl. They'd come to blows twice, but been separated each time by Big Tenner, their huge ten-man section leader. Since then, they had avoided each other as much as was possible when sharing a tent. Quintus knew, however, that it would only be a matter of time until they clashed again. As much as anything, the scar on Macerio's cheek would see to that. He was grateful to be in the five-man sub-unit led by Urceus, with whom he'd become friendly, while Macerio was in Big Tenner's lot. Little Tenner, the diminutive but charismatic leader of the century's other ten-man section, was with his men some distance off to their right, while the remaining twenty velites were scouring the ground to their left. Sets of short, high-pitched whistles and runners kept the groups in occasional touch.

'We move out. South, same as before. Keep your eyes peeled,' said Urceus, rising. 'Stay at the same height. Big Tenner's men are working the slope below us.'

The undergrowth was too dense to see the rest of the velites, but Quintus glanced anyway. Macerio was out there somewhere, and he wouldn't put it past the whoreson to lie in wait for him with a javelin. Such things happened in war from time to time, and if there were no witnesses, no one would ever be the wiser. The thought of that made him lick his lips and grip the light spear in his right hand a little tighter. Like the ones in his other hand, it had an ash shaft and a narrow, pointed head. Under Corax's hard gaze, Quintus and his companions had spent hours throwing them at bundles of straw. He'd worked hard not to let his experience with a spear show; it appeared to have succeeded.

They wormed their way through the bush in a well-worked pattern, making little noise. Urceus took the centre; Quintus walked about twenty steps to his right, with Rutilus another score beyond that. The two others were in similar positions to Urceus' left. For the most part, it was boring work. The chances of encountering any of the enemy were slim. The Carthaginians were some distance to the south, and all they were interested in was farms and estates, not empty countryside. Inevitably, perhaps, Quintus' attention began to wander. Dead leaves rustled underfoot. A snake slithered away as his tread disturbed it from a sunny patch of earth. Lizards watched him with beady eyes before skittering to safety over the rocks. At last he looked up. He could see vultures, lots of them. His stomach turned, dragging him back to the present.

The Carthaginians' savage tactics meant that vultures had become a common sight overhead, drawn by the rich pickings. There were so many corpses that Flaminius had ordered that, upon discovery, they were to be left unburied. It was a directive that greatly angered his soldiers. Urceus reckoned that that had been the consul's intent, and Quintus was inclined to agree. He was increasingly eager to confront the enemy army in battle. Yes, it would be good to wait until they met up with Servilius and his legions, but if the right opportunity came about, it would be foolish not to take it. How many innocents had to die before Hannibal was stopped?

A series of short whistles, the signal that one of Big Tenner's men was approaching. Without a word from Urceus, the five came to a halt. Despite the fact that the call had been from one of their own, each veles lifted his shield and readied a javelin. As Corax had drummed into them, they always had to be ready to sting like a bee and flit away like a fly, and to do the reverse with equal aptitude. Quintus glanced at Rutilus, who shrugged. 'Who knows what it could be?'

The sight of Macerio sloping towards them made Quintus scowl. Macerio made straight for Urceus.

'What is it?' Urceus demanded.

'Believe it or not, a party of Numidian cavalry.'

Urceus was as surprised as everyone else. 'On the road?'

'Yes. I saw them first.' Macerio shot a spiteful look at Quintus, as if to say, 'You wouldn't have noticed them.' Quintus pretended not to notice.

'How many?' Urceus asked.

'Only six.'

A disapproving hiss. 'They're probably just outriders for a bigger party. We'd best not go near them.'

'They're on their own. They're all pissed.' The insolence in Macerio's tone was just perceptible. 'Maybe they got left behind when their unit was tearing apart a farm. Drank themselves stupid, only woke up this morning.'

'Hmmm.' Urceus looked tempted, and Quintus cursed silently. Why did it have to be Macerio who'd seen them?

'Big Tenner agrees with me.'

'Fair enough,' said Urceus with a feral grin.

'Has he sent for Little Tenner or any of the others?' asked Rutilus.

'For six men? There's no need,' Macerio retorted scornfully.

'True,' added Urceus. 'It'll piss off the others as well, when they discover that we got to blood our spears when they didn't. What did you see, Macerio?'

'One of their horses has gone lame, so they've stopped while its rider tends to it. If we move fast, we can spring an attack from in front and behind,' Macerio announced with another triumphant glance at Quintus.

Fuck you, Macerio, thought Quintus. It's not as if this turns you into an amazing general.

'I like the sound of it! C'mon then, or we'll miss the party.' Urceus indicated that Macerio should turn around.

They began to run. A new urgency lent speed to their feet. A devilment took Quintus, and he placed himself right behind Macerio. It gave him immense satisfaction that the result was to make his enemy cast frequent looks over his shoulder. Down the slope they went, side by side at times, or making their own path through the dense vegetation. Skidding their heels on the dry earth. Avoiding branches that whipped past their faces. Cursing as a bird flew up, making its alarm call.

Big Tenner was waiting for them in a tiny clearing, his broad face twisted into a ferocious grimace. Of his three remaining men, two were visible, watching the road. 'You sound like a herd of fucking cattle. A deaf man could hear you a mile away!'

Macerio flushed.

'It wasn't that bad,' growled Urceus.

'Just as well the shitbags are pissed, or they'd have been long gone.' Big Tenner waved them closer. 'Take a look.'

Urceus padded to a gap in the bushes and disappeared. An instant later, his head popped out. 'Best come and see,' he said to Quintus and the others. 'Then we'll all know what way the land lies.'

It didn't take long to appraise the scene. Some thirty paces below them was a short straight section of the road that led south to Lake Trasimene. Under the shade of some tall strawberry trees opposite was a party of Numidian cavalry, all dismounted. As Macerio had said, there were six. Two were wrestling with a horse, one holding it by the bridle while the other repeatedly tried to lift its left back hoof. Their four companions were sitting in the road, their slouched positions and loud comments giving away much about their state. That, and the amphora that was passing from hand to hand, convinced Quintus that Macerio's hunch was correct. It was a perfect opportunity to strike. They had numbers, sobriety and surprise on their side.

'You take your lads about twenty paces to the rear. We'll stay here,' said Big Tenner. 'Creep down until you're within javelin range. I'll give you enough time. When you hear my whistle, give them a volley, and then another one. After that, charge. None must escape, or we risk being hunted down like dogs by the rest of their comrades.' His stare moved around the group. 'What are you waiting for?' he whispered. 'Go!'

Urceus led them into position, his feet moving silently over the earth. Quintus and his companions followed. When they had come within some thirty paces of the oblivious Numidians, Urceus gestured that they should spread out. The four didn't need to be told twice. The tension in the air could be cut with a knife. Quintus dried the palm of his spear hand on his tunic, and chose his victim.

'Be sure to pick different targets,' Urceus ordered.

'Mine's the one with the amphora,' Quintus hissed.

'I'll take the man to his left,' said Rutilus.

'The ugly one on the right for me then,' rumbled one of their companions.

Urceus looked to the last man. 'We'll both aim for the horse first. It will panic the filth even more.'

A trace of pity entered Quintus as he eyed the Numidians, who were laughing over a shared joke. His gaze focused on the amphora and a burning rage took him. Where had it come from? Whom had they murdered to take possession of it?

Peeeeeeep! Big Tenner's whistle shredded the air.

Quintus cocked his arm back, and let fly. To either side, he heard the grunts as his comrades launched their weapons. He transferred another javelin to his right hand without looking, aimed and threw before the first had even landed.

'Go!' roared Urceus as the first screams hit their ears.

Quintus tore forward, the third of his spears ready to throw. Branches whipped his cheek, half blinding him, but then he was free of the vegetation. He leaped down on to the road, a drop nearly his own height. Rutilus and the others were half a heartbeat behind him. The scene was utter chaos. Javelins were raining in from all directions. Two, three, four of the Numidians were down or dying. The lame horse had been struck twice and was rearing up, shrilling its agony to the world. The other mounts were whirling in panic or galloping off to the south, sending up dust trails. Big Tenner and his men were driving forward from their position. Quintus' eyes flashed from side to side. Where in Hades were the last pair of Numidians?

Then he knew. His feet took him towards two horses that had not yet fled. They were wheeling and turning some twenty paces to his left, but they hadn't run – because someone was talking to them, soothing them. Even as Quintus drew near, a man scrambled up on to the back of the furthest, a small roan. An urgent glance over his shoulder, and then the Numidian pulled on the reins and drummed his heels into the horse's sides. Quintus skidded to a halt and threw, but in his haste, he launched the javelin at too high an arc. It arched up and came down beyond the Numidian. *Shit.* He only had one javelin left. 'Over here!' he bawled. 'Two of them are escaping!'

Whom to aim at? The man he'd missed was already thirty paces away, lying low over his galloping horse's back as they headed north. Quintus cursed again. In the madness of battle, Urceus and the rest hadn't seen him. It was not the direction in which Hannibal's forces lay, but if the Numidian made it, he would have no difficulty in doubling back through the fields. Quintus blinked sweat from his eyes and let out another oath. He wasn't a good enough shot to make such a throw. That meant the last cavalryman was the one to go for. He'd have to be quick. Spotting a hand gripping the bottom of the last horse's neck, a black, his eyes shot to its back. Yes! There was the outline of a bare foot, halfway between its withers and its hip. The Numidian was hanging on to its far side, using its body as cover as he urged it to follow its companion. 'Here! Over here!' Quintus sprinted to get around the horse, which was fast moving from a walk to a trot.

A moment later, he caught sight of the Numidian, a lithe figure in a sleeveless tunic clamped to his mount's chest and belly. Quintus' breath caught in his throat. If he threw at this angle and missed, his javelin would strike the black. But it couldn't be helped. It was that or a second man would get away. He closed one eye, took aim and hurled his spear with all his force. It shot through the air and drove into the Numidian's back with a meaty *thump*. A scream of agony, and the man's grip failed. He dropped to the dirt. Freed of its load, the black galloped off. Quintus was relieved to see no signs of blood in its coat. If Big Tenner had thrown, he thought, the javelin would have skewered the Numidian and horse both.

Dragging out his gladius, he ran towards the Numidian. He had gone only a couple of strides when he felt a stinging sensation slice across the top of his left shoulder. A whoosh of air and the javelin had gone, driving into the ground by the Numidian's feet. 'Clumsy bastard! Watch where you're throwing!' Quintus shouted. He spun to see who had made such a stupid mistake.

From a short distance away, Macerio's baleful gaze met his. Death was in his eyes.

Quintus could have sworn that the blond man was about to throw another spear, but then Urceus and Rutilus were shoving past, roaring curses at the Numidian, finishing him with savage thrusts of their swords. Without a word, Macerio trotted back to where the other enemy riders were being dispatched. At once Quintus' attention was taken by Rutilus and Urceus, who came over to congratulate him on hitting the last Numidian. He let out a gusty sigh of relief. It was over. They had won. The tension in his shoulders eased, and he suddenly felt drained. Yet the combat had lasted mere moments. In that short time, five Numidians had been slain. Two horses needed their throats cut to end their suffering, but the others were long gone. Nonetheless, the ambush had been a resounding success. Around him, men were giving each other pleased, relieved looks.

Big Tenner remained focused. 'No hanging about on the road,' he barked. 'Gods know who might come riding along. The Numidian who escaped might have friends nearby. Search the dead if you wish, quickly, and then let's get out of here.'

Urceus made a beeline for the amphora, which was lying on its side, its contents leaking on to the earth. He peered inside. 'There's still plenty left,' he announced with satisfaction. 'That's all I need.'

There were whoops as coins and rings were emptied out of purses found on the Numidians' bodies. Quintus' amusement was soured by the sight of the dead being rifled. But any valuables present were Roman by right, he thought.

Rutilus saw him looking. 'Whoever owned that stuff is dead.'

'It still seems like stealing.'

'Come on! If our lads don't take it, someone else will.'

Rutilus was correct, but that didn't mean Quintus liked it one bit.

'Time to move!' Big Tenner clapped his hands. 'In case you ladies had forgotten, we've still got a patrol to finish.'

With good-natured grumbles, they withdrew to the shelter of the trees. As each five-man section split up again, insults were thrown, ridiculing various individuals' poor javelin throws and the fact that one of the enemy had escaped. The amphora that Urceus had swiped was passed about. Quintus' comrades were grinning from ear to ear, but unhappiness settled over him like a wet blanket as he watched Macerio vanish into the trees. He had only seen the look in the blond man's eyes by chance, but he had not missed its meaning. Macerio had tried to murder him. Frustration mixed with Quintus' anger. He had no way of proving what had happened. An accusation would result in Macerio denying everything. Killing him before he tried again would work, but Quintus didn't have the stomach for slaying a man in cold blood – even someone like Macerio. Better to keep quiet, and stay alert. Urceus' amphora was thrust at him, but he refused it with a word of mumbled thanks. From now on, brooded Quintus, he would need to make sure that he had company all the time. It was bad enough having the Carthaginians to worry about without having an enemy in his own camp.

Yet that was his new reality.

Chapter VII

Capua

From the first time that they had met formally, Aurelia had liked Lucius well enough. He was attentive and courteous; he clearly found her attractive. Once this had become clear, her mother had postponed their departure for the farm. A week had become two; that time had since been extended to a month. Aurelia didn't mind. This was infinitely better than living at home, where, since Quintus and Hanno had left, nothing ever happened. Every day, there had been something new and exciting to look forward to.

Typically for a Roman man, Lucius was poor at compliments, but she had never been given so many gifts. A smile of pleasure, and a little guilt, traced her lips as she touched the jet and carnelian necklace at her throat. It had been hers from the moment she'd made a casual comment while walking with Lucius through the city. Her little jewellery box, formerly bare, was now overflowing with earrings and bracelets. She had a stunning fan made from the tail feathers of an exotic bird called a peacock; he had even tried to buy her a little monkey as a pet. With her mother as chaperone, she and Lucius had walked around the forum, taken a boat trip along the River Volturnus and watched chariot-racing at the local amphitheatre. They had been to the theatre twice, and taken an overnight trip to the coast. The time since the confrontation with Phanes had been a veritable whirlwind of activity. There was even talk of visiting the island of Capri. While she wasn't sure that she wanted to marry Lucius, Aurelia was having the time of her life. Why was it then that she wasn't enjoying herself more? Agesandros wasn't around to upset her. Atia had sent him back to manage their estate.

Aurelia knew well the reasons for her disquiet. Every night she thought about them until her head hurt. First was the fact that she didn't find Lucius that attractive. He was a decent, likeable man, but he was so . . . what was the word she was looking for? Earnest. That was it, she thought. He was too *earnest*. Well meaning, intelligent, well educated, good-looking in his own way. Sadly, all those qualities didn't stop him from being a bore. She'd initially had that thought when, during their boat trip, Lucius had begun expounding on the fish life in the River Volturnus. At the time, Aurelia had pretended to be fascinated, shoving away the idea and berating herself afterwards for even allowing it into her head. Whether or not she wanted to know the differences between freshwater fish and those that dwelled in the sea, it was wrong to think ill of him. She had every reason to find him physically attractive – the way she did Gaius, and had Hanno. No matter how hard she tried, though, her feelings would not change. She regarded Lucius as a friend, but nothing more than that. It didn't help that, staying in Martialis' house, she saw Gaius every day. If anything, her crush on *him* had intensified.

Her second problem was that her mother had taken a real shine to Lucius. It turned out that Atia's father had been friends with his grandfather; the pair had served together in the first war against Carthage. Not only were his family cultured, they were also big landowners, with estates given over mainly to the production of olives. As Atia had whispered approvingly to Aurelia during a dinner with Lucius and his father, 'The olive crops haven't suffered like the wheat has of recent years. Olive oil is like liquid gold if you have enough of it, and they do.' She had tried to tell her mother that she wasn't interested, but Atia was having none of it. 'You like him; he wants you. I understand that he's been under considerable pressure from his father to marry. It's time that he provided his family with an heir. That's more than enough grounds for a marriage. Where there is friendship, love can grow,' she had said firmly. 'Lucius is a good man, from good stock. Your father would approve.'

'Father doesn't know a thing about him,' Aurelia had protested. 'He has to give his approval before any match can be made.' Her hopes had plummeted with her mother's answer.

'I've already sent a letter to your father, telling him that Lucius is the perfect husband for you. If all goes well, we could hear back within a month or two, and the betrothal can be formalised.'

Defeated, Aurelia had lapsed into a gloomy silence that even Lucius could not lift. Furious, Atia had taken her home, pleading a headache. The lecture she had delivered at Martialis' house afterwards still rang through Aurelia's mind. Lucius was no older man, no Flaccus; he was of a similar age to her. He was not arrogant, or pompous, as Flaccus had been. He lived nearby, not in Rome, so she would be able to see her family regularly. He wasn't interested in serving in the army – and there was nothing wrong with that – instead, he had decided to study law, after which he would enter politics. Lucius' career choice meant that he would not, unless things grew far worse, have to leave as other young nobles would. There was little risk that he would die in battle, as her father and Quintus might. Why was she continuing to try and sabotage her planned betrothal, a god-granted path to salvation of the family's fortunes? If she succeeded, Atia ranted, she would be condemning her own family to penury and worse. Was that what she wanted? Did she wish for a man like Phanes to assume the ownership of their estate?

Aurelia had been reduced to tears by the effectiveness of her mother's words. She'd wanted to run to Gaius – the only friend she had in Capua – and throw herself into his arms, and tell him of her feelings. She had wanted to run away and take ship to Carthage, there to find Hanno. The latter was nothing but a dream – Hanno wouldn't even have been there – but she could have chosen to go to Gaius' room. Yet she had not. She had wiped her face, and agreed to her mother's demands, telling herself that marriage to a man such as Lucius could be a good thing. Plenty of women had to live with worse matches than she. Best to count her blessings, and accept her lot.

The day after, trying to take her mind off the whole affair, Aurelia had asked permission to pay a visit to the temple of Mars, there to pray for her father and Quintus. With a new betrothal looming, she felt their absence more than ever. To her relief, Atia had reluctantly acquiesced, with the stipulation that two of Martialis' male slaves accompany her for security. 'Phanes has given me a month's grace, but I still wouldn't trust him, or any of the other leeches, not to harass you in the street, or worse,' she said with a scowl. 'If you see as much as a hair on his head, turn around and head in the other direction.'

Promising that she would, Aurelia set out. She stopped to buy a plump hen at the market – a suitable offering – before making her way to the temple. All went well within. The priest, a young, intense man with a beard, commented on the bird's healthy plumage and bright eyes, and its apparent lack of fear. It died without a struggle, and its organs were free of blemishes of any kind. Mars had accepted her gift, and would keep his shield over her father and her brother, the priest assured her. Aurelia wasn't as religious as she ought to be; she often forgot to say her prayers or kneel at the lararium in their house, but the ritual and his words gave her a good deal of comfort that morning.

Her spirits high, she slipped the last coin that Atia had given her to the priest and prepared to leave the temple. At that moment, Gaius entered in full army uniform: Boeotian helmet, bronze cuirass, linen pteryges and leather boots. He was a magnificent sight, and her stomach fluttered. Suddenly shy, she ducked her head so as not to be seen.

'Aurelia? Is that you?'

She made a show of adjusting her necklace before looking up. 'Gaius! What a surprise.'

'I could say the same thing, seeing you here.'

'You're very handsome in your uniform,' she ventured.

He grinned, looking boyish. 'Do you think so?'

Aurelia wanted to pay him more compliments, but she could feel a tell-tale flush beginning on her cheeks. 'I came here to ask Mars to grant Quintus and Father his protection,' she said quickly.

His face grew serious. 'I thought as much.'

'The priest was happy with the sacrifice, and the omens were good.'

'Mars be thanked! I shall include them in my prayers too, as always.'

She wanted to kiss him, but all she said was, 'You're a good man, Gaius.'

'Quintus is my best friend, and your father has always been kind to me. It's the least I can do.'

'What brings you to the temple, and in uniform too?'

'You've heard how Hannibal's rabble has been laying waste to Etruria?'

She nodded, grateful that Capua was hundreds of miles from the conflict.

It didn't bear thinking about what might happen if the war came further south. 'It's dreadful.'

'I won't tell you some of the things I've heard,' he said with a frown. 'But the good news is that the consul Flaminius is shadowing the enemy. He's trying to push Hannibal into a position where he and Servilius can strike him from both the rear and the front.'

'That is worth praying for,' she said, determining to ask the gods more often that Rome was victorious.

'It's not just that.' He gave her a conspiratorial wink. 'There are rumours that the local contingent of socii troops is to be mobilised.'

Shocked, she didn't take in his meaning at once.

'Soon I might be sent north, with my unit. Aren't you pleased for me?'

Aurelia felt lightheaded. How could she be pleased? She wanted to rage and scream, to beg him not to leave her as well. 'It's so dangerous. Quintus and Father, they—'

'They're still alive, despite the setbacks our forces have suffered. The gods protect brave men such as they. With any luck, they'll do the same for me.' His eyes were bright with courage and enthusiasm.

'I will miss you, Gaius.' *If only you knew how much.*

'I'm not going yet. But when I do, your new friend will keep you company. I've heard all about him from your mother.' Another wink. 'You won't even notice I've gone.'

Aurelia felt even worse. He didn't seem jealous of Lucius. 'I shall pray for you,' she whispered. *What if he never comes back? I have to say something, I have to.* 'Gaius, I—'

Gaius was so excited that he didn't hear her last words. 'By your leave, I'll go inside to make my offering.'

'Of course.' She watched him go, her heart thudding off her ribs. Surely, any chance she had of winning him over had just vanished.

'Quite the dashing young soldier, isn't he?'

She spun in shock. Phanes was watching her from the shadow of the colonnaded walkway that ran around the temple's courtyard. How long he had been there, Aurelia didn't know. She hadn't noticed him on her way in. Despite the slaves who stood behind her, fear coursed through her, and she studied the gloom to either side.

'Don't worry. I've left Smiler and Achilles at home.'

'How long have you been watching?' He hadn't been there when she went in, she was sure of it. What had he heard?

'Long enough. I thought you spent all your time with Lucius Vibius Melito nowadays,' he said slyly. 'That's Martialis' son, isn't it?' He strolled forward. Sunshine glittered off his oiled hair.

'What if it is?' She wanted to leave, but her fear that he had noticed something between her and Gaius froze her every muscle.

'A handsome lad, as you said.'

'He looks good in uniform, like my brother. Like most men.'

'You seem worried that he might be sent to war.'

'He's dear to me. I've known him since I was a child,' she said casually. 'He and my brother Quintus are best friends.'

'May the gods protect him if he is sent north. Rome has lost too many sons in recent months,' said Phanes, his tone oozing sincerity.

'He's Oscan, not Roman.' She could not bear his calculating eyes on her any longer. 'Mars will give our forces victory, and Gaius will be there to celebrate it,' she declared, moving past him, and grateful for the slaves' presence at her back.

'My compliments to your lady mother,' he called.

Aurelia didn't deign to reply. She just wanted to get away.

Phanes launched his final barb. 'Does Melito know your friend?'

Despite her best efforts, Aurelia stiffened. She forcibly relaxed her shoulders and turned with a surprised look. 'But of course. He will miss Gaius too.'

Phanes nodded as if she'd given him the answer he expected. 'I'm sure he will.'

She left him to it. All the way back from the temple, Aurelia's unease grew. Phanes had put two and two together about her feelings for Gaius – why would he have made such a comment if he hadn't? Had she done enough to allay his suspicions? Gods, don't let him tell Lucius, she worried. If there was even a seed of doubt in Lucius' mind about her intentions, he would never consent to a betrothal. If all things were equal she wouldn't have minded that, but it would bring ruin down on her family. *Curse him!*

Eventually, Aurelia managed to achieve some sort of calm by telling herself that the Greek could not have read too much into the situation. She couldn't quite shake her disquiet, however. Phanes probably had spies throughout Capua. As she neared Martialis' house, she watched the people in the street sidelong: a boy selling fruit juice from a handcart; a stonemason and his apprentice repairing a wall; two old men gossiping in the warm sun; a woman selling trinkets from a small stall. Any one of them could be in his employ, she thought bitterly. As the Greek had already proved, even in Martialis' house she was not beyond prying eyes.

Aurelia felt like a rat in a trap.

She made up her mind. From now on, she would have to avoid Gaius, and make much more of Lucius. She had to, for her family's sake. It felt as if the last of her liberty had been taken away. Before, she had at least been able to play at being free to make her own decisions. Not any more.

Near Lake Trasimene

'Tell me what you saw again,' ordered Corax. The bright moonlight lit up his features but not his deep-set eyes, making him look even more forbidding. Quintus, who had been ordered to attend him along with Big Tenner and the rest of their section, was glad that the centurion was on his side.

'As you know, sir, the ground opens out after the pinch point to the east of our camp,' said Big Tenner.

'Yes, yes.'

'The area is half-moon shaped and about a square mile in area, sir. At the eastern end of it, another ridge comes down to the water's edge. Hannibal has put his camp on the heights there, overlooking the road. We scouted along the shore towards the enemy for about half a mile, but then we started seeing groups of Numidians. If we'd gone any further, they would have ridden us down.'

'You saw nothing on the hills to the north?' asked Corax.

'No, sir. On the way back, I even sent a five-man section to search the lower slopes. They didn't find a thing.' As Corax chewed on that, Big Tenner let out a little sigh. Quintus knew why. Tenner had reported when they'd returned to the camp, which lay just to the west of the entrance to the narrows. Then he had had to repeat it all to Flaminius himself. Now

Corax was making him do it all over again. Behind Tenner, Quintus shifted on his haunches. Rutilus glanced at him as if to say, 'How much longer will this take?' Even in the poor light, Urceus looked downright pissed off. It was unsurprising. They had been scouting since early morning. All of them were tired, sunburned and thirsty. Quintus' stomach rumbled with hunger, but he said not a word. Until their centurion dismissed them, they had to sit tight. Surely, though, the grilling would not go on for much longer.

'What's the whoreson planning?' mused Corax. 'He must be aware, like us, that Servilius is marching this way from Ariminum. If he stays where he is, with the lake hemming him against the hills, his army could be crushed.'

'Knowing that, they'll probably move off tomorrow, sir,' Tenner ventured.

Corax barked a laugh. 'Aye, I dare say you're right.' He gave the velites an approving nod. 'You've done well today, all of you. You have earned a drink, and some food in your bellies.' They rumbled in agreement, and he clicked his fingers. A servant hastened over. 'Fetch an amphora of my second-best wine and a round of cheese to these lads' tent lines.'

'We're grateful, sir.' Tenner was grinning from ear to ear.

'Thank you, centurion,' the rest chorused.

'Enjoy it, but don't stay up too late,' warned Corax. 'You'll need fresh heads in the morning. Flaminius is set on an early start. Dismissed.'

The velites trudged away, their spirits restored by Corax's generosity. 'He's a good officer,' muttered Quintus. 'I wouldn't mind standing in line with him.'

'He's just given us some food, not a promotion!' said Rutilus. 'It'll be a year at the earliest, probably two, before you're even considered for the hastati.'

'I know, I know.' Quintus buttoned his lip. Part of the reason he wanted to leave the velites was because of Macerio, whose latest tactic was to spread malicious rumours about him among the men. 'Crespo pissed in the river. It fouled the water. That's why men are falling sick.' 'Crespo would have fallen asleep on sentry duty if I hadn't woken the dog up.' 'Crespo is a coward. He'll run the first time we really have to fight the guggas.' And so on. Quintus was sick of it. Fortunately, most of the men in his section didn't believe the lies. They had been there during the ambush on the Numidians. But they seemed to have taken root with some of the other velites. If he moved to the hastati, he could start anew. *Don't be stupid.* Macerio also stood to be promoted into the legionaries' ranks. What was to say that they wouldn't end up in the same unit, where the bullying would start all over again? Quintus clenched his jaw in frustration. It was a moot point anyway, because he was still a veles, and would remain so for the foreseeable future.

'Forget about everything except that wine and cheese,' advised Rutilus. 'That and a dip in the lake before bed.'

Quintus smiled. The idea of filling his belly and, after it, washing off the day's dust was so appealing that it was easy to obey.

Tomorrow was another day.

Following Hannibal's orders, Hanno and his men had moved into position when there was scarcely any light in the sky. They and the rest of the Libyan spearmen were the bait in the trap for the Romans. They had been deployed on the slopes of the hill below their camp and across the road where it ran into the defile on the eastern side of the half-moon-shaped plain. The phalanxes were in full sight of anyone approaching from the west, and an open invitation for Flaminius to seek battle. More than an hour had passed since they had blocked the passage east, and the skyline was paling fast. Hanno studied the eastern horizon for the hundredth time. Red, pink and orange mixed in a glorious riot of colour. Normally, he would have taken the time to appreciate such a beautiful dawn. Today, though, his gaze quickly returned to the west.

Sudden delight filled him. No one could have predicted this! Everything was vanishing beneath a blanket of grey. It was as if the Carthaginian gods had decided to act in unison, favouring Hannibal, he thought, watching the thick, oily banks of fog that were creeping in off the lake. Already some of the flat ground had been covered; it would not be long before the low hills were also encased. It was fortunate that the area had been reconnoitred the previous day; that Hannibal had ordered everyone into position so early. By now, the entire army should have been deployed.

Hanno had seen glints from sunlight flashing off metal a few times as the Gauls moved on to the slopes opposite, and the Numidians on to the hills to the north, but that had been it. His guts clenched with excitement and fear. He hardly dared admit it, but he even felt a touch of elation. Before, their ambush might have been revealed if the Romans had sent in scouts in advance of the legions. With the arrival of the fog, however, the enemy had no chance of noticing the waiting Carthaginian soldiers, scouts or not. Don't be over-confident, he told himself. Everything could still go wrong. If the Gauls did something stupid before the majority of Flaminius' army had marched through the pinch point, they would only catch a fraction of the enemy's number in their trap. He prayed that Hannibal's trust in the Gauls, his most undisciplined men, would be repaid in full. Bostar had told him of the tribal chiefs' joy at being given such an important task, as they had at the Trebia. To them, the possibility of suffering heavy casualties was as nothing compared to the honour of leading the attack. Yet that didn't mean some fool among the Gauls wouldn't give the game away by yelling a war cry too soon.

The gaming pieces were in place. The contest was about to begin. It was pointless worrying about it, but Hanno did anyway. Restless, he walked along the front rank of his spearmen, nodding, smiling, murmuring names, telling them that victory would be theirs. They gave him fierce grins in return. Even Mutt's doleful face cracked into a smile as he approached. It had been the same since Victumulae. Hanno's fingers felt under the strip of cloth that protected his neck from the edge of his cuirass. He could trace the outline of the 'F' still; he would be able to until his dying day. Perhaps the torture and pain had been worth it. His survival against all the odds at Victumulae had turned him into a sort of good-luck charm for his men, and those of the other phalanxes. Apparently, some of them maintained that he couldn't be killed. Tanit grant that that be true for today at least, he thought wryly.

'Ready, sir?' asked Mutt.

'As I'll ever be. This is the worst bit, eh? Waiting.'

'Aye,' grumbled his second-in-command. 'Let's get it over with and have done.'

Hanno clapped Mutt on the shoulder and moved on. At the edge of his phalanx, he glimpsed Bostar, who was talking to Sapho and their father. Seeing him, they beckoned.

'Father.' He nodded at Sapho and Bostar. 'Brothers.'

Malchus' gaze moved across the trio. 'This is a proud day, my sons.'

They all smiled, but Bostar and Sapho did not look at each other.

'Who'd have thought that we would ever be standing in northern Italy as part of a Carthaginian army?' asked Malchus. 'That another Roman army would be about to walk into our trap?'

It did seem a touch unreal, thought Hanno. Not too many months before, he had been a slave. Memories filled his head. *Don't think about Quintus.*

'Don't tempt the gods, Father,' said Bostar, glancing at the heavens. 'We haven't won yet.'

Sapho eyed his brother derisively. 'Are you scared we'll lose?'

Rather than reply, Bostar clamped his jaw. Malchus intervened. 'Overconfidence is not a quality admired by the gods, it is true. Pride comes before a fall. Far better to ask for victory with humble hearts.'

'All I ask is that those bloodthirsty Gauls keep silent for long enough, until the Roman vanguard reaches us. We'll do the rest,' said Sapho. 'Eh, brother?' He aimed a nudge at Hanno.

Don't try and use me in your fight with Bostar, thought Hanno angrily. 'I'm sure that all four of us will play our part. Fulfil our duty to Hannibal.'

In the distance, trumpets blared. The hairs on Hanno's neck prickled. There *would* be a battle today.

'They're coming!' breathed Bostar.

'Blindly, into the fog. Baal Hammon be thanked for their arrogance.' Malchus bared his teeth. 'Back to your phalanxes. I will see you when it's over, gods willing.'

With fierce grins, they parted.

Tiny pearls of moisture covered the iron of Quintus' javelins and his shield rim. His skin was clammy, his tunic damp and, thanks to the wet grass, his feet were soaking. Pangs of hunger rose from his empty stomach, and he wished he'd taken a chunk of bread to eat while marching, as some of the others had. Yet his physical discomforts were the least of his worries. The visibility was growing worse, he was sure of it. The grey fog lay heavy on the land. Rutilus and Urceus were a few steps to his left and right, but he could barely make out the men beyond them. At least Macerio was as far away from him as possible, at the end of the line. Nonetheless, it was unnerving to walk into the gloom, knowing that the enemy was only about a mile and a half away. 'Is this a good idea?' he muttered. 'We can't see a damn thing.'

Urceus heard him. 'Flaminius thinks the fog will lift by mid-morning. So did Corax and so do I. That good enough for you?'

'Corax wasn't exactly ecstatic about the order to march,' replied Quintus. *Nor can he be happy that we are only fifty paces ahead of the vanguard. Normally, we'd be half a mile out at least, and the cavalry would be beyond that.*

'An officer of his experience isn't going to be. He knows that some of his men may well be killed and injured today, but it's his duty to obey orders. Like it is mine. And yours, Crespo.'

Quintus caught the warning tone in Urceus' voice. He decided not to mention his concern about the cavalry. Saying it would just aggravate Urceus further. So he said, 'Don't worry, I'll do my bit.'

An irritable grunt. Urceus glanced to either side. 'Pass the word. Go slow. Stay abreast of each other, no more than five paces apart. I don't want any of you getting lost, you hear?'

Quintus repeated Urceus' words to Rutilus, who did the same to the man on his right.

From behind them came the heavy *tramp, tramp, tramp* of thousands of legionaries following their trail. Trumpets blared in the distance as the units far to the rear manoeuvred into the long marching column. The sounds were magnified by the ridge that pressed Quintus and the velites against the side of the lake, deafening their ears to anything else. It was unsettling, but the loud rhythm was also reassuring. And intimidating. That will send the fear of the gods into the Carthaginians, Quintus thought. If they had not left, that was. Part of him recklessly hoped that the enemy had stayed put. Hearing their enemies approaching, but not being able to see them, would be terrifying. They won't advance to meet us – in the fog, that would be madness. They'll wait on the slopes of the hills until we've come a lot closer. By then, the haze will doubtless have started to burn off. Things will be clearer.

They walked on, swishing dark, damp trails through the calf-high grass that lined each side of the narrow road. No one talked. Every man's attention was locked on the ground before his feet, on the impenetrable fog before his eyes, straining for any indication of the enemy. But they heard nothing. Saw nothing. Came across nothing. They were alone in the clammy gloom. It felt eerie, and Quintus was glad of his comrades to either side. He had never walked so far in such conditions. Without the others, his unease might have mastered him.

Absent the sun, all sense of time vanished. Gradually, though, it grew a little brighter. Morning had arrived, but he couldn't be more accurate than that. At the start, Quintus had tried to keep count of his footsteps, but thoughts of the Carthaginians and Hanno kept breaking his concentration. He had long since given up. It would sound nervous to keep talking about how far they had come, so he didn't say a word. Eventually, however, he could bear it no longer, and asked Rutilus.

'No idea. A mile, perhaps?' came the reply.

'What do you think, Urceus?'

Their section leader hawked and spat, quietly. 'I'd say a mile was about right. We'll be getting close now.'

They peered suspiciously into the murk. 'Nothing,' whispered Quintus.

'They might be gone,' ventured Rutilus.

'Aye, and they might not,' growled Urceus. 'Keep your eyes peeled and your wits about you.'

It was as if Urceus had sensed Big Tenner's thoughts, and those of the centurions behind. Not fifty heartbeats later, an order came down the line to Urceus, who repeated the command at once. 'A runner's come from the legions. We're to slow even further. Have a javelin ready to throw. Spread the word.'

Quintus' stomach twisted sharply, but he threw a grin at Rutilus. 'Ready?'

'Yes.' Rutilus glanced at the man to his right and raised his spear. 'Go slow. Ready to loose? Pass it on.'

The order raised the tension and fear several notches. Rutilus was scowling. The tip of Urceus' tongue was visible between his lips. Quintus moved his throwing arm back and forth, back and forth, making sure that the javelin was well balanced. He pricked his ears. The only thing audible was the cadence of the legionaries' feet, but it was much slower now. *Tramp*. His heart hammered out a few beats. *Tramp*. His eyes lifted to where the sky should be. Still fog, everywhere. *Tramp*. No, wait. The grey overhead was lighter than it had been, but only a fraction. Damn fog! Jupiter, Greatest and Best, please make it lift, he prayed.

It was easy not to lose count of his steps now. Ten paces. Twenty. He couldn't see a thing in front of him. Thirty paces. Fifty. A hundred. Quintus' scalp prickled from the sweat that had built up under his felt helmet liner. Runnels of it trickled down the back of his neck. His scar itched, but there was no chance of scratching it, just as there'd be no opportunity to empty his suddenly full bladder. A quick glance at his companions. Their tense faces and white knuckles mirrored his own jangling nerves. At 150 paces, the fog thinned a little, shrinking from an all-enveloping soup to white tendrils that writhed in slow motion over the grass. Then, a glint of sun from above. Quintus' spirits lifted. *At last*.

'Thank the gods,' muttered Rutilus with a sigh.

'*Shhhh!*' hissed Urceus, glaring.

Rutilus flinched. Silly bugger, thought Quintus. With any luck, though, no one had heard. No one being the enemy.

Ahead, looming out of the fog, he saw treetops. The ridge. They were near the second ridge. His eyes flickered to Urceus, who had seen it too. Eyes front again, thought Quintus, take another step. Was it his imagination, or was the fog opening out? Two more paces. Then, a hint of brown perhaps fifty paces to his front. Bushes, or was it a dead tree?

Without warning, the fog came to an end. One moment, Quintus was surrounded by clinging grey fingers, and the next, he was in the open air. The transition was startling enough, but what made his heart leap into his mouth was the massed ranks of enemy troops not fifty paces in front of him. Conical helmets, large round shields, long spears. Libyan spearmen, the soldiers that Hanno had commanded. Could *he* be here? Quintus wondered. Above the Libyans were groups of men in simple tunics, carrying slings. His gaze shot from left to right. There were thousands of the bastards, standing there. Just waiting.

For them.

'Look out!' he roared. 'They're here! They're here!' Without waiting to see if his comrades had heard, Quintus darted forward. This is what velites were trained to do. The closer he was, the more likely his javelins would find a target. He was safe from the Libyans' spears, which were used for thrusting. In just a few heartbeats, however, the slingers' stones would start landing. His stomach twisted into knots as he neared the enemy lines. 'Roma! Roma!' he shouted. At thirty paces, he took aim at an officer in the first rank and launched his first javelin. Despite himself, he hoped that it wasn't Hanno. Without looking to see where it landed, Quintus transferred his second shaft to his right hand. A bearded soldier caught his eye. Draw back, aim, loose – just as he had been trained. His third javelin was already in his fist when he heard the characteristic whistle of an incoming slingshot. And then another, and another.

Quintus flinched. It took every bit of his self-control not to look up. First shots are never accurate. They're nervous too, he told himself. *Thump. Thump. Thump.* The stones were landing all around him. He chose his target and threw, seized his last javelin and hurled it as well. Now, the air was filled with humming noises, as if a swarm of bees was approaching. Quintus fought his panic as he turned to flee. The way back would be fraught with danger. Slingers could make accurate shots for hundreds of paces. He had seen the evidence of that with his own eyes at the Trebia. *Stop it.* He wheeled, taking in Rutilus, Big Tenner and the rest of the section all close by, weaving, ducking, throwing their javelins. His heart lifted. He was not alone, not the only target for the enemy.

But it was time to run. During his training, Quintus had often wondered how it would feel to retreat from the enemy on foot rather than on horse-back, as he had done before. Now he knew, with his heart hammering off his ribs and the acid taste of fear in his throat. It was far worse. Gut-churning. Bloody terrifying. Without thinking, he lifted his shield over his helmet so that it protected the back of his head and his shoulders. He would look ridiculous to the oncoming legionaries, but he didn't care. *Thump. Thump. Thump.* His ears rang with the deadly sound. He could see stones landing everywhere: in front, to the left and right and at the edges of his vision.

He had gone perhaps fifty paces when a sharp cry made him look back. A short distance behind him, Rutilus had dropped to one knee, clutching at his right hip. Charging back into the storm of stones would be suicidal, but he couldn't just leave him. Gritting his teeth, Quintus sprinted back, holding his shield before him. His arm jarred as it was struck. White-hot pain lanced through him as a slingshot hit his left shin. He spat a curse, and kept running. A moment later, he skidded to a halt beside Rutilus. 'Stand up!'

Rutilus groaned. 'Are you trying to get yourself killed?'

'Shut your mouth and get up.'

'We'll never make it.'

'Jupiter's cock, Rutilus, do you want to live or not?'

Rutilus struggled to his feet, grunting with pain. 'Throw your arm over me,' Quintus ordered, slipping his own around Rutilus' shoulders. 'Come on, damn you! I don't want to risk my life for nothing.' His friend did as he was told. Quintus lifted his shield over his helmet again, and together they began to move.

'They'll target us even more now,' said Rutilus.

'I know.' Rather than let his fear master him, Quintus stared at the ground and concentrated on each step. They were doomed, but this gave him something to do. Better than dwelling on the harsh realisation that he was going to die in his first action as a veles. Left, right. Left, right. Four steps. Left, right. Left, right. Eight steps. The flesh on Quintus' back crawled. This was worse than retreating from the enemy on horseback – far worse.

But they were still moving at fifty paces. Then, somehow, it was a hundred. Quintus' leg muscles were burning with the effort of supporting Rutilus, whose limp was growing worse. He didn't know how much further he could go on. The sling bullets were still raining down around them, clattering off his shield. It was only a matter of time before one struck him a deadly blow.

'Look,' grunted Rutilus.

Quintus' head lifted. He blinked. Emerging from the fog was the front of the column. There, in the front rank, he could see Corax. The centurion was shouting orders, and his men were spreading out into battle formation. Quintus' heart leaped with joy, and not a little relief. Already he could sense that they were no longer the slingers' main target. He began angling to the right of the soldiers. If they went left, there was every chance of being pushed into the lake. 'Move it, or we'll get in the way.'

Rutilus responded with a burst of energy. 'They'd best get into position quickly. Otherwise those phalanxes will smash them apart.'

'There'll be time. Those spearmen are going nowhere. Why would they give up the high ground?' countered Quintus.

Before Rutilus could answer, the air rippled with a new, unearthly sound. *Parr-parr-parr. Zẓẓeyrrp. Parr-parr-parr. Zẓẓeyrrp. Booooooooo.* Beneath it, thousands of voices began to chant. Metallic clashes signalled the clattering of weapons off shields. The back of Quintus' throat filled anew with bile. The noise was coming from a long distance to their rear, from far over on the right, where the first ridge ran down to the water's edge.

'Hades below, what is that?' The fear rippled in Rutilus' voice.

'Carnyxes. Gaulish trumpets,' said Quintus, who had heard them before, at the Trebia.

'They're behind our men,' whispered Rutilus.

From another location on the right, where the hills ran down on to the hemi-lunate area of ground, a chorus of high, yipping cries added to the Gauls' cacophony. The ground trembled with the hammering of hooves. 'That's the Numidians!' Quintus let go of Rutilus' arm and ran straight for Corax, his arms pointing to the rear. 'AMBUSH, SIR! AMBUSH!'

Despite the overwhelming din, the centurion heard him. Quintus saw the realisation burst in Corax's eyes. In his gut, though, he knew it was too late. Far too late. Hannibal's trap had been well and truly sprung.

Only the gods would determine who survived what was to come.

A dark joy had suffused Hanno as the small group of enemy scouts emerged from the fog to be confronted by the sight of the Libyan spearmen, and to their rear, the Balearic slingers. They had been close enough for him to see their utter consternation. To be fair, the forty-odd Romans had not flinched from their duty. One had immediately sprinted forward to the attack; he had been followed by his comrades. Their javelin volleys had caused few casualties; the Libyans' large shields afforded great protection. Veterans all, the spearmen had not wavered much as the missiles fell. They had known, as Hanno had, that the slingers' replies would soon be raining down on the Romans. The Balearic men were famed throughout the Mediterranean, but hearing stories of their skill was very different to witnessing it with his own eyes. Their concentrated shooting was similar to watching a storm of hailstones hit a small patch of ground. Few of the enemy scouts had been killed, but more than a dozen had been injured, some seriously, before they had withdrawn behind the protection of the legionaries.

The real fighting had begun a short time later. Encouraged by the noise of the Gauls and Numidians launching their attacks on the Romans further back, the Libyans had been difficult to hold in position. Hanno and Mutt had had to break ranks and stalk up and down before the unit, bawling threats. He had seen other officers doing the same. The idea of charging down the slope to hit the disorganised enemy had been immensely appealing, but phalanxes were far less manoeuvrable than Roman maniples. If the legionaries had managed to break open one of their formations at the very start, things might have taken a different turn.

As it was, the fighting had been intense and brutal. Some of the centurions at the front of the column possessed real initiative. The ambush meant that not enough men would reach them to form the classic *triplex acies* formation. Knowing this, the Roman officers had led an immediate assault on the three phalanxes nearest them. Hanno and his spearmen had watched, fascinated, throats tight with tension, as the scouts and legionaries had advanced in good order. As before, there had been a shower of light spears from the scouts, who had then withdrawn through gaps in the infantry formations. Two volleys of javelins from close range, and the legionaries had charged uphill into the solid Libyan shield wall. It hadn't taken long for the Libyans to repulse the attack, but another bigger one had come soon after, when the enemy's numbers had been swelled by the arrival of more maniples. Hanno's phalanx had fought then, and in the three subsequent attempts to smash their line.

They had thrown each one back, causing heavy casualties among the Romans. After the most recent, the centurions had opted to give their battered men a breather, encouraged no doubt by the sight of fresh maniples arriving, with triarii among them. Hanno was grateful for the respite. Those of his men who had broken their spears or damaged their shields had had time to replace them from the fallen or their comrades to the rear. The injured had been helped out of harm's way and given what care was available. For some, it was a slug of wine and a friendly word. Others, too far gone, were comforted as they slipped into oblivion. A few, the screamers, were helped on their way by him or Mutt. He had done it before, at the Trebia. A prayer to the gods, a few reassuring words in the ear and a swift blade across the throat. Hanno stared at his right hand, which was crusted with blood. It trembled slightly. *Stop it.* Killing the wounded was a thankless task, but it had to be done. Few things were worse for morale than bleeding, filthy men roaring in pain and calling for their mothers.

When it was done, Hanno resumed his place in the front rank. A soldier handed him a skin of wine and he accepted it with a grateful nod. Despite his thirst, he limited himself to a couple of mouthfuls. His eyes roved the lakeshore and the open ground, which had cleared of fog, exposing the raging battle. Thanks to his position on the hill, he had a view of some of what was going on. Excitement gripped him. The Romans appeared to have failed to form their battle line anywhere. The most distant point, where the Gauls had sprung from ambush, was obscured by a dust cloud, but from within it, the carnyxes' weird booming continued unabated. Hanno had little doubt that the tribesmen were giving better than they got. Their memories of defeat by Rome and thirst for revenge were fresher than for anyone in the Carthaginian army. At the battle of Telamon, just eight years before, seventy thousand of their fellows had been massacred by a much smaller Roman force. When he talked with any of the Gauls, that was all they seemed to care about. Today they would be out to turn the waters of the lake red with blood.

Closer to hand, Hanno could see groups of Numidians wheeling and turning in graceful arcs as they attacked the disorganised mass of Romans by the shore. Fascinated, he watched a squadron of perhaps fifty riders come galloping in from an oblique angle towards a block of legionaries. Now and again, he could make out their high-pitched, yipping cries through the din of battle. Even at a distance, their skill was staggering. Hanno could not even imagine charging an enemy bareback on a horse that had no bit or bridle. Similar to a little cloud of midges, the Numidians closed at speed.

They infuriated the Romans not with bites, but a volley of well-aimed spears. Hanno grinned as a handful of tiny figures – enraged legionaries – broke ranks to try and close with the enemy. In a flash, they were enclosed by the horsemen. Dust swirled, obscuring what was going on. A few heartbeats later, the riders cantered away, leaving nothing but bodies sprawled in the dirt. Everywhere he looked, similar things were happening. The battle was going well for his side. It wasn't tempting fate too much to think that the outcome had already been decided.

If he and the rest of the Libyans could hold the enemy vanguard in place until the rest of their army hit the Romans from the rear, the result would not just be victory, but a total massacre. Another defeat for Rome, his people's bitterest enemy. An image of Quintus came unbidden, and Hanno found it impossible not to wish that whatever the outcome, his former friend survived. He fingered his scar. As for the rest of them, well, they could go to Hades, the Roman bastards. If Pera still lived, Hanno hoped that he would be among the dead by the day's end.

Despite what was happening elsewhere, their task would not be easy. The legionaries below had been rallied and re-formed into three large blocks. Good numbers of triarii had been positioned in the front ranks. Alongside them, Hanno could see the characteristic crests of centurions' helmets. Orders were bellowed and each of the three units formed a triangle, aiming its point up the hill at the Carthaginians. They've formed the 'saw', he thought, his belly clenching. It's an attempt to smash through. The attack would fall upon his phalanx and those of his father and brothers. For them, this was when the real battle would begin.

'They're really going to try and break us this time, lads,' he roared. 'We can't have that, can we?'

'NOOOOOO!' his spearmen screamed back at him.

'Hannibal wouldn't be too pleased if we failed him, would he?'

'NOOOOOO!'

'That's what I like to hear. Close order, all ranks!'

The men at the front shuffled together, making sure that their shields overlapped. The soldiers to their rear shoved in behind, forming a tight mass of equipment, weapons and sweaty flesh. There was very little room to move now, but that was the strength of the phalanx. When their spears were raised, the formations presented an armoured wall to the foe, a wall that was impregnable to most attacks. Whether it would prove effective against the saw, he would shortly find out. Thus far, the gods had seen fit to lend them their aid. As the Romans began to climb the slope, Hanno prayed that they continued to do so.

The centurions led their men steadily uphill. Hanno could hear them shouting orders similar to his own. 'Steady, boys!' 'Keep your position!' '*Pila* ready!' Ahead of the infantry, the velites trotted, their few remaining javelins ready to throw. Hanno's men hurled abuse as they drew near; the phalanx had suffered almost no casualties from the spears of the enemy light infantry. He even heard wagers being made about which of the velites would first get struck by a slingshot. They were brave men to attack yet again, he thought, as the whistling sound of hundreds of stones passed overhead. Even when the first volley landed, they didn't turn and run. There were fewer than a score of the velites left, but they advanced into the hail of sling bullets, coming nearer than they had ever done before. *What in Baal Hammon's name are they doing?* wondered Hanno in alarm. It was as if the velites wanted to die. More and more of them were falling, but that did not stop their assault. Closer and closer they came, shouting war cries and throwing their spears.

Their action was nothing but a diversion. By the time Hanno had realised this, the nearest saw point had changed direction. Now it was aimed directly at the junction between the right edge of his phalanx and the left edge of Bostar's. He was about to order his men to move to the right, thereby sealing the gap, when he glanced at one of the other saw points. It was moving straight for the junction between the leftmost part of his phalanx and the right of his father's. 'Damn them for devious bastards,' he swore. If his men moved either way, they risked making the situation worse. 'Mutt!'

From his left, 'Sir?'

'Do you see what they're at?'

'Yes, sir.'

'Pass the word back, quickly. The slingers are to concentrate their shooting on the saw points. I want the men at the front taken down at all costs. Clear?'

'Aye, sir.'

'You heard what I said. Send the word back. Now!' Hanno growled at the soldiers directly to his rear. 'Mutt!' he called again.

'Sir?'

'The men on our left edge must see what's about to happen, but pass a message to them anyway. They have to hold!' Hanno glanced at the spearman to his other side. 'Spread the word to the lads on the right. The Romans must not break through!'

Scowling, the spearman did as he was told.

Hanno eyed the Romans, who were now less than fifty paces away. He had warned his men. Done all he could do. He chafed to be in the middle of the action, but he couldn't break ranks without damaging the integrity of the shield wall, something the Romans might capitalise on. Agonising though it was, he had to stay put.

From then on, every moment dragged. Even when the legionaries began to run the last short distance, it was as if Hanno saw it one dramatic image at a time. The last of the velites pulling back, limping, bleeding, but still defiant. The hail of slingshot that darkened the sky overhead. The unbelievable sight of the bullets landing in and around the tip of the saw point. *Thunk. Thunk. Thunk. Thunk* went the stones as they rattled off shields and helmets, fractured skulls and caved in cheekbones. Holes began to appear in the Roman line here, there, everywhere, yet men shoved their way forward into the spaces, willingly stepping over their comrades' bodies and into the withering rain of stones. The high-pitched screaming of the injured did not stop the legionaries from coming. 'On! On! On!' shouted the centurions. 'Roma! Roma!'

Hold them! Hold them! Hanno wanted to scream, but his words would be lost in the maelstrom of sound. 'HANN-I-BAL!' he shouted, clashing his spear tip off his shield rim.

His men responded with alacrity. 'HANN-I-BAL! HANN-I-BAL!' All along the Carthaginian line, the chant was taken up. The noise of it was absolutely deafening.

The Roman advance checked for a moment and hope flared in Hanno's breast.

It didn't last. With great shouts of encouragement and not a few curses, the centurions got their men moving, even increased their speed. With an almighty crash, the saw point to his right collided with Hanno's soldiers. The immense force of it rippled through the men. A heartbeat later, a second blow reverberated through the phalanx as its left edge was struck. 'Steady, steady!' Hanno shouted. He craned his neck forward, desperate to see what was happening. *Let them hold, please let them hold!*

'HANN-I-BAL!' cried the men who weren't fighting for their lives.

Hanno longed to have a target for his spear; to be able to sink the sharp iron deep into Roman flesh and somehow halt their advance. Instead he had to remain where he was, mad with rage and frustration as the 'V' of the saw point punched deep into the gap between the phalanxes. He pictured the confusion of his men, whose unprotected sides were now exposed to the Romans. The spearmen of the other phalanx would be able to fight back – but only if they had wheeled around to face left, rather than forward. Hold them! he prayed. Screams, shouts and bawled orders in Latin and Carthaginian mixed with the clash of metal on metal. The Romans whom Hanno could see did not move for some moments, but then they shoved forward a few steps. Then a few more. His heart sank. Once the phalanxes had been split apart, there would be no way for them to regroup.

Confusion reigned as the impact of the blows from either side spread through the ranks. Around Hanno, soldiers shouted, pushed and fought to stay on their feet. Many were driven to their knees or had their arms dislocated as their shields were ripped away from them. The front rank buckled, and then broke up. Men moved forward, breaking formation. Hanno was among them. There was no enemy directly in front, and the phalanx had shattered anyway. His mind raced, fighting panic. What to do? Ordering his men to attack the side of the saw might slow down the Roman attack, but there was every chance that the legionaries could break ranks and wheel around to their rear. That would be even more disastrous.

A glance downhill, and his heart sank further.

More groups of legionaries were pounding up the slope, clearly intent on pushing through the holes in the Carthaginian line. They would arrive long before the broken phalanxes had had time to regroup. There was no chance that the Balearic slingers could do what the Libyans had failed to. These Romans were going to get away.

Hanno lifted his eyes to the bright blue sky. Why? Why are you doing this to us? he screamed silently.

There was no answer.

Quintus had never been more glad to have Corax as his commanding officer than during the latter part of the brutal fighting on the hill. Big Tenner had been slain and Urceus injured in the third or fourth attack – when exactly, Quintus couldn't remember. From that point on, his section of velites had struggled to maintain their morale in the face of the over-whelming barrage of stones from the Balearic slingers. Every man among them knew that they were dying for nothing; their javelins weren't capable of penetrating the Libyans' shields. He'd actually wondered if some of them were about to run – Macerio in particular had looked very unhappy. Run to where? Quintus had wondered cynically. The gods only knew what was going on to their rear, but it didn't sound good. The carnyxes' sound had a new, manic tempo, which implied that the Gauls at least were winning. It was as if Corax had known how close to the edge the eighteen uninjured velites were. He'd gathered them together, out of range of the deadly sling bullets. He had praised them to the skies for their efforts thus far, which had brought smiles to a few of the weary faces. Then he had revealed his and Pullo's plan to escape. 'We can't do it without you lads,' he'd growled. 'You will be the stinging horseflies that send the gugga whoresons mad. They'll be so busy watching you that by the time they see what we're up to, it will be too late.'

'By then, we'll all be dead,' Macerio had muttered.

Corax's eyes had been like two chips of ice as they bored into the blond-haired veles. 'You will call me "sir", soldier.'

Macerio's gaze had fallen away. 'Yes, sir.'

Despite his dressing down, Macerio's words had remained hanging in the air.

The centurion knew it too. He had glanced at each of them in turn. 'Macerio is a cheeky prick, but he's right. You might be killed if you go up there again. I can tell you one thing for nothing, though. It's down to the triarii now. If they can't help us to break past those bastards, we'll all die anyway. Twenty years of war have taught me one thing, and that's to recognise when a master tactician is on the field. There's one here today, and sadly, it's not Flaminius. The ambush was pure fucking genius. It won the battle at a stroke. We're just trying to get our arses out of here before it's too late.'

They had stared at him numbly, none prepared to answer. Which was worse: certain death by charging at the enemy again, or certain death in an hour or two by being overwhelmed by Numidians or Gauls? Remembering the heads he'd seen dangling from the harness on Gaulish horses at the Trebia, Quintus had known which he'd prefer. 'I'll go, sir.'

'Me too,' Rutilus had added.

When the injured Urceus had insisted on going as well, the others had been shamed into volunteering. Corax hadn't berated them for their lack of enthusiasm; he'd nodded and smiled. 'Good. Make this your best effort, boys, and I swear to you that we'll get out of here.'

Fire had flared in their eyes then – weaker than before, but present all the same.

Gods, but they'd needed every last part of that fire, thought Quintus wearily. The Balearic slingers had long since found their range. Their bullets hit their targets more often than not, or so it had seemed. The front man had gone down before they'd gone twenty steps, his forehead smashed in. Only fourteen velites had come within javelin range of the Libyans. There had been eleven of them by the time they'd launched one volley, and just eight when they'd heard the *crash* of the first saw point hitting the enemy line. At that stage, Quintus had seen no shame in taking to his heels. He had sprinted to the back of the nearest formation of legionaries and squirmed into the rearmost rank. Rutilus, Urceus and two others had joined him soon after, but that had been it. How many of the twenty velites attached to Pullo's century remained alive, he had no idea.

It had seemed the most natural thing in the world to grab the scutum of a fallen hastatus. Rutilus did the same. For close-quarters fighting, its size and weight made it far superior to their own light shields, which they discarded. There had been little initial need to use them, however, for which they were both relieved. The repeated attacks on the enemy had sapped Quintus' strength, and he had been grateful to pound along behind the mass of legionaries as they pushed through the broken phalanxes. On the other side, the officers had rallied the men for a moment, and then charged the slingers. The Balearic warriors had taken one look at the bloodied and battered Romans before running for their lives. Few soldiers could stand up to armoured infantry, least of all skirmishers.

After that, the advance had slowed, as the physical toll of their efforts struck home. Quintus had hated Corax then, because they had been allowed the briefest of rests before the centurion had ordered them to continue uphill. Yet it had been the right decision. Their formation had been the only one thus far to succeed in breaking through the enemy line. If they'd stayed, they would have died. So they had slogged through the hills for at least a mile, until there was no sign of the enemy. Corax had ordered a halt then, just as men began to drop with exhaustion. The site, a small exposed hilltop, gave them a bird's-eye view of what was happening by the lake. It wasn't pleasant viewing, but once he'd made Urceus as comfortable as possible, Quintus could not tear his eyes away from it. Rutilus stood beside him, also transfixed.

'Most of them have been driven on to the shore,' announced a voice by his elbow.

Quintus glanced around, surprised to see Corax. 'Yes, sir,' he said with a sigh. 'They're being hounded by Gauls and Numidians alike.'

'Poor bastards,' said Rutilus.

'Their lines were broken long ago; the units will all be mixed up with one another. Most of their officers are probably dead or injured. They're surrounded, confused, panicked.' Corax scowled. 'Fuck it all. There's nowhere for them to go but into the lake.'

Quintus peered down at the battlefield again. Was it his imagination, or was there a strange tinge to the shallows near the fighting? He blinked in horror. No, the water *was* turning red. His overwhelming thirst vanished for a moment. Even if he'd been able to drink his fill from the lake at that very instant, he wouldn't have. 'What will happen to them, sir?'

'To the ones down there? They're dead meat. Nothing we can do about it either. Going back down there would get every one of us killed, double quick.'

Quintus and Rutilus exchanged a sober but relieved look. If a man such as Corax said it was all right not to play the hero, then who were they to argue? Quintus prayed that his father was safe – that the cavalry hadn't had time to pass through the pinch point before the ambush began. And at least Calatinus wasn't present.

'What we've got to concentrate on is not letting the same thing happen to us. My guess is that the guggas will be after us as soon as they can get organised.'

'Ready to leave when you are, sir.' Rutilus stuck out his chin.

An approving look. Corax eyed Quintus' scutum. 'How do you like the feel of that?'

'It's heavy, sir, but I can manage it.' Another silent prayer, this time one of thanks that his arm had fully recovered.

'And you?' The centurion looked at Rutilus.

'Same, sir.'

'Picked them up from lads who'd gone down, eh?'

Quintus nodded.

'Did you have to use them?'

'No, sir. We were at the back,' Quintus replied, expecting Corax to tell them off twice over.

'It was good thinking to arm yourselves with them. Those little round things you velites carry aren't worth the steam off my piss when you've got to slug it out with other infantry. Hang on to them for the moment.'

Quintus and Rutilus grinned in surprise. 'Yes, sir!'

'You and your mates did well earlier too,' said Corax in a tone of gruff approval. 'It's no easy thing to keep running up a slope with those bastard slingers raining death down on you. Keep that type of behaviour up, and you'll both make hastatus sooner rather than later.'

'Thank you, sir!'

'Make the most of this break. We're leaving soon. We need to get as far from here as possible by sunset.'

'Will we make it, sir?' Quintus asked.

'If the gods wish it, yes.' With a tight nod, Corax moved off.

Quintus' pride had been stirred by the centurion's praise, but his final words had turned it to ash in his dry mouth. He could see the same emotion writ large on Rutilus' face. He lifted his gaze to the heavens, searching for inspiration. Surely the gods wouldn't let them survive the hell they'd just been through only to see them slain by other Carthaginian troops? After a moment, he looked down, angered by the absence of a sign.

'The damn gods never answer. Never,' whispered Rutilus. 'Even when you need them most.'

'I know.' Quintus felt bone-weary. 'We'll just have to soldier on.'

Chapter VIII

Capua

'Aurelia.'

She clamped the pillow tighter against her head. Go away, she thought miserably. Mother has only sent you because she knows I won't talk to her.

'I know you're in there,' said Gaius.

Despite the pillow, Aurelia could hear every word he said.

'Open the door. Please, Aurelia.'

With a sigh, she lifted her hand away from her head. 'What do you want?'

'To talk.'

'Mother sent you,' she accused.

'She did ask, yes, but I wanted to talk to you too. I'm worried about you.'

'I'm fine.'

'No, you're not.' He knocked again. 'I won't go away until you let me in.'

She lay on her bed for a moment longer, before she got up and lifted the latch. Perhaps he could lift her mood.

'You've been crying,' he said, entering.

She wiped her reddened eyes. 'What do you expect? Hannibal has defeated our armies yet again. Thousands of our soldiers have been killed. If Flaminius was killed, it stands to reason that Father and Quintus could have been slain too. And I'm – I'm supposed to be getting married?' Her tears began again in earnest.

'Come here.' He took her in his arms, which is what she'd wanted him to do since the night at her house. But not in these dreadful circumstances. Aurelia didn't fight him, though – she needed all the comfort she could get.

Three days before, a letter from her father granting his permission for her to wed Lucius had arrived. Aurelia had expected that. What she could never have envisaged was reading that Quintus had recently disappeared en route from Flaminius' camp to Capua. Fabricius' assertion that every effort was being made to find him had done little to ease her or her mother's distress. It was too easy to assume that Quintus was dead, killed in a fall from his horse, by bandits or by an enemy patrol. Two days later – the previous morning – their lives had been turned upside down a second time when the shocking details of the battle at Lake Trasimene had reached Capua. Atia's face had gone grey when she'd heard; she'd spent much of the time since on her knees at the temple to Mars. Gaius had been training on the Campanian plain, unaware, but the normally ebullient Martialis had been reduced to a brooding silence. Aurelia had been devastated. Deep in her gut, she knew that her father was among the thousands of dead. He had given his blessing to her betrothal, and then he had been killed in battle. It was as if the very gods were laughing at her.

'The news from Trasimene was dreadful,' Gaius began, which made her sob even harder, 'but from what I've heard, most of our casualties were taken by the legionaries. Flaminius didn't send any cavalry ahead of the vanguard, so they hadn't passed through the narrows by the lake. From the moment that the fighting began, the press was so great that they couldn't join in. When the tide turned, they were able to ride away without any difficulty.'

She pulled away, incredulous. 'When did you hear this?'

'Only this afternoon. I spoke with a second rider, who'd arrived from Rome. The Senate sent him with advice for the city's leaders.'

She needed him to say the words. 'So you're saying that Father might be alive?'

He kissed her on the forehead. 'He's probably planning your wedding as we speak.'

'The gods be thanked.' *How could I have doubted them?* She managed a wan smile. 'Have you told Mother?'

'Yes. She said that I should be the one to tell you.'

Then Aurelia thought of Quintus, and her misery resurged. 'What about my brother?' she whispered.

'Just because he disappeared doesn't mean he's dead.'

'Why would he not come home, though?'

'I don't know, Aurelia, but he must have had a good reason. Quintus is no coward, you know that. He wouldn't do something like this on a whim.'

'I know. But what could his reasons have been? A girl?'

'They'd been marching for weeks. He wouldn't have had the time to get to know any.'

They gazed at each other, thinking the same thing.

In an effort to distract herself from how close Gaius was, Aurelia voiced the thought first. 'Could it have been to do with Hanno?'

'I don't see how it could have been. How would he ever make contact with Quintus? They're in opposing armies.'

'And even if he did, what would make Quintus run away?' She shook her head in frustration. 'It doesn't make any sense.'

'But thinking about it logically has cheered you up a little.' He gave her an affectionate squeeze. 'Quintus will reappear sometime, never you fear.'

'Thank you, Gaius.' Aurelia smiled ruefully, feeling better than she had for many hours. Why can't Lucius be more like you? she thought, looking up at him in admiration. Her head moved a fraction towards his. He didn't move away, and her breath caught in her chest. She dropped her gaze until all she could see was his nose and lips. A fingersbreadth closer. Still he didn't pull back. His breath was warm on her face. Gods, but she had never wanted to kiss someone so much. Their lips brushed, sending a jolt of energy through every part of her.

'Who did you say was here?' Carrying in from the courtyard, Atia's voice was loud with displeasure.

The slave's reply was pitched too low to be discernible, but by then the magic had vanished. They moved apart awkwardly, not looking at each other.

'Show him in. He'll only wait outside if I don't see him,' Atia ordered.

Gaius frowned. 'Who could that be?'

'Phanes,' spat Aurelia.

'Who?'

'He's a moneylender.'

'What would someone like that want with your mother?'

Gaius would find out sooner or later, she thought. Besides, what did it matter if he knew? Quickly, she filled him in on what her mother had told her.

'Why didn't your father ask mine for help? Or your mother?'

'Could you, in a similar situation?' she challenged.

'It's not easy to ask a friend for a loan, I suppose,' he admitted.

'I want to hear what he has to say.'

'I don't suppose that Atia will be too appreciative of that idea.'

'What she doesn't know won't harm her,' replied Aurelia as she padded to the door and peered outside. Her mother was facing the tablinum door, waiting for her unwanted visitor. Aurelia watched for a few moments. Phanes eventually appeared, accompanied by Martialis' major domo. Atia greeted him in a cold voice; she made no move to welcome him further into the house, forcing the Greek to stand in the doorway. Aurelia wanted to stamp her foot. Her bedroom was too far away to be able to hear a word. She slipped out, ignoring Gaius' hiss of dismay.

The courtyard had been designed in typical fashion, with statues and plants – vines, olive, lemon and fig trees – throughout. Using these as cover, Aurelia darted forward until she was close enough to eavesdrop. A glance behind her revealed that Gaius had accompanied her. She crouched down behind a large statue of Jupiter Grabovius, an Oscan version of the god revered by Romans, one whom Martialis also worshipped. Gaius crowded in behind her; she relished the feel of his chest against her back.

'I sent a message informing you of the new arrangements. The first payment will be with you next month,' Atia muttered.

'When first we talked, you promised that I would have the money within a month. To try to change our agreement without consulting me about it is unacceptable,' said Phanes sharply.

A pause. 'It has been more difficult than I thought to raise the funds.'

'As well it might. We live in times of war. What assurance have I, however, that you will meet this new deadline? I would be entirely within my rights to bring proceedings against you at once.'

'Gods above, what more proof do you need than my word?'

Aurelia could hear the strain in her mother's voice. Anger coursed through her, but she too was helpless. Martialis, who might have come to their aid, had gone on his daily outing to the baths and wouldn't be back for hours.

'Do you want my jewellery, is that it?' Atia's bracelets clinked off one another as she began stripping them from her wrists.

'Keep your trinkets. They are of little consequence against a debt of this size,' retorted Phanes, his tone thick with contempt. 'I will agree to the later date on the condition that the interest rate is increased to six drachms in every hundred. Calculated weekly.'

'That's daylight robbery!' cried Atia.

Aurelia felt Gaius tense with fury. Her own blood was boiling now. She peeked around Jupiter's foot. Phanes had still not replied. He was just looking at her mother, a little smile playing across his thin lips. 'Call it what you will,' he said at last. 'That's my offer. You can take it or not, as you wish. If you refuse, I will instruct my lawyer to petition the courts this afternoon.'

A short silence.

'You leave me no choice,' said Atia, her shoulders sagging. 'I agree to your terms.'

The low-down prick, thought Aurelia. Her anger was so all-consuming that she didn't realise she'd leaned too far forward until it was too late. The next thing she knew, she was sprawling forward and landing flat on her face. She looked up to find her mother regarding her with horror. Phanes was smirking.

'Have you been eavesdropping?' demanded Atia.

'Clearly,' said Phanes. 'And not very well either.'

'I-I'm sorry, Mother,' stuttered Aurelia, getting to her feet.

'You will pay for this! Go to your room!'

Before Aurelia could move, Gaius had stepped out from behind Jupiter. 'My pardon, Atia, it is I you should blame.'

Atia's lips thinned, while Phanes' expression verged on delight. 'Explain yourself,' hissed Atia.

'We heard voices. Aurelia recognised that of the *moneylender*.' He loaded the word with disdain. 'She'd told me of your . . . difficulties . . . and wanted to listen. She was scared to, but I encouraged her. It was wrong, and I apologise.' He stuck out his chin a little.

'I see.' Atia's gaze shot from Gaius to Aurelia and back again. Both were careful not to look away. She scowled, momentarily defeated. 'Your father will hear of this shocking behaviour. I do not expect to be eavesdropped upon whilst I am dealing with my family's private business matters.'

Gaius bowed his head in acceptance. 'No, of course not.'

'Leave us, both of you,' ordered Atia.

Aurelia began to breathe again. She turned to go, but Phanes' voice coiled around her as a whip might. 'Touching how close the two of them are, is it not?' he asked.

'What is it to do with you?' Atia's tone was glacial.

'Nothing, nothing at all. I merely wonder if Melito is aware of their . . . *intimacy?*'

'You go too far, you piece of filth!' shouted Atia. A slave on the far side of the courtyard, who was watering the plants, looked up in surprise. She lowered her voice. 'How dare you impugn my daughter's honour?'

'I would never do such a thing,' protested Phanes, but his eyes told a different story.

'Get out, before I have the slaves throw you on to the street!' Atia pointed towards the atrium.

'I am at your command.' Phanes made as if to go, but then turned back. 'I wonder how well Melito will take it when he hears how his betrothed cavorted with a family friend before my very eyes. The first time I saw them together, I told myself I had to be imagining it, but there is no denying their fascination with each other now.' He bowed. 'I will expect the first payment by the date agreed.'

Atia let him go.

Aurelia was stunned that her mother could react in this way. When Phanes told him, Lucius would break off their betrothal, she was sure of it. Gaius' expression said the same thing. Whether Lucius believed Phanes or not, it wouldn't matter. Jealousy was a terrible beast, her mother said. Once its claws sank into someone's flesh, they never came out. The Greek was nearly at the door now. He hadn't looked back once.

'Phanes,' Atia called out.

He turned.

'What would it take for you not to speak with Melito?'

A smirk. 'And I thought you had nothing to hide?'

'I don't! How much?'

Now, a broad grin. 'The interest rate will be ten drachms in every hundred. It will also be calculated every week. Do you find that acceptable?'

'Yes,' said Atia. She sounded very tired.

Phanes gave her a mocking bow. To Aurelia's horror, he winked at her. And then he was gone.

Atia's gaze was baleful as it fell on Aurelia. 'Why could you not have stayed in your room? You have ruined us, child.'

Guilt-ridden, overwhelmed, Aurelia heard her mother's voice as if through a long tunnel. Her knees gave way, and she crumpled to the floor in a dead faint.

The Adriatic coast of Picenum

Hanno shifted from foot to foot, excited, but also hot and sweaty in his full uniform. He eyed the glittering blue sea, which lay tantalisingly close. Off-duty soldiers were splashing about in the shallows, shrieking like happy children. The contrast to the last body of water he'd seen – Lake Trasimene, during the aftermath of the battle – could not have been more stark. Hanno's men and the other Libyans had been too exhausted to pursue the Roman legionaries after they had broken through their lines. Leaving Mutt to take charge of the injured, he'd walked down to the lake, where the battle had been won.

The first shock had been the immeasurably vast area of water that had been stained red. When Hanno had managed to drag his eyes from that horror, they had been drawn to the shoreline, which had been crowded with thousands of bloody, mutilated corpses. Velites and hastati, principes and triarii, centurions and other officers had sprawled ignominiously together, their ranks irrelevant in death. Gauls and Numidians had been roaming the scene in their hundreds, killing any living Romans and looting the dead. Headless corpses lay everywhere, the grisly handiwork of warriors who wanted the ultimate trophy. That hadn't been the worst of it, though . . .

Plenty of legionaries had still been alive. With nowhere else to go, they had retreated into the water, where, if their armour hadn't pulled them under, they'd served as sport for the enemy cavalry. Hanno had seen men making wagers with each other over who could hit a particular legionary in the head with a spear from twenty paces, or who could slice off a head as he urged his horse past. Some legionaries had slain one another rather than end their lives so miserably; others had simply walked out into the deep water to drown. Despite his hatred of Romans, Hanno had been repulsed. What other choice had they had, however? he thought harshly. They couldn't have taken them all prisoner, and Rome had to learn its lesson for the humiliations that it had heaped upon Carthage in the past. If they didn't learn something from the loss of fifteen thousand legionaries and one of their consuls, and three days later, more than four thousand cavalry, they were damn fools. Deep in his belly, however, Hanno knew that their latest victory wouldn't be enough. More blood would have to be spilled, more defeats inflicted on their old enemy.

'It'd be good to have a swim now, eh?' whispered Sapho.

He jerked back to reality. 'Yes. Hopefully, we can have a dip after Hannibal's done with us.'

'That would be good. I've hardly seen you in days.'

'You know how it is. There's so much to do after each day's march. The injured need extra care. So too do the rest of the men. Thank the gods for the stores of oil Bostar found on that farm. Adding that to their food seems to have improved their health.' The whole army had been exhausted by the long march from Cisalpine Gaul, the swamps and the battle, during which their rations had not always been good. Men had been complaining of aches in their joints; of feeling fatigued all the time; others had had badly bleeding gums. Yet Hanno knew that he was dodging the issue – and his brother. For some reason, he couldn't shake his memory of the look on Sapho's face when he'd fallen into the pool. There was no one he could talk to about it without feeling like a traitor. Sapho was his flesh and blood.

'True enough. Let's change that this evening, though.'

'Good.' He caught Bostar's eye. 'Fancy a dip later?'

'Maybe,' answered Bostar with a smile. 'It depends what Hannibal has in mind for us.'

'Do you know, Father?' asked Hanno.

Malchus, who was standing a few steps away with Bostar, Maharbal – Hannibal's cavalry commander – and a group of other senior officers, looked around. 'Even if I do, I'm not telling you. Wait until your general gets here.'

The mention of Hannibal made Hanno wish he could vanish. He had felt awkward enough as it was around his general, but since the battle at the lake, he had avoided him if at all possible. He told himself that he was being stupid. Their victory had been resounding; moreover, the vast majority of the six thousand legionaries who had battered through their units had been surrounded the following day. In a magnanimous gesture, the non-Roman citizens among them had been set free with the message from Hannibal that he had no quarrel with their peoples. Apart from a few senior officers held as captives, the remainder had been slain. Why then did he feel such a failure? Even their father had told him that no one was to blame; Sapho and (particularly) Bostar had agreed, but Hanno fancied he could see the same unease in his brothers' faces that he felt inside. The Libyan spearmen – their spearmen – had been the only units in the entire army to fail at the task set them by Hannibal.

'Here he comes,' muttered Bostar.

Hanno's eyes followed everyone else's. He saw the block of scutarii first, some of Hannibal's black-cloaked crack troops. They went every-where with the general, unless he was on one of his regular undercover missions, when he would don a disguise and go among his soldiers to gauge their mood. The scutarii came to a halt; their ranks parted and Hannibal strode forward. Today he had left his armour and weapons behind. Few men would mistake him for anyone else however. His confident bearing, deep purple tunic and the similarly coloured strip of fabric that covered his right eye made him stand out a mile. Close up, it was evident that Hannibal had also suffered during the previous weeks. His brown complexion was pastier than normal. There were new lines on his broad face, and grey hairs that had not been there before in his short beard. Despite this, his one remaining eye still danced with energy. 'Thank you all for coming,' he said, acknowledging their salutes. 'It's more pleasant to meet here than my tent. Sun. Sea. Sand. What more could a man want?'

'Perhaps a few women, sir?' suggested Maharbal with a cheeky grin.

Hannibal's eyebrows rose.

'Chance would be a fine thing. What's wrong with your horses?' called a voice from the gaggle of soldiers who had been drawn by the presence of their general.

Maharbal pretended to scowl. 'They all have mange! Haven't you seen us bathing them in the old wine?'

'Is that where it's all gone? Meanwhile, our tongues are hanging out with thirst.'

'If you like, you can have the wine to drink after the horses have been washed in it,' declared Hannibal.

The anonymous soldier went silent, while his companions fell about the place, hooting with laughter.

'Lost your thirst?' shouted Hannibal.

No answer.

'Stand forth, soldier.'

There was a moment's pause.

'Do I have to say it twice?' Hannibal's voice was cold.

A short man with a slight limp pushed his way to the front of the group. He looked most unhappy.

'Don't you fancy the horses' wine?' asked Hannibal lightly.

'Yes, sir. No, sir. I don't know, sir.'

More laughter, but it was a little uneasy this time. For all of his charisma, their general was known for his toughness.

'I'm joking with you,' said Hannibal warmly. 'The horses have to be treated, you know that. They're vital to us.'

The men nodded.

'Now I need to talk to my officers. In private.'

'Yes, sir. Thank you, sir,' muttered the short soldier.

'You're good men.' Hannibal glanced at his scribe, who stood alongside, parchment and stylus in hand. 'See that these soldiers are issued with a small amphora of wine from my personal supply. Small, mind,' he added with a smile as the men began cheering.

'Me and the lads will follow you anywhere, sir. Even if it's to hell and back,' cried the short soldier.

His comrades shouted even more loudly. Hanno never failed to be impressed by his general's leadership. With a few words and a little wine, Hannibal had just turned his men's resentment into adoration once more. 'He makes it look so effortless,' he whispered to Sapho. Instantly, he realised that it was a mistake. Sapho's face twisted with bitterness.

'It's a skill, little brother. Some people have it, some people don't.'

'I wish I had it,' said Hanno, fully aware that Sapho led his men through fear, not devotion, whereas he tried to emulate his father and Bostar, who led by example.

'So do I,' said Sapho, giving him a suspicious glare.

'Gather round,' ordered Hannibal.

Hanno felt a momentary relief that Sapho would not be able to jibe at him, but it didn't last. There were no Gaulish chieftains or Numidian officers present, only Carthaginians. He felt sure that Hannibal was going to talk about the battle, and his and his family's failures. The brunt of the blame would fall on him, because his phalanx had been the first to crumble. How would he be punished? Demotion seemed most likely. He steeled himself for the inevitable.

'Our victory at Lake Trasimene was well earned,' said Hannibal, eyeing them all.

'Your plan made it easy, sir,' said Maharbal. 'It was a stroke of genius to set the trap as you did.'

Hannibal smiled. 'A general is only as good as his officers and men. Which is why we're here.'

Bostar glanced uneasily at Malchus, whose jaw was clenching and unclenching. Sapho flushed. Hanno studied the ground between his feet. Every officer within sight, apart from Maharbal, was doing something similar.

'Everything went according to plan at the lake, except for one thing. As you know, the Libyan phalanxes broke before a sustained assault by thousands of legionaries.'

Hanno looked up to find Hannibal staring at him. Him, when he could have looked at a score of others. His mouth went as dry as a bone. 'I'm sorry, sir. We should have held them,' he began.

'Peace. I do not know if even I could have stopped the Romans breaking through,' said Hannibal, surprising him entirely. 'The phalanx has been used for hundreds of years, by generals who led their armies to victories at places such as Marathon and Gaugamela. But those battles were fought against soldiers who also fought in phalanxes. The Roman legionary fights in an altogether different style. He's more mobile, and can instantly respond to a change in his orders. The men of a phalanx cannot do that. They've never been able to and they never will.'

Hanno could not believe his ears. Were they being absolved of blame? He didn't dare to look at Malchus or his brothers for confirmation. All his attention was locked on Hannibal. What use were the Libyan spearmen if they could not defeat the enemy?

'Your Libyans' – here Hannibal eyed them, one by one – 'are among the finest soldiers I have. Their failure at Lake Trasimene is not a thing to be ashamed of. You could have done no more than you did.'

'Thank you, sir,' said Malchus, an uncharacteristic gruffness to his voice. Hanno felt as if an immense weight had just been lifted from his shoulders. His failure had not been down to poor leadership. He threw a look at his brothers, who seemed no less relieved than he felt.

'Yet the same cannot happen again,' warned Hannibal. 'On a different day, what happened at Trasimene could have signalled disaster. The ship I sent to Carthage yesterday might have been carrying an altogether different message than the one it does.'

'How can we serve you better in future, then?' asked Malchus.

'A man must always use the tools to hand,' replied Hannibal with a sly grin.

He had them all now, thought Hanno, scanning the ring of intent faces. His own stomach twisted with excitement – and with admiration for his leader, who always seemed to have another trick up his sleeve.

'Many of your men took mail shirts from the dead after the battle, which was an intelligent move. As you know, I ordered that the shields and swords of the enemy fallen also be collected.' Hannibal smiled at the gasps of surprise. 'Yes, I would have you train your troops to use *pilum*, gladius and scutum. If we cannot beat Rome with the phalanx, then we shall beat it by turning our Libyans into legionaries. After we have done that, we shall march south. Like the Gauls, the inhabitants of the southern part of the peninsula have no love for Rome. Moreover, their lands are fertile and will keep us in supplies. When the legions come to meet us again, we shall be well fed, better prepared and have allies at our backs.'

Around Hanno, the other officers were chuckling and muttering excitedly to each other. He grinned and pretended to listen to what his father was saying to him and his brothers. South. How far south would they go? he wondered. To Capua? He thought of Aurelia. 'Come back safely,' she'd said to Quintus. Then she had looked at him and whispered, 'You too.' With a thumping heart, he had answered, 'I will. One day.' Hanno had thought his promise would not be feasible for many years, if ever. He had buried his confused feelings for Aurelia deep. Now, he felt them take flame again. Gods, but it would be good to see her! Despite the intrinsic dangers, the possibility had just been made real. And that felt very good indeed. So too did finding out what had happened to his friend Suni.

The Apennines, on the Via Latina, southeast of Rome

A burst of laughter made Quintus' head turn. Through the darkness, it was still possible to make out the maniple's tent lines, some distance away. Orange glows marked the fires built by each contubernium. In the dim light beyond, he could see the glitter of the mules' eyes from the animal pens. By counting carefully, Quintus was able to make out the canvas shape that was his tent. Like most troops in the camp, his comrades – his men, he corrected himself – were sitting around outside, talking and drinking whatever wine they had managed to buy or steal that day. He had no desire to share their company. Urceus would have been a logical choice to lead the ten-man section, but his injuries had meant he'd been left behind at Ocriculum, where the battered survivors of Trasimene had marched to meet their new commander, Quintus Fabius Maximus, recently appointed as dictator by a panicked Senate. Rutilus had been chosen by Corax to become the section leader, but it had been even more of a surprise when

Quintus had been elevated to lead a 'five'. When he had protested, Corax had told him to shut up, that he had earned it. Eyeing the new recruits, who had looked scared and as green as young saplings, Quintus had done as he was told. The strip of wolf skin on his helmet had barely been in place for a week.

Macerio had been incandescent with jealousy at being passed over; their enmity had grown even deeper as a result. Rutilus was now Quintus' only friend in the unit, and he had formed a relationship with Severus, one of the new arrivals. Quintus barely saw him any more, except when they were marching. His father was alive – a couple of sneaky trips to the cavalry tent lines had established that Fabricius had come through Trasimene unscathed – but Quintus couldn't exactly approach him for a friendly chat. With no one to turn to, he had grown to prefer solitude. In the midst of an army, that wasn't often possible. The hours after the day's duties ended were therefore his favourite time. As soon as the evening meal was over, it had become his norm to steal away to the camp's rampart for some peace and quiet. As long as he kept out of the way of the duty officer, the sentries let him be.

In the blackness, he could grieve and let his guilt gnaw at him afresh. Several weeks had passed since the defeat at Trasimene, but the magnitude of those events and what had happened since still hadn't quite become real. Against all the odds, Corax had led them through the surrounding ring of enemy troops after their breakout during the battle. More than five thousand of the legionaries who'd followed in their footsteps had not been so lucky; apart from a few senior officers, the citizens among them had been slain. Quintus felt a burning fury about their deaths, as he did about the thousands more who had died by the lake. He was sorry too that Big Tenner was gone – he'd been a decent man. But by far the greatest sorrow – and remorse – that he felt were reserved for Calatinus.

His friend was dead. He had to be. Shocking news had come a few days after the battle. Servilius' four thousand cavalry had been annihilated. Hearing of Flaminius' defeat, the other consul had sent his horse to reconnoitre the area. They had been ambushed by an enemy force and virtually wiped out. The very thought of it made Quintus feel sick with remorse. Despite his father's orders, he should have been with Calatinus and the rest. For his friend to survive the Trebia only to be killed a few months later seemed too cruel. It proved how capricious the gods could be.

Quintus Fabius Maximus seemed of the same mind. Upon his appointment as dictator, he had ordered the priests to consult the Sibylline Books. Like the election of a dictator – a magistrate with supreme power over the Republic – this was something that was only done in times of great crisis. Innumerable other religious rites had been performed; dedications and vows had been made in an attempt to win the gods' favour. None of it had made Hannibal disappear, thought Quintus bleakly. The bastard was still leading them a merry dance. The last he'd heard, the Carthaginian was laying waste to half of Apulia. That was bad enough, but what if Hannibal led his army over the Apennines and into Campania? Fabius had ordered that unfortified towns and farms near the enemy were to be abandoned, and all property and crops that could not be removed should be destroyed, but Quintus couldn't envisage his mother leaving their home, let alone torching their stores of grain and wine. She was too stubborn. He closed his eyes, imagining a band of Numidians – like the men they'd ambushed – riding up to their farm. That made him feel guilty about not obeying his father. Jupiter, never let that happen, he prayed with all his might. By way of reply, he heard nothing, felt nothing, saw nothing. As usual. He wanted to shriek his frustration, to curse the gods, but he did not dare. Had they abandoned Rome altogether? Much of the time, it felt like it. Quintus wondered about sending his mother a warning letter, something that his father might have done already. It would serve a second purpose, that of telling her and Aurelia that he was alive. But he wouldn't be able to tell them about joining the velites, so they would think he was even more of a coward. The idea increased his misery.

'I thought I'd find you here.'

Rutilus' soft voice made Quintus jump. 'Hades, you're as quiet as a cat.'

His friend grinned. 'I can be silent when I want to. Feel like some company?'

Quintus bridled. 'Won't Severus miss you?'

'He's asleep.'

'I should have known that would be the reason.'

Rutilus thumped him on the arm. 'You know what first love is like – when you can't get enough of the other person. When every spare moment has to be spent together.'

'I've heard it talked about.' Quintus could feel Rutilus' eyes on him, but he didn't turn his head to meet them. Instead he stared out beyond the rampart, angry at himself for resenting Rutilus – and Severus – and the fact that he'd never been in love.

'You've never been with a woman?'

'I didn't say that.' He thought longingly of Elira, the attractive slave at home whom he'd bedded on countless occasions. 'I haven't been in love with one, that's all.'

'One day, it will happen to you. Eros' arrow will strike, and your life will never be the same again.'

'Not while this damn war is on, it won't.'

'Meeting women in the army is hard,' Rutilus agreed. 'You could always seek out male company.'

Quintus spun. Rutilus' smile made him even angrier. 'Stop making fun of me!'

'My apologies. I was only trying to lift your mood.'

Quintus didn't answer. They stood in silence. Overhead, a shooting star shot across the heavens and winked out. It's gone, just like Calatinus, he thought sourly.

'What has you so downhearted?' asked Rutilus after a while. 'That's why I'm here.'

His anger eased. Rutilus *was* a good friend. 'You have to promise not to tell a soul.'

'Your secret is safe with me.'

'Not even Severus, Rutilus, I mean it.'

'What have you done, raped a Vestal Virgin?' Rutilus saw his mood and nodded. 'All right, I swear it, before Jupiter, Juno and Minerva.'

Mention of the sacred triad was reassuring. 'My name's not Crespo. It's Fabricius. Quintus Fabricius.'

Rutilus' surprise was palpable, even in the gloom. 'Why did you use a false identity to join the army? Did you commit a crime?'

'You could say that. I am – I was – a cavalryman, but my father ordered me home months ago. I hadn't been discharged from the cavalry, so by enlisting in the velites, I broke my original oath.'

Rutilus' eyes were wide. 'You're an equestrian?'

'Shhhh!'

Rutilus came closer. 'Why in all the gods' names would you want to become a veles?'

'It's complicated.' In low tones, Quintus sketched him a brief outline of his past.

'Well, that's a story and a half, and that's no mistake,' said Rutilus when he was done.

Quintus' guilt felt more raw than ever. 'Do you think the gods will punish me? Strictly speaking, I am still in the cavalry.'

'The gods have already had the last laugh, by letting you join the velites!'

'I'm serious.'

'So am I. If the gods can't see that you're a loyal servant of Rome, then there's no hope.'

'I should have been serving with Servilius' cavalry. I should have been there when they were ambushed. A good friend of mine is dead, Rutilus. I should be too.'

'But your father ordered you home, didn't he?'

'Yes,' muttered Quintus.

'So you wouldn't have been there anyway. Even if you had been with your friend, you wouldn't have deserted him if you'd known about the ambush. Would you?'

'Of course not! I would never have left Calatinus on his own.'

'Stop blaming yourself, then. For all you know, you might die in the next battle against the guggas. It's not your choice when or how it will happen.'

Quintus cast his gaze up to the stars. 'I hope you're right.'

'I am, so cheer up,' ordered Rutilus. He raised the wine skin he had been holding by his side, unseen. 'Let's drink a toast to your dead friend, Calatinus.'

The wine was probably stolen, but Quintus didn't care. He took the skin and carefully poured a libation on to the ground below, offering a prayer for Calatinus as he did so. 'To all the others who died at the lake as well.' He took a deep swallow, enjoying the warm sensation as the liquid swept down into his belly. Wordlessly, he handed it back to Rutilus. They passed it to and fro for some time, honouring the dead and savouring the silence.

'I've often thought your accent was better bred than you let on,' said Rutilus eventually, 'but I had no idea that you were nobility. And friends with a gugga!'

'Don't call him that,' retorted Quintus, remembering the time he had used the insult on Hanno.

'Come on! All Carthaginians are guggas, surely?'

'No! The term means "little rat", Rutilus, remember? I knew Hanno for almost a year. Whatever he is, he's not a gugga.' He related the story of Flaccus, and the ambush where he had died.

Rutilus chewed on that for a moment. 'If a man prefers men to women, he's often judged harshly by others. It's something I've always hated,' he mused. 'I suppose the same applies to the Carthaginians. Hanno showed real honour in letting you and your father go free. They're not all monsters, eh?'

Quintus felt a strange relief to hear another offer respect towards Hanno. 'No. They're enemies, but they are worthy men.'

'What will you do if you meet him again?'

'I hope that that never happens.'

'But if it does?'

'I'll kill him, as he'd kill me,' said Quintus savagely. Deep inside, he wasn't so sure that he could, but he wasn't going to admit that to anyone.

'Gods will it that you never have to,' muttered Rutilus. He nudged Quintus. 'Never thought I'd be serving with someone whose dead brother-in-law was so important!'

'He wasn't my brother-in-law. The marriage never took place.'

Rutilus hadn't even heard him. 'The brother of our new Master of the Horse related to a lowly veles, imagine that!'

Quintus' protest died in his throat. He'd heard Marcus Minucius Rufus mentioned often enough of recent days, but the name's relevance had passed him by. Caius Minucius Flaccus and he had been brothers. Now and for the next six months, Minucius was the second-highest-ranking man in the land, subordinate only to Fabius, the dictator. 'I hadn't thought of that.' Another pang of guilt as he imagined the social and political advancements that that powerful family might have brought to his own if Aurelia's wedding to Flaccus had taken place.

'You will have to introduce me to him,' said Rutilus, his tone mock-earnest.

Finally, Quintus laughed. 'I told you, Aurelia did not marry Flaccus, so I'm not related to Minucius!'

Rutilus snorted with amusement. 'Even if you were, I'd bet you wouldn't introduce your comrades to him. Can you see someone as important as Minucius chatting to the likes of us?'

'I can't even see him talking to me. Anyway, it will never happen. I just hope that Minucius has more sense than Flaccus. He was an arrogant fool. It was his stupid idea to go on that patrol in the first place.'

'Let's be grateful that Fabius is more senior then,' said Rutilus, looking a little worried.

'They say he was slow-witted when he was a boy, don't they? Now, he's known for being cautious,' said Quintus, repeating the gossip he'd heard. 'But he's twice been consul and once dictator. He should be able to keep Minucius in line.'

'Course he will!' Rutilus raised the skin high again. 'To our new dictator. May he prove to be an able leader and a skilful general, who brings us victory over Hannibal!'

'Before too long,' added Quintus, thinking again of his mother and Aurelia.

'Corax says the word is that he's not going to rush into anything. To do so with so many new recruits and insufficient cavalry would be madness. The plan is to harry the Carthaginian foraging parties. Kicking the enemy in the stomach is nearly as effective as killing him in battle, Corax says, and far less dangerous. I'm not going to argue with that!'

Quintus had heard the talk. Although it was hard to swallow, it was difficult to disagree with Fabius' and Corax's logic. He could remember his father talking about the Hellenistic principles of generalship, which men such as Alexander had followed. If a general could not realistically be certain of winning a battle, then it was best that he avoid confrontation until such time as his forces had increased sufficiently in strength. It could easily take Fabius and Minucius the full period of their office to do that. 'Gods, let Hannibal stay east of the Apennines,' he muttered. He felt

Rutilus' eyes on him. 'I'm from near Capua. My mother and sister are still living on the family farm.'

'If Hannibal does cross the mountains, your mother will abandon the property for the safety of Capua. She'll be protected there.'

'You don't know my mother. She's as stubborn as a mule with a bad temper.'

'Your father might have sent her a letter.'

'I hope so.'

'Why don't you write one as well?' Rutilus sensed his uncertainty. 'Tell her that you're fighting with the socii or something of the kind. Even if your father hears that from her, he won't have time to look for you in every section of the army.'

That could work, thought Quintus. 'Writing her a letter doesn't mean she'll pay any heed to it.'

'No, but it might. And it will ease your worries a little, so do it.'

'Thank you, Rutilus,' said Quintus gratefully. His friend was right: he should make the best of the situation rather than revel in misery. All the same, a knot of worry for his mother and Aurelia remained in his guts.

Chapter IX

Near Capua

As the walls of Capua receded into the distance, Aurelia wondered for the twentieth time if she was being wise. I'll do what I want, she thought fiercely. My mother can go to Hades! One of Martialis' two slaves threw her another questioning look, but her immediate scowl made his gaze drop. Her mixture of cajolery and threats had got the pair beyond the gate; she hoped that it would take them as far as the family farm. Aurelia wished again that Gaius were around; he would have accompanied her. No, it was better that he wasn't here, she decided. She was to marry Lucius now. There was no point putting any more temptation in her way. Besides, Gaius was long gone, sent with his unit to bolster Fabius' forces. Lucius might have come if she'd asked, but she didn't want his company. He was part of the reason that she was going.

If only her mother hadn't been so assiduous in winning over Lucius' father, she thought. But Atia had been like a dog with a bone. She and Lucius were to wed within the next few months. Aurelia had grown somewhat resigned to that fact – her father had given his blessing to the union, so there wasn't much she could do about it – but she was determined to savour her last months of relative freedom. As a married woman she would live at her husband's command. This might be her last chance of visiting the place where she'd grown up, of being alone with her memories of Quintus and – if she admitted it – Hanno. She had been spurred into action by something she'd overheard literally the night before. Since her disastrous attempt to listen in on her mother and Phanes, Aurelia had become a master at eavesdropping. Atia and Martialis tended to talk in the evenings, after she was supposed to be in bed. The previous night, Aurelia had been shocked beyond belief by what she had heard. Martialis' loan had only placated Phanes for two months, her mother had lamented. Martialis had expressed his horror and repeatedly apologised to Atia. The regret had been thick in his voice. 'I don't have any more money to lend you.'

Aurelia had bitten her lip at her mother's next words. Unless Fabricius was able to help, which seemed unlikely given the fact that he was in the field, shadowing Hannibal's army, the farm would either have to be sold or signed over to Phanes. Given the uncertainty gripping the area, the latter seemed more likely. Aurelia stuck out her jaw, trying hard not to cry at the memory. Because of her, Phanes would soon own her father's farm. She'd had dark thoughts about having the moneylender killed, but didn't know how to organise such a thing – even if she had the money to pay for it, which she didn't. A gusty sigh escaped her. Her family would soon be beggared and there was nothing she could do about it.

'Where are we going, mistress?' asked the older of the two slaves, a stoop-shouldered man with foul breath. His companion, a swarthy Iberian with a moustache, also turned.

'To my family's farm,' said Aurelia curtly. 'It's not far.'

'And the master knows that we're going there?'

'Of course he does,' Aurelia lied. 'As if it mattered! He ordered you to accompany me everywhere for my safety, did he not?'

He looked unhappy. 'That was within Capua, mistress.'

'I do not recall Martialis saying that we were to remain inside the walls,' she snapped, knowing full well that that *had* been what he meant. It was for that reason that she'd had the pair, and a mule for her to ride, at the east gate as soon as it opened, a time when Martialis would still have been abed. He was probably only stirring now, while they were more than a mile from the city. 'Do you?'

'N-no, mistress,' he replied sullenly.

'Less of your insolence then, and more attention to the road. Because of the war, there are more *latrones* about than ever. Keep your eyes peeled for bandits and your cudgels ready.'

The slave exchanged a look with his companion before buttoning his lip.

Good, thought Aurelia, urging her mule on with her heels. That should keep them quiet for a few miles. After that, I'll tell them that it's only another short distance. By the time they find the courage to question me again, we'll practically be there. She tried not to think about the wooded area through which they'd have to pass some five miles hence. It was a favourite spot for travellers to be robbed. She rallied her courage. Nothing had ever happened to her or her family when travelling to or from Capua. Even if there were latrones in the woods, two sturdy slaves with clubs would be sufficient deterrent.

If Quintus were here, I'd feel safer, she thought with regret. There was no chance of that – she had no idea where he was. However, her brother was alive. Learning that had been the only thing to leaven Aurelia's recent misery. The arrival of his letter – a month or so after Trasimene – had been a complete shock to her as well as her mother. Aurelia had wept for joy as Atia had read it aloud. She didn't care that Quintus had argued with Fabricius, or that he had joined the socii contingents as a foot soldier rather than return home. All that mattered was that he was not dead. 'Do not tell Father,' Quintus had written. 'He will not find me, no matter how hard he tries.' Despite her obvious disapproval of his actions, Atia had also been unable to hide her joy at the news. She had even seemed to take in Quintus' warnings about leaving the farm, even though it hadn't been necessary. The urgency of her quest to marry Aurelia to Lucius had ensured that mother and daughter had not returned home since the confrontation with Phanes. The farm was too far from Capua for any wooing, or courting of Lucius' father's favour, to take place, so in Martialis' house they had remained. 'Agesandros is more than capable of running the place,' Atia had said dismissively when Aurelia asked.

She wasn't looking forward to meeting the overseer again, especially because she was on her own. Since Agesandros had killed Suniaton, she had never allowed herself to be alone with him. He scared her too much. He had done it ostensibly to protect the family, but it was really because he hated Carthaginians. Suni had done nothing! Aurelia thought sadly. He was a gentle soul who didn't even want to become involved in the war. If I'd kept my mouth shut, he might still be alive. Remembering her slip of the tongue made her feel considerably worse. The journey began to drag even more. The temperature rose as the sun climbed into the azure sky. Aurelia's dress clung to her back; sweat prickled her scalp, making her regret that she had not brought a hat. Her mule was as stubborn a beast as she'd met, refusing to walk faster than a steady plod. The slaves made one more attempt to question her authority before giving up, but they paid her back with resentful expressions and a shuffling pace that scarcely kept up with the mule. What Aurelia liked least, however, was the empty countryside.

The area was scattered with the farms and estates of her family's neighbours. Normally, the fields were full of slaves at work. Today, there was barely a soul to be seen. Most of the wheat and barley had been harvested, but areas of blackened ground showed that a decent proportion of it had been burned instead. Some people were taking Fabius' advice at face value, thought Aurelia scornfully, even though no Carthaginian soldiers had been seen within miles of Capua. Her contempt was somewhat of a pretence. By all accounts, it was only good fortune that had prevented enemy foragers from raiding this far to the north and west. She was glad to be living in Capua with its strong stone walls. Whatever Hannibal's skill in the field, Lucius was fond of saying, he had no siege engines. Without those, he had no chance of taking a town the size of Capua. 'Unless he had help from the inside,' Martialis had once said quietly, shocking Aurelia. She was used to thinking of the old man and Gaius as Roman, but of course they were Oscans first. The Oscan people had lived in the area for hundreds of years, and had only acceded to Rome's rule a few generations before.

'What are you saying?' she had asked.

'It was just an old man's little joke,' Martialis had murmured, smiling.

Well, it would never come to that, Aurelia decided, dismissing the idea as ridiculous.

Nonetheless, unsettling thoughts of Carthaginian soldiers filled her mind for the rest of the journey. When the familiar outline of the family's villa and farm buildings appeared in the distance, relief filled her. To her surprise, one of their herdsmen was in position by the front gate, several of his large dogs by his feet and a bow sitting across his knees. It turned out that Agesandros had set armed guards all around the farm's perimeter, their mission to alert everyone else in the event of any enemy troops being seen.

One whistle blast meant a small group and a stand to arms; two blasts signified larger enemy numbers, necessitating a wholesale evacuation to the woods. Aurelia did not let Agesandros see how impressed she was. Instead she nodded as if she'd have done the same thing.

'And your mother knows that you are here?' he asked for the second time.

'She does.' It wasn't a complete lie. By now, Atia would have found her note. She prayed that her mother hadn't made the discovery until it was too late to set out in pursuit.

'It is a little out of the ordinary for her to allow you to travel here with only two slaves as protection. These are dangerous times to be abroad, even for the legions.'

'It's not for me to question my mother's decisions.' *Nor for you to do so either* was the implication.

Agesandros took the hint. 'How long will you be staying?'

Aurelia bridled, but it wasn't an unreasonable question. 'Only one night.' Any longer than that and her mother would probably arrive. She wanted to avoid the indignity of being dragged back to Capua. As it was, Aurelia wouldn't be surprised if she met Atia on the road the following morning. Even that would be better than Agesandros seeing her chastised. She glanced at him, seeing his curiosity. Let him wonder why I'm here, she thought fiercely. It's none of his damn business. He'll find out about my wedding soon enough – from Martialis' slaves, most likely.

'While you are here, I would ask that you stay close to the house.'

'Why?' demanded Aurelia, her temper flaring. It had been her intention to walk to the clearing where Quintus had taught her to use a sword.

'Need I spell it out? An estate ten miles south of here was pillaged and burned a week ago. Only the arrival of a strong Roman patrol stopped the guggas from raiding more properties in the area. The patrol has moved on since, which means the threat of attack is as severe as it ever was. If you were to be found alone in the woods, the gods only know what kind of fate you would have.'

'Who are you to tell me what to do? I shall do what I please!'

To her surprise, he did not get angry. 'You know my family's story,' he said, his dark eyes full of pain. 'I will not have the same happen to you. Aside from what your parents would do to me, I could not bear it myself.'

Aurelia found herself feeling a little sorry for Agesandros. During the previous war against Carthage, his wife had been raped and then murdered, together with his young children, by Carthaginian soldiers. That was still no reason to kill Suni in cold blood! she thought angrily. Yet the stiff cut of his chin told her that he was capable of holding her in the house against her will. A tickle of fear licked the base of her spine. Perhaps he was right to be so cautious. 'Very well. I will stay close to the house.'

He gave her a penetrating look; then he nodded in satisfaction.

To Hanno's right, the Apennines ran from north to south in an unbroken line. In the bright sunshine, their slopes were a mottled mixture of brown, green and grey. He had grown to love their look, despite the fact that it wasn't Carthage, wasn't home. The countryside here was a stark contrast to his homeland, which had few peaks. There were mountains far to the south and west of Carthage, but he had never set eyes on them. As far as he'd seen, it was impossible to stand anywhere in Italy and not see some. To his left, an occasional peak pushed up towards the sky. It had been the same since they'd come down from the Apennines. The largest he'd seen was Vesuvius, which had risen an impressive distance from the surrounding plain. The mountains here were smaller, and the terrain was mostly open farmland. It ran down towards the sea, a day's ride to the west. He had never visited here in his life, but it felt familiar. For good reason. Fabricius' farm lay no more than ten miles away. His life had turned full circle, Hanno reflected. The last time he'd been in the area, he had been a runaway, fleeing for his life. Now he was part of an invading army, with nearly two hundred spearmen under his command.

Part of Hanno burned to march to the farm: to see if Aurelia was there; to kill Agesandros; to show them all that he was no slave. But the rest of him was glad that Zamar, the Numidian cavalry officer with whom he was patrolling, had deemed it too risky. Zamar's scouts had reported the presence of enemy forces to the north. The Romans had a new policy of shadowing their foraging parties and ambushing them, and Hanno didn't want to suffer the grisly fate of a number of other patrols. Hannibal's orders were that, if a situation appeared risky, discretion was the better part of valour. Hanno and the Numidian had conferred with Mutt earlier in the day, and accordingly taken the decision to turn back towards their army in the morning. There was every reason to do so. Their mission had been an unqualified success. All contact with Roman troops had been avoided; their mules were laden down with sacks of grain and amphorae of wine and oil; close to five hundred sheep and five score cattle were penned up in the temporary enclosures beside their camp. His men had slain plenty of Roman farmers, but not too many women and children; as far as he knew, there had been little rape. Achieving that had been no mean feat.

Hanno scowled. By rights, he should be a happy man. But he wasn't. The sensible thing would be to leave this place and never look back. If I do that, he thought, I will never have the opportunity to see Aurelia again. To ask her about Suni. All day, that awareness had been rattling around in his head like a stone in a gourd. He took another look to the north. She might not even be there; the majority of the farms in the area had been abandoned. It didn't matter, he decided. If he didn't seize this chance, he would always regret it. If he borrowed a horse from Zamar, he could make good time. Thanks to the war, the roads around were empty of traffic. When it got dark, the night sky would still be bright enough to follow the road to Capua. The turn-off to Fabricius' farm was easy to find; so too was the property itself. If things went well, he would be back before dawn. No one apart from the Numidian and Mutt would be any the wiser. A fierce grin split Hanno's face at the thought. He hadn't been this excited since . . . since he couldn't remember when.

The gods were smiling on Hanno that afternoon, and he made good time from his camp. The only travellers he encountered were a priest riding a mule, and his acolyte, who trudged along in the dust behind his master. Both stared suspiciously at Hanno, but after his hearty greeting, the priest let out a mumbled reply. Neither party stopped to talk. It was good that he'd donned some nondescript clothes and taken one of Zamar's more scruffy mounts, Hanno decided. To the unsuspecting eye, he was no Carthaginian. True, he was abroad when few others were, but what would an enemy soldier be doing on his own?

There was yet light in the sky as he came up the road that led to Fabricius' farm. The entrance lay about half a mile further on. It would have given Hanno considerable satisfaction to ride up the avenue to the house, but there was no point being foolish. If Agesandros was about, and he had no reason to think otherwise, his first greeting would be a hurled spear. Best to travel the last distance on foot. A patch of buckthorn and juniper that formed the junction between two properties was the perfect spot to secrete and hobble his horse. Then, hand on sword hilt, he crept through the fields towards the farm, joining the track that led to the villa halfway along its length.

The oddness of the situation sank in as Hanno saw buildings outlined at the end of the line of cypresses. His heart thumped in his chest with excitement, but he forced himself to walk at a snail's pace. If the place hadn't been abandoned, Agesandros might have set guards. Or dogs! Too late, Hanno thought of the huge hunting hounds that Fabricius used, great slavering things the size of a boar, with temperaments to match. They were usually let out at night. Sweat slicked down his back. Why hadn't he thought of the damn dogs before? They'd tear him to pieces.

His head twisted to and fro, gauging the distance to the property's boundary. It was a few hundred paces at most. There hadn't been a sound from the villa. If he retraced his route, there was every chance that he'd get away. He turned, but made no more than a dozen steps before his feet dragged to a halt. *What kind of coward are you? To get this close and not even try to see if Aurelia is there?* Hanno swallowed down the bile that had risen to the back of his throat. The dogs tended to run in ones and twos. If they attacked, he would be able to kill one and then the other. With any luck. Slipping his blade from the scabbard, he began creeping towards the group of buildings once more.

He reached the last pair of cypresses without difficulty. Their branches moved in the light air, filling the air with a gentle creaking. A memory slowed him. The last time he'd stood here in darkness, it had been after Quintus had set him free. That debt had been repaid, he thought harshly. He's an enemy now. Then why are you trying to see his sister? came the instant response. To that, Hanno had no answer. All he knew was that the compulsion burning him up was impossible to ignore.

A movement in the shadows between the farm buildings and the villa; the excited whining of dogs. The villa had not been abandoned, far from it. He shrank against the trunk of the nearest cypress.

'Ho, Zeus! Ho, Mars! You're eager to run tonight, aren't you?' A chuckle. 'You two are always the same. Bear and Fang are always the ones to hang back a little. Still hoping for another scrap of food, aren't you? Sorry to disappoint you, boys, but it's the same routine as usual. No food for you until the morning. Hunger makes your noses keener, or I'm no judge.'

I know that voice! thought Hanno in amazement and rage. That's Agesandros, the bastard.

'Good boys, good boys. Just let me unclip your leads, and you can run free.'

Shit! Hanno cursed his stupidity for pushing his luck this far. The hounds were so close that they'd catch his scent within a few moments. He began tiptoeing backwards. The further away he got before they were released, the better. If he had any favour remaining with the gods, the dogs might run off in a different direction. Then one of the hounds barked, and fear seized him. That notion was downright foolish. He seized the lowest branch of a cypress, knowing it would do little good. Without a doubt, the dogs would tree him. When Agesandros realised, he would force him down at the point of a spear. A howl; and then another one. All hope left him as he swung himself up on to the first limb. Tanit, do not desert me now, he prayed. Don't let me die here, like this. It was an instinctive response, a rhetorical question. Divinities did not intervene like that, at least not in his experience.

'Agesandros?'

Hanno froze. *No. It can't be.*

'What are you still doing outside, Aurelia? It's late.'

Aurelia *was* here? Hanno nearly fell out of the tree with surprise.

'I want to sit outside for a while,' she said.

'I was just about to set the dogs loose.'

'That can wait, can't it?'

'I'd be happier if they were running about now—'

'If I'm here, all they'll do is hang around, looking for treats. Please, Agesandros. I won't be long.'

A short pause. 'Very well. I'll return them to their pen. Find me in my room when you're coming in.'

'Thank you.'

Hanno was so astonished that he almost expected to see Tanit herself urging the Sicilian away. He watched with delight as Agesandros' shape returned to the yard. It seemed beyond belief, beyond all possible coincidence that she should be here on the very night he had crept in. Yet, as he breathed, Aurelia stood not twenty paces away. He longed to call out, but what could he say? She would have no idea that it was he. Her most likely response would be to scream for Agesandros and the dogs. He peered at her again, and was relieved to see that she was walking closer. Where was she going? Hanno dropped lightly to the earth, placed his sword on the ground and waited. As she drew alongside, he darted out behind her. Grabbing her waist with one hand and her mouth with the other, he whispered into her ear, 'Don't make a sound. It's me, Hanno!'

She writhed beneath his grasp, but he held on to her for dear life. 'I swear it to you. It is I, Hanno. I have come to see you.' She wriggled again, but Hanno detected less resistance than before. He was suddenly aware of the warmth of her back and buttocks against his flesh, and of the feel of her breasts heaving against his hand. Was that perfume she was wearing? A wave of desire rushed over him; it was followed by huge embarrassment. Without thinking, he released her and stood back, every nerve jangling.

She spun, mouth open in shock. 'H-Hanno?'

He took a step towards her; then he stopped. 'Yes.' Words failed him.

'What? Where? How did you get here?' The words tumbled from her mouth.

'I rode.' It sounded so stupid, a giggle left his lips. 'From my camp. It's only ten miles away.'

'Oh gods. Are you going to raid the farm?' Her voice was full of terror.

'No, no, of course not. Aurelia, I would never—'

'I'm sorry,' she interjected. 'Some of the stories I've heard have been terrible.'

'I know. I'm sorry too.' He wanted to add that her people had done the same and worse to his in the previous war, but there was no point.

'These things happen in war,' she said sadly. 'But I don't want to talk about that. I can't believe you're here again, when I am too. I've been living in Capua recently. But seeing you, it's so unexpected – but wonderful! I have prayed for you.'

'And I for you.' He still couldn't believe his eyes.

They smiled at each other, suddenly shy because they had both changed so much in the time since they'd last seen each other. She's become an adult, thought Hanno. She's beautiful. Little did he know, but Aurelia was thinking similar things of him.

'Is Quintus alive? Have you heard from him?'

'He's fine. We heard about how you captured him at the Trebia and set him and Father free.' Her voice caught a little. 'That was good of you.'

'It was the least I could do, after what he'd done for me. And your father?'

'He is also well, thank the gods. May the gods keep them both safe.'

'Yes indeed.' He asked for the same for his own family. 'I wouldn't have slain Flaccus,' Hanno felt impelled to say, 'but my brothers overrode my decision. Our orders were to kill all enemy troops who fell into our hands.' He remembered the resentment he'd felt at the discovery that Flaccus was to marry Aurelia.

'I don't blame you. I was relieved,' she whispered. 'I scarcely knew him. We had only met once.'

'You deserve a better man than Flaccus,' he said gruffly. 'A man like Suni, maybe. Was it long before he left the shepherd's hut?' She didn't answer at once. Hanno cursed to himself. 'If I offended you, I'm sorry,' he said awkwardly. 'It's just that Suni is a gentle soul. He would make a good husband to you.' Still she didn't speak. He began to feel uneasy. 'Aurelia?'

'I-I don't know how to say this. How to tell you.'

'What?'

'Suni is . . .'

'Not . . . dead? No. No.' He staggered back a step.

'I'm so sorry, Hanno.'

'But his leg was healing!' he cried, raising his voice.

'Shhhh. Someone will hear.'

Hanno took a deep breath. 'He would have had a bad limp, but that's all,' he whispered. 'What in Melqart's name happened?'

In a trembling voice, she told him.

'Agesandros,' he muttered in disbelief. 'That whoreson killed Suni?'

'It's my fault. I should never have brought him into the house.'

'You're not to blame. If you hadn't taken him in, he would have died at the hut.'

'Didn't you hear what I said? If I hadn't spoken his name, Agesandros might never have realised. Suni might still be alive.' She began to weep.

Before he knew it, he had stepped forward to take her in his arms. 'It was a slip of the tongue, nothing more. Anyone could make the same mistake. Besides, you know what Agesandros is like. He would have discovered Suni's real identity sooner or later.'

'I was so terrified the whole time.' She pressed herself into his chest. 'It was even worse when Suni was gone. Agesandros had no reason to harm me, but that's not how it felt.'

'I ought to go in there and kill him right now,' Hanno said from between gritted teeth.

'No, please don't. He has armed all the male slaves. At least three are on watch in the yard. I couldn't bear it if you were killed, when you've only just returned from the dead.'

Hanno doubted whether a few agricultural slaves could stop him, but Aurelia's heartfelt request held him where he was. 'The filthy dog will have to pay for what he did one day,' he swore.

'The gods will see to that.'

Or I will, thought Hanno grimly. There was no way that he could let the murder of his best friend go unanswered. Already his mind was racing at the thought of raiding the farm once Aurelia was gone. He discarded the notion at once. He knew and liked many of the slaves here. Unless a good number of them were to die, he would have to keep his soldiers away.

'It is so good to see you.'

Hanno's attention shot back to Aurelia. She was looking up at him, her face so close that he could see every detail. The strands of black hair on her cheek. Her eyes, fixed on his. Her half-open lips. The pulse at the base of her throat. It was mesmerising. He felt a great urge to kiss her.

'Since you and Quintus left, and Suni was killed, I have been so lonely. Mother and I fight all the time. There's been no one for me to talk to. Gaius was here for a while, but he's gone now too.'

'Quintus' friend? The one who helped Suni to escape?'

'Yes. He serves with the socii cavalry.' Aurelia felt guilty at the mere thought of Gaius. Had she fantasised about him because she'd thought never to see Hanno again? She wasn't sure about that. What she *was* certain of was how good it felt to have Hanno so close to her. Bitterness took Aurelia. What did it matter? There was a war on. Hanno could not stay, and she was to marry Lucius.

'Gaius is a good man. The gods will protect him as well.' That didn't seem to make her any happier. Hanno bent his neck the tiniest fraction, towards her. She didn't pull away. 'Do you know why I came back?'

'No. Why?' Her breath came fast and shallow.

'Because you asked me to. Do you remember?'

'Of course. I cried myself to sleep that night.'

Hanno could take it no more. He crushed his lips to hers, felt them melt beneath the pressure. His tongue darted out and was met by hers. They kissed long and hard, their hands roaming all over each other's bodies. Aurelia moulded herself against him; he could feel her breasts against his chest, her groin against his stiffness. Hanno cupped her buttocks with both hands, felt her gasp with desire. It was all he could do not to tear off her dress and take her right there. Yet that was not how he wanted it to be. It was also far too dangerous to linger. 'Come away with me,' he urged. 'We could be back at my camp before dawn.'

'You're not serious!' She stared into his eyes. 'You are.'

'I'd never say such a thing if I didn't mean it.' Even as the words left his mouth, Hanno knew them for utter madness. Women followed Hannibal's army, it was true, but they were whores every one. Aurelia would never survive the cutthroat nature of that existence. Soldiers and, in particular, officers were not allowed to have women live and travel with them. Hannibal himself had set the example by leaving his own wife to lead the campaign. He was guiltily grateful, therefore, when she whispered, 'I cannot leave with you.'

'Why not?'

'A woman has no place in an army that is at war. Especially when that woman is one of the enemy.'

'No one would lay a hand on you. I'd kill them!'

'You know it would never work, Hanno.' She smiled at his strangled protest. 'Even if you could take me, I would not go.'

He recoiled, hurt. 'Why not?'

She guided his fingers to her left hand in silence. There was a ring on her third finger.

He recoiled from the warm metal. 'You're betrothed to another? Already?'

'Yes. Mother organised it. His name is Lucius Vibius Melito. He's a good man.'

'Do you love him?' he spat.

'No!' She caressed his cheek. 'It's you I truly care about.'

'Then why can't you come with me?' Who knew if they two could be happy together, but Hanno couldn't bear the idea of her living her life with a man she didn't even love.

She was grateful that the darkness concealed the flush that coloured her cheeks. 'If I don't wed Melito, my father will be ruined.' In a low voice, she explained. 'So you see, I have no choice. Once I am part of a powerful family, the moneylender will back off. That will give enough time for my father, and possibly Quintus, to win promotions. Then the debts can be paid off.'

Hanno thought that a dubious way of trying to earn money. What if either – or both – of them were killed? he wanted to ask. 'Is it just one moneylender?'

'One man holds the vast majority of my father's debts, yes. Phanes, he's called.'

'He's a sewer rat. Shame he isn't here. I'd give him a reason to write off the money.'

She touched his cheek. 'Thank you. You can't do anything about him, though. Let's not talk about him. We have little enough time.'

Grumbling, Hanno stored away the name for future reference. He lost his train of thought as she pulled him into another, prolonged kiss. Her fingers caressed his shoulders, moved on to his neck and before he could stop her, under the cloth that protected his scar. Feeling the puckered flesh, she tensed. 'What happened to you? Were you wounded?'

The familiar fury filled Hanno. He wanted to rant about what Pera had done to him, but there was no point. Aurelia wasn't responsible, so instead he said, 'In a manner of speaking, yes.'

'You were lucky to survive.' Her voice trembled. 'A wound in a place like that, well . . .'

'It took a few days to recover, that's all.' He kissed her again, and she responded with fierce passion, as if by her actions she could undo the harm. Hanno's heart filled, and he returned her urgency with his own hunger. His fingers gently tugged down the shoulders of her dress to expose her small breasts. He bent his neck and took one of her nipples in his mouth. 'Gods,' he heard her murmur. 'Don't stop.'

'Aurelia?'

It was as if someone had dumped a bucket of cold water over them both. Hanno straightened, mouthing a curse, frantically reaching for his sword. He melted into the darkness by the nearest cypress as Aurelia struggled to pull up her dress, to regain her composure. 'Agesandros? Is that you?'

'Who else?' came the dry response. 'Where are you?'

'I'm here.' An urgent whisper to Hanno: 'I have to go. I will try to come out again later.'

'I can't wait,' he said, his voice thick with regret. 'The dogs will find me.'

'Why are you hiding there, under the trees?' Agesandros called.

'Hiding? I was just walking back to the house,' cried Aurelia brightly. She threw Hanno a look full of longing. 'I would that this meeting could have lasted forever,' she whispered. 'May the gods always watch over you and keep you safe.'

'And over you too,' replied Hanno passionately.

'I will keep him talking as long as I can, but you had better move fast. If the dogs catch your scent—'

'They won't. Goodbye, Aurelia. I will always remember you.' He watched miserably for a moment as she walked away; she didn't look back. Then he retreated into the darkness. The instant that Agesandros was no longer visible, he began to run. Sorrow gripped him as he sped through the trees. This visit was supposed to have been an exciting one, a joyful one. Instead it had proved to be more heart-rending than he could have imagined. To have been reunited with Aurelia against all the odds had been astonishing – like a very gift from the gods. Yet like so many apparently divine interventions, it was double-edged. Their encounter had been brutally brief, and there was to be no happily-ever-after. Aurelia was soon to be wed to another man. Sadness filled Hanno.

What about Suni? he thought. To Hanno's shame, his grief over what had happened to his old friend kept being overwhelmed by thoughts of Aurelia. Yet, even if another meeting could be engineered with her, what was the point? Before long, she would be a married woman with a new life ahead of her. Compared to that, he could offer her nothing at all – not even a life on campaign. It would be best – for Aurelia as well as him – to wish her well and forget her, he decided.

But as he scaled the boundary wall, found his horse and rode in the direction of his camp, Hanno found that impossible to do. He found himself reliving every moment, every touch, every word she had spoken. It was, he realised in the days that followed, a type of mental torture: momentary exquisite pleasure from the memories of their intimacy, followed by hours of pain from the knowledge that it would never be repeated. After his return to the main body of the army, it had been the turn of other units to go out on foraging missions. That was bad enough, but as the host turned south in search of fresher areas to pillage, the permanence of his separation from Aurelia was hammered home. After that, the only ways for Hanno to achieve any kind of peace were in combat – scarce enough to find at that time, with the Romans refusing any offers of battle – or at the bottom of an amphora of wine.

At times, he wished that he'd never ridden to the farm, never met her, not discovered Suni's fate. Somehow, though, the pain was worth it. Deep in Hanno's heart, an ember of hope still burned that, one day, he might meet Aurelia again in happier circumstances. It was so fragile, so small that he scarcely dared acknowledge its existence. But it helped him to go on. That, and the burning desire to bury his sword in the hearts of men such as Agesandros and Pera.

Chapter X

The Volturnus valley, northeast of Capua, autumn

The entrance to the valley was about half a mile wide. The forested peaks on either side formed a tunnel for the wind that scudded constantly across the Campanian plain from the sea. At the height of summer, it would have provided welcome relief from the heat, but the season had changed early. Once it got dark, temperatures dropped fast and the breeze just added to the chill. Cloaked and wearing two tunics, Quintus was grateful that he had a fire to crouch over. The blaze at which he and his comrades were warming themselves was just one of many strung across the valley's entrance. A few hundred paces to his right, the line of light – and the valley itself – was split by the dark band of the River Volturnus, which ran down to Capua and the west coast. To be illuminated and in such an exposed position felt most uncomfortable, but that was Fabius' precise intention. Although Quintus felt a little like a piece of iron upon the anvil just before the smith is about to strike, the dictator's decision made perfect sense.

With the harvest taken in, and Campania stripped bare, Hannibal needed to march his army to the east once more. There were few routes out of the area, and Fabius had covered them all. Strong forces had been posted, weeks before, astride the Via Appia and the Via Latina, and at the mouths of a number of passes. Quintus was one of four thousand legionaries and velites to be posted here, in the perfect place to block one of the larger paths to the east. This, while Fabius' main strength continued to shadow Hannibal's army, up and down the edge of the Campanian plain, sticking to the mountain slopes and avoiding battle at all times. The two weeks

Quintus had spent here had dragged beyond belief. Less than fifteen miles from Capua and a similar distance from his home, he had been unable to do a thing about it. Even a day's leave was out of the question, and, thanks to the quadrupling of the sentries at night, desertion was downright dangerous. If truth be told, that wasn't why Quintus had stayed. Although he'd longed to slip away for a night or two, to try and see his mother and Aurelia, a loyalty to Rutilus and Corax, and even his new comrades, had held him back. If he had missed a big battle, he would never have forgiven himself. At this stage, his loved ones *had* to be safe inside Capua. From the gossip Quintus had heard, the countryside was empty, abandoned. This news had given him much solace. Hannibal wasn't about to lay siege to Capua. As long as the farm hadn't been raided in the weeks prior, his mother and sister were fine.

Whether he and his comrades would be was another matter. Hannibal's host was camped not two miles distant, on the plain. He had seen it with his own eyes, an immensely long column that had taken the entire afternoon to arrive. Now, a thousand pinpricks of light in the distance marked the enemy fires. Quintus' stomach clenched at the sight of it. Would the Carthaginians attempt to break through this pass? And if so, when? Those were the questions on every man's lips.

'There are a lot of them, eh? At least we're not alone. The rest of the army is close by,' said Rutilus as he stamped in from the vantage point fifty paces to the front.

'I know,' muttered Quintus. 'It doesn't feel like it, though.' It *was* hard to believe that Fabius, his four legions and an equal number of socii troops were nearer than the enemy. Their encampment was on a hill less than a mile away.

'It certainly doesn't.' Rutilus spat in the direction of Hannibal's forces.

'They'd get here quick enough if we're attacked,' declared Quintus with a confidence he didn't quite feel. 'It takes hours to form an army up to march. Hannibal's men are no different.'

'So you think Fabius will actually fight?' asked Rutilus with a snicker.

Quintus knew what his friend meant. After an entire summer of marching and training, training and marching, and chewing on the dust left by the marauding Carthaginians, most soldiers were champing at the bit to fight the invaders of their land. Trebia was a distant memory; even Trasimene didn't seem such a terrible defeat when one considered that they had been outnumbered nearly two to one. Apart from the time spent in the field, the main reason for this newfound confidence was that Fabius and Minucius, his Master of the Horse, now led more than forty thousand men. 'That's more than enough strength to smash the guggas,' soldiers said to each other daily. 'It's time to teach Hannibal a lesson.' Quintus had been brooding on it too. 'This pass is easy to defend. If the enemy begins an assault, I think he will, yes. The time is right.'

'Ha! I'm not so sure. Old "Warty" wants to avoid confrontation no matter where we are. He's got no taste for battle. I'd wager my left bollock that—'

'That what, soldier?' Corax emerged from the shadows, his eyes glinting dangerously.

'N-nothing, sir,' replied Rutilus.

'Did I hear you calling Fabius "Verrucosus"?' Corax's voice was silky. Deadly.

'I, er . . .' Rutilus' gaze flickered to Quintus and back to the centurion. 'Yes, sir. You might have done, sir.'

Corax's response was to punch Rutilus in the solar plexus, dropping him to the ground like a sack of grain. Rutilus' mouth opened and closed, like a fish out of water. He gasped in a choking breath. 'I'll pretend I didn't hear you this time,' Corax growled. 'But if I ever hear you insult our dictator in future, I'll have you scourged within a pubic hair of your life. Do you understand?'

Unable to speak, Rutilus just nodded.

Corax wheeled on Quintus, who had to force himself not to flinch. 'You're not as much of a fool as your friend here.'

'Sir?' asked Quintus in confusion.

'We've had our orders. If the guggas come at us, the entire army *will* march into battle.' A wolfish grin. 'No more moving out of the way.'

'That's great news, sir!'

'I thought so.' Corax threw Rutilus a baleful glare. 'When you catch your breath, I want you back on sentry duty – for the rest of the night.'

Quintus began to relax – a fraction too soon.

'You can go with him, Crespo. Make sure he doesn't fall asleep.'

Quintus knew better than to protest. He glowered at Rutilus as the centurion walked away. 'We're going to freeze our balls off all bloody night thanks to you. Why couldn't you just keep your big mouth shut?'

'Sorry,' Rutilus muttered. He didn't grumble when Quintus told him to bring along the skin of wine that he'd been saving for a special occasion.

All the same, Quintus thought sourly, it would be a long time until dawn.

Despite the cold, it was possible for one of the pair to try to doze a little from time to time. Corax came to check on them once or twice, but by the third watch, it was clear that he'd left them to it. Quintus wasn't sure if there was much benefit in closing his eyes and snatching a few brief moments of standing rest. He was so chilled that it was almost impossible to fall asleep. Every time he did, a gust of wind would sweep under his cloak, waking him anew. The wine helped, but it soon ran out. They traded dirty jokes for a while, but then they ran out of new material. Rutilus started droning on about Severus and how much they had in common. Quintus was still pissed off with Rutilus, though, and rudely said he wasn't interested. He tried thinking about the warm bed in his old bedroom at home, but that made him even more grumpy. Imagining the battle that might take place the following day had a similar result. Infuriatingly, Macerio's position was close to theirs and the blond-haired soldier spent his time making obscene gestures at Quintus or spitting in his direction. Quintus did his best to ignore the taunting, but it was hard. By the time a few hours had passed, he was in an utterly foul mood. His face and feet were numb, and so too were his lower legs, where his cloak didn't reach. The rest of his body was a little better, but not by much. Stamping up and down was preferable to standing still. Staring at the fires to the rear didn't just ruin his night vision, it made him feel far worse. With a fixed scowl on his face, he marched to and fro, his gaze fixed on the enemy's camp.

The first flares of light did not register for a few heartbeats. When they did, Quintus blinked in surprise. Had a tent caught fire? It wasn't unheard of for that to happen. The glow spread, and he knew that he had been mistaken. No blaze could spread that fast. What in Hades was going on? 'Rutilus? Do you see that?'

'Can't a man take a piss in peace?' Rutilus glanced over his shoulder. His eyes widened. Swallowing a curse, he shoved himself back into his undergarment and sprinted to Quintus' side.

'What do you think it is?'

'It's soldiers, getting ready to march,' replied Quintus as realisation dawned. 'They're all lighting torches at once.' Around him, he could hear the alarmed voices of the other sentries. No one had expected this. Attacks at night were not something that the Romans undertook, so they didn't expect them of their enemies.

'The bastards aren't waiting until the morning to move!' cried Rutilus, stating the obvious. He was already a few steps away. 'I'll fetch Corax.'

Quintus watched with increasing nervousness as the illuminated area before the enemy camp grew in size. Thousands of men were involved, he thought. Would it be the whole of the enemy host or just a section? Was a rapid assault on their position about to be launched? That could break through. The four thousand soldiers blocking the pass were spread thinner than soft cheese on a piece of bread. If the Carthaginians moved fast, there was no possible way that Fabius and the rest of the army could reach them in time. At best, they would be swept aside; at worst, annihilated. A knot of fear twisted in Quintus' stomach. As at Trasimene, he felt the sickening certainty that he would die. A short time later, when the torches began to move, he was almost relieved. Death, when it came, would be swift.

'Scheming gugga dogs,' snapped Corax.

Quintus had never been more glad to see his centurion. 'Yes, sir. Rutilus went for you the instant we saw the lights.'

'They're moving already.'

Nausea roiled in Quintus' belly, but then he saw that the line of torches wasn't coming towards them. His head twisted, eyes searching the darkness. 'The saddle. They are heading for the saddle, sir!' On the far side of the peak to their right, the slope was less precipitous. Quintus had seen it as they marched into position. 'The climb from the plain to the ridge between it and the next summit to the north isn't difficult.'

'Yes, I know it. From there, they'll be hoping to pick up the trail that leads through the Apennines. So they're trying to outflank us, eh?' Corax laughed. 'The fool Hannibal has misjudged the distance. If we move now, we can scale the peak near us and after that, the ridge, before his troops. Denying them the passage with a good advantage of height shouldn't be hard. Spread the word. I want four men out of every five assembled by the riverbank and ready to march as fast as they possibly can. I'll be back soon.'

'Yes, sir!' Quintus' heart thumped against his ribs. His weariness fell away; even the cold was no longer an issue. He and Rutilus set about gathering the velites who were on duty and passing on his orders to the legionaries present. When Corax returned with Pullo and the other centurions, the soldiers were formed up in maniples. Corax gave him a tiny nod of approval before eyeing his men. 'You've all seen what's going on, boys. Hannibal thinks he's being smart. He thinks we're asleep! Well, his men are going to get the surprise of their miserable lives. When they reach the ridge, we will be waiting there for them. Won't we?'

'YES, SIR!'

'Fabius is relying on us. Rome is relying on us to throw the guggas back. If they can't get out of Campania, the shitbags will starve. And then we'll have them!'

As the men around him began shouting, 'Roma! Roma!' Quintus remembered the talk of kicking an army in its stomach. That was all very well, he thought with a touch of bitterness, but the lands that would be laid to waste if Hannibal's troops were denied the passage were those of Campania, his home. Thus far, the area east of the Apennines had escaped the brunt of the enemy's depredations. There was nothing wrong with them taking their turn. Yet Quintus felt guilty for even entertaining the idea. It was time to fight, he thought, not to give in just so his home region could be spared.

'Crespo. Rutilus.' Corax and the other centurions called the velites' section leaders into a quick huddle. 'You lot can move faster than the hastati or principes. You're to go in front. Run like the wind. I want you up there before the guggas at all costs. Give them a welcome that they won't forget. Understand?'

'Yes, sir,' Quintus replied, his pulse racing. The air filled with growls of acknowledgement from the others.

'This is your opportunity to prove that you're not the fool I think you are,' said Corax, glaring at Rutilus.

'You won't be disappointed in me, sir,' replied Rutilus fiercely.

'What are you waiting for?' cried Corax. 'Get moving!'

They hurried to their comrades. Quickly, Quintus explained what they had to do. 'Ask Hermes for his help on the way up. It's a broken ankle that you need to be most worried about, for now at least.' That garnered him a few chuckles, but Quintus didn't smile. He ignored Macerio's sneering, scarred face too. 'I'm serious. Watch your footing. If you fall, you will have to fend for yourself. I want every able-bodied man ready to fight the instant we reach that saddle.' There were grim nods then, reassuring him. He glanced at Rutilus. 'Ready?'

'I'd have been halfway up the hill already if you hadn't talked so much.'

'You're full of shit!'

'And you love it. See you at the top.' Clearly keen to win Corax's favour once more, Rutilus jumped straight into the river, spears and shield in hand. His men followed.

'We can't let them steal a march on us!' shouted Quintus. 'With me!' He sprinted after Rutilus, all thoughts but reaching the top and throwing back the Carthaginians gone from his mind. Fortunately, the Volturnus was no more than knee deep. Even so, the chill in the water struck him like a blow in the face. He scrambled across, his sandals slipping a little on the smooth stones of the bottom. And then he was up on to the opposite bank, the damp grass brushing off his legs.

They ran at full speed across the flattest portion of the valley floor. It wasn't long before they caught up with Rutilus and his men. Insults were thrown about who could sprint the fastest, and despite his nerves, Quintus grinned. The badinage was a good sign that morale was high. As the incline began to rise, the grass was replaced by small trees, bushes and rocks. The ascent became a matter of scrambling over boulders and shoving through thick scrub. An orange-yellow harvest moon hung low in the sky, while overhead countless stars glittered.

Moving slowly would still have posed some risk, but their urgency meant that it was impossible to avoid harm. Curses rang out as toes were stubbed and flesh ripped open by thorns. Now and again, Quintus heard the impact of a body hitting the ground. It was difficult to see who had fallen but there was no time to stop and help. He had to trust that the unlucky men would only be lightly injured. Every spear would count at the ridge.

By the time he reached the peak, Quintus was vaguely aware of a bruised shin and a long, bleeding graze on one arm. To his left and right, the panting shapes of men emerged one after another. All his attention, however, was on the mass of enemy soldiers ascending from the plain. 'Jupiter's cock, they have moved fast,' he swore.

Rutilus materialised by his side. 'It will be a push to get to the saddle before them.'

'We can do it, damn it!' A glance back down the slope and Quintus' unease lessened. The dark shapes of the legionaries were only a couple of hundred paces below them. The fight would just have started by the time they arrived. 'Come on, lads,' he cried, moving before his fear took a greater hold. Rutilus was more than equal to the challenge and took the lead once more. Quintus was determined not to be left behind. Neck and neck, they barged down the slope, trusting that their comrades were following. Afterwards, he would wish that he had checked. They were perhaps halfway down when someone gave him a tremendous shove in the back. He stumbled forward and his vision spun as he lost control. He saw stars, Rutilus' back, burning torches and then the ground. His head slammed against a rock and Quintus knew no more.

He came to with someone slapping his face. Blinding pain was radiating from a spot above his left eye, and Quintus groaned.

'He's alive.'

'Can you get up?' The voice was low and urgent.

'I think so.' Strong arms raised him to his feet. Quintus was grateful that they didn't let go of him at once. His knees shook from the effort of standing upright. It was odd, but he thought he could hear the bellowing of cattle.

'You're lucky that one of the lads saw you,' said a burly hastatus. 'What the hell happened? Did you trip?'

Macerio. It must've been he who pushed him, thought Quintus fuzzily. His wits were scrambled, but he knew better than to accuse a fellow soldier of something he had no way of proving. 'Yes, I think so.'

'Can you fight?'

He raised a trembling hand to his head, gingerly feeling where it hurt. His fingers came away sticky with blood. Quintus wiped them on his tunic. 'Of course I can,' he said. He looked down; confusion filled him. Then the bellowing he'd heard made sense. Hundreds and hundreds of cattle were stampeding across the saddle. A weird light flared from their heads.

'Clever, eh?' snarled the hastatus. 'They've got torches tied to their horns. From a distance, each beast looks like two men.'

Quintus goggled. Around the sides of the herd darted the enemy: men armed with spears and little else. Other figures, which had to be Roman, were being massed at the bottom of the slope while others, the velites probably, hurled javelins at the Carthaginians. 'It's a trick, to get us out of the pass,' he said stupidly. 'Why didn't we see it?'

'Your lot did,' replied the hastatus grimly. 'They started shouting, but we couldn't hear. The centurions kept us moving. At the top, we were packed like salted fish in a barrel. Even when we got the order that most men were to return to the river, it took an age to turn everyone around. That was when the second enemy unit hit us with a volley of javelins and slingshots. There was complete chaos.' A bitter laugh. 'They knew we'd charge for the saddle like a bunch of excited children.'

'What's happening now?' asked Quintus as dread filled him.

'There's fighting on two fronts: here and on the other side of the peak. Meanwhile, Hannibal's entire fucking host is marching through the pass under arms. Even if we do succeed in crossing the river again, it will be too late.'

'That was his plan all along,' muttered Quintus.

'I'll give that gugga bastard one thing,' admitted the hastatus. 'He's damn clever.'

'His luck will run out one day.' Quintus tried to ignore his relief that Campania would be spared further pillaging. 'Fabius will finish him.'

'Aye, or Minucius, more likely,' retorted the hastatus.

Rutilus wasn't alone in thinking that Fabius was too cautious, thought Quintus. He, on the other hand, favoured Fabius, not least because Flaccus had been an arrogant fool. Hanno worried that Minucius was cut from the same cloth. 'One of them will get lucky in the end,' he said diplomatically.

'Gods willing. Best go and lend a hand, eh?' The hastatus punched him on the arm. 'Take your time down the slope. You're probably still seeing stars. One javelin more or less isn't going to change the outcome.' With a cynical laugh, he and his companion moved off.

Grateful for the respite, Quintus sat on a large boulder. His head *was* still killing him. The fighting below looked to be growing more vicious. The cattle continued to stream by. Was there no end to Hannibal's tricks? he wondered. It appeared not. Yet this was no Trebia, no Trasimene. There would be some casualties, but not many thousands. This had not been a defeat, merely a case of being outmanoeuvred. It was a sting to Rome's pride, not a blow to its vitals.

Far below, a man with blond hair lobbed a spear at the enemy. It was Macerio. I need to watch my back better from now on, thought Quintus soberly. Fortuna must have been smiling on him earlier. Macerio probably thought that the fall *had* killed him, or perhaps someone else had come upon the scene, preventing his enemy from finishing the job. Either way, it had been a lucky escape. Soon after, this truth was brought home to him even harder. On his way down to the saddle, he came across Rutilus' body. That was upsetting enough, but the fact that his friend's mortal wound was in his back made Quintus' blood boil with rage. It would not be a coward's injury; Rutilus was no lily-liver. The chances of an enemy striking such a blow were slim to none. Wounds in honourable combat tended to be on a soldier's front, or side. No, it was far more likely that Macerio had turned on Rutilus after pushing *him* down the slope. It was a cowardly act that would be impossible to prove. Where is the devious bastard? Unsure that he was strong enough to fight but desperate for revenge, Quintus scanned the area. In the confusion of battle, there was no sign of the blond-haired man.

He forced himself to calm down. His best tactic would be to pretend nothing had happened, to lull Macerio into thinking that he had got away with it. Next time, though, he would be ready. And it would be Macerio who ended up dead, not him.

North of Capua

Dawn had come. Aurelia could tell. She had been lying awake for hours – if she had slept at all – and through her closed eyelids the light had been increasing for some time. Still she refused to open her eyes. By doing so, she would be forced to acknowledge that this was her wedding day. Lying rigid on the bed, taking only shallow breaths and thinking of everything but the celebrations to come, she could continue the pretence that she and Lucius were not to be husband and wife by the day's end. That she would never see Hanno again. The thought of *him* brought tears to her eyes once more. Before his unexpected arrival on the night at the farm, she had been gradually reconciling herself to the idea of wedding Lucius. Since seeing Hanno it had been impossible. Her every waking moment, and many of those when she was asleep, had been consumed by passionate thoughts of him. The preparations for the wedding: being fitted for her bridal dress, ordering the orange veil that she would wear, deciding whom should be invited, had passed her by in a blur. Any time that she was forced to concentrate and things had seemed more real, Aurelia had told herself she was preparing to marry not Lucius, but Hanno. Yesterday, however, her efforts at denying what was happening had begun to unravel at last. Accompanied by her mother, Martialis and a party of slaves, she had travelled north of Capua to the house of one of Lucius' relations. Because of the risk of marauding Carthaginian soldiers, it had been deemed too dangerous to hold the wedding at her family home as tradition dictated. Instead, it would take place in this villa, a house that she had never set foot in until the previous day. All night long, Aurelia had tried to deny the truth of what would happen in the coming hours. But the pretence was coming to an end. She tried to curse Hanno for appearing in her life, for opening her heart to feelings of love, but she couldn't. May the gods protect you, wherever you are, she prayed.

'Mistress?' Elira was outside the door. 'Are you awake?'

And so it begins, thought Aurelia wearily. 'Yes. Come in.'

The door opened and Elira slipped inside, smiling. 'Did you sleep well?'

Aurelia wondered whether to lie, but before she could speak, the Illyrian had seen her mood.

'Melito is a good man. A kind man. He will give you many children.'

There was no point trying to explain. 'I know,' replied Aurelia, forcing a smile of her own.

They both started as the unmistakable sound of a pig squealing carried from outside the house. It was customary to slaughter a pig early on a wedding day so that the entrails might be read by a soothsayer.

'Let us hope that the omens are favourable,' said Elira.

Aurelia found herself murmuring in agreement. For all her misgivings, she did not want to add bad luck to the impending proceedings. She eyed her old dress, lying over a stool, and a few of her childhood toys, brought with her from Capua just so she could ritually set them aside the day before. From this moment, she would never wear a girl's dress again. She would don a bridal tunic; later she would become a woman – in the truest sense. Her cheeks flushed at the thought.

'Your mother will be here soon to help with getting you dressed. She says to start by dressing your hair.' Almost shyly, Elira raised the iron spear head in her right hand.

'Very well.' Aurelia threw back the covers and swung her legs on to the floor. 'There is more light in the courtyard,' she said, picking up another stool.

The moment that they were seen, the two began to attract attention. By the time that Elira began using the spear head to separate Aurelia's hair into the traditional six plaits, a handful of slaves had gathered to watch. Their approving smiles and murmurs of appreciation did nothing to improve Aurelia's mood, but she did not frown or throw disapproving looks. This would be a long day, but she was determined to maintain her family's honour throughout. After the way she had contributed to her parents' problems, it was the least she could do. Marrying Lucius was the only way that the threat of Phanes could be kept at bay.

Aurelia was standing just outside the open doors of the tablinum. She was alone apart from Elira. This was it, she thought, her guts churning. There was no going back now. Apart from Lucius, who would be last to arrive, everyone else was waiting for her in the atrium.

'It's time,' whispered Elira.

Aurelia's head turned. Through her *flammeum*, or veil, Elira was orange. Her whole world was orange. It was most disconcerting, even more than her simple, white wedding dress, saffron-coloured cloak and sandals. Her fingers rose to touch the knot of Hercules that tied the girdle just beneath her breasts – it could only be undone by her husband – and she fought the urge to weep. It felt like a waking nightmare.

'Mistress.' Elira's voice was urgent.

Freeing her traitorous limbs by sheer strength of will, she began to move forward. The scent of marjoram from the wreath at her brow was strong in Aurelia's nostrils. It was one of her favourite smells, and she inhaled deeply, trying to take strength from it. Into the tablinum, across the black and white chequered mosaic, past the pool that collected rainwater from the hole in the roof. By the wooden partition that separated the room in which she stood from the atrium, she paused. Her heart was beating like that of a bird in her breast, faster than she could count. Nothing she did made any difference. Get on with it, she thought. Prolonging the agony will make it worse.

Inside the atrium, her mother and Martialis waited with the priest and eight other witnesses. As she entered, Aurelia heard their murmurs of approval. Her appearance at least was satisfactory. Trying to move gracefully, she walked to stand before the priest, the most senior from the temple of Jupiter in Capua. A stern-looking man with a narrow face and little hair, he gave her a tight nod. Atia and Martialis stood to his right; the others, to his left. Aurelia's eyes moved to her mother's face, which bore a pleased expression. She looked away, holding in the anger that bubbled up in response. Martialis gave her a kindly smile. Apart from Lucius' father, she didn't know the eight further witnesses. She supposed that they were friends and relations. Gods, but she wished that her father and Quintus could have been among them, if not to stop the proceedings, then at least to give her moral support.

They didn't have to wait long for Lucius to appear from the other entrance to the atrium. He was dressed in a new white toga and garlanded with flowers. He looked very handsome, Aurelia had to admit. Even so, she couldn't help imagining Hanno in his place. Accompanying Lucius were more relations and a band of his friends. She trembled as he reached her side. It was a relief when the priest began to speak at once. He thanked the gods for the favourable auspices seen in the entrails of the sacrificial pig, welcomed everyone present to the marriage ceremony, offered gratitude to Lucius' father and the shades of the family's dead ancestors. A few words about marriage, children and a few more about Lucius. None about her, other than to mention she was of good stock. Aurelia fought her bitterness. By becoming Lucius' wife and the woman who would bear his heirs, thus continuing his bloodline, she was also helping *her* family.

'Repeat after me the sacred words,' intoned the priest.

So soon? Aurelia wanted to scream.

'As long as you are Aurelia, I am Lucius,' said the priest.

Lucius echoed the words in a strong, clear voice.

The priest's gaze moved to her. 'As long as you are Lucius, I am Aurelia.'

Her eyes flickered to the side. Lucius was watching her. So was everyone in the room. Her breath caught in her throat; the muscles in her legs trembled. Somehow, she regained control. 'As long as you are Lucius, I am Aurelia.'

'To symbolise this union, witnessed by the gods, the couple's hands must be joined by a married woman, who will represent the goddess Juno,' declared the priest. This was Atia's moment. She glided forward to stand before Aurelia and Lucius, who turned to face each other. Taking both of their right hands, Atia brought them together. Aurelia steeled herself as Lucius' fingers gripped hers; she glared at her mother through her flammeum. I'm doing this for you and Father, she shouted silently. If she saw, Atia gave no sign. Wordlessly, she withdrew.

The remainder of the ceremony passed by as if in a dream. Aurelia walked forward to the temporary altar that had been set up by the household lararium; sat with Lucius on a pair of stools that had been covered with one sheepskin; watched as the priest made an old-fashioned offering of spelt cake at the altar. She paced around the dais, holding hands with Lucius, and repeated the blessing spoken by the priest; heard the applause as they were declared married; listened, numb, as, one by one, the guests offered their congratulations. She barely touched a morsel at the feast afterwards; she had no appetite. Only when Lucius encouraged her did she try some of the suckling pig, and the baked fish that had been especially shipped in from the coast.

'It's delicious, eh?'

They were almost the first words Lucius had said to her. To be fair, there had been no chance to talk, but that had suited her. 'Yes, it is.'

'Have some more.' He skewered a large piece of pork with his knife and deposited it on her plate.

'Thank you.' Aurelia felt boorish that she didn't have more to say to him, but nothing sprang to mind. And the lump of greasy meat made her stomach turn. She was grateful when Lucius' father, on a nearby couch, called his name and drew him into conversation. Toying with her food, she tried not to think of the night to come. No matter how hard she tried, however, her thoughts kept returning to what would happen, inevitably, after they had made the short journey to Lucius' family's house and retired to the bridal bed. Her mother's lecture, delivered the previous day, returned to haunt her. Aurelia hadn't been at all prepared for the graphic nature of it, particularly coming from her mother. During her childhood, she'd seen enough farm animals mating to know how the physical aspects of intercourse worked, but the concept of having to lie there while Lucius did the same to her was revolting and horrifying. 'Won't it hurt?' she'd asked. Atia's face had softened; she had patted Aurelia's hand. 'At first, a little, maybe. Lucius is not like many men, though. He will be gentle with you, I am sure of it.'

She shot a quick glance at her husband. The wine he'd drunk lent a warm flush to his cheeks. Alcohol made some men more aggressive, but there was no sign of that with Lucius. If anything, he seemed more jovial than ever.

'In time, you may even come to enjoy it,' Atia had gone on. The memory made Aurelia blush for the second time – simultaneously angry and embarrassed. As if that were possible! She would hate every moment of it, would endure it because that was her duty. There would be no pleasure involved; with luck, it would not take long. Despite the pork she'd just tried, there was a new, bitter taste in her mouth. It was easy for her mother to talk in this manner: she had been blessed in marriage, for she had wed Aurelia's father not by formal arrangement, but in a love match that had been disapproved of by both their families. Maybe I *should* have run off with Hanno, Aurelia reflected, left my old life behind to make a new one with him. The fantasy lasted no more than a few heartbeats. Her conscience would not be silent. And leave Phanes to beggar your parents? it asked. A knot of emotion closed her throat. She could not have lived with herself if that had happened. It was partly her fault anyway. If she hadn't been discovered eavesdropping that day, her mother might have kept up with the payments to the unscrupulous moneylender. Stop it, she thought. The whole argument is futile. If Lucius hadn't come along, another suitable husband would have been found. It was so unfair!

There was one consolation, if it could be called that. According to her mother, if she became pregnant, Lucius would not try to have sexual relations with her. Nor would he while she was breastfeeding a baby. 'As you're unhappy about this match, it's all the more reason to get with child. Once you have provided him with at least one son, but preferably two or even three, he will leave you alone, should that be your wish.' Aurelia could scarcely imagine giving birth once, let alone multiple times. It was not something that she'd dreamed about, as she knew other girls did. If given the choice, riding horses and training with a sword – both activities prohibited to women – were preferable to her than the drudgery of rearing children. But it would be best to forget that Quintus had ever taught her to do either. She would never do them again. Nor would she roam through the woods with him and Hanno.

'Once you have had three children, no one could complain if you discreetly took a lover. But not before then,' Atia had warned. Hanno might have been a lover, thought Aurelia with regret, if only he weren't one of the enemy. According to everyone, the Carthaginians – she refused to call them guggas – were absolute savages. Aurelia only knew Hanno, and he certainly wasn't like that. Nor had Suni been. She doubted their families were either. Quintus was about the only person who might understand her feelings for Hanno – to all intents and purposes, he and Hanno had been friends – but she doubted if even her brother could bring himself to approve. For the rest of her days, it would have to remain her dark secret.

Aurelia realised with a start that Lucius' father had been speaking for some time. He expressed regret that her father and brother could not be present, offered his respects to Atia and Martialis, who was standing in for Fabricius, and gave thanks to the gods for the auspicious omens pronounced by the priests that day. Aurelia's mouth went dry as he turned with a wink to Lucius. 'And so the highlight of the ceremony is nearly upon us.'

'Stand up.' Atia was right by her. Aurelia did as she was told. Her mother had explained what would happen, but her heart still began to race once more. Atia's embrace had never been more welcome as Lucius stood up and said in a loud voice, 'I am here to claim my wife.'

There was an immediate, loud chorus of cheers, catcalls and sexual innuendoes from the other guests.

'You will not take her,' declared Atia.

Aurelia wished with all her heart that that were true, but it was all part of the ritual.

Lucius rose from the couch and took hold of Aurelia's hand. 'She is my wife, and I claim her.'

The hooting and crude references to the night's activities grew even louder. Lucius began to pull Aurelia away. The reality of her situation sank in fully and she clung to her mother with her free hand like a child who didn't want to go to its lessons. Lucius looked puzzled, and then annoyed. He tugged harder, but Aurelia resisted.

'Let go!' hissed Atia in her ear. 'You will disgrace yourself and our family.'

Aurelia's resistance crumbled and she allowed Lucius to drag her away. Her mother wailed theatrically at the 'parting', and the guests, who hadn't noticed a thing, roared with approval. She let him lead her through the atrium to the front door, where slaves waited with burning torches to accompany them outside. There, two small boys were waiting. The first darted to her side and took her left hand. As tradition dictated, he was the son of two living parents, Lucius' sister and her husband. The second child held a torch and a hawthorn branch; he would walk before them on the road to Lucius' house, which lay about a mile away. The couple waited as the guests spilled out into the night air around them. A pair of musicians with flutes appeared and began to play rousing tunes. Aurelia tried to ignore the barrage of lewd jokes and songs, but it was impossible. They continued to be shouted and sung as the procession set off. She might not have cared if she'd drunk some wine, but custom dictated that women should not drink much, if at all.

'You look beautiful.'

Lucius' voice startled her, even more so because he had paid her the compliment. Typically, he did not do so, at least in public. 'T-thank you.'

The cacophony made it easy to journey the rest of the way in silence.

At Lucius' house, Aurelia anointed the doorposts with oil and animal fat, and tied woollen threads to each side of them. Lucius carried her over the threshold to much applause and they walked to the atrium. The guests followed in a loud, drunken gaggle. There he gave her the formal gifts of a beaker of water and a burning lamp, which welcomed her into his home. Using the torch borne by the boy who'd led the procession, they together lit the twigs which lay ready in the fireplace, symbolising their new life together. Without further ado, they continued to the bridal chamber, one of the bedrooms, which sat off the courtyard and had been specially prepared for this occasion. A large bed dominated the room, numerous lights hung from an ornate bronze stand. In a corner sat an ugly statue of the ancient fertility god, Mutunus Tutunus, with his massive phallus. More suggestive comments filled the air. Lucius' lips twitched, but Aurelia eyed it with dread, grateful that the old practice of new brides having to lower themselves on to the stone member had long since been discontinued. She allowed her mother to divest her of the flammeum and her shoes, flushed red at her ceremonial advice and watched with relief as Atia and the other guests withdrew. Lucius closed the door behind them.

Of course the moment that they were alone, her mental anguish grew even greater. Aurelia didn't know which way to look — at the bed, the statue of the priapic god, or Lucius. She shuffled her bare feet and gazed at the floor, too scared even to move. When Lucius touched her arm, she jumped. Unwillingly, she lifted her eyes to his. His expression was gentle, which almost made her disquiet worse.

'Sit on the bed,' he said in a kind voice.

She obeyed. He stooped to untie the knot beneath her breasts. Aurelia watched as if she were someone else. His hands went to the hem of her tunic, and she blurted, 'Shouldn't I pray first?' Atia had drilled into her how things had to proceed.

He stood back and smiled. 'If you wish. I for one have had a bellyful of prayers for today.'

Partly to conceal her shock, partly to delay the inevitable, she closed her eyes and asked Juno, the guardian of maidens, and Cincia, the goddess to whom the loosening of the knot was consecrated, for their blessings and their help in the hours to come. All too soon, she had finished. Lucius gave her an enquiring look, and Aurelia found herself nodding. She was too weary to fight.

Rather than undressing her, he surprised Aurelia by next taking off his toga. He was attractive, she had to admit. His muscles were as sculpted as those of an athlete and he had a belly like a race hound. Clad in just his licium, he approached again. 'You have the advantage on me now,' he said softly. 'Stand up.'

'Yes, husband.' She tried not to tremble as he lifted the hem of her tunic up and over her head. It fell to the floor unnoticed as he slipped down her undergarment. Aurelia was mortified. She had not been naked in front of a man since well before her monthly bleeds had started. With an effort, she did not cover herself. His eyes drank in her body, and she did her best not to recoil when he reached out and touched a breast. Under his licium, she could see him swelling.

'Get into bed,' he said.

Relief for a moment as she escaped his touch. Sliding under the covers, she watched him extinguish the lights one by one. Blackness coated the room when he'd finished, but there was no comfort in it – as there might have been if she had been alone. Aurelia heard him move to the other side of the bed and undress. Her anxiety reached new levels. If the build-up to the ceremony and the event itself had been hard to take, this was torture. As he got in, she slid herself to the furthest edge of the bed and turned her back to him. When he reached out and touched her shoulder, she flinched.

His hand stayed where it was. 'We're married now.'

'I know,' she said miserably.

'Wife, I know that you married me only because of your parents' insistence.'

Guilt flayed at her. He deserves better than me, she thought. 'I—' she began.

'Don't lie.' For the first time, his voice was harsh.

A long-drawn-out pause. Feeling even worse that he had seen through her, Aurelia tried to think of something to say. 'You are a good man, Lucius,' she whispered eventually.

'And you are a kind and beautiful young woman. I hope that you can learn to be happy. Marriage is about begetting children and running a household, but it doesn't have to be entirely miserable. Or so my father says.'

What would he know? Aurelia thought furiously. Yet when he moved closer, sliding his naked body against hers, she did nothing. His chest was warm and soft, in stark contrast to his stiffness, which pushed against her buttocks. It was all she could do not to jump up from the bed, screaming. She didn't move. This was the final part of the test. It had to be endured, for her family's sake. As Lucius fumbled down below, she thought of Hanno, which helped a little. The first thrust inside her was shocking, however. It hurt, because she was dry, but Aurelia didn't say a word. She bit her lip instead. Lucius moved to and fro, easing himself deeper, letting out small sounds of pleasure. Aurelia's pain grew a little worse, but it was bearable. The feeling of him inside her was far harder to accept. Be brave, she thought. Quintus has to risk his life in battle, has to slide his spear into other men's flesh. I only have to do this.

Lucius reached around to squeeze her breast, shoved harder a few times and let out a strangled cry. His body juddered and relaxed; he pulled away from her. She felt his stiffness diminishing, and then it was out of her. At once she felt a sticky sensation between her thighs. It would be his seed and her blood, mixed. Aurelia felt a long, slow breath escape her chest. Was it relief, or satisfaction that the act had been done? She wasn't sure. Lucius moved away from her without a word and she brought her knees up to her chest, as a baby would. A bath would have felt like heaven, but she knew that was out of the question on this of all nights. Silence cloaked the two of them, their bed, the room, like a heavy weight. At least the gods have been appeased, Aurelia thought. The marriage had been consummated.

It was as if that was enough for Lucius, whose only further words to her were a sleepy, 'Good night, wife.' Soon he was snoring.

The same was not true of Aurelia. She lay wide awake, staring into the blackness. Let his seed have taken hold, she prayed. Although she had no desire to have a child, pregnancy would protect her from more of what had just taken place – at least until that child had been weaned. If that didn't happen, she would have to submit to Lucius as often as he wished. Never had Aurelia felt so helpless. A sob escaped her. She managed to swallow the next but then another one came, and another. It was too much for her. The tears that had been threatening all day began to flow at last. They poured out of her in a great tide of sorrow, soaking her pillow and the sheet below. She did her best to cry quietly, but after a while she no longer cared if Lucius heard. Maybe it would make him sorry that he'd touched her. If he saw how upset she was, maybe he wouldn't touch her again. Aurelia even rolled over to lie beside her husband, to see if her weeping would wake him. All he did, however, was to roll over and snort as he settled in a new position.

At this, Aurelia's desolation knew no bounds. Hanno, she thought. *Hanno.*

Many hours passed before sleep overtook her.

Chapter XI

Apulia, a month later . . .

'Stop looking at me like that,' ordered Hanno irritably.

'Like what, sir?' Mutt made a pretence of a happy expression.

Hanno waited for the inevitable. A moment later, like a fat man's wine belly that has been sucked in, Mutt's face sagged back down into its normal doleful position. 'Like that,' Hanno said, pointing. 'You're not happy that I'm going, but you're not going to stop me.'

'I can't stop you, sir,' replied Mutt mournfully. 'You're my commanding officer.'

'But you won't tell anyone about this when we return from patrol?'

'Of course not, sir. The men won't say a thing either, you have my word on it.' Mutt's lips pursed, but then relaxed.

'You will keep quiet, but you don't approve,' said Hanno, perplexed.

'That's right, sir. Women have their place, and it's not in the middle of a war.'

Hanno glowered. He'd felt obliged to tell Mutt his reasons for leaving. It was impossible to argue; his second-in-command was right. What he was planning was reckless, even bordered on lunacy. Yet his mind was made up. Like many other units, his phalanx had been sent on patrol by Hannibal, their mission to protect the Carthaginian foraging parties that scoured the land for supplies. Fabius had continued his tactic of attacking these groups, often with considerable success, meaning that their job had become even more important. Abandoning his men for what would probably be several days would not be regarded favourably by Hannibal, or any other senior officer for that matter. Hanno could all too vividly remember the disciplining he had received from his general after disobeying orders once before. 'Good. Because if Hannibal finds out about this, he will crucify me.' It was weird, he thought. Even that knowledge couldn't deter him from making another attempt to see Aurelia before she was wed. Since the night at the farm, he had hardly been able to sleep for thinking of her. If he could kill Agesandros on the same journey, all the better.

'That's the main reason I will say nothing, sir. Plus, I owe you.'

'I'm grateful.'

A snort of amusement. 'It's not just that you saved my life near Victumulae, sir. You're a valuable commodity. There are so few other officers around. If you die, there will be no time to train another one. This war is hotting up, and when the next big battle comes, I don't want to die because the unit doesn't have a commander.'

Hanno had to chuckle at Mutt's pragmatism, which felt mildly insulting but made sense. 'What if I don't come back?'

'Then I'll curse you for a damn fool, sir, and regret not tying you up right here and now.'

'You're a good man, Mutt. Thank you.'

'Why don't you piss off, sir? The sooner you leave, the sooner you'll be back.'

'I'll find you at the road junction we talked about, three days hence.'

'We'll be there, sir, unless a Roman patrol has slaughtered us all.'

Hanno gritted his teeth and tried not to think about that eventuality. 'Fare well,' he said, swinging up on to his horse's back.

But Mutt was already walking away, back to their camp.

Deflated, Hanno clicked his tongue and aimed his mount's head west, towards Capua. It would all be worth it when he saw Aurelia again, he told himself; when he revenged Suni's murder. Deep in his gut, though, Hanno knew that this wasn't really about Suni. He wanted vengeance for his friend, but seeing Aurelia came before that. Scourged by his conscience at that admission, he made an oath to ride past Fabricius' estate as well. Despite what she'd said, Aurelia might be there again. Making that additional detour would mean Hanno risked missing the meeting with Mutt and his men, but the chance might never come his way again. The whole enterprise was insane, he thought. Was he making the biggest mistake of his life?

His misgivings grew over the following day and night. Even when he crossed the Apennines, things did not get better. The marks of war were everywhere, from the burned-out villas and farmhouses to the empty villages and roadside inns. He grew used to the scatters of crows and vultures that congregated over dead animals and humans alike, rising lazily into the air at his approach. At the Trebia and Trasimene, Hanno had seen more corpses than he could have dreamed of. After those horrors, he'd thought that he had become inured to the sight, but he was mistaken. The warm weather had returned, causing the bloated bodies to rot fast. The sight of maggots in a child's eye sockets, purple tongues that no longer fitted in mouths and the overwhelming stench of rotting flesh turned his journey into an ordeal. Many of the rivers and streams had also been fouled by corpses, meaning he did not dare to drink from them. Instead he forced himself into the yards of abandoned houses once a day in search of a well. Water was all Hanno needed. The sights he saw quelled his appetite more thoroughly than a dose of the flux.

There were other perils as well. More than once, he spotted Roman patrols. They were only small, doubtless because Fabius' main strength was east of the mountains, but Hanno was on his own and an easy target. He took to riding through the fields, parallel to the roads. In this way, he was able to avoid contact with the enemy by hiding in patches of woodland. The added benefit was that he did not have to meet any other travellers – not that there were many. Early one morning, spotting the figures of men hiding in a roadside ditch, he realised that his tactic had also prevented him from being waylaid by latrones.

Finding Aurelia's home empty was not a complete surprise, but it let him off the hook with regard to Agesandros. Yet how could he know where the Sicilian had gone? Capua was the most logical place, because that was where Aurelia and her mother would be, but how would he find Agesandros – or, come to that, Aurelia – there? The idea of entering a city brought home the madness of what he was about to do. It was as foolish – and possibly as dangerous – as standing on the tail of a venomous snake. There was little chance of being personally recognised but his foreign accent, dark complexion and green eyes stood out. It would take but one denunciation by a suspicious citizen for him to be seized and interrogated before enduring a lingering and painful death. Only the gods knew whether he would come through the experience alive. He had not prayed as much since being washed out to sea from Carthage. As Hanno drew nearer to Capua, his unease grew. Strong parties of socii troops grew common, sent out to protect the farms close to the city. None gave him more than a passing glance, but his stomach was in a constant state of anxiety. Three things kept him riding. The memory of Aurelia's kisses, the thought of what Mutt would think if he returned in failure, and a stubborn refusal to admit defeat.

It was around midday on the second day when Hanno arrived at the main gate on the west side of Capua, the point at which travellers from the coast would arrive. Seeing the mighty stone walls again reminded him why Hannibal wasn't attacking cities. Reducing such a place would take many months, as the siege of Saguntum had shown, time in which the Romans would be free to cut off all supply routes and thus the Carthaginians' ability to remain in the field. Far smarter to do as Hannibal had, and to fight the Romans in open battle. The number of guards at the arched gateway made Hanno's stomach clench. None of the other travellers were keen to talk, which suited him. There was time for a prayer that no difficult questions would be hurled his way. When his turn came, the sentries seemed satisfied with Hanno's explanation, delivered in his best Greek accent, that he worked for a merchant who had recently landed at the nearest port. He slapped his saddlebags and pronounced them full of letters for his employer's customers. The guard studied him for a moment, his eyes moving to the horse. Hanno began to sweat. Not only were his saddlebags empty, but his short sword was lying hidden under the saddlecloth. Then, to his relief, the man waved him in without further query, even giving him advice about where to find stabling for his horse.

Their information was as good as any, he decided. A short time later, having secured a small bedchamber and a place in the stables for his horse in a rundown establishment called the Sheaf of Wheat, Hanno headed out to get his bearings. He left his blade under the mattress in his room. After so long away from centres of population, the experience was a shock to the senses. The narrow, unpaved streets were jammed with a mass of humanity, their speed reduced to that of a snail. Capua, it seemed, was filled to bursting point with refugees from the surrounding countryside.

The effect on the city was noticeable. The shops had less on offer than he would have expected. He heard prices bellowed for ordinary goods such as bread and fruit that were eye-watering. A burst sewer at one junction spewed liquid filth that was spreading in every direction. The smell was overpowering, and that was without the run-off from the dungheaps in many alleyways. Beggars lounged in every available space, hands outstretched, and gaunt-faced children ran hither and thither, grabbing purses and stealing what they could from the food stalls. Because of the press, the enraged shopkeepers could do little but throw abuse after the thieves.

Realising that his decision to come to Capua had been rash indeed, Hanno wandered aimlessly at first. He had no clue where to start. Think, he told himself, think. Buying a fresh flat loaf at a baker's, he moved to the doorway of a temple and racked his brains as he ate. Quintus' friend had been called Gaius. But what had his family name been?

It wouldn't come to him.

Frustrated, he wandered on, hoping for a sight of Aurelia, her mother or even Agesandros. His luck was not in, however, and his mood wasn't helped when he stumbled on to the slave market. The war hadn't stopped business here. Lines of naked men, women and children, their feet chalked and with chains around their necks, filled the roped-off area behind the forum. Prospective buyers walked up and down, assessing the specimens on offer. Bad memories flooded back. This was where he'd been sold for the second time. Parted from Suniaton. Met Agesandros, who would make his life a living hell.

'Looking for a slave? A pretty girl?'

Startled, he found a pox-scarred dealer with lank grey hair regarding him. He indicated his slaves, half a dozen girls who ranged from no more than six or seven up to adulthood. They all seemed terrified. Hanno curled his lip. 'No.'

A greasy smile. 'You prefer boys? A friend of mine has several who might interest you. Come, come!' The dealer beckoned.

Hanno could feel his temper rising. Keen not to make a scene, he turned his back and strode off. Unsure where to go next, his feet took him down a street that he'd not been on before. A blast of warm, moist air from a doorway to his left made his head turn. Above the lintel, he read the words 'BATHHOUSE. JULIUS FESTUS, PROPRIETOR. HOT WATER AT ALL TIMES. PRICES REASONABLE.' He could hear the chatter of conversation within and a voice calling, 'Fresh pastries, fresh pastries. Just baked! A quarter of an *as* each, or five for one as.' Hanno stopped, but not because of the food. He hadn't had a proper bath in many months – and if Carthage was anywhere to go by, there was no better place to eavesdrop on conversations. He was about to duck inside when something made him glance to his right. A pair of bruisers were leaning nonchalantly against the wall of the forge opposite. They scowled; Hanno averted his gaze. No point picking a fight when there was no need.

A pasty-faced fat man was sitting behind a desk by the entrance. On top of the desk lay a tabby cat, which was cleaning its face with its paw while the attendant stroked its ears and whispered to it. Hanno waited for a moment. The cat cocked its head at him, but the man did not look up. Irritated, he cleared his throat.

Finally, an uninterested glance. 'Wanting a bath?'

'Yes,' he growled.

'One as. That includes a drying cloth. Two asses if you want a strigil and oil as well.'

'That's bloody robbery!'

'Times are hard. That's the price. If you don't want to pay . . .' His eyes flickered to the right, and Hanno spotted the other doorman, a grinning brute with no teeth who gripped a club as thick as his thigh.

'Fine.' He slapped down two bronze coins.

The attendant eyed Hanno again. 'If you're after a massage, the slaves, male and female, offer other *services* as well, but they cost more—'

'A bath will be sufficient.'

'As you wish. The *apodyterium* is that way.' He waved at the door on the far side of the little room, his attention returning to the cat.

Hanno didn't bother to reply. Throwing a scornful look at the brute, he made his way into the rectangular changing room beyond, which was nicely decorated with a mosaic floor and swirling aquatic murals on the walls. At once a pastry-seller – whose voice he must have heard – lifted his platter in Hanno's direction, but he waved it away. There were a couple of other men undressing; they handed their clothes to a slave who placed them into individual numbered partitions on the wooden shelves that hung at eye height. Hanno was about to start disrobing himself when a sudden realisation froze him on the spot. His scar. He'd forgotten his damn scar! Anyone who saw it would take him for a slave. Devilment and irritation made him decide not to walk out. If he left the strip of fabric that protected his neck in place, no one would see the incriminating 'F'. If asked about the cloth, he would explain it away with a story about a non-healing wound. The surgeon had told him to keep it covered, especially in the baths.

He stripped and handed his garments and sandals over. 'I want nothing stolen while I'm bathing.' It wasn't his imagination that the slave sniffed. Hanno's lips quirked. 'They might smell ripe, but some thieves will take anything.' He handed over an as, and the slave's expression warmed.

'I'll keep good watch over them, sir. Would you like your clothes laundered?'

'Maybe another time.'

The slave threw a curious glance at his neck, but Hanno was already heading for the *frigidarium*. He didn't intend to spend long there: few people tended to linger in this room. Sure enough, there was only one occupant of the cold pool – one of the other customers he'd seen in the apodyterium, a middle-aged man with a shock of white hair and a beak of a nose. They exchanged nods; his neck cloth got another inquisitive look. To keep up the pretence, Hanno was careful not to get it wet. He waded quickly from one side of the pool to the other and climbed out. The *tepidarium*, the next room, would be more to his taste. The brief immersion had brought up goose bumps all over him.

In the tepidarium, he took a seat on one of the long wooden benches that ran down each side of the room. The air was pleasantly warm; the walls were decorated with images of dolphins, fish and sea monsters. A number of men sat nearby, or opposite. Three were talking together in low tones while supping wine from clay beakers; a pair were playing dice on the floor; one leaned back against the wall, dozing. Hanno closed his eyes and pretended to do the same. In reality, he was listening with all his might.

'A drachm on the next roll, as before?' asked the first gamer.

'Aye, I suppose,' said his companion none too happily.

'Two fives! Beat that if you can, my friend!'

'Did you go down on Fortuna last night?' asked the second man sourly. 'She's giving you all the luck.' He rolled the dice. Then, a triumphant cry: 'A six and a five! I win at last.'

The pair continued to play and bicker, and Hanno's attention moved on to the three men who were sitting together. Because they were opposite him, he continued to pretend that he was asleep. Thanks to this, or perhaps the wine, their tones gradually became louder.

'The damn war shows no signs of ending,' grumbled the oldest, a greyhair with knobbly jointed hands and feet. 'No doubt it will drag on as long as the last one did. I remember—'

'Calavius, have some more wine,' said the man on the left, a short individual with brown eyes and oiled ringlets. 'Your cup is empty.'

Although he had interrupted, Hanno noted that his manner was obsequious. There was a difference in social status here: his companions were possibly nobles. This added hugely to his frustration. Capua was not that big a city. These men probably knew Aurelia's parents. If only he could ask them where she was!

'My thanks.' Calavius held out his beaker.

The short man raised his own vessel. 'A toast: to our brave leaders, that they may defeat Hannibal before too much longer.'

The third man, broad-shouldered and with a casually handsome look, sat back without doing the same. 'Our leaders, you said. You're not a Roman, still less a Campanian. You're a damn Greek.'

'That's neither here nor there, surely. I live here, I pay my taxes,' said the short man, looking a trifle uncomfortable.

'You're no citizen, though.' The third man's voice had a hard edge to it. 'You'll never be conscripted into the army. Never have to fight the guggas, like my son, or Calavius' nephews and grandsons.'

Calavius' brows lowered. 'It's as my friend says.'

'My apologies,' came the swift reply. 'I meant no offence.' He lifted his cup again. 'May the gods guide and protect the Republic's leaders in their quest to defeat Hannibal. May they also keep safe all the sons of Rome who fight the enemy.'

The two others were mollified by this. They all drank a toast.

However, the peace didn't last long. When the two Romans began talking politics again, the Greek couldn't help but throw in his opinion. The third man looked even more irritated than he had before. 'Enough of this, Phanes. You're here to curry favour, that's clear, but I'm not interested in your opinions on the Roman political system. Understand?'

As Phanes fawned and grovelled, Hanno's brain raced. The name 'Phanes' was familiar.

'Why *are* you here, Phanes?' asked Calavius. 'It's not just to share your wine with us.'

'Well . . .' The Greek licked his lips. 'I have a number of debtors who have fallen severely behind on their payments.'

The moneylender! realised Hanno. The one with the stranglehold over Aurelia's mother. Gripped by fury, he listened even harder.

'That's unsurprising. There's a war going on, in case you hadn't noticed,' snapped the third man.

'Peace,' said Calavius. 'You may disapprove of his profession, but he and his fellows provide a service to the city. Let him speak.'

'Fine. I'm for the *caldarium* then.' With a courteous nod at Calavius and a scowl at Phanes, the third man got up and walked out. A moment later, he was joined by the man who'd been dozing. Hanno snorted as if stirring, but then pretended to fall asleep again. There was a short pause before, apparently happy, the Greek spoke again.

'I would like to approach the courts for permission to seize their properties in payment for their debts. I was wondering whether, perhaps, the judges' decision would be made easier if they had a little *guidance*. A word or two in the right ears would ensure that my appeals were heard favourably.'

'Are any of these people nobles whom I would know?' asked Calavius. An awkward cough. 'Some, yes.'

Atia could easily be on Phanes' list, thought Hanno, seething with anger. In his mind, the first seeds of a plan began to sprout.

'I could not countenance that,' said Calavius sharply. 'In these straitened times, those who have fallen on hard times must be afforded some leeway. More time to pay.'

'But—'

'No, Phanes.'

A short pause.

'I do not like to mention it, but there is the small matter of your son-in-law,' muttered Phanes.

'That is none of my affair,' snapped Calavius.

'Not quite true. How would it look if it were to come out that one of Capua's most illustrious magistrates was father-in-law to a degenerate – a gambler who has wagered away his entire family's wealth? A man who spends his time in the city's lowest taverns and fleshpots? Your chances of re-election might suffer considerably in the light of that information.'

'Curse you, Greek!' hissed Calavius.

'You give me no option. I am entirely within my rights to ask for a court ruling on these debts,' protested Phanes.

'You're still a bloodsucking parasite!' Calavius let out a heavy sigh. 'What is the price for your silence about my son-in-law?'

'As a gesture of goodwill, I will write off his debts in their entirety. Not a word shall pass my lips about him either. In return, I ask for not a drachm. As I mentioned, all I need is for the judges to approve the list of properties that I wish to have seized.'

'I want to see the names first,' said Calavius.

'It will be delivered to your house by the end of the day.'

'Then I believe that our business is done. I seem to have lost my taste for your wine.' Without another word, Calavius rose and stalked off.

Hanno sensed Phanes' gaze rest on him. He kept his breathing slow and regular, and after a moment he heard the Greek rise and leave the room. After an acceptable amount of time had passed, he decided to enter the caldarium himself. It was far busier than the tepidarium had been. The air was intensely warm and moist. Nearly a dozen men were relaxing in the hot pool, among them Calavius and the big noble; others were using strigils and oil to scrape the dirt from their skin or performing stretches; several were lying face down on waist-high stone benches while slaves massaged their muscles. There was no sign of Phanes, and disappointment filled Hanno. Then he heard a woman's voice from one of the cubicles off to the side and he remembered the attendant mentioning the other services on offer. It was a gamble that the Greek was engaged in such activity, but it was better to stay where he was. If Phanes had gone through to the next room and he followed too soon, his quarry might grow suspicious. Hanno climbed into the pool, avoiding eye contact.

After so long without a bath, the hot water was unadulterated bliss. He longed to immerse himself up to his chin, but conscious of the charade with his neck cloth, he lounged against the side with his arms stretched out along the tiles. The chatter here was all about the war: about this man's son and the unit he was serving in; how Fabius was too cowardly to fight Hannibal; what a blessing it had been when the Carthaginians had headed east once more; how the numbers of refugees were filling the city to bursting point; and so on. Hanno was too far away to eavesdrop on Calavius and the third man, and he heard no mention of Atia or Aurelia. Patience, he thought. If his plan came off, Phanes would be able to tell him where they lived. It wasn't long before there was a friendly query from his neighbour about the strip of fabric. His explanation was accepted without question, but Hanno moved off soon after. He had no desire to enter into conversation with anyone. After he had cleaned his body with a strigil, he dried himself off and went to pick up his clothes. It was imperative that he was outside before the Greek.

The two thugs were still parked opposite the bathhouse entrance. It was the best spot for observing who entered and left and so Hanno was forced to take a seat at an open-fronted restaurant a short distance away. Picking through a plate of tasteless gruel that was being sold as 'meat stew', he kept a regular eye on proceedings and wondered if it would be more prudent to continue his search for Aurelia. It didn't take long to make up his mind. At this late stage, being sensible had nothing to do with it. Just coming to Capua had been an insane notion. Now that he was here, he had a definite link to Aurelia through Phanes, which was more than he'd discover by wandering around like a fool.

When the Greek emerged, Hanno was annoyed and dismayed to see the two heavies fall in line behind him. Why did they have to be *his* bodyguards? he railed silently. His plan to interrogate Phanes was slipping away before his eyes. With a grudging nod at the stallholder, he paid for his food and sidled after the trio. It was soon apparent that the moneylender was making the rounds of some debtors. The reactions of the shopkeepers who saw him was uniform: one of surprise and dismay. Yet their attempts to avoid Phanes, or to shut their premises, all failed. His two companions were adept at jamming their feet in doorways or seizing men by the scruff of the neck and pinning them up against a wall. This was done in the most upfront of ways, without even a look as to how the passers-by might react. Any thoughts that Hanno might have had about tackling the pair disappeared. Not only were they armed with short cudgels, but they were well able to handle themselves. To have any chance of tackling Phanes, the Greek would have to leave his men behind. Morose because this did not seem likely, he dogged their footsteps for more than an hour.

By this stage, Hanno was no longer paying such close attention. On a less busy street, he had nearly caught up with the bodyguards when he noticed the Greek's absence. Hastily, he feigned interest in the display of ironmongery outside a shop. On impulse, he bought a small but sharp knife. When he turned, the bruisers' gaze was locked on the staircase that led up to the shrine's entrance, which told him where Phanes had gone. Slipping the blade under his tunic and into the waistband of his undergarment, he walked right past them. There was little room to pass on the stairs. Soothsayers promised readings of the future, men were selling hens suitable for sacrifice, or votive lamps and trinkets to leave as offerings. Half an as bought Hanno a tiny clay amphora; anyone who glanced at him would assume he was another worshipper. At the top, six mighty fluted columns supported a triangular, richly decorated portico. In the centre was a painted figure of a winged woman standing with a sceptre in her hands. On either side sailors in ships reached up to her in supplication. Fortuna, he thought. The moneylender prays to Fortuna for good luck. It felt quite apt.

Great wooden doors framed the entrance to the *cella*, the long narrow room that formed the main part of the temple. A group of people clustered there around a stout, robed priest with a beard, listening as he held forth on the goddess' intent for Capua and its citizens. There was no sign of Phanes. Hanno padded inside, wary and alert. His eyes adjusted slowly to the gloom, which was alleviated by an occasional oil lamp on a bronze stand. The chamber's walls had been decorated with panelled murals of Fortuna: she stood with her father, Jupiter Optimus Maximus, and other deities; presided over fields of ripe wheat as the goddess Annonaria; watched chariots race at a stadium while men placed wagers. Hanno did not like the last depiction, that of Mala Fortuna, in which she stood over the entrance to Hades, watching as those who had died through bad luck filed past with miserable faces. Although she was not one of his gods, he offered her a prayer nonetheless, asking that his fortunes remain good – while he was in Capua at least.

At the far end of the room stood a low altar. Behind it was an enormous painted statue of Fortuna, her lips curved in an enigmatic smile. It was a little disquieting that her dark-rimmed eyes seemed to follow Hanno as he wove his way through the throng, but he told himself it was just his imagination. The other devotees were a mixture of men and women, young and old. Everyone needed Fortuna on their side, thought Hanno, from the crone who needed money to buy food to the man who was fond of gambling and the wife who could not conceive.

Phanes was standing near the altar, his head bowed. Hanno slipped in behind him, grateful for the loud prayers of an elderly woman nearby. He moved past the Greek to place his figurine on the altar among the other offerings, confirming with a sidelong glance that he'd found his man. Poised behind his quarry once more, his heart began to race. Whatever he did would have to be rapid and brief. It had to take place within the cella and in a manner that didn't alarm those around them. He doubted that anyone would intervene but if the two brutes outside were alerted to what was going on, he'd be lucky to escape with his life – even though he was now armed. Steady, he thought. It will go to plan. Soon Atia will have less to worry about, and I will know where to find Aurelia. That thought was calming.

He reached under his tunic and took hold of the knife's hilt, readying himself. When Phanes began to turn, Hanno slid forward on the balls of his feet. He grabbed the Greek's left hand and twisted it behind his back, at the same time tickling the skin over his right kidney with the blade's tip. With his lips against Phanes' ear, he whispered, 'Keep turning. If anyone looks, smile at them. Do not cry for help, or I'll slide this iron in so deep that it comes out of your filthy chest.'

Phanes obeyed. His head twisted. 'Who in Hades' name are you? What do you want?'

Hanno shoved him forward a step. 'That's an odd question for a stinking moneylender to ask. I'd wager you have plenty of enemies. That's why you employ those two apes outside.'

'They'll gut you when this is done,' hissed Phanes. He squawked with pain as Hanno pushed the knife hard enough to draw blood.

'Shut your mouth. Keep walking,' ordered Hanno, smiling at an old man who was gawping. He guided the unresisting Greek over to the side of the room, where there were fewer people. By the mural of Fortuna at the games, he paused, as if to admire it. 'Are Gaius and Atia Fabricius familiar to you?' Phanes stiffened and his heart leaped.

'Yes.'

'They owe you money.'

'A great deal,' agreed the Greek.

'Are their names among those that Calavius will receive later?'

Phanes' head twisted again, this time in surprise, and Hanno poked him again with the knife. 'Keep your eyes to the front. Answer the damn question.'

'Yes. They're on the list.'

'No, they're not!' Hanno gave the blade a vicious little twist, and Phanes had to bite back a moan. 'You are going to leave their names off it. If you don't, I will hunt you down and cut you into little pieces. That's after I've cut your balls off and fed them to you. The same will happen to you if you harm them or any of their family. Understand?'

'Y-yes.' The Greek sounded confused as well as terrified.

Hanno could see beads of sweat trickling down through Phanes' oiled hair, which pleased him immensely. 'Good. Do you know their daughter as well?'

'Aurelia?'

'Where is she?'

'I would have thought you'd know that,' muttered the Greek. 'You seem aware of everything else.'

'Tell me,' demanded Hanno.

Phanes let out a little *phhh* of contempt. 'I believe that she's living with her husband, on his land, to the north of the city. They were married a short time ago.'

Hanno closed his eyes. Disappointment washed over him. These were two eventualities that he hadn't counted on. That Aurelia would already be married and that not all citizens were too scared to remain on their properties. It was as if the Greek sensed his dismay. With a powerful wriggle and twist, he jerked free of Hanno's grasp. Whirling, he slammed Hanno's hand against the wall. The knife clattered to the floor and Phanes clawed at Hanno's eyes with hooked fingers. As Hanno lurched backwards, the Greek snatched at his neck cloth instead. It wasn't knotted, so it came away with ease. A heartbeat's pause; a disbelieving gasp from Phanes. Hanno could almost feel the 'F'-shaped scar itching.

'You're a runaway slave?' The Greek's voice was loud and shrill.

The game was up. Hanno ran for the door, shoving past everyone in his way.

'Stop that slave!' Phanes cried. 'He attacked me with a knife. Stop him!'

A middle-aged man stepped into Hanno's path, arms outstretched. Hanno roared a war cry, and the man abruptly changed his mind.

Hanno pounded towards the entrance, elbowing a youth who grabbed at him in the face. There were a few ineffectual attempts to seize him by the tunic, but he was running at full tilt now. Past a goggle-eyed old woman and into the open air. From behind him, Phanes' voice, growing louder. Hanno cursed. Unless the Greek's bodyguards were deaf, they would be waiting for him at the bottom of the steps.

Slowing, he walked to the top of the staircase. Sure enough, the heavies were staring upward, scowls on their faces and cudgels in hand. Every face in between was watching too. Don't alarm any of them, Hanno thought. He needed the men on the steps to remain calm and Phanes' thugs to feel confident. With a casual smile, he began to descend. 'I'll come down to you,' he called. The bodyguards glanced at one another, grinning with delight. So far, so good, thought Hanno. His stomach was tying itself in knots, but he waited until he was three-quarters of the way down before making his move.

Grabbing a large woven basket full of poultry from a startled boy, he hurled it straight at Phanes' men. Loud curses, a crash, the sound of splintering wicker. Feathers flew. The air filled with the distressed squawking of hens. Hanno didn't wait to see what happened next. With a great leap, he bounded down the last few steps and into the crowd. Worming his way between the passers-by, he was careful not to look at people's faces. To his relief, no one tried to stop him. Ten paces, twenty, then thirty, forty from the base of the staircase. He slowed his pace, assumed a casual gait. Already few would realise that he was the one being sought. All eyes were on the temple.

Nonetheless, at the first alleyway, Hanno decided to leave the main thoroughfare. Pausing at the corner, he looked back for a moment. Phanes was just visible on the temple steps. His face was purple and he was screaming abuse, no doubt at his hapless bodyguards. Hanno smiled as he turned and sped away. A fresh strip of cloth ripped from his tunic would cover his neck; he would soon become just another member of the crowd. His satisfaction didn't last, though. It was not safe to remain in Capua. Phanes would not rest until he was found.

There was a bitter taste in his dry mouth. What need had he to stay when Aurelia was not here? There was no point either in heading off on a wild-goose chase to find her. She was a married woman now, with a whole new life that he could never be part of. Any chance of finding Agesandros had vanished too. His best option was to return to his phalanx and his duty, and to forget them both. *Try* to forget them.

Fortuna was so capricious, he thought ruefully. He had threatened Phanes and made good his escape, but in the process been denied a chance ever to see Aurelia again. He hardened his heart. Mutt was right. There was no place for women in war. From now on, his only focus would be the Carthaginian cause.

Yet for all his resolve, Hanno felt a deep sadness as he walked away.

Chapter XII

North of Capua

Aurelia regarded her own face in the bronze mirror. Her complexion was good at the moment: her face unmarked by her inner turmoil. Even her hair, which Elira was brushing, had a lustrous gloss to it. It was as if her body had decided to act in the opposite manner to the way she felt, which was isolated and miserable. There was another reason that might lie behind how well she looked, but Aurelia didn't want to think about that. Better for the moment to wallow in her loneliness – her new and constant companion. It wasn't surprising. Her new abode was in the countryside, in a household of slaves whom she didn't know. Lucius' mother had long since passed away, and his father was a crusty old man whose only interest lay in the running of his estates. Lucius, whose company she now felt wary of, was rarely present either. Family business and political dealings kept him in Capua much of the time. When he was home, he tended to spend his days with his father, or out on the farm. They slept together, but the bedroom activity tended to be physical rather than verbal. Aurelia didn't know why this was. She suspected it was because that they were now man and wife. Other than trying to get her with child, there was no need for him to make any effort with her. Although she still didn't love Lucius, she missed the attention he had showered upon her. It was possible that she had the power to change the way he acted towards her, but Aurelia wasn't ready to share her secret with him yet.

There was an occasional dry letter from her mother, which helped a little. Her father was alive; he was serving with the legions who shadowed Hannibal's forces; there had been no further word from Quintus; the olives had been harvested, and preparations for winter on the farm were going well. There had been no sign of enemy troops in their area of Campania, which justified Atia's decision to return home with Agesandros and the slaves. Not a word about Phanes, which she hoped meant that her mother was managing to meet his payments. The news eased Aurelia's isolation only a fraction. If it hadn't been for Elira, who had stayed with her after the wedding, her loneliness would have been unbearable.

Despite sharing many confidences with the Illyrian, Aurelia had not yet let her in on her innermost thoughts either. Her eyes flickered, studying Elira's profile behind her, brush in hand, deft strokes freeing her hair from the tangles that had formed overnight. She would have to mention it soon, she decided, or Elira would guess. She wouldn't be able to conceal her pregnancy much longer. At first, Aurelia had been unsure. Lucius had lain with her enough times but she had somehow felt sure that his seed would not have taken root. That had been but wishful thinking. A second month had gone by without the usual bleeding and her confidence had turned to anxiety. Of recent days, her belly had begun to tighten a fraction. Some mornings, she felt a little nauseous. The last of her doubts had been dispelled. Before long, the swelling would be impossible to miss, especially when she bathed. Soon, thought Aurelia, I will have to tell Elira soon. And Lucius. Or to act. Guilt filled her that she could even contemplate such a thing, yet the thought wouldn't go away. Aurelia didn't wish the baby any harm; the idea kept popping up because she had not resigned herself completely to the cold reality of her life as Lucius' wife. Thus she had not been able to stop herself eavesdropping on the kitchen slaves talking about ending unwanted pregnancies: they used rue, but Aurelia had no idea where to find such a plant, how to prepare it or even what dose to take. There were old women in back alleyways in Capua who dealt in herbs and potions, but she had no pressing reason to go to the city. Her duty was to remain here, unless Lucius took her with him. Stop it! she commanded herself. Her pregnancy had not come about through violence or mistreatment. There was no point in trying to terminate it. Apart from anything, the process was dangerous. Her mother had told her once of a slave who had bled to death after a botched attempt at abortion.

And if she lost the baby, she would just have to get pregnant all over again. That would be Lucius' – and everyone else's – wish. Her purpose now was to provide his family with a male heir, and as soon as possible. Atia's words came back to her. If she could carry a baby to term, and, even better, swiftly produce a second and a third child, her existence would become much easier. Lucius would leave her alone. Her life would be filled with the joy of raising her family. If Fortuna granted her favour, she might even find a lover, someone who thought of her not as a brood mare, but a woman. It was hard not to think that doing nothing was the best course of action. An image of Hanno came to mind, but, ruthless, Aurelia shoved it away. The bitter truth of it was that she would never see him again. Would never spend her life with him. It had to be better to accept her situation as it was. Otherwise she would condemn herself to a life of utter misery, in which the only fleeting happiness to be had was in her head – and that was the path to madness.

It was for the best that she was expecting Lucius' child, she decided. That was part of her job now. Slyly, she slipped a hand to her belly. A thrill of excitement – of joy – touched her. It still didn't feel real that she could have a baby growing within her. I will carry this child to term. For all that it is Lucius', it will be mine too. And I will love it and cherish it, boy or girl. That will be my task in life. The decision pleased her. This was an area that lay, as so much else did not, within her control.

'You look happy, mistress,' said Elira.

Startled, she masked her expression. 'Do I?'

The Illyrian regarded her through the mirror. 'Yes. I thought I saw the hint of a smile, and the gods know that you don't do that often.'

Aurelia scrambled for a plausible lie. 'I like you brushing my hair. It looks good.'

'You don't normally smile when I do it.'

'Well, today I am enjoying it,' Aurelia declared in a tone that brooked no argument.

Elira's eyebrows arched, but she said nothing.

Aurelia considered telling the Illyrian now, but immediately decided against it. They were in too public a place: just outside the marital bedroom, which gave on to the main courtyard. To have any chance of beautifying herself well – something she had taken to doing since her marriage – Aurelia needed daylight, hence her current position, on a stool. She had grown used to the slaves' stares and, in time, they to her ritual. The majority now didn't give her a second glance as they moved to and fro, performing their daily duties, but that didn't mean they wouldn't eavesdrop on her conversation. It could wait until later, when she took her usual walk with Elira to the nearby river.

Deep in thought, she paid no heed to Statilius, the thin major domo, as he minced around the walkway from the tablinum. It was only when he gave a polite cough that she looked up. 'Yes?'

'Mistress. Your lady mother is here,' he announced.

Aurelia blinked. 'My mother?' she repeated foolishly.

'That's right, mistress,' he said, full of self-importance. 'She has come on a visit. I've already sent a slave to find the master and let him know.' He eyed the tablinum doors, which were open. 'I offered her refreshment, a room to change, but she refused both.'

Still trying to take it in, Aurelia rose, gesturing Elira to stop. Atia swept into view a moment later. A body slave scurried behind her.

'Mother.' Although things had been awkward between them when last they met, Aurelia felt a rush of warmth towards Atia. She fought her urge to run. That was what a child would do. She walked instead. 'What a surprise! What a pleasure!'

Atia's lips turned upwards in reflex, but her eyes remained cold as they kissed. 'Daughter.'

Aurelia's stomach lurched. Something was wrong. 'Have you had word about Father, or Quintus? Are they all right?'

'I assume so. There have been no letters since I last wrote to you.' Atia pulled her dark green woollen cloak closer around her shoulders. 'It's so cold out here. How can you bear to sit in just a dress?'

'There's better light,' Aurelia explained, her mind racing. Why then was her mother here? 'Come. One of the reception rooms has underfloor heating and a fire.' To Elira, she said, 'Fetch some warmed wine.' To Statilius: 'See that a suitable lunch is prepared.'

The reception chamber was a well-decorated room used to entertain guests. Everything about it oozed wealth. The plaster on each wall had been painted red; over this background, exotic scenes portrayed images from myths: Aeneas meeting Dido for the first time; Orpheus looking back at Eurydice at the gates of the underworld; Romulus and Remus sucking the wolf. There were hardwood dressers, comfortable couches and a mahogany table with an ornately carved top. A silver candelabrum hung from the ceiling. Aurelia saw none of it. As soon as they were within, she closed the door. Her mother's face was still cold, unnerving her. 'You are always welcome, Mother, but your visit comes as a complete surprise. Why did you not send word before you?'

'There was no time.'

'I don't understand.'

'How could you, living out here, far from the city? It's Phanes.'

There was a rush of blood to Aurelia's head. Lightheaded, she put out a hand to the wall to steady herself.

'Are you well, child?' Atia was by her side, her tone at last that of a mother.

'Y-yes. I'm fine. You mentioned Phanes.'

'I haven't mentioned the piece of filth in my letters because there was no point. Somehow, I was managing to keep up with the payments. There was no contact with him, which suited me.' Atia took a deep breath. She looked older and more vulnerable than Aurelia had ever seen her.

She touched her mother's arm. 'Please go on.'

'I was in Capua last week, buying supplies. As usual, I was staying with Martialis. Phanes must have eyes everywhere, because he appeared at the house the day after I arrived. He told the most outlandish story about being attacked in a temple in the town.' Aurelia's mouth opened, but a frosty look from her mother silenced her. 'While he was worshipping, someone slipped in behind him with a knife. It was no robbery. They told him he had to forget all about our debts.'

'Just our debts? No one else's?'

'He mentioned only our family.'

Confusion filled Aurelia. 'Who was it that attacked him?'

'I thought you might have the answer to that.'

Hanno? thought Aurelia. No, it couldn't be. 'Agesandros?'

'No. He's on the estate. Every slave in the place can vouch for him.'

'Gaius?'

'He would never do such a thing! Besides, he's away with the army. Phanes said it was a slave. There was a struggle. He managed to break free and rip a scarf from around the man's throat before the wretch fled. There was an "F" branded into his flesh. I know of only one slave who would potentially do such a thing. As far as I can recall, however, Hanno didn't have a mark like that.' Atia's eyes searched Aurelia's. Somehow, she kept her face impassive.

'No, he didn't. Anyway, how could it have been him?' Aurelia exulted even as pain stabbed into her heart. *He must have come back to try and find me! So that was how he came by such a terrible scar. Why didn't he tell me what had happened to him?*

'I don't know, child. Hannibal's army wasn't so far away at the time,' snapped Atia. 'Besides, what other slave would assault Phanes on our behalf?'

'I have no idea.' It had to be Hanno, thought Aurelia. There was no one else it could have been. Her heart leaped with joy, and a crazy notion of travelling to Capua to find him filled her head. Her mother's unhappy expression soon made her delight dissipate, however. 'What else did Phanes say?'

'That he would not be threatened in such a way. He laughed and told me that his bodyguards were more than capable of dealing with one rogue slave. Then he doubled the repayments with immediate effect. When I protested, he waved the loan agreement in my face. Because we have missed so many monthly instalments, he can charge what he likes, when he likes.'

'You couldn't pay that much!' cried Aurelia in horror.

'I had three days to raise the money,' said Atia heavily. 'In the end, the only thing I could do was to sell part of the farm.'

'No!'

'I had no choice, child. It was that, or Phanes would have gone to the court to have the whole property seized. As it is, I won't be able to meet the next payment without selling another parcel of land. I've written to your father, but I doubt that there is anything he can do to help. Martialis can't either. He has almost beggared himself already lending us money.'

A chasm of despair opened at Aurelia's feet. What did you do, Hanno? she shouted inside her head. Instead of making things better, you've made them far worse. 'What are you going to do?'

A helpless shrug. 'Sell off pieces of the farm a bit at a time. Try to get the best prices I can, although few men are buying at the moment. Perhaps I can hold on to some land until such time as your father can pay Phanes off.'

'There must be something we can do!'

'Pray,' said her mother. 'Pray that a lightning bolt strikes down that motherless cur before we're ruined. He'd suck the last drop of blood from a corpse, I'd swear it.'

'I can speak to Lucius,' said Aurelia on impulse.

'I won't hear of it. It's shameful enough that the family will be ruined. Asking for help is beneath us.'

'Surely it's better than losing the farm?'

'No, it is not. Your father will win enough glory in the war to renew our fortunes.'

'How do you know that? What if he's killed? Then where would you be?' Aurelia expected her mother to slap her, but it was Atia who looked as if she'd been struck. It made her realise how fragile was the façade that her mother presented to the world, and how easy it was for her, with a husband who was not away at war. 'I'm sorry,' she whispered. 'I shouldn't have said that.'

'No, you shouldn't.' Atia's voice shook. 'The gods will protect Fabricius, as they did before. Quintus too. That is what I believe.'

'And I also,' said Aurelia in as confident a tone as she could manage. Praying was her only method of helping her father and brother, but there *was* something tangible she could do about Phanes. The seed of a daring plan had germinated in her mind. Her mother couldn't stop her from asking Lucius to help. The timing couldn't be better either. He would be delighted when she told him about her pregnancy. Pleased enough perhaps to bring pressure to bear upon the moneylender? Aurelia wasn't sure, but she had to do something to defend her family. What a pity it was that Hanno hadn't just killed Phanes, she thought savagely. Yet to have done so might have placed him in mortal danger. Despite the repercussions of his actions, she was intensely glad that that hadn't happened. Let his gods keep him safe too, she pleaded.

Elira arrived with the wine. Once it was poured, Aurelia was quick to dismiss her. Who better to tell first about her pregnancy than her mother? It would lift Atia's mood too. 'I've got some news for you as well,' she said, suddenly feeling shy. 'Good news, for a change.'

'You're with child!' said Atia, quick as a flash.

'How did you know?' gasped Aurelia.

'A mother's intuition.' At last, a warm smile. 'How many months are you gone?'

'Two, I think.'

'Very early days, then. You mustn't be complacent about it. A lot can happen in the first three to four months. It's common to lose the baby.' Aurelia's face fell, and her mother took her hand. 'We shall ask all the gods and goddesses to make sure that that doesn't happen! It's still wonderful news, my child. Does Lucius know?'

'Not yet.'

'When are you going to tell him?'

'Soon. For now, I want it to be our secret,' said Aurelia with a wink. She would wait until her mother had left before speaking with her husband. In fact, she would delay it until he had bedded her before doing so. Perhaps Elira could give her some advice on pleasing him? Her cheeks warmed at the immodest thought, but her resolve did not weaken. She would do everything within her power to aid her family. Aurelia didn't know the exact details, but she had heard Quintus and Gaius talking and laughing with one another on enough occasions to know that bearing children wasn't the only way to please Lucius. She just hoped that her newfound eagerness didn't arouse his suspicions.

Aurelia's opportunity came less than a week later. Atia had departed after just a few days, citing her need to return to the estate. Their relationship had improved in the short time together and they had taken an emotional farewell of each other. The day after, Lucius returned from a successful trip to Neapolis. He arrived with a rare gift for Aurelia, a gold necklace decorated with tiny rubies. She was delighted with it, especially as it gave her the pretext of seducing him by way of thanks. Lucius' good humour was increased by the warmth of Aurelia's welcome, the lavish dinner that was served that evening and the keen manner with which she drew him to bed afterwards. Once there, Aurelia was glad of the courage granted her by the sly cup of wine she'd consumed before leaving the dining room. When Lucius tried to roll on top of her as usual, she swiftly moved away, pushing him on to his back. Before he could do or say much, she had begun kissing his chest and belly, using her fingers to roam all over his hips and thighs. His surprise was clear as she let her mouth roam down to his groin, where it had never been before, but he did nothing to stop her. The little gasps that left his lips in the moments that followed, and the pressure of his fingers on her head, told Aurelia that Elira's advice had been accurate.

Afterwards, he took her in his arms, which was rare in itself. Aurelia nestled against him, delighted by his evident pleasure. Deliberately, she said nothing.

'That was quite a welcome,' he murmured.

'I've missed you.'

'Clearly.' His voice was wry.

A silence fell, more comfortable than any between them before. Lucius gently stroked her hair, another new development. Aurelia wondered if it was time to tell him about her pregnancy, but emboldened by her success, decided to follow more of Elira's counsel. A little while later, her hand casually strayed downwards again. A few strokes and she felt him stiffen.

'Gods, but you are eager tonight!'

Panic bubbled up inside Aurelia but she did not let her fingers stop. 'I have missed you. That is allowed, isn't it? And I love my new necklace. Besides, you are more than rising to the occasion, husband.'

He laughed and lay back, closing his eyes. It was just the opportunity Aurelia wanted. If he'd been looking at her, it would have been much harder to climb on top of him and ease his rigid length inside her. The moment she did, however, his eyes jerked open. 'What are you doing?'

Rather than answer, Aurelia moved her hips to and fro, as Elira had told her. To her surprise, it felt very good – better than anything they had ever done before. Her enjoyment was enhanced by the way that his face kept morphing into Hanno's. She felt a momentary guilt, but it was too pleasurable to banish the image.

'Aurelia?'

'Only trying to give you pleasure,' she whispered. 'Shall I stop?'

A faint groan; a muttered word that might have been 'No'. Gaining confidence, Aurelia found her rhythm, rocked backwards and forwards as he writhed in ecstasy beneath her. When his hands reached out to grasp her buttocks, she let him guide the speed at which they moved.

It wasn't long before Lucius climaxed. He made more noise than ever before. Aurelia felt a deep satisfaction as she rolled off him, not least because if their coupling had been that enjoyable, it could only be better with Hanno.

'Where did you learn to do that?' he asked, intruding on her fantasy.

'My mother gave me some advice,' lied Aurelia, knowing that he would never dare mention it to Atia.

A sleepy smile. 'I'm in her debt.'

'And I in yours.'

His eyebrows rose. 'Why's that?'

Moving to lie her chin on his chest, she gazed into his eyes. 'You are to be a father.'

A confused look; then a surprised one. Last of all, an expression of unadulterated joy. 'You're pregnant?'

She nodded, smiling with satisfaction. 'Only two months so far, but I thought you'd want to know.'

'Ceres and Tellus be praised – that's wonderful news!'

She chuckled as he touched her belly. 'There's nothing to feel yet.'

'How can you be sure then?'

'I've missed two cycles. Besides, a woman knows these things.'

'You told your mother when she was here?'

'Of course. But you're the only other person who knows.'

He squeezed her to him, before self-consciously loosening his grip.

She pulled his arm back around her. 'You won't cause me any harm!'

He gave a sheepish grin, which made him look very young. 'Let's not say a word until you begin to show. It can be our secret.' And then he was off, waxing lyrical about how proud his father would be, his favourite boys' names, the games he would teach their son.

Aurelia joined in from time to time, agreeing with everything Lucius said. She offered up a silent prayer that the child was indeed male. The second baby could be a girl, but the first, for a multitude of reasons, had to be a boy. When he was done, she kissed him on the lips. 'You'll make a fine father.'

'And you will give me a strong son!'

The iron was hot, thought Aurelia. It was time to strike. 'It is such a shame that my mother wasn't able to enjoy the wondrous news.'

'I don't understand. Her visit went well, did it not?'

'Yes, it did.' She let her voice tail away.

'What then was the reason? Is she ill? Has there been bad news of your father or brother?'

'No, it was nothing like that.'

'Tell me.' His voice was commanding but gentle.

Fortuna help me, pleaded Aurelia. 'It's nothing that concerns you. Just a family problem.' She kept her gaze averted from his. A blaze of hope warmed her insides as he took her chin and tilted her face upwards.

'You can tell me.'

Out it all came, told in suitably sorrowful tones. How her father had borrowed from Phanes after a few years of disastrous crops. He had kept up with his payments until going off to war. The subsequent pressure her mother had been under. Phanes' threats; his increase of the interest rates; how Martialis had helped as best he could. She didn't mention the attack on the moneylender – bringing Hanno into the equation was not something she wished to do – merely relating that of recent days Phanes had raised the monthly amounts so high that her mother had had to sell part of their farm. 'I'm sorry,' she said, putting a tremble into her voice. 'I shouldn't have told you. Mother and Father would be so angry with me if they knew.'

'I won't mention it to a soul,' he promised. 'If it's money that they need, I can lend them—'

'Thank you, but no. They're too proud to accept even a single drachm from you. Martialis practically had to force my mother into taking his money, and he's known the family for thirty years.' Aurelia didn't say any more. Instead, she prayed that Lucius would come up with the notion of pressuring Phanes himself and think of it as his idea. Long moments went by. Her heart thudded off her ribs so fast that she worried he might feel it.

'Phanes, you say his name is?'

'That's right.'

'And he lives in Capua?'

'Yes.'

'I'll see if someone can't pay him a visit. Persuade him to think again on your family's debts.' He smiled as she looked up at him. 'It'll be nothing illegal. The dog just needs to reduce the payments to a fraction of their current level, so that your mother can continue to pay them. That's not unreasonable, given that there's a war on. Once your father returns, no doubt laden with honours from the Senate, the situation can be reassessed.'

'You would do this for me?'

'Of course! You are going to bear me a son. Besides that, it's but a small thing.'

Genuine tears of gratitude and joy flowed from Aurelia's eyes then. 'Thank you,' she whispered.

'I will have a slave carry a letter to Capua tomorrow. There are people in the city who can look after this matter for me. Consider it done.'

She kissed him with real feeling. When her hand moved downwards from his chest, however, he stopped her. 'A man needs his rest! Wake me again in the morning and I'll be happy to oblige.' Content that she had done enough, Aurelia relaxed into his arms. Lucius was a good husband, she thought. For the first time, she wondered if their life together could actually be *happy*. Yet that didn't stop her thinking of Hanno again. Didn't stop her fantasising that it was he who lay beside her, not Lucius. Fuelled by thoughts of how she had just behaved, her imagination ran riot. The temptation to ease the throbbing feeling in her groin grew too great. Moving with great care, she rolled out of Lucius' embrace and on to her own side of the bed. He moved a little and then settled down again. When she was sure that he had not woken, Aurelia lay back. Her eyes closed, and an image of Hanno, naked, entered her mind. Her hand slipped down of its own volition, dipped into the wetness between her legs, began to rub.

As she reached the heights of ecstasy, she felt no guilt.

Calena, Samnium

It was a cold, blustery afternoon. The sun had vanished behind banks of grey cloud. Looming, swirling, ever changing in shape, they filled the sky from one horizon to the other, as they had since daybreak. The gale had risen at some stage during the night, and it showed no sign of abating. The Roman troops had learned to expect such weather. Mid-winter storms off the Adriatic were a regular occurrence in this part of Italy. The camp's position on high ground didn't help. Gusts of wind battered the tents, alternately pulling taut and slackening the guy ropes in a way that threatened to see at least some become airborne before the day's end. The bitter air meant that the only soldiers who were abroad were those who had to be. Sentries on the ramparts of the large camp huddled below the level of the wooden battlements, with barely their heads visible. An occasional messenger hurried down one or other of the avenues. A mule-driver led his charges back from whatever scant grazing they'd found that day. Groups of unfortunate legionaries, who were being punished for misdemeanours, manoeuvred miserably to and fro on the open ground beyond the defences, threw javelins or went at each other with wooden swords and shields. Their officers stood in thick woollen cloaks nearby, pouring scorn on their efforts.

In the lines of Corax's and Pullo's maniple, everything was quiet. Men huddled in their tents, only venturing outside to answer a call of nature or to fetch fuel for the braziers that the more resourceful *contubernia* had obtained. Like his comrades, Quintus was not on duty – he had been on a two-day patrol that had returned the previous evening. He was inside too, lying in the midst of the nine other men who shared the tent. As the most senior, he had the best spot, by the small, three-legged brazier. Even better, he had a number of sheepskins to lie on: some bartered for, others the winnings from dice games – or plain stolen. Three months in camp with just an occasional skirmish against the Carthaginians meant that the priorities in life had changed somewhat. They were now all about how to make one's existence in a leather tent in the cold and damp of winter more bearable. Fuel and bedding were always needed; so too were rations that warmed a man's insides. Choice items like cheese or wine fetched premium prices.

Quintus had soon discovered that Severus, Rutilus' former lover, was a born scavenger. It didn't seem to matter what was needed; Severus could find it. Quintus had learned equally quickly to turn a blind eye to his soldier's pilfering. The reason for this was simple. Everyone in the camp was at it; the trick was never to be caught. It helped that experienced centurions such as Corax tended 'not to notice' what was going on. At the start of winter, he'd made one pronouncement: that anyone caught stealing from their own maniple or those that directly neighboured it would receive thirty lashes. It hadn't taken much to read between the lines that the units further away, or property outside the camp, were fair game.

There had been a tasty stew for the midday meal: the best food Quintus had had in days. Luxuriating in the comfort of his warm bedding, he lay back and let the chatter wash over him. For the first time in he couldn't remember how long, he didn't want to brood over Rutilus. That was all he'd done since the fight at the pass: simmer, and plot how he could revenge himself upon Macerio. Trouble was, it was hard to accomplish such a thing when there was no fighting going on. In the camp, everyone lived cheek by jowl; a man could barely take a shit without half a dozen others watching. The best opportunities to be had were in the thick of combat. At times like that, most men didn't see what was happening five paces away, let alone ten. To his frustration, the war had ground to a halt since the onset of winter. That was the way it would remain until the fine weather returned in the spring. I'll get the bastard eventually, thought Quintus. One way or another. Until then, it wasn't a crime to relax a little in the safety of his tent mates' company. To distract himself, he focused on what was going on around him. Five of the men were loudly playing dice. Filthy jokes filled the air; many concerned the farts one of them was emitting. Severus was whispering with two of the others, no doubt planning an expedition to thieve something new. The last man was dozing. At moments like this, Quintus reflected, life wasn't too bad.

'Crespo!' The voice came from outside the tent.

With a silent curse, he ignored it.

'Crespo! Corax wants you. Now.'

The request was unusual enough, but why was Macerio the messenger? Wide awake now and full of suspicion, Quintus sat up. His men were staring at him. 'Don't just look at me,' he barked. 'One of you unlace the flap!' To Macerio, he growled, 'I'm coming.' Quickly, he strapped on his sword belt and donned his helmet. Throwing on his cloak, he stepped over the huddle of bodies and blankets to the entrance. Caution stopped him from exiting the tent. Was Macerio capable of trying to kill him in broad daylight, in the midst of their own unit? Surely not. Quintus could feel his men's eyes on his back, and he began to move. The danger from Macerio was small, and he could not be seen to be indecisive.

'What the hell are you at?' Macerio's voice dripped scorn.

'I'm here,' he growled, emerging. He made an obvious show of keeping his hand on his sword hilt.

Macerio regarded him mockingly. He was also wearing a woollen cloak, but his hands were empty. Quintus flushed, but he didn't move his hand. Not after what had happened to Rutilus. His eyes flickered left to right, and behind him, over the tent. He saw no one. Relaxing a fraction, he glared at Macerio.

'Looking for someone?'

'Fuck you, Macerio. You know what I'm doing, and why,' he said, almost amiably. 'What does Corax want?'

'Buggered if I know. I was on the way back from the latrine trench, minding my own business, when he collared me by his tent. Told me to get you, double quick.'

Quintus grunted, unwilling to admit his confusion. Macerio said no more, and the conversation died. In silence, they walked past the tents of the hastati. To Quintus' even greater surprise, Corax was waiting for them by the entrance to his tent. An enigmatic smile played across his face. 'Crespo. Macerio.'

Stamping their feet, the pair snapped to attention. 'Sir!' they bellowed in unison.

'You're probably wondering why I ordered you here on such a miserable bloody day, when you've only just returned from patrol.' Corax's smile broadened. 'Course you're both too smart to say so. Well, I've got a little surprise for you. Step inside.' He indicated that they should enter.

Forgetting their enmity for a moment, Quintus and Macerio exchanged an astonished look. Neither had ever received such an invitation.

'Come on, come on. All the heat is escaping.'

Quintus expected to find Pullo within, but instead he found a familiar figure with prominent ears. Beside him, he heard Macerio's gasp of shock. 'Urceus!' Quintus cried. 'You're back.'

'Didn't think you could try to end the war without me, did you?' Urceus limped forward and embraced Quintus.

Even Macerio's perpetual sour expression eased into a grin. 'Welcome,' he said warmly, clapping Urceus on the shoulder. 'You're recovered, then?'

Urceus stepped back with a grimace. He rubbed his left thigh. 'This still pains me, but I can fight. And I wanted to get back to you boys. All of you.' His face darkened. 'I was sorry to hear about Rutilus.'

Not half as sorry as you'd be if you knew what happened to him, thought Quintus, feeling his grief scraped raw yet again. 'He will always be missed,' he said.

Beside him, Macerio muttered something that at face value sounded genuine.

'Many good men have already died. Plenty more will lose their lives in Rome's service before Hannibal has been defeated,' said Corax sombrely. He moved to stand before them, with his back to the brazier that stood in the middle of the large tent. 'But none of us will rest until the job has been done, will we?'

'No, sir!' the trio chorused.

'You're good soldiers, the three of you. That's why you are here. You are veterans too, not just of this summer's campaign, but of Trasimene as well. Urceus, you were also at the Trebia.'

Quintus wished that he could reveal the same about himself.

'Men like you are in short supply right now,' the centurion went on. 'You'll have heard that they're raising new, larger legions in Rome. The socii are enlisting many thousands more, but the vast majority of these new soldiers will be raw recruits. I don't know when the day to face Hannibal on a battlefield will come around again. But I do know that when it happens, we'll need soldiers with real backbone to stand and meet his troops. A rabble they might be, but they're not short of courage.'

'We'll fight, sir. Have no fear of that!' said Quintus.

Urceus and Macerio loudly voiced their agreement.

'Aye, you will,' cried Corax. 'And as hastati!'

For a moment, a shocked silence filled the tent. It was broken by the centurion's laughter. 'Aren't you pleased?'

'You're promoting us to hastati, sir?' Quintus' voice was incredulous.

'That's what I said.'

'It's a great honour, sir,' said Urceus gruffly. 'Thank you.'

'I'm very grateful, sir,' added Macerio. He shot a spiteful look at Quintus. 'As you know, when Urceus and I enlisted, we had to prove our income and, with it, our right to promotion to the infantry. Shouldn't Crespo here have to do the same?'

Quintus' stomach lurched. *The filthy bastard.* Macerio couldn't know his real background, but he knew well enough that Corax had taken him into the unit with few questions. It must have roused Macerio's suspicions. If he were questioned now, he could say nothing about his true identity without the risk of being thrown out of the velites and returned to his father's authority. That might not be quite what Macerio had intended, but it would still wreck his chances of staying in the infantry.

Corax's brows lowered. 'That won't be necessary. Crespo here has earned his salt, and he's proved his courage enough times for me to accept him at face value. In any case, I spend my time looking at damn paperwork. I have no desire to look at any more. He can produce the necessary details when this is all over.'

'As you say, sir,' Macerio said, failing to conceal his unhappiness.

Quintus threw the centurion a grateful look. 'I'll be sure to do that, sir.'

'Have yourselves an evening off duty,' ordered Corax. 'See the quartermaster. Tell him that I have promoted you. You might be able to persuade him to give you an advance on your pay.' He gave them a broad wink. 'The three of you can start training with the hastati in a couple of days, when your heads have stopped pounding.'

The three stood, not quite believing what they had just heard.

'Dismissed!'

They saluted and beat a hasty retreat. 'It's not that far to Larinum,' said Urceus the instant that they were outside. 'I say that we head there and get pissed out of our heads.'

'Sounds good to me,' replied Quintus. He glanced at Macerio, dreading that the blond-haired man would come along too. He couldn't think of anything worse than having to spend an evening in his company. To his relief, Macerio made some excuse about having a bellyache; he congratulated Urceus upon his return again and headed back to his tent, there 'to get some rest'.

Urceus gave an expressive shrug. 'All the more wine for us, eh?'

Quintus' loud agreement was as much from relief as a desire to get drunk. Nonetheless, he'd stay on his guard in Larinum. A dark alleyway there would be as good a place for Macerio to strike as in the middle of a battle.

Chapter XIII

In the event, Quintus' and Urceus' visit to Larinum passed off without incident. If Quintus were to be cynical about it, he knew that did not mean Macerio had not been lying in wait for him somewhere. The fact was they had both got so drunk that they each ended up taking a whore to the tiny rooms over the inn where they'd been drinking. They had spent the night there. Afterwards, Quintus couldn't remember if he'd actually lain with the woman, an attractive Gaul; she had told him with a knowing wink that he'd not been up to it but that if he wanted to come back another time, she'd only charge him half price. It appeared that she had been telling the truth, because when Urceus contracted a nasty bout of the pox soon afterwards, Quintus was (to his relief) unaffected. The incident reminded him of the advice his mother had given him once: if visiting brothels, it was best to frequent the more expensive ones.

Even if Quintus could have afforded such establishments, there was no chance of searching any out in the weeks that followed. Their move to the hastati proved so physically demanding that all he and Urceus wanted to do when they were off duty was sleep. Corax had always been a hard taskmaster, but now that they were *real* infantrymen, as he was fond of telling them, they actually *had* to be tough instead of just *thinking* they were. Velites were soft in comparison, he roared as they and the rest of the new recruits floundered along muddy tracks, carrying more armour and weapons than they'd ever had to in their lives. The centurion's forced marches happened at least two times a week, and were up to twenty miles in distance. On the intervening days, Corax had them train using wooden swords and shields that were twice as heavy as the real thing, swim in the nearby river, despite the temperature, or exercise by wrestling and running.

Sometimes the centurion let them have a 'day off' – which consisted of marching in formation with the rest of the hastati and learning to respond to the trumpeters. If anything, that was harder than the other activities, but eventually Quintus and the others learned to assume close order, form the 'saw' and charge at a moment's notice, stopping only to hurl their javelins. Teaching them to assume the position they would take in the triplex acies formation also came high on Corax's list of priorities. Maniples marched into a battle situation one century in front of the other. At a signal, the rearmost century had to be able to move rapidly to stand along-side the other century, ready to fight. The soldiers had to learn how, if things were going badly, to do the reverse in order to let the principes advance to the attack, and how, after a period of rest, they might be expected to return to the fray through similar gaps in the principes' maniples. The centurions had the hastati do this over and over again, sometimes on their own, and the rest of the time in concert with other maniples of principes and fellow hastati.

It was hardly surprising therefore that Quintus was delighted to be eventually given three days' sentry duty with Urceus, watching over the tent of one of the legion's tribunes. Two contubernia had been assigned the job: theirs and that of Macerio. The remaining soldiers, thirteen youngsters from the farmland to the south of Rome, were no less pleased at what was regarded as a soft duty. 'Guarding this is a damn sight better than training. Or having to keep the via principalis clean, like the others in our maniple,' said Urceus happily.

Quintus murmured in agreement. It was the second afternoon of their duty, and, as it had the previous day, the sun was shining from a pale, watery blue sky. The temperature wasn't warm, but as long as he walked to and fro, it was acceptable. Macerio and his comrades were stationed at the rear of the tent, so he didn't have to worry. After weeks of hard training, anything was better than sweating his balls off while Corax stood nearby, roaring abuse and bringing down his vine cane on anyone who didn't do exactly as he'd ordered. He didn't have to suffer the barbed comments of the hastati whom Macerio had befriended either. Quintus wondered if he had missed a trick when he had been promoted by not bothering to make himself popular within the maniple. His enemy had lost no time in ingratiating himself with soldiers who'd been in the unit for a while. So far, nothing had come of it, but there were half a dozen men who had taken a dislike to Quintus purely because of Macerio's poison.

There were other benefits to sentry duty, Quintus mused. Here they were able to observe the comings and goings of very senior officers. They had even seen Gnaeus Servilius Geminus, the surviving consul, and his colleague, Marcus Atilius Regulus, who had been elected to replace Flaminius. These two men had led the army since the dictator Fabius and Rufus, the Master of the Horse, had left office near the previous year's end. The evening before, both consuls had ridden past as dusk was falling. As usual, a large troop of *extraordinarii*, the best of the allied infantry and cavalry, had accompanied them. Quintus had looked for Gaius, but not seen him.

'Who d'you think will replace the consuls in March?'

Urceus looked at him as if he were mad. 'How should I fucking know? Who cares anyway? They're all the same as each other' – here he lowered his voice – 'a shower of arrogant arseholes who think they're better than us.'

Quintus snorted with laughter. There had been a time when he would have partially fallen into that category. Living as an ordinary infantryman had been an eye-opener, and often in a good way. Men such as Urceus and Rutilus had taken him at face value; he had learned to do the same. 'Fabius was all right.'

'He didn't needlessly throw our lives away, I suppose,' Urceus admitted. 'He probably looks down his nose at the likes of us, though.'

'Course he does,' said a familiar, mocking voice. 'They're all the same, those bloody senators and equestrians.'

'What are you doing here?' demanded Quintus, bridling at the mention of his own class. 'You're meant to be at the back of the tent.'

Macerio looked unconcerned. 'Corax isn't about, nor is the optio. The new lads have things covered. I thought I'd keep you company for a while.'

'You can piss off, more like,' snapped Quintus.

'Nice welcome, eh?' said Macerio to Urceus, who shrugged his shoulders. Once again, Quintus wondered if he should have confided in Urceus, told him what he thought – *knew* – had happened to Rutilus. It was almost as if he'd lost his chance, though. Macerio had acted the instant that Urceus had returned, seeking out his company, sharing his wine, treating him like the oldest of friends. Urceus, pleased by this welcome, had taken greatly to Quintus' enemy, which had made Quintus feel a little like an outsider. He worried that accusing Macerio of murdering Rutilus now might endanger his friendship with Urceus. That was not something he wanted to happen. The short, jug-eared man was now the only real comrade he had left. He got on well enough with Severus, but it wasn't the same as it had been with Rutilus, or even Big Tenner. Gods, but he missed Calatinus, and Gaius, his old friend. He even missed his father, if truth be known. But Calatinus was dead, and so too were Rutilus and Big Tenner. There was no way of contacting his father without endangering his position in the infantry. Quintus hardened his heart. He was immensely proud to be a hastatus, and he was not about to throw that away.

As Macerio fell into conversation with Urceus, Quintus tried not to let his displeasure show. The sooner an opportunity presented itself for him to slip a blade between his enemy's ribs, he thought, the better. The clatter of hooves brought him back to the present. As a small party of cavalrymen rode up to the tribune's tent, he was stunned to recognise Calatinus. Older, leaner, with new lines on his thin face, but still the same sturdily built man whom he'd known since before the Trebia. Quintus turned his head so that Calatinus wouldn't see him. Whatever happened, Macerio must not get so much as an inkling that they knew each other. One of the riders jumped down from his horse and approached. Quintus saluted. Beside him, he heard the others do the same. He eyed the man, similar in age to his father, whom he was relieved not to recognise. 'Can I help you, sir?'

'Is the tribune about?'

'No, sir. You'll find him at the camp headquarters.'

'I see. My thanks.' He turned away.

'Sir.' Quintus looked at the ground, willing Calatinus not to see him. A moment or two passed; he heard the rider who'd questioned him mount up and tell his companions what had been said. The horses began to move off. A relieved breath left Quintus' lips.

'Soldier!'

Quintus froze. It was Calatinus' voice.

'Soldier! A word.'

'One of them's calling you,' said Urceus.

Quintus made a show of appearing surprised.

'Best go and see what he wants,' advised Urceus.

'Get a move on, or we'll all find ourselves on a charge thanks to you,' added Macerio spitefully.

Quintus threw his enemy a filthy look and walked towards Calatinus, his heart pounding. He was grateful that the other cavalrymen had already ridden off. 'You called me, sir?' he asked loudly.

Calatinus made a show of lowering his voice a fraction, as if being conspiratorial. 'Where might a man find an extra supply of wine round here?'

From the corner of his eye, Quintus saw Macerio's and Urceus' knowing smiles. That was clever, he thought, as they began talking to each other. 'Well, sir,' he said, moving closer to Calatinus' horse, 'the man you want to talk to is . . .'

'Hail, Quintus!' whispered Calatinus, struggling not to smile, and failing. 'I prayed that you had made it this far.'

'Gods, but it's good to see you!' Quintus couldn't stop grinning either. He was glad to be holding his pilum and shield, otherwise the impulse to pull Calatinus into a bear hug might have been overwhelming. 'How is it that you survived the ambush after Trasimene?'

Calatinus' face darkened. 'Fortuna's tits, I don't know! The dogs came out of nowhere. My horse threw me when it was hit by an enemy spear. I was knocked out by the fall. When I woke up, there were two bodies on top of me. It was dark, and the enemy had vanished. All I had to do was crawl off into the woods and walk away.' Shame filled his eyes. 'I didn't even strike a blow.'

'That's not your fault,' hissed Quintus. 'I'm glad. Because of what happened, you're here.' He glanced at Macerio, who was watching again. His stomach twisted. 'As I say,' and he pointed, 'you'll find him in the quartermaster's offices.'

Calatinus realised at once what he was about. 'Near the quaestor's tent?'

'That's the one, sir,' Quintus replied.

'Let's have a talk tonight. My unit's tents face on to the *via praetoria*. We're the third lot in from the *porta decumana*,' said Calatinus in an undertone. Then, at full volume, 'I'm grateful, soldier.' A silver coin flashed into the air.

'I'll find you,' muttered Quintus, catching it. 'Glad to be of service, sir,' he added for Macerio's and Urceus' benefit. Calatinus rode off without as much as a backward glance; Quintus walked back to his comrades. He brandished the coin, a drachm. 'That was easily earned!'

'The things a man will do for the produce of the vine,' said Urceus with a wicked grin.

'It took a long time just to tell him where to find someone who'll flog him some wine.' Macerio's eyes were bright with suspicion.

'He asked me a few other things as well.' Quintus tapped the side of his nose. 'But they're between him and me.'

'Not happy with the arse bandit Severus, eh?' jibed Macerio. 'Urceus, he's looking to be a cavalryman's wife!'

Quintus thumped his scutum into Macerio's, sending the blond-haired man stumbling backwards. 'Watch your fucking mouth!'

'Can't you take a joke?' taunted Macerio.

'Peace, lads.' Urceus stepped between them. 'We can't be seen brawling outside a tribune's tent. Not unless you want to spend the rest of the winter digging latrines.'

At that moment, Quintus didn't care. His pilum was already levelled at Macerio. If his enemy moved, he would skewer him through his shield.

'Crespo,' Urceus cried, 'calm down! Someone will see. Macerio, step away.'

Quintus shook his head, regained control. Urceus was right. It wasn't worth being caught fighting by an officer. A few steps away, Macerio was already smiling as if nothing had happened. 'It was just a joke,' he said with a laugh.

No it wasn't, you whoreson, Quintus thought. I'll get you, one day.

'What's got into you, Crespo?' demanded Urceus. 'Macerio was only trying to get a rise out of you. Everyone knows you're not interested in men, like Severus or poor old Rutilus.'

'Rutilus, eh?' Quintus' temper boiled over again. 'Why don't you ask Macerio here about him?'

Urceus looked confused. 'Ask him what?'

'How he came to die from a wound in his back,' said Quintus from between gritted teeth.

'Well, there's only one reason that men take an injury like that,' replied Macerio smoothly. 'And we all know what it is.'

'You piece of filth!' cried Quintus, pushing against Urceus. 'Rutilus was no coward. He would never have run from the enemy.'

'What are you saying then?' growled Urceus, glancing from one to the other.

'He's just trying to cover up for his arse-loving friend,' said Macerio with a snicker.

The approach of the tribune whose tent they were guarding cut off all conversation. From then on, there were regular comings and goings, and Quintus had a chance to calm down. By the time Urceus asked him again and Macerio had returned to his post to the rear of the tent, he was able to explain what had happened the night that Hannibal had stampeded the cattle over the mountains.

Urceus swore loud and long. 'Can you prove this?'

'Of course not!'

'How do you know it was Macerio then?' Urceus gave him a sympathetic look. 'Just because Rutilus had never run before doesn't mean that he didn't that night. Stranger things have happened, you know.'

'It was Macerio. I'm sure of it,' said Quintus adamantly. He recounted what had happened when they had ambushed the drunk Numidians, a lifetime before.

Urceus became thoughtful. 'It was stupid to throw so close to you, but it must have been a mistake. I've made throws like that during combat myself. Macerio and you have never got along, right from the beginning, but he's a good lad at heart. He's not the type to try and murder a comrade, let alone two.'

Quintus could see that he was banging his head against a wall. 'You believe the best of people, that's why you don't understand,' he said. 'Macerio is a snake in the grass.'

'I'm sorry you think that.' Urceus shook his head. 'It'd be easy enough to sort out your differences over a few drinks. I'd make sure you didn't come to blows.'

'I'd rather throw myself off the Tarpeian Rock!'

'Fair enough,' replied Urceus regretfully.

An awkward silence fell. It lasted for the remainder of their duty. Quintus fell to thinking about Calatinus. The knowledge that his friend was alive and well lifted his spirits no end. Tonight, they'd be able to catch up with one another. He'd bring some wine; it would be just like old times, when they had got pissed together in Cisalpine Gaul. For an instant he sobered, remembering that he and Calatinus were the only survivors of the four tent mates from that period, a year before. When the war started again, how long would it be before either – or both – of them were also killed? All the more reason to live in the present, Quintus told himself, for tomorrow we die. A jar of wine and a good natter with Calatinus – that was what counted at this moment.

Quintus cast frequent but casual looks behind him until he was out of sight of the maniple's tent lines. He made towards the open space that lay inside the earthen wall. From there, he could go straight to the porta decumana and then up the via praetoria. Moving between the tents would have been quicker, but he risked breaking his neck on guy ropes in the dark. He'd told Urceus that he was going to chat to a possible contact who could obtain sheepskins at a reasonable price. 'This will help me get a good bargain,' he had said, waving the beaker of wine. Urceus hadn't argued; used to his comings and goings, the rest of the contubernium had hardly noticed him leave the tent.

Other soldiers were about too; searching out locations where there was gambling or wine to be bought, or just talking outside their tents. There were even some madmen sprinting against each other, watched by a cheering crowd of their friends. The atmosphere was relaxed, even party-like. Quintus felt much the same way. Everyone knew that there would be no real fighting until the spring; with their day's duties done, it was time to relax. Soldiers were free to come and go until the second watch of the night, so why not make the most of it? For those who were on duty, however, it was a different matter. Atop the wall, the sentries – velites all – marched to and fro. Quintus was grateful that he no longer had to perform this, the coldest of duties.

It wasn't hard to find the cavalry tent lines, which, apart from the first unit, faced on to the via praetoria. Their rectangular layout was the same as those of the infantry: an open side, two lines of tents opposite each other and, at the far end, the pens for the horses making up the fourth side. Counting carefully, Quintus made his way to Calatinus' section. It was here that he began to feel self-conscious, and a little wistful. As a cavalryman, he had taken his elevated status for granted. Now he was a lowly hastatus, far below the social status of Calatinus and the rest of his *turma*. Life would have been much easier if he'd stayed where he was. That fantasy lasted until Quintus thought of his father, and his intention to send him home. Squaring his shoulders, he made for a group of figures standing outside one of the tents. Engrossed in conversation, they did not notice him approach through the gloom.

Quintus coughed. No one noticed. He coughed again, with the same result. 'Excuse me,' he said loudly.

A ring of surprised faces regarded him. Several twisted with scorn. 'A hastatus. What's he doing here?' demanded one man. 'Tell him to piss off,' added another. 'But not before he gives us that beaker of wine.' Loud chuckles met this comment, and Quintus really had to bite his tongue. *Arrogant bastards!* He was grateful when one of the cavalrymen asked him what he wanted in a civil tone. There were curious glances when he replied that he was looking for a rider called Calatinus. Nonetheless, he was directed to a tent in the line opposite. Halfway across the open space, a familiar voice stopped him in his tracks. Quintus was grateful for the darkness that concealed his face. Not ten paces away, his father was talking to a decurion. His heart twisted. Despite the bad terms they had been on before he had vanished, he loved his father. In that instant, Quintus realised how much he had missed him. How good it would be to walk up and greet him. *As if he'd welcome me!* Quintus ducked his head and cut off at a different angle, putting as much distance as possible between them.

A sour-faced man emerged from Calatinus' tent as he approached.

'Is Calatinus inside?'

That got him a jaundiced grin. 'Who's asking?'

'My name is Crespo, hastatus.'

Now, a lip curl. 'What might Calatinus want with the likes of you?'

Quintus had had enough. 'That's my own business. Is he there or not?'

'You impudent—' began the cavalryman, but he was interrupted by Calatinus shoving his head outside.

'Ah, Crespo!' he cried. To his companion, 'Leave us, will you? I've got some business to deal with.'

The man walked off, grumbling.

'Come in!' Calatinus beckoned.

With a last look at his father, Quintus entered. To his relief, there was no one else in the tent. Calatinus laced the flap behind him, and then waved him to a stool by the central brazier. 'Welcome, welcome. Crespo – is that your name now?'

'I couldn't use my own, could I?' Quintus grabbed him in a bear hug. 'I thought you were dead, damn you,' he muttered in Calatinus' ear.

Calatinus squeezed him back. 'It takes more than a few guggas to kill me.'

They grinned at each other like fools before Calatinus pulled away and produced some wine. When Quintus offered his own, his friend retorted, 'We can have that afterwards. There's a whole night's drinking ahead of us.'

'Won't your tent mates return soon? I got enough strange looks just asking where to find you.'

'Don't worry. Luckily for us, the turma next door is holding a party. No one will be back for a long time yet.'

'My father was outside, talking to a decurion,' Quintus blurted. 'I didn't expect that.'

'Vulcan's hairy arse! Did he notice you?'

Quintus shook his head. 'It was a real shock, though. I wanted to talk to him, but I couldn't, obviously. I realise that I have missed him – more than I thought I would.'

'He has missed you too,' said Calatinus soberly.

'How do you know?'

'We talk now and again.' Calatinus saw Quintus' surprised look. 'He seeks me out. I think it's because he knows that you and I were' – a grin – 'are friends.'

'What does he say about me?'

'He wonders why you disappeared, and if you were killed by the enemy.' Calatinus hesitated, and then said, 'I'm not sure, but I think he wonders if he was too harsh on you.'

Quintus started forward. 'Why do you think that?'

'The sadness in his eyes when he talks about you.'

Quintus swallowed the unexpected lump that had formed in his throat. 'I see,' he said.

'Why don't you come back to the cavalry? I don't think your father would be too hard on you. He'd be so glad to know you're alive.'

It was an appealing prospect in many ways. Comrades such as Calatinus. More glory. Better rations. Best of all, no Macerio. Quintus shoved away the idea. Don't be a coward, he thought harshly. Only cowards run away, forgetting their friends who were murdered. 'He hasn't heard from my mother then? I sent a letter, telling her that I was all right.'

'He's mentioned nothing like that.'

'He'll hear eventually. I'm not leaving my unit. Not now, when I've just been promoted to the hastati.' Not when I've got Macerio to kill, he added silently.

'What are you trying to prove, Quintus?'

'I don't want to talk about it,' he retorted. This was something he had to do on his own, for himself. For Rutilus. 'Let's drink some of this wine, and you can tell me properly how you survived when so many others were killed.'

'Fine. But only if you tell me how you managed not to end up as fish food on the bottom of Lake Trasimene.'

They both grinned, the randomness of their still being alive making the reunion all the sweeter.

Quintus woke with a start, blinking away the nightmare in which Macerio had been attacking him with a sword while he'd had nothing to defend himself with. There was a sour taste of wine in his mouth and a thick-headed feeling encasing his brain. Wiping a dribble of saliva from the corner of his lips, he sat up. An empty amphora lay beside him. The oil lamps had gone out. By the brazier's dim glow, he could see Calatinus flat on his back, a few steps away, snoring loud enough to wake the dead. Quintus kicked him. A grunt. He kicked him again. 'Wake up!'

'Huh?' Calatinus' head lifted.

'What time is it?'

'How should I know?' grumbled Calatinus, struggling on to one elbow. 'Gods, but my mouth is bone dry.' He reached for a water skin and sucked at it greedily.

Quintus peered at the tent fabric. No trace of light. 'It's still dark. I'd best be heading back.'

'I'll walk with you.'

'No need, thanks. Besides, it isn't a good idea for us to be seen together. In fact, it's best if we don't do this again for a while. People would start asking questions.'

'If anything was said, I'll maintain that you were the son of a tenant on our estate at home.'

'That might work once, but not after that. When was the last time you drank with an ordinary citizen?' retorted Quintus. 'I don't like it any more than you, but there's not much we can do.'

'I suppose we could meet outside the camp, especially when the weather gets better.'

'That might work,' admitted Quintus. He rose to go, shrugged on his cloak and patted the handle of his dagger. 'Stay safe, my friend.'

Calatinus struggled up to embrace him. 'You too.'

Quintus had reached the tent's entrance when Calatinus spoke again. 'Shall I say anything to your father?'

'Of course not! He would disown me as likely as anything else.'

'I just thought you could let him know—'

Quintus, still befuddled with drink, grew angrier. 'How, Calatinus? Just call by his tent and deliver him a letter?'

'I'm sorry, Quintus,' said Calatinus, looking crestfallen. 'I only wanted to help.'

'I know.' Quintus let out a heavy sigh. 'It's too risky, though.'

Calatinus waved a hand in weary acknowledgement.

Feeling bad for reprimanding his friend and guilty about not making contact with his father, Quintus ducked outside. Apart from the raucous noise from the tents of the neighbouring turma – the party was clearly still going on – all was quiet. His breath plumed before his face; a moment later, he felt the chill night air creep under the bottom of his cloak. The wind of earlier had died down, allowing a frost to form. Moonlight glittered off the frozen, hard-packed earth of the via praetoria. His head turned from left to right, searching for a patrol of the watch. Nothing. Quintus padded out on to the wide avenue. This was riskier than walking back through the tent lines, but he trusted his sense of balance even less than he had earlier. As long as he kept a close lookout, he'd keep out of sight of hostile eyes. Or so he thought.

Brooding about his father, melancholic from the wine, he didn't see the four figures steal out behind him. The first thing he knew was when the strip of cloth was fed over his head and jerked backwards into his mouth. Quintus staggered backwards; he nearly fell. Even as his hands reached up to free himself, they were pinioned by his sides. His gaze shot from side to side to the man in front of him. Shock filled him. One was a new recruit from Macerio's contubernium; the other two were veteran hastati from his own maniple. As the dreadful realisation sank in, a familiar voice whispered in his ear, 'I take it that the equestrian has finished fucking you?'

Macerio! Frantic, Quintus tried to free his arms. He bit down on the gag, tried to spit it out, all to no avail. Legs kicking, he was bundled between lines of tents to a gap between two sets of horse pens and thrown to the ground. A few of the mounts nickered and most moved away from the fence, but here, Quintus realised with a sick feeling, there was far less chance of anyone hearing what was done to him. Up, I have to get up, he thought. Before he could even get on his knees, however, the kicks and stamps rained down on his chest, head and belly. Quintus went down hard, agony radiating all over his body. When the blows stopped, he drew in a ragged breath, fought the urge to vomit. Looked up at his attackers.

'I always knew you had to be a man lover,' hissed Macerio, kicking him again. 'Who else would befriend a *mollis* like Rutilus?'

'Are you sure this one isn't a Greek?' asked one of his companions, sniggering.

'He should be,' agreed Macerio, spitting on Quintus. 'Renting out his arse to an equestrian just like one of the lowlifes you'd find in the worst type of brothel. Filthy mollis!'

Quintus tried to rise again, but a hefty kick to the face felled him. Stars burst across his vision; he felt a dull crack as his cheekbone broke. You're attacking the wrong man, he wanted to scream. I'm not the one who murdered one of my own – Macerio is! The only sounds he could make, though, were muffled groans that made no sense to anyone. Before long, he began to lapse in and out of consciousness. With a supreme effort, Quintus formed a coherent thought. He had to act, to do something. Otherwise this beating would be the death of him, if not from his injuries, then from lying outside all night after it.

His fingers scrabbled uselessly on his tunic. Felt the outline of his baldric. Followed the leather down to the hilt of his dagger. He squinted up at his attackers, outlined against the sky above. None seemed to have noticed. Quintus' stomach twisted. There would be one chance only. He tugged the blade free, lifted his arm and hammered it into the nearest piece of flesh he could make out.

A shriek of agony. The knife was wrenched from Quintus' hand as his victim jerked away. The kicks stopped. Another bellow of pain. A man stooped over him and tugged at his foot with a savage oath.

'Shut up, you fool!' Macerio's voice.

'He's stabbed me in the fucking foot!'

'I don't give a shit! You'll bring down the damn watch on us.'

The dull glint of silver as Quintus' blade was lifted high. 'I'll finish him now, then. Can't talk if he's dead, can he?'

'Do it,' said Macerio with a cruel laugh. 'But be quick.'

With the last of his strength, Quintus rolled to his left. His feet collided with something – a man's legs, a post? Pulling in his knees, he kept rolling. Under the fence and into a pen full of horses. The smell of manure filled his nostrils. All he could see were hooves, dancing uneasily around him. He rolled on regardless, desperate to put as much distance between himself and his attackers. Whinnies filled the air. Hooves stamped on the ground. There were curses too, from beyond the fence. And then, the most welcome thing Quintus had ever heard: 'Hey! What in Hades' name are you lot doing?' Another voice: 'Arm yourselves, boys! Someone's trying to steal our horses!'

More oaths; then the sound of men running away.

Quintus sagged on to the cold ground with relief. The last thing he saw was the starlit sky, arching overhead in a glittering display of light. How beautiful it was, he thought, before oblivion claimed him.

Pain. Waves of pain from his cheek, his ribs, his groin. They alternated in a sickening rhythm, an unending cadence that bore Quintus irresistibly along. A pulse hammered off the back of his eyelids, at the base of his throat, deep inside his head. He felt sweat trickle down the side of his head, between his hairline and the corner of his eye. I must still be alive, he thought fuzzily. His eyelids felt as if they had been stuck together with glue, but he forced them open to find a dark-skinned man studying him. Behind him, Quintus could see Corax, who didn't look happy at all.

'Good. You've woken.' Corax moved forward, but the surgeon lifted a hand. The centurion frowned, but he stopped.

Quintus tried to speak, but his tongue was as thick as a plank.

'Drink some of this.' A cup was held to his lips.

The watered-down wine tasted like nectar. After a couple of swallows, the surgeon took it away. 'Not too much. I don't want you vomiting.'

'Where am I?' asked Quintus.

'In the camp hospital,' replied Corax. 'Along with your friend.'

Quintus turned his head carefully from side to side, but was pleased not to see the hastatus in any of the beds nearby. The soldiers he could see were pretending not to listen, but he had no doubt that their ears were twitching. 'My friend, sir?'

'The piece of shit whom you stabbed in the foot. I assume it *was* you who did that?'

With a displeased look, the surgeon moved back to let Corax take his place. 'You're not to talk to him for long, sir,' he chided. 'He needs to rest.'

Corax didn't even reply. The Greek backed away, lips pursed.

'Well, Crespo?' The centurion's eyes were like chips of flint.

'I stabbed him, yes, sir.'

'Why?'

'He was going to kill me.'

'Why in damnation would he try to do that, in the middle of the night, so far from our tent lines? Eh?'

Quintus tried to collect his scrambled thoughts. He wanted to tell Corax everything but as before, when Macerio had attacked him, he felt wary. For one thing, too many men were listening. Whether they heard or not, ratting out would make him a total outcast in the maniple. It didn't matter that Macerio and his cronies had tried to murder him. Maintaining the unit's code of silence was vital to keeping the other soldiers' respect. He'd have to sort out his vendetta with Macerio without official intervention. By himself.

'I asked you a question, soldier!' Corax bent over the bed. 'I don't give a shit what the surgeon says about you needing rest. Answer me, or you'll be stuck in this place for a month after the beating I give you!'

Corax must have talked to the hastatus already, thought Quintus. What would he have been told? He clawed for a credible response. 'We were having an argument, sir.'

Corax's lips thinned. 'Clearly. Tell me more.'

'You know how it is, sir. He's a veteran; I'm not. He was taking the piss out of me. We came to blows. I came off worst.'

Silence. Quintus tried not to squirm under Corax's scrutiny.

'You'd been drinking?'

'Yes, sir.' Grateful that Corax didn't interrupt, he hurried on. 'I bumped into the filth on my way back from a friend's tent. That's how we ended up fighting.' Aware of how implausible that sounded, but unable to think of a better story, he stopped.

'What a pile of horseshit,' said Corax coldly. 'The soldiers who heard the fight said that several men ran away. Did you see any of their faces?'

'No, sir,' said Quintus stolidly, avoiding Corax's gaze.

'You have no idea who they were?' The centurion's tone was disbelieving.

'That's right, sir.' Quintus glanced at Corax, his heart thumping. Had his version been anywhere near to the hastatus' version of events?

A long pause.

'Luckily for you, Crespo, the hastatus says the same thing, that you were just brawling for no particular reason. Don't think I don't know that you're both lying through your teeth. The instant that you get out of here, you're on latrine duties for a month. That's as well as having to cook for your contubernium every day for the same period. You'll also report to me each morning at dawn for a ten-mile run, in full kit. Consider yourself lucky that I'm not demoting you as well.'

'Yes, sir. Thank you, sir.' Let the hastatus receive the same, he prayed.

For once, his request was answered. 'In case you're wondering, your friend will be doing the same as you once he's discharged from the hospital.' Corax paused before adding, 'He's also to receive ten lashes.' ⸗

Curiosity and delight mixed in equal measure. 'Why's that, sir?'

'He's a veteran, for Jupiter's sake! He should have been able to thrash the living daylights out of you, not get stabbed in the damn foot. The whipping might teach him not to be so fucking useless.'

Quintus almost thought he imagined Corax's fleeting wink. Almost. He tried hard not to smile. 'I see, sir.'

'Report to me when you get out.' Corax was all business again. 'The surgeon estimates that will be in two to three days.'

'Very good, sir.' Feeling slightly happier despite the punishment that awaited him, he watched Corax go. There was no way of proving it, but his gut told him that the centurion was more on his side than that of the hastatus, which meant in turn that Macerio and the others would have to watch out. If Corax caught them doing anything untoward, Quintus had no doubt that they would live to regret it. That didn't mean he could relax. Macerio was too dangerous. Anger filled him that he had been ambushed so easily. That was three times now. It must not happen again. It was time for him to surprise Macerio, once and for all. Yet even as sleep claimed him, Quintus knew that would not be easy. Corax would also be watching him like a hawk.

Two days later, the surgeon pronounced him fit for active duties, as long as he avoided weapons training for six to eight weeks. The reason for that, the Greek explained, was that a blow to his face could permanently cave in his cheek, making it difficult to speak or eat. Quintus was relieved when Corax didn't argue with the surgeon's directions. His healing injury made no difference to the extra duties – all light – laid upon him by the centurion, however. Quintus sweated from dawn until dusk, running or digging latrines, watched by either Corax or one of the junior officers.

273

Evenings were spent with his tent mates, who had grown fiercely protective of him since the fight. Even if Macerio had wanted to do anything, there would have been no chance of doing so.

There was no sign of the hastatus for about three weeks; when he did appear, complete with a limp, Corax had him whipped and then set to shovelling earth on a different latrine trench. After a day or two, Quintus happened to catch the other's gaze. The veteran scowled at him, and he returned the look. Next time, I'll stick the knife in your chest, Quintus mouthed. In reply, he got an obscene gesture. There was scant comfort in the mini-confrontation; Macerio and the two other hastati also gave him hard looks at every opportunity.

Perhaps the best thing to come out of it was the fact that Urceus now believed Macerio was a serious threat. The first time he'd visited Quintus in the hospital, the jug-eared man had demanded an account of the night's activity. He had listened in silence to Quintus' tale of selling some of the wine that they had stockpiled to an equestrian for a healthy profit. Even when he'd revealed who it was that had attacked him, Urceus had not interrupted. When he had finished, his friend had sat for a few moments, drumming the fingers of one hand off his cheek. 'You don't have to tell me what you were really doing in that part of the camp. That's your business. I don't believe the nonsense about you being a mollis either. Arse-lovers don't eye up whores the way you do.' He'd held up a meaty hand to stop Quintus replying. 'I'm sorry that I doubted you about Macerio before. I've seen the looks he and his mates have been giving you since you got out of the hospital.'

'Do you believe me about Rutilus too?'

A heavy sigh. 'I don't want to, but yes, I do. If the bastard's prepared to try and kill you on the sly, he's capable of doing the same in the middle of a battle.'

'It won't end until one of us is dead. And it's not going to be me.'

'I'll help make damn sure of that,' Urceus had growled.

Knowing that he now had a friend to watch his back eased Quintus' burden. It helped him to sleep better at night, although he was often troubled by nightmares about Macerio. The sooner he could end the feud, the better. He wondered if it would be when the month of punishments was up, but there was no let-up in the officers' supervision of either him or the hastatus. A couple of other soldiers in the maniple who were caught fighting were severely flogged. Corax was letting them all know what to expect, Quintus surmised. The worst of the winter weather passed, and the days grew longer. Bands of enemy soldiers were spotted more often, resulting in an escalation of Roman patrols. Quintus never found himself on the same mission as Macerio or his cronies, which made it even more likely that Corax knew of the enmity between them. Whatever the reason, it distracted him from the problem, for a while at least. As the weeks passed, he buried his hatred of Macerio for another time. Vengeance for Rutilus' death could wait, but the war with Hannibal could not.

And war it would be once more. Although Servilius and Regulus still led the army, and had followed their instructions from the Senate not to engage significantly with Hannibal during the spring, the gossip that ran through the camp daily was of only one thing: confrontation with the enemy. When Lucius Aemilius Paullus and Gaius Terentius Varro, the new consuls for the year, arrived to take charge, they would bring with them four newly raised legions and the same number of socii troops. Together with the soldiers who were encamped near Gerunium, they would command a total of more than eighty thousand men. With that vast force, the braggarts cried, defeat was impossible. Quintus found it hard to argue with such logic. As the days lengthened and the temperatures rose, their training renewed with added ferocity. A number of clashes with the enemy went the Roman way too, and his spirits rose along with everyone else's. There would be no rest until total victory had been achieved. It would come soon, before the summer's end – which meant that if he survived, the possibility of autumn leave would become real. He could potentially be reunited with his family. For all that he wanted to walk his own path, Quintus also longed to see his mother and Aurelia again. His father too, if he admitted it. If he distinguished himself in the battle that saw Hannibal defeated, perhaps his father would forgive him for disobeying his orders? Quintus suspected that that thought was a wishful fantasy. Nonetheless, he guarded it jealously, telling no one.

Chapter XIV

Hannibal's camp, outside the town of Gerunium, Samnium, spring

Hearing Sapho's voice close by, Hanno scowled. It was too late to leave his tent without being seen. What did Sapho want? he wondered.

His relationship with his eldest brother had always been prickly, but during the period of his enslavement, he had largely forgotten the details. When he had been reunited with him, Hanno had fancied things had changed between him and Sapho. They had got on famously for a short while, but then the pair had fallen into their old pattern of clashing regularly.

Most recently, there had been the look on Sapho's face when he had nearly drowned. As he had before, Hanno had convinced himself that that had been his imagination running riot. Had Sapho not revealed Hannibal's plan to him before the battle at Lake Trasimene? They had also spent many subsequent nights drinking wine together. Which was why his brother's reaction when Hanno had returned from patrol with Mutt and his men the previous year had not been what he expected. Sapho had looked smug, to say the least. Knowing, as well. That hadn't surprised Hanno overmuch. What *had* was the edge to Sapho's voice. 'Emptied your balls, have you?' his brother had repeatedly asked. Startled and angered, Hanno had denied everything, but Sapho had persisted until he'd demanded to know who in his phalanx had been telling tales. Sapho had winked and said he had his source, who'd told him that their commander had vanished in the direction of Capua. 'Gone for three days, I hear. It must have been a good whorehouse to risk your skin like that!'

Despite the double edge to this comment – Sapho could have meant the threat of either the Romans capturing him or Hannibal finding out what he had done – Hanno had breathed a sigh of relief. He hadn't thought it was Mutt who had informed on him, but this was proof. Sapho didn't know why he'd left his soldiers; he had been making a shrewd guess as to the reason. Yet Hanno had felt most uneasy that someone had spoken out of turn. If Sapho knew, others might also find out. Hanno had no doubt, either, that his brother had been showing his power over him: if he said a word to any of the senior officers, Hanno's life was over. When he'd challenged Sapho about it, his brother had laughed it off, saying he'd never do anything of the kind.

Why does he always have to make such jokes? thought Hanno angrily. Bostar doesn't. For all of his veiled threats and sarcasm, however, that time Sapho had been right. It *had* been rash to leave his command and seek out Aurelia. Naturally, Hanno wouldn't ever admit that to Sapho. A quick grin sloped across his face. He didn't want to end his life nailed to a cross, that was for sure, but part of him was still glad about what he'd done. If only he had managed to see Aurelia in Capua! Stop it, he told himself. Months have passed. She's married now, and you'll never see her again. Best to forget her. Doing that, though, was easier said than done. He had tried to do so before and failed.

'Ho! Hanno, where are you?'

'I'm in here.' He lifted the tent flap and grimaced. 'What is it?'

'That's a strange welcome for a man's brother,' said Sapho, scowling. 'Aren't you going to invite me in?'

'Of course,' replied Hanno. Now he felt bad. He stood aside so that his brother could enter. 'Take a seat.'

Sapho sat on one of the two stools and extended his feet towards the glowing brazier with a happy sigh. Spring had arrived, but the temperatures still dropped considerably at night. 'Got any wine?'

'A little.' Taking a pair of plain clay beakers from the bronze tray that sat on his clothes chest, Hanno gave them a quick wipe with a rag. He filled them both from the jug that sat alongside. 'Here.'

Sapho saluted him with his cup. 'To our general Hannibal, and victory over the Romans!'

Hanno echoed the words, and they both drank. He wanted to ask what brought Sapho to his tent, but that would be too direct. It wasn't easy to think of something else to say. For all that Hanno was his own man, Sapho still had a way of making him feel like his little brother. Relax, he thought. Enjoy his company. He's merely come for a friendly chat. 'How are your men finding the new formations?' he asked. His had done little but complain since the order had come down that they were to arm themselves with Roman weapons and learn to fight like legionaries.

'It took a while, a few lashes of the whip, but they're proficient now,' growled Sapho. 'And yours?'

'Getting them to react as one when I shout an order has taken a bloody age,' admitted Hanno. 'They're getting there, I suppose.'

'If you need any help or advice—' Sapho began, but Hanno interrupted. 'I'll manage, thanks.'

'I know you will,' said Sapho with a warm smile.

Again Hanno felt bad for being so prickly. *He trusts me. He knows I'm a man now.*

'You say that there's no prospect of a battle, yet that doesn't mean we can't bloody some Romans' noses from time to time.'

Hanno's ears pricked. 'On patrol, you mean?' Hannibal's army went through a vast amount of food every day, and through the winter it had become harder and harder to find supplies. The soldiers who were sent out on these missions often had to range quite far afield and were therefore the most likely to see combat.

'Yes. Hannibal has ordered me to accompany a foraging party tomorrow. He's had reports of a large estate, as yet unplundered, and with a large amount of grain. It's about fifteen miles to the northwest of here, on the other side of the river. A lot of men and mules will be needed to carry the wheat, so a strong force is required. I'm to ask another phalanx commander to come along. I thought of you. But if your men aren't ready—'

Fiercely eager, Hanno cut him off. This was another chance to fight the enemy, to win Hannibal's favour. 'They would jump at the chance of getting out of camp! So would I. If we happen to clash with a few Romans, we'll teach them a damn good lesson.'

'You're sure? If something happens, I don't want to see your men taking to their heels and leaving us in the shit.'

'I give you my word,' swore Hanno. 'My phalanx is made up of veterans, remember? They crossed the Alps with you and the rest. Learning how to fight with new weapons is just a reason to grumble. You know what soldiers are like. When it comes to a fight, they'll stand as firm as any man in the army, I guarantee it.'

'Fair enough.' Sapho raised his cup once more. 'We shall march out together, and return with sufficient grain to feed the entire army for weeks. And may the gods have pity on any Romans who are foolish enough to cross swords with us!'

Hanno laughed with anticipation. 'Hannibal will be pleased.'

'He'll also see what a fine soldier you are,' added Sapho.

Hanno beamed at this rare compliment. The wine tasted even better as it ran down his gullet. He poured refills for them both.

'I'd like nothing more than to get hammered,' said Sapho as they drank another toast, 'but we'll need clear heads tomorrow.'

'Just what I was going to say,' replied Hanno, although he'd been fully prepared to keep drinking. He was grateful that Sapho, who must have seen that in his face, made no comment. A warm feeling towards his eldest brother flowed through him. Hanno was sure now that he'd been wrong about Sapho. 'We can get pissed when we get back.'

'I'll see if I can persuade Hannibal to come as well.'

'He wouldn't bother with the likes of us, surely?' asked Hanno in surprise.

'I don't know. I've had the honour of sharing wine with him a few times; if he decides to put his cares aside, he's quite a sociable type. Leave it with me,' said Sapho with a wink.

Impressed and pleased, Hanno beamed at his brother. He was ever more determined to prove himself on the patrol.

Indicating to Mutt that his men should keep marching, Hanno stepped out of line. As ever, his purpose was to scan the horizon behind them. To his relief, he saw nothing. It was almost too good to be true. Thus far, the raid had gone without any major hitches. They had left the army's main camp well before dawn. The Numidian cavalry sent to escort them had set out at the same time, reporting back regularly that they had found no signs of enemy troops in the surrounding area. They had reached their objective by mid-morning and met almost no resistance; as soon as the elderly owner realised how large was the force sent against him, he had surrendered. Hanno had been impressed by Sapho's restraint towards the man, who had been executed without torture after he'd revealed the contents of his farm buildings. The slaves had not been harmed.

In the space of an hour, the place had been ransacked. The sheds had been emptied entirely and Hanno, Sapho or their officers had ensured that the most valuable items were taken from the residential quarters. The mules had been loaded up with sacks of grain, sides of cured meat and hundreds of amphorae full of wine and oil. Only a handful of soldiers had had to be disciplined for drinking some of the wine. Hanno suspected that a number of female slaves had been raped, but he had seen no direct evidence so there had been no point in trying to do anything about it. The purpose of the mission was to gather supplies and return safely with them, not to concern himself with the plight of a few unfortunate women.

Satisfied that there was no pursuit, Hanno hurried back to his position at the front of his phalanx. The road was narrow, but his troops could march six abreast, which satisfied him: wide enough for them to fight if needs be, as well as to manoeuvre. Clouds of exhaled breath billowed above the files of marching soldiers. Frost crunched beneath their sandals. Mail shirts jingled, spear shafts knocked off other men's shields. Although no one had given the order to do so, conversation was muted. Still unused to their new appearance, which was similar to that of Roman legionaries, Hanno studied them as he passed by. Most were wearing their original conical bronze helmets, a small but pleasing detail. As usual he followed his father's advice and offered greetings here, gave out praise there, laughed at the ribald jokes that were being told. Unsurprisingly, spirits were high. Hanno was grateful for that (although he was careful not to allow it to take control) for it was infectious and helped lift his own mood. He had been keen the day before, but now that he was in the situation, his nerves were jangling. It was commonplace for their foraging parties to be attacked, and not unheard of for them to suffer heavy casualties. He would not relax until they reached the Carthaginian camp at Gerunium. And watching the file of laden-down mules ambling along before them, Hanno knew *that* would not come to pass until near sundown.

'See anything, sir?' asked Mutt.

'No.'

'Happy?'

Hanno glanced at Mutt, wondering if his dour second-in-command felt any of the misgivings he did. 'Not entirely,' he said in an undertone.

'Thinking about the river, sir?'

'Among other things, yes. That would be the best place to attack us.'

'It would, sir. All being well, nothing like that will happen.' Here, a characteristic sigh. 'It doesn't hurt to wish that the cavalry are as alert as they were on the outward journey, though. If they are, they'll soon root out any nasty surprises.'

Hanno grunted, wishing that the cavalry captain, a swarthy man whom he hadn't met until that morning, were Zamar. Stop thinking like that, he told himself. The fellow must be more than capable, or Sapho would not have chosen him.

'Never thought I'd say this, but the cold weather has done us a favour,' commented Mutt, jerking a thumb at the frozen ground. 'Imagine the dust that we'd be breathing in if this were summertime. For all that this is the position of honour, we would be cursing Sapho for taking the vanguard.'

Surprised by this outburst, for Mutt often went miles without saying a word, Hanno smiled. 'True enough, it wouldn't be pleasant. Marching in the cold isn't so bad, eh?' He tapped his scutum and his bronze cuirass with the shaft of his spear. 'All this doesn't feel as heavy as it does in Africa.'

'Careful, sir,' warned Mutt. 'You'll be turning into a bloody Roman next.'

'There isn't much chance of that happening,' said Hanno with a sour chuckle. He rubbed at the base of his neck. 'It was a Roman who gave me this, remember? I will never forget that, nor will I stop seeking revenge for it until the day I die. If I'm blessed, it will be Pera, but any other Roman will do.'

'Sorry, sir. I had forgotten,' said Mutt, with a look of respect.

Hanno nodded. Deep inside, his conviction was not quite as absolute when it came to Quintus and, more particularly, Aurelia, but he was not going to admit that to a soul. The chances of him ever being tested on it were slim to none, which meant that he could wholly concentrate on two things: exacting retribution from every other Roman who came within reach of his sword – something he positively looked forward to – and doing his duty, which was to fight for Hannibal and Carthage. He would do that until the very last drop of blood drained from his veins. Pera's torture had not done that to Hanno. There were other, much older reasons for his loathing of Rome. Throughout his childhood, his father had inculcated into him the details of every defeat suffered against the Republic in the first great struggle between it and Carthage. The loss of that twenty-three-year war, as well as control of the Mediterranean and Sicily, had been immensely humiliating. Yet Rome had not been content to leave it at that, forcing Carthage to pay immense reparations as further punishment. More evidence of the Romans' perfidy had come a few years after the first war's end, when Hanno's people had been coerced into ceding Sardinia and Corsica to Rome as well. Yet with a little luck, there would be no fighting today. Hanno scanned the horizon to either side once more, but saw nothing. Despite his wish to kill the enemy, escorting the mules and their precious cargo back to the camp was more important than adding a few more casualties to the list of the Roman dead. Bringing back the grain and proving to Hannibal that he was capable was what counted.

Time passed, and the patrol edged its way south towards the river that separated them from the rest of the army. An air of anticipation became palpable. The pace picked up a little, even among the mules. It was as if they sensed that once across the watercourse, they would be safe, thought Hanno. Roman soldiers had not been seen on the far bank – the Carthaginian side – for some time, and with good reason. Squadrons of Numidian cavalry patrolled the area daily, ensuring that any enemy forces were discovered and wiped out. Hanno could feel his soldiers' excitement growing; his spirits also rose. Once the mission had been accomplished, there was no way that Hannibal could fail to acknowledge what Sapho and he had done. Perhaps this expedition would fully restore him to his general's favour? He had felt that Hannibal's poor opinion of him was easing, but at a slower rate than Hanno liked.

The column came to a sudden halt. It was perhaps a mile from the river. Hanno chafed with impatience as they waited for information. Soon a rider brought the expected news that Sapho's phalanx had reached the bank. A small number of his men had begun to cross; the remainder were guarding the approach to the water, where the mules were being gathered by their handlers. It would not be long, said the messenger, before the mules also began to enter the ford. Hanno and his men were to act as a rearguard until the last of the vital supplies had been transported to the other side.

'What are you to do?' Hanno asked, hoping that some of the cavalry at least would remain on this bank to act as his eyes and ears.

'The bulk of us have been ordered across the river, sir,' replied the rider apologetically. 'I am to remain with you as a messenger; so too are five of my comrades. They'll be here any moment.'

This development was unsurprising – Hannibal's horsemen were among his most valuable troops and therefore exposed to as little risk as possible – but that didn't stop Hanno's stomach from clenching. Without scouts on their flanks and to their rear, they had to remain in their current position, blind. He mightn't have minded as much if there hadn't been trees pressing in on both sides. Bare of leaves, they afforded little shelter for potential ambushers, but their effect was still to funnel the Carthaginians together more closely than he liked. 'Very good,' he said with an attempt at nonchalance. 'Tell Sapho that we'll withdraw gradually as the mules go across. Order your companions to ride back along the road for a distance and make sure that there has been no pursuit.'

'Yes, sir!' The Numidian was already wheeling his horse back the way he had come.

'Have the men turn to our rear,' directed Hanno. 'Let's be cautious. I want the first two ranks on each side facing the trees. They're to walk sideways. We'll move in that fashion to the river.'

Mutt didn't bat an eyelid at this odd command. 'Yes, sir!' He stalked off, barking orders, leaving Hanno to watch. He was pleased by his soldiers' response to their orders. The change in formation was assumed with few mistakes and minimal fuss. A new sense of urgency and excitement settled over the phalanx. Men began to mutter prayers to their favourite gods, to rub the amulets that hung from their necks or to make over-loud jokes.

Hanno clashed the tip of his javelin off his shield to gain their attention. 'This is just a precaution, lads. There is no need to worry. The nearest Romans are miles away,' he shouted. 'The mules are going to start crossing any moment. Our job is to act as a screen until they are safely over. Then we'll do the same. When we get back to camp, I will see to it that you have enough wine tonight to drink yourselves unconscious.'

That got him a loud roar of approval. 'All the same, I want you to go over your equipment as usual.' There were a few grumbles at this, but he saw many more nods of approval. Satisfied, Hanno went through the little ritual that had become his routine before a battle. Wipe his hands clean of sweat. Check that his helmet straps were tight. Loosen his sword in its scabbard. Test the edge on his spear head with a thumb. Ensure that he had a firm grip of his scutum. Lastly, a quick glance at his sandals to make sure that the lacing wasn't about to come undone. His father once told him the story of a soldier who had tripped on his own laces and been killed by an enemy; it was a stupid mistake that Hanno had resolved never to make for himself.

The pounding of hooves drew his attention like a wasp to a piece of overripe fruit. It was the Numidian who had just spoken to him, and his companions. At least they would have some eyes now, he thought. He raised a hand to beckon the riders.

A soft whirring sound filled the air. Long, dark shadows hissed in from the edge of Hanno's vision. Instinctively realising what they were, his throat closed with horror. In slow motion, his eyes swivelled, taking in the swarm of arrows arcing towards his men and the group of figures in the trees to his left, who stood with bows still raised. 'Ambush!' he roared. 'All ranks, raise shields!' He lifted his own scutum and ducked down behind it. Where the hell had the archers come from? One thing was certain in his mind: they would not be alone. He would have to seize control, warn Sapho if the situation were not to turn disastrous. A wary glance around the side of his shield made him curse bitterly. It was already too late. Of the six Numidians, only one remained astride his mount. The others were dead, wounded or had been thrown by their injured mounts. Frantic neighs. Bucking, rearing. Roars of pain from the wounded men. Even as Hanno's mouth opened to order the last horseman to tell Sapho what was going on, a flurry of arrows struck him with soft, sinuous thumps. He went down screaming.

Through the trees, Hanno could see the shapes of men closing in. Legionaries. Scores and scores of the bastards. It was the same on the other side. Already they were outnumbered, and this would be a fraction of the force facing them, of that he had no doubt. Whoever had sprung this ambush had known what he was doing. Like their own trap at Lake Trasimene, it had been timed to perfection. 'If we fight, we die. Retreating to the river is our only chance,' he muttered.

'And if we don't retreat, the whoresons will stop the mules from crossing, sir,' added Mutt, appearing by his side.

'Let's move. This lot will have orders to cut us off,' said Hanno. He cupped a hand to his mouth. 'About turn! The men on the flanks are to keep their shields high. Those inside, lift yours over your heads. If you want to live, do it fast!' He shoved his way into the press of soldiers, becoming part of the formation, looking south towards the river. Mutt joined him. Hanno could taste the fear in the air, could see it in some men's eyes. How quickly the mood could change, he thought, moving his tongue round a suddenly dry mouth. Yet Mutt's steady presence by his side was calming, and the situation was far from lost. 'Close order! Forward!' he shouted. 'Back to the river, at the double. Back!'

They began to run.

The instant that the Romans saw their purpose, they also charged, towards Hanno's men. Amid the bouncing of shields and weapons, Hanno observed that these were no new recruits. Everywhere he looked, he could see mail shirts, crested helmets and plenty of long thrusting spears. These were not just principes but triarii, the cream of the Roman fighting force. 'They're fucking veterans,' he growled.

'The consuls must want to give us a real bloody nose, sir.' Mutt's grin was feral. 'It's a compliment of a kind.'

'A compliment I'd rather not receive,' retorted Hanno, although the knowledge gave him a surreptitious thrill.

The first Romans were spilling on to the road perhaps fifty paces ahead of them. They paid no heed to the last of the mules, who were being whipped onwards by their terrified handlers. Instead they began to form a shield wall, blocking the passage to the river. Hanno could hear their officers roaring encouragement to the men still in the trees. Their chance to break through was slipping away before his very eyes.

'Form a point, behind me!' he bellowed, moving to take the most forward position. Hanno could taste the sharp tang of fear in his mouth, but he pushed onward anyway. His men needed to be led from the front. If their resolve wavered, all would be lost. There was a moment when he could feel no one to his rear, and his heart hammered out a new, nervous rhythm. Then Mutt was there, and with him four, five, six others. Relief filled Hanno as the few men became a tide, and their formation assumed an arrowhead shape. He was at the very tip, the most dangerous place to be. That was because they *had* to succeed. If they didn't reach Sapho's phalanx to help defend the mules and their drivers, their plunder would all be lost. The army would go hungry. Worse than that, in Hanno's mind, Hannibal would know that they had failed. That was not something he was prepared to let happen. Even if it cost him his life. 'Come on!' he yelled. 'They're only one or two ranks deep.'

Hanno aimed for the centre of the Roman line. As they drew closer, he had his troops slow down and throw a volley of javelins. They were moving again even as the legionaries responded in kind. 'Shields up! Draw swords!' Hanno bellowed and moved on. He was desperate to close with the enemy, but he did not run. If the impact when the two sides met was too powerful, it would knock many men over. Even so, they hit the legionaries with an almighty crash. Hanno hoped that wherever Sapho was, he heard it. Not that his brother would do much about it. The grain was more important than a small number of soldiers. That was the last coherent thought Hanno had. His world narrowed to the few paces in front of him. To the crazed grin on the face of the triarius opposite him, and the spear head that came shoving in, threatening to take out one of his eyes. He raised his shield, felt the *thump* as the sharp iron struck it.

The triarius tugged on his spear; Hanno held fast to his shield. He realised a heartbeat before his opponent that the blade was stuck. Up he came, like an uncoiling snake. With all his force, he sent his right arm out and around the side of the legionary's scutum. Metal grated off metal; the tiniest delay, and then his sword was driving deep into the triarius' belly. Hanno twisted his wrist for good measure, slicing the man's guts to ribbons. The pressure on his shield suddenly slackened as the screaming triarius let go of his spear. Hanno ripped his weapon free and shoved forward a step with his useless shield. There was no resistance from his dying enemy, yet that did not stop the man in the rank behind from trying to skewer Hanno with his spear. It took every bit of Hanno's strength to keep up his scutum. A powerful thump; his arm trembled; another impact, which he also resisted. He cursed; the legionary laughed and stabbed at him again; the blade whistled overhead. His enemy had all the advantage; his thrusting spear had a far greater reach than Hanno's sword. In addition, Hanno would not be able to hold up his shield for much longer; it was front-heavy, thanks to the triarius' weapon buried in it.

Bending his knees, he drove forward, pushing the mortally wounded triarius backwards and into his current opponent. The startled legionary took a step backwards to avoid being knocked over and Hanno used the opportunity to shove at him again. At this point, the wounded triarius' strength gave out and he collapsed to the ground. Hanno was ready; dropping his shield, he trampled over it and the triarius, straight at his comrade behind. Grabbing the rim of the shocked soldier's scutum, Hanno stabbed him through his open mouth. An odd, choking noise. Spittle and pieces of broken tooth flew; a crimson tide flowed from the man's lips. His eyes opened wide in momentary disbelief before the light left them forever. Hanno's blade grated off bone as he tugged it free. Blood sprayed all over his arm: he barely noticed. A quick glance over his shoulder as the legionary collapsed. Mutt was right there; so too were the rest. His heart lifted. They had punched a hole in the Roman line, and their charge yet had momentum.

Eyes to the enemy again. Burning hope filled Hanno. There were only three Romans remaining before him, and they didn't look too happy. He bared his teeth and roared his fiercest war cry. They flinched, so he added, 'HANN-I-BAL! HANN-I-BAL!' The cry was taken up at once by his men, and Hanno felt the whole Roman line waver a fraction. The men facing him did not move to the attack, giving him the chance to flip over an undamaged enemy scutum and pick it up. Thus armed, he renewed the fight. His next opponent, a princeps, looked visibly scared but that didn't mean he was going to run. A brave man, thought Hanno. They went at one another like men possessed, Hanno eager to break through, and the legionary desperate to prevent him from doing so. *Clatter, bash. Bash, clatter.* Their shield bosses smacked together over and over, each of them trying to destabilise their opponent. One man would thrust; the other would dodge or block the blow. Then the reverse happened. Back and forth they swayed, neither giving ground, neither managing to wound or disable the other.

Hanno's moment came when the man to the legionary's right was killed. Hearing his companion's death rattle, the Roman was unable to stop his eyes from swivelling to see what was happening. Hanno reached down with his sword and stabbed him in the foot. When the legionary staggered backwards, bawling with pain, he followed through with another savage thrust to the belly. There was no mail shirt to stop it this time – the princeps wore only a square pectoral plate – and his blade slid in below it, almost to the hilt.

That was enough for the last legionary, who had been standing just behind his companions. He retreated several steps. Hanno pulled his sword free, stepped over the princeps and into open space. His heart beat even faster. There were still Romans pouring in from either side, yet the road to the river lay wide open now. 'Mutt!'

From right behind him, 'Yes, sir?'

'How are the men doing?'

'Still moving, sir. A moment or two, and they'll be through.'

'FORWARD, LADS!' Hanno yelled. 'To the mules!'

An inarticulate roar. He sensed movement behind, took a glance and saw any Romans left in the way being swept aside. Keep moving; they had to keep moving, he thought. Praying that not too many of his men had been lost, Hanno took off at a steady trot. Pila scudded in, but they caused few casualties. A half-hearted charge was made on their left flank by the men emerging from the trees, but it was beaten back by the invigorated Libyans. Hanno grinned, a mad delight coursing through him. He had made it, unharmed. They had taken on veteran legionaries and beaten them!

His pleasure did not endure for long. Their main battle had yet to be won, and from the sounds that carried from the riverbank, the fighting between yet more Romans – the main enemy force, probably – and Sapho's troops had already begun. He had to stay calm, but it was damn hard. To the rear, he could hear the frenzied shouts of the Roman officers, urging their men to pursue them. Hanno fought his fear. He thought of the grain, and of its importance to the army. He imagined Hannibal hearing of how they had failed. New determination filled him.

He needed every last bit of it as they left the trees. On the far side, he could see a few Libyans, the Numidians and perhaps ten wagons. Nearer, chaos reigned. Slowing, Hanno shouted a curse. The river was clogged with carts trying to get across. Some of the panicked drivers had urged their mules into the water outside the fordable area, forcing them to swim as they pulled their carts. At least one team was in serious difficulty. Men shouted, cracking their whips to no avail. Sprays of water rose up as the mules kicked and struggled against their traces. Frustration coursed through Hanno but he could do nothing about that situation. He wrenched his eyes away, evaluating the rest of the scene. The majority of the wagons were still on his side of the river, clustered in the shallows or on the bank nearby. Sapho's soldiers were spread out in a thin, protective arc around the vehicles and their precious cargo. Between Hanno and his brother's phalanx were several hundred Roman legionaries, more triarii and principes from the look of them. Yet more were spilling from the trees to either side. Hanno took solace from the fact that they were still some distance away. He turned, looking for Mutt, and was pleased to find him not two steps away. 'Move fast and we can hit the lot who are engaging Sapho before the others reach them.'

Mutt produced a rare smile. 'Sounds like a good idea, sir.'

That was all the encouragement Hanno needed. He eyed the nearest men, gave them an approving look, before raising a hand to his lips. 'I'm pleased with you so far, lads,' he cried.

They cheered him for that.

'The fight's not nearly over, though. The wagons are still in danger. We've got to smash through to our comrades. Think you can do that?'

Their answering shout was twice as loud as the previous one.

'Quickly, then! Form up, twenty men wide, ten deep, fast as you can! Soldiers without shields and those with wounds are to move back several ranks.' To Mutt: 'I want you at the front, five men in from the right edge. I'll be the same number in from the left side.'

Mutt nodded, the understanding clear in his eyes. They were to use themselves as focuses for the soldiers at the very front, none of whom would be any further than five men away from either. If the strategy worked, it would ensure that their line held.

If it didn't, they were damned, thought Hanno. 'What are you waiting for?' he bawled, seeing the enemy reinforcements picking up speed. They had been spotted. 'Move!'

They covered the distance to the river at full pelt. Shields high, swords ready, screaming blue murder at the Romans. Cheered by their success in smashing through the triarii, they forgot how much their armour and weapons weighed, allowed the temporary madness of the charge to take over. Hanno had to give the legionaries credit; they reacted fast, the rear-most soldiers wheeling about to face them with minimal fuss. There seemed to be no triarii present, for which he was grateful. As he'd just discovered, the thrusting spears used by those veterans were deadly at close quarters against men armed with swords.

As Hanno had hoped, Sapho led his troops forward as he and his soldiers struck the Romans from behind. Despite the fact that their comrades were advancing from the trees, the phalanxes' combined strength was enough to panic the legionaries, who broke away after just a short period of fighting. Scores of casualties were left behind. Ordering that the enemy wounded be killed, Hanno sought out Sapho. They would have a brief chance to confer before the Romans regrouped and attacked again.

'We could have done without this,' growled Hanno.

'Baal Hammon damn their eyes. Their scouts must have seen us, or a quick-thinking farmer. They weren't far away either, to be able to get into position so fast. Still, we'll hold them until the grain gets across, eh?' His brother's eyes had a dangerous glint to them.

'We'll have to,' replied Hanno grimly. He'd seen that the carts with amphorae were being held back so that those laden down with wheat could go first.

'Good.' Sapho thumped him on the arm.

'What about the wine and oil?'

A harsh laugh. 'Let's see how the land lies then!'

'Fine.' Hanno asked the gods that no more enemy troops arrived other than the ones already present. With a little luck, they would manage to see every wagon to the far bank *and* escape themselves. The Numidians' presence would severely reduce the likelihood of any pursuit. If any Romans were foolish enough to ford the river, they would be met by a cavalry charge. That would be followed by a frontal assault by both phalanxes. Get to the other side, and we'll be fine, thought Hanno. That's all we have to do. Yet the enemy soldiers massing not a hundred paces away were evidence that doing so would not be quite that simple.

'I want your phalanx on the right. I'll take the left. Don't give any ground if you can help it. The wagons need plenty of space to move around each other.'

'We've got our orders, men,' shouted Hanno, pointing. 'Form up in lines. About face so that you're looking at the Romans. Then I want you over this way. Move it!'

His soldiers needed no further prompting. In good order, they did as he'd ordered. With Mutt's assistance, Hanno directed them to their new position, which extended in an arc from the riverbank outside the last wagon to the midpoint of the road, where they came up against Sapho's troops. There were sufficient numbers to stand three deep, no more. It wasn't enough, thought Hanno, doing a rough head count, but he now had only 180 or so men. Ten Libyans were held back as a reserve. It was a pitiful number but even those few weakened his lines more than he liked.

They had barely finished when a couple of trumpets blared and the Romans began to move forward. There were hundreds of them, perhaps twice as many as the two phalanxes combined. Hanno sensed rather than saw his soldiers' apprehension. 'Hold the line, boys!' he roared. 'If that grain gets recaptured, we'll definitely go hungry tonight.'

'What about the wine, sir?' yelled Mutt. 'Surely that's more important?'

That raised a laugh, and Hanno threw his second-in-command a grateful look.

'To some of you drunkards, perhaps! If you want that as well, we'll have to hold the crossing for a while yet.'

'We can do it, sir,' cried Mutt, beginning to clash his sword off the metal rim of his scutum. 'WINE! WINE! WINE!'

The delighted Libyans began to copy Mutt. 'WINE! WINE! WINE!' they shouted.

Hanno couldn't help but smile. If that was what would make them stand, so be it. To uncomprehending ears such as the Romans, the refrain sounded as fearsome as many a battle cry. He let them shout for a few moments before he held up a hand for quiet. 'Anyone with pila, pass them to the men in front. Wait for my command to throw.' When that had been done, he glanced to either side with a smile and roared, 'WINE!'

They continued to hurl their challenge at the Romans until there were no more than fifty paces between the two sides. Then it died away. At once, fear tinged the air. Hanno clenched his jaw. He didn't like the unnerving silence with which the legionaries advanced either. 'Ready javelins,' he yelled, dragging his men's attention back to him. 'Throw when I say, not a moment before. To help your aim, I'll give a measure of wine to every man who hits one of the enemy.'

The Libyans still with pila began to whoop with excitement, mocking their companions who were without.

Hanno studied the legionaries closely as they advanced. Thirty paces was about the furthest a man could expect to hurl a javelin with any accuracy. Even closer was better, but that required more nerve, and the distinct possibility that an enemy volley would land first, with the potential to cause mayhem. Not yet, he told himself. Not yet.

On the Romans came. Hanno's mouth was dry again, damn it, and his heart was hammering out a beat like a maniac smith on an anvil. Twenty. Finally, the enemy came within range. He hadn't uttered a word when a single pilum soared up into the air. It came down just short of the Roman front rank. Derisive laughter from the legionaries followed in its wake. Hanno leaned forward, glaring at the men to his left, whence it had come. 'I said, wait for my order! Every bloody missile counts!'

Another ten steps and the Roman officers had their men launch a volley of pila. Hanno roared the command to raise shields; he heard Sapho doing the same. The javelins came humming down in a blur of wood and metal. *Thump. Thump. Thump.* A few soldiers in Hanno's phalanx were wounded; only one seriously. With their missiles thrown, the Romans began to move faster, but Hanno was ready. 'Quickly now, boys. LOOSE!'

The Libyans' pila rose up in answer; they arced down, banging into shields – and a few unlucky legionaries. The volley had little impact on the Roman formation, Hanno saw, but at least it had kept his men focused on the task at hand. 'Close order!' he shouted. 'WINE! WINE! WINE!'

His soldiers took up his chant with gusto.

The moments that followed were a blur. Hanno traded blows with a number of Romans. He thrust with his sword and battered with his scutum, bared his teeth and shrieked at the top of his voice. He even spat in the face of one legionary in an attempt to anger him enough to make a mistake. The ruse worked. When the furious man raised his arm to hack at Hanno, Hanno was able to slide his blade into the man's armpit, ending his life at a stroke. Blood from the resulting wound spattered him in the face, but Hanno had no chance to wipe it away. The space occupied by the legionary had already been taken by another man. That fight went his way when the Roman lost his balance on something underfoot – his comrade's body? – and Hanno chopped a savage wound in the side of his neck. He was vaguely aware that the couple of soldiers to either side were holding their own but he had no idea what was happening beyond that. A large part of him didn't care. He'd begun imposing Pera's features on each of the men he faced. Hanno wanted to kill every last one of them. Managing to dampen his rage after downing his third opponent, he ordered the Libyan behind him to take his place. Hanno shoved his way back to a spot where he could see what was going on.

Their line was bowed in a couple of places but, to his amazement, it was holding. So was Sapho's. His head swivelled to the river. The carts that had been in difficulty had been pulled out. Another ten or so wagons had crossed. Perhaps twenty remained, half of which contained sacks of grain. The rest were loaded with wine or oil. Go on! Hanno willed them all to make to the other side.

A sudden commotion to his right; he looked, cursed and ordered the reserve to the attack. Led by an officer in a horsehair-crested helmet, a handful of triarii had smashed through his lines close to the river. Hanno led the way, aware that if the group weren't contained immediately, they would enlarge the hole that they'd made and the battle would be lost. Hanno was proud of his soldiers in the short, savage bout that ensued. No mercy was asked for or given. The Libyans fought like demons, cutting down every Roman with the loss of only one of their own number. Covered in even more blood than before, sweat running down their faces, chests heaving, they looked at each other in disbelief when it was over. Hanno was the first to start laughing. He was aware that there was a note of mania to his voice, but he didn't care. In a heartbeat, his men were also roaring with laughter, as if they'd seen a hilarious practical joke played on someone.

There was another breakthrough almost at once. Hanno stayed with the reserve from then on. That attack and another one were repulsed before his strength began to falter. His shield felt as if it were a wooden practice one, his sword as if it were made of lead. Eyeing the others sidelong, he saw the exhaustion creeping into their faces too. The Roman attack showed no signs of abating. Trumpet calls even signified that reinforcements might be arriving. Fingers of desperation tickled the back of Hanno's neck; bile rose in his throat. His gaze moved to where Sapho's phalanx stood. They looked no less hard-pressed. If anything, they had given way a little: their lines were closer to the remaining wagons – seven in total – than his soldiers were.

As he wondered what to do, the decision was taken from his hands.

'Cavalry, sir!' Mutt roared. 'Cavalry coming!'

Hanno elbowed his way through to where Mutt stood. His heart sank as he took in the horsemen trotting from the point where the road exited the trees. In good order, on fresh mounts, armed with thrusting spears, they would be unstoppable. 'Shit.'

'A big fat, smelly shit, sir,' said Mutt in his usual sombre tone. 'What shall we do?'

'Start to fall back,' replied Hanno at once. He would have preferred to confer with Sapho, but by the time he did that, the enemy horsemen would be upon them. 'I want deeper ranks – five would be good. Any pila on the ground are to be picked up. Have the men at the front use them to keep off the cavalry. The phalanx is to move back at an angle so that the last few wagons have a chance to reach the ford. Sapho will see what we're doing, if he's not already doing the same.'

'Aye, sir.' Mutt moved out of rank and off to their right, bellowing orders. Hanno did the same to his left. He kept glancing over his shoulder at the enemy. Hope gripped him. The legionaries were holding back, clearly waiting for the cavalry to charge before they attacked again. If they seized their chance, they might pull it off yet. 'Assume five-rank depth, quickly. Grab any javelins you see,' he growled. 'Hand them to the men at the front. When you've done that, I want you to start walking backwards, towards those wagons. Keep your eyes on the enemy. Be ready for the Roman horse.'

His soldiers moved fast, but that didn't stop Hanno's stomach from twisting in knots. Perhaps one man in three had a pilum now, and that wasn't enough to stop a cavalry charge. To stand against such an attack, infantry formations needed so many spears protruding that they resembled a hedgehog. Without that protection, foot soldiers *would* break before a sustained cavalry assault. Hanno hated the inevitability of it. Unless they could make it to the river, many of them were about to die. Baal Hammon, watch over us, he prayed.

They shuffled towards the ford, Hanno directing operations from the left of the front rank, Mutt aiding him from a similar position on the far right. Hanno thanked the gods when he saw that Sapho's phalanx was also retreating. He twisted his head to eye the soldier behind him. 'What are the wagons doing? Pass it on.'

The word moved swiftly to the back rank, and returned as fast. 'Five wagons left on this bank, sir, the first of which is about to enter the water.'

The grain was across, thought Hanno with satisfaction. Yet part of him didn't want to give up until all of their booty had been transferred to the far bank. Was there time? His gaze returned to the front; he cursed. There were mutters of dismay from among his men, and their lines wavered a little. The enemy cavalry had seen through their plan and were advancing at a walk. After a few paces, this became a trot. 'Back,' roared Hanno. 'Move back. Closer to the wagons!' Against them, they would have some chance of holding back the Roman horses. A fierce hunger to succeed against the odds swelled in his heart.

That was when he glanced to his left and was stunned to see the other phalanx breaking apart. Sapho's soldiers were turning and running. They were perhaps thirty paces from the water's edge, so there was every chance of making it before the Roman cavalry arrived. For an instant, Hanno watched in utter disbelief. Why hadn't he been told? It felt as if they had been abandoned – and that was without the thought that they could have held the Romans back. Furious now, he tried to catch a glimpse of his brother amid the chaos, but failed. He dragged his attention back to his own unit, which was further from the water. Despite his wish to save the last wagons, Hanno would have to copy what Sapho had done, or he risked not just enflankment by the enemy on his unprotected side, but being completely overrun.

His mouth had opened to issue the command when horror filled him. The Roman horse had been urged into a full charge. The ground rumbled with the thunder of hooves. Interspersed in the din, he could hear the cavalrymen shouting encouragement at each other. If he ordered his troops to retreat now, they would be cut down in their droves. What other choice did they have, though? Fuck you, Sapho, he thought furiously. Why didn't you wait? If we had regrouped around the wagons, it would have given most of the men the opportunity to ford the river. Now, he had no choice.

'Retreat!' he shouted. 'Retreat! Into the river! Retain your weapons!'

The Libyans did not need telling twice. They spun, cursed as they banged into one another, elbowed slower men out of the way. Then, in a disorganised mass, they ran. Many disregarded Hanno's order and dropped their shields and swords. He cursed them roundly, but it was easy to understand their panic. There were few troops in the world who could stand fast against a wave of charging horsemen. The fact that most horses would not crash into a mass of soldiers was irrelevant. The threat of being trampled to death was enough, Hanno thought bitterly as men streamed away to either side. He would not run, however. 'Give me that!' He made to grab a pilum from a bearded Libyan, one of his oldest veterans. Shamefaced, the man paused. 'What are you going to do, sir?'

'Stay here. Defend my men.'

'That's a death sentence, sir.'

'Maybe so.' Hanno tugged on the javelin shaft, but to his surprise, the Libyan didn't let go.

'I'll stay as well, sir.'

Hanno could see the fear bright in the soldier's eyes, but his chin was firm. He released his grip. 'Very well. Grab a couple of others if you can. Only those with javelins. When the Romans get close, run right at them, screaming like a lunatic. Take down the riders, but if you can't, stab their horses. Do it quick, and move on to the next one. Kill or wound as many as you can.'

'Yes, sir.'

Hanno gave him a tight nod, and the man vanished. A glance at the Romans. A savage oath. They were less than fifty paces away, pounding in at a full gallop. Hanno tried to ignore his fear and thought of how many of his men might get away if they could just break the enemy line. It was an insane thought, but something wouldn't let him run. Hannibal would have to acknowledge his bravery if he did this. Sheathing his bloody sword, he scooped up a discarded pilum. He caught the attention of another Libyan who had not fled. This man was wounded in the leg, which explained why he'd stayed. Hanno gave him a fierce grin. 'Ready to give the whoresons a bloody nose?'

An eager nod. 'Aye, sir!'

Just before the Romans hit, Hanno saw Mutt nearby. A handful of men armed with pila were clustered around him. He felt no surprise, just an overwhelming sense of comradeship with his dour second-in-command. One last look over his shoulder: a sense of relief. Perhaps half his men were already in the river. Sapho's troops, who had been closer to the water, would be faring even better. Their total casualties would not be catastrophic. By anyone's standards, the patrol had been a success – even if he didn't survive it. Hanno readied his javelin as if it were a spear, preparing to sell his life dearly.

The Romans were very close now. He could see their faces clearly, hear their triumphant war cries. They were definitely citizens, not socii. Their mounts were of good quality, sturdy little horses that looked well trained. Most of the riders wore Boeotian helmets and mail shirts; a good number were armed with *gladii* as well as thrusting spears. All carried small round shields. They rode close together, their mounts' shoulders only a few paces apart. It was like facing a fast-moving wall of metal and muscle. Hanno's bladder threatened to empty itself, but he shoved the urge away and raised his shield. 'They won't like foot soldiers launching a counter-attack,' he shouted to the injured Libyan. 'Forward!'

It felt insane not to turn and run, but he advanced anyway. From the corner of his eye, Hanno saw the Libyan limping after him. Beyond that, Mutt and his companions were also moving forward. A cracked, manic cry left Hanno's throat. It was born of fear, desperation, the shreds of his courage, and a tinge of sheer bravado. Aiming his javelin at the rider who looked most likely to strike him, a long-legged man close to his own age, he trotted on. 'WINE! WINE! WINE!' he yelled.

The Roman looked startled to see him running in, but he quickly regained control. He levelled his spear at Hanno's head. His horse whinnied and slowed down, however, disconcerted by the approach of a screaming man bearing a large shield. Hanno drew nearer, still shouting and praying the other enemy horses didn't knock him down, or their riders stab him in the back. 'WINE! WINE! WINE!' He could scarcely hear his own voice above the sound of pounding hooves.

The Roman's spear came thrusting down at his face. Hanno met it with his shield, at the same time peeping around its side. A quick jab with his javelin and the head sank into the cavalryman's thigh. A piercing cry of pain rent the air; the spear fell from the man's nerveless hand as he toppled off his mount. Hanno didn't go after him; instead he wheeled and plunged his pilum into the chest of a passing horse. It was a foolish move. Although the beast staggered and threw its rider, it wrenched the javelin from his hand. He caught a brief glance of its shaft bending in two as the horse rolled over and then it was gone.

His eyes shot over the ground, between the legs of passing riders and steeds, searching frantically for another weapon. A whistle in the air. Hanno ducked instinctively, and the spear that would have skewered him between the shoulder blades screeched off the top of his helmet instead. Even as he tried to turn, a massive weight barged him sideways, unbalancing him. He saw sky, a horse, a snarling face, and then the ground hit him very hard. A hoof clashed off his helmet.

Hanno's world went black.

When he came to, the Roman riders were still riding past, so he couldn't have been unconscious for long. Some hundred paces away, a line of legionaries was advancing in his general direction. Shouts and the clash of weapons carried from the riverbank. Stars spun across his vision, and his head felt as if it were about to burst. There was a massive dent in the top of his helmet, but it was still in place, which was probably the reason he was alive. With difficulty, Hanno undid the chinstrap and eased it off. Cool air ruffled his sweat-soaked hair. The movement sent knives of pain lancing into his brain, and he bit back a curse. Yet it had to come off. Any legionary who saw its shape would know him for a Carthaginian. Without it, in his cuirass, he could perhaps pass for a Roman officer. He had to play dead first, though. The enemy riders had passed by; he just had to escape the infantry's attention. With a few tugs, he managed to pull the corpse of a cavalryman on top of himself. It was a relief to close his eyes. Hanno wanted to go to sleep, to have his headache disappear, but there was no chance of that. The harsh taste of fear was too strong in his mouth. If a single Roman stopped to look at him, he was a dead man. *Stay calm. Breathe slowly and deeply.*

The best thing to do might have been to lie there until it was dark, but Hanno felt that to be the act of a coward. He wanted to cross the river, be there with his men when they marched back into their camp, when they received Hannibal's accolade. He listened with all his might, not moving a muscle as the legionaries tramped past, some distance to his right. When the sounds had diminished, he waited a little longer before shoving the body to one side. Lifting his head a fraction, he peered around. To his relief, he was entirely behind the Roman troops. There was no sign of any more emerging from the road or the trees either.

Hanno struggled to his feet, drew his sword, picked up a scutum. A few paces away, he spotted the body of the bearded Libyan; beside him lay the man who'd been wounded in the leg. Both were covered in wounds. He felt sad but proud of the pair. Welcome them into the afterlife, Hanno asked the gods, for they have earned it. Throwing back his shoulders, he tramped after the enemy soldiers as confidently as he could. Anger flared in his belly. In front of the legionaries, the shapes of the cavalry swirled back and forth, the riders hacking down with their swords from time to time. Some of his Libyans clearly hadn't made it into the water. The infantry would be closing in, intent on finishing them off. Hanno wanted to run, to join in the fight, but he knew that for a pointless way to die. His purpose was to survive. He ensured that his pace was measured, regular.

As he reached the mass of Roman troops, his heart rose to his mouth but to stop might draw attention, so he kept moving, right into the midst of the enemy. The fighting seemed to have eased or even ended, and their formation had broken up. Small groups of men trotted to and fro, killing wounded Libyans or looting the dead. Others were being directed by their officers to turn the carts that had been abandoned around. A few had even downed their shields and were slaking their thirst from wine skins. Everyone was intent on his own purpose. Muttering a prayer for himself this time, Hanno ducked his head and threaded his way through the confusion. It didn't take him that long to near the riverbank. A generous coating of bodies, both dead and injured, covered the ground. Unsurprisingly, most of them were Libyan. Hanno's eyes studied each as he passed; his heart bled as he recognised numerous soldiers from his phalanx. To his immense relief, he saw none with non-mortal wounds. He didn't know if he could have left such a man behind.

On the other side, the wagons were moving off, guarded by some of the Libyans who had made it across. A rearguard remained, safely out of javelin range, perhaps a hundred soldiers and all of the Numidians. Hanno recognised a familiar figure at the Libyans' head: Mutt. At least his second-in-command had made it, he thought with some satisfaction. He glanced at the ford. None of the Romans were attempting to cross, but there were far too many of them standing around for him to be able to enter the water at that point. There was nothing for it: he would have to swim. That meant taking off his cuirass. In his current state, Hanno didn't feel strong enough to brave the crossing with its extra weight. By removing his armour, however, he would expose himself as an enemy. The Romans would turn on him like a pack of feral dogs. He swallowed. Just act as if everything is entirely normal, he decided.

Heart pounding, Hanno walked to a point on the bank where there were fewer legionaries, shedding his baldric as he did. At the water's edge, he didn't look back. Fiddling with the buckles at the side of his cuirass, he undid them. He reached for the upper ones. The effort – and the pain that caused – was too much for him. He paused, waiting until his strength returned a little.

'You! What in Pluto's name do you think you're doing?'

Panic constricted Hanno's throat. With a final effort, he managed to undo the last buckle. The breastplate dropped from his arms, landing at his feet with a metallic thump. Angry shouts came from his rear; he heard the noise of men running towards him. He didn't dare to check how close they were. Taking a deep breath, he jumped in, feet first. The river was much colder than he'd remembered. Coming up to the surface in a fountain of water, he took in a lungful of air and began swimming for the opposite bank. By now, he could hear a chorus of angry voices behind him. Don't let any of them come after me, he begged. He hadn't the reserves left to fight another man, out of his depth. A familiar sound, a rush of air, and a pilum hit the surface not five paces to his left. His head twisted. A line of legionaries had formed, several of whom had javelins. Wagers and jokes were being traded over who would hit him first. Nausea washed over Hanno. They were no more than fifteen paces away – easy killing range.

Damn them all, he thought, turning away and kicking his arms and legs. On he swam, expecting with each heartbeat to feel the agony of a pilum striking him in the back. Five strokes. Ten. In the distance, Hanno heard more shouts. They might have been from the Carthaginian side of the river, but he wasn't sure. Another javelin hit the water behind him. At last he drew close enough to the bank to try putting his feet down. The feeling of mud beneath his feet was incredible, euphoric. Only the luckiest of throws would hit him at this stage.

'Let's get you out of there.'

Shocked, Hanno looked up to see a hand reaching down to him. Incredibly, it belonged to Mutt.

The hand beckoned. 'It's not a bath you're having! Come on, sir.'

'Thank you!' Grinning like a fool, Hanno reached up and accepted the grip. As Mutt heaved him on to dry land, he saw a dozen or more Numidians riding up and down, hurling abuse and spears in equal measure at the Romans. The legionaries had prudently withdrawn out of range. 'I reckon that makes us even, eh?'

A rare smile. 'Maybe, sir.'

'You saw me, then?'

Mutt led him away from the bank. 'One of the lads did, sir. I thought he was making it up, but the spray of water you sent up gave the lie to that. Only one of our lot would have jumped in the water, so I told the Numidians to give whoever it was covering volleys of spears. For all Sapho's orders, I couldn't just ignore the poor bastard – you, sir.' Mutt chuckled. 'Begging your pardon.'

'Sapho's orders?' repeated Hanno stupidly.

'Yes, sir. Once we'd reached this side, I sent word to him that you weren't with us and asking for permission to lead a group back over to look for you.'

Hanno's heart filled. 'Wanting to die today, were you?'

'I didn't get the chance, sir. Sapho said that the grain was all that mattered now and that we had to move it fast, in case the Romans crossed the river.'

'Harsh, but true,' muttered Hanno. He caught the way Mutt's mouth turned down. 'What?' There was no immediate answer, so he asked again.

'He didn't seem overly concerned that it was you I was talking about, sir,' admitted Mutt reluctantly. 'It was as if you were just another soldier, not his brother.'

'I wouldn't worry about that,' said Hanno, brushing it off. 'It's not as if he had time to sit and think about it. There was every possibility that the Romans would counter-attack, that he might still lose the grain. His priority was to see it delivered to our camp, nothing else.'

'If you say so, sir.' Mutt's face told a different story, however.

Hanno refused to give credence to the idea that Sapho might have wished him ill when he'd ordered his phalanx to retreat without warning. It was too shocking, too harsh. He shoved the matter from his mind as they walked slowly towards the rearguard. The grain and wine had not been lost; the army would be fed. He was alive. Not too many of their men had been lost. Hannibal would be pleased.

That was what was important. That was enough.

Chapter XV

Sapho's face was the picture of surprise when he first saw Hanno appear. Hanno wondered if there was a flicker of another emotion in his brother's eyes, but it was gone so fast that he could not be sure. Sapho enveloped him in a bear hug, gave thanks to every god in the pantheon and insisted that they crack open one of the amphorae that they'd seized. 'We'll drink as we march,' he shouted. 'After an adventure like that, we deserve it!' Hanno's head was still thumping with pain, but, delighted at his semi-miraculous escape, he again buried his concern that Sapho might have intended him to die. Yet he welcomed the dulling of his senses granted by the wine. Mutt and the rest of the officers were also thirsty. Once it was clear that there would be no pursuit, they let the men start drinking too. The march back to the camp passed in a blur of singing, bawdy jokes and increasingly inflated versions of what they had all done. By the time that Hannibal arrived to take a look at the wagons, they were both the worse for wear.

Hanno's palms grew slick with sweat as their general came to hear their account. What would the punishment be for drunkenness? he wondered. His worries were unfounded. Hannibal listened attentively to Sapho, smiled as Hanno recounted his mad charge at the enemy cavalry and clapped him on the shoulder when he'd finished. 'Not only have you brought back all the grain, which is much needed, but you did it even when ambushed by a superior force. Casualties?'

'Between fifty and sixty men, sir,' replied Sapho. 'Plenty of walking wounded, but most of them will recover.'

'I can ill afford to lose my Libyans,' said Hannibal, 'but it seems that today I was lucky not to lose more. Both of you have done well today. My thanks.' His gaze moved to Hanno's water skin. 'I presume there's wine in that?'

'Er, yes, sir.' Hanno felt his cheeks redden.

'Does a man have to die of thirst around here before he gets offered a drink?'

'Of course not, sir.' Grinning with relief, Hanno handed it over.

And that had been that. Hannibal had shared a drink with them and, with a last congratulation, departed, calling for his quartermaster. 'The wagonloads of grain, oil and wine need to be divided up.'

Hanno had needed no further excuse to get uproariously drunk. He was grateful to Sapho for asking him on the patrol, to Mutt for rescuing him and to Hannibal for recognising what they had done. For the moment, all was well with the world and it seemed as if things could only get better. There was the matter of Aurelia, of course, but he drowned out thoughts of her with more wine. He was vaguely aware of Mutt helping him back to his tent long after sundown and that was it.

Hanno woke with a bad hangover and a mouth that tasted as if something had died in it. The pain from the blow to his head was no worse than it had been the day before, which told him that no lasting damage had been done. Regretting the excesses of the patrol's aftermath a little, he struggled outside his tent and emptied a bucket of water over his head. There were knowing smiles from a few of his men, but he was too weary to care. Even officers were allowed to relax now and again. A few mouthfuls of wine and a piece of stale bread taken sitting in the sun restored him somewhat. His duties were calling, but Hanno decided that they could wait. Mutt would be taking care of things anyway. The new equipment he now needed would still be in the quartermaster's stores later on. For the moment, he could rest on the laurels of what they'd done the previous day.

'Here he is, the hero of the hour. Dozing!'

Hanno's eyes jerked open. Sapho was standing over him, the trace of a mocking smile playing over his lips. He fought his irritation. 'There's nothing needs doing that Mutt can't deal with right now.'

'How's the head?'

'Not too bad. And yours?'

Sapho shrugged. 'A little tender, but it will soon pass.'

'We did well yesterday,' said Hanno.

'Indeed we did. You're not a boy any longer.'

'No, I'm not. I've been through too much since I was washed out to sea with Suni that day.' Hanno fingered his scar. Many of his memories were dark and unpleasant and better forgotten. 'Maybe I should have listened to you, eh?'

Unbelievably, Sapho's chest puffed up. 'Well, I haven't said so before, but—'

Hanno's irritation became real anger. 'Piss off, Sapho! You always know best, eh? You didn't have a clue a storm would blow up that day any more than I did. Admit it: you were just being your usual overbearing self by trying to stop me and Suni going fishing.'

Sapho's face went bright red. 'How dare you speak to me like that?'

'I'll do as I please,' Hanno retorted, getting to his feet. 'Just fucking try and stop me. I'll soon put you right.'

'Don't tempt me.' Sapho's eyes glittered with anger.

Breathing hard, they glared at each other. Hanno was not prepared to back down. He'd had enough of being the younger brother, the one who was patronised. After the patrol's success, he'd assumed that Sapho would see him through different eyes. Clearly not. In that moment, all his concerns about his brother's previous actions returned to haunt him. Did Sapho yet hold a grudge against him? he thought furiously. He wanted to leap upon his brother, fists pounding, but to his surprise, Sapho made a conciliatory move.

'I didn't come here for an argument,' he said.

'I didn't invite you in for one,' Hanno admitted. He stuck out his jaw, unwilling to give any more ground without good reason. 'What *did* you come here for?'

'I was going to invite you on a hunt. The mountains on the peninsula to the east are reported to be rich in game.'

'Now?' Riding all day was the last thing Hanno wanted to do, hunt or not.

'No, tomorrow.'

'We'd need permission to go that far, surely?'

Sapho couldn't stop his smugness from returning. 'There's no need to worry. Mago is coming too.'

'Mago?' Hanno had been in the same tent as Hannibal's brother a number of times, but never done more than exchange polite greetings with him. Sapho, on the other hand, had been with Mago – and Bostar – when he'd led two thousand men to ambush the Romans' rear at the Trebia. They must have hit it off well since, Hanno thought. Sapho's star was indeed rising if he now hobnobbed with one of the most senior officers in the army.

'Yes. He tried to persuade Hannibal to join us, but had no luck. Our general is too busy. He's given his blessing to the expedition, though,' Sapho drawled. 'Says it will do us all good. Especially for you and me, after the patrol.'

'Who else is going?'

'Bostar, Cuttinus. A few other phalanx commanders. The Numidian Zamar will be there too. That was his condition for lending us the horses.'

Hanno's enthusiasm grew. He got on well with Bostar. Zamar and Cuttinus, another phalanx commander, were good company too. 'Father?'

'No! You know what he's like,' answered Sapho with a laugh. 'He's far too serious.'

Hanno chuckled at the truth of that. 'I'd love to tag along.'

The tension eased at once. Sapho slapped a hand off his knee. 'Excellent. The more, the merrier.'

'Have some more wine,' said Hanno, leaning over to pour.

'I don't mind if I do.' Sapho smacked his lips after swallowing. 'That's not bad stuff. Where did you get it?'

'It's some of what we took on the patrol.'

'You didn't steal it from the whorehouse then?' Sapho smirked, and Hanno fought his irritation again. 'Peace,' said his brother, raising a hand, 'I don't want to start fighting again.'

Hanno grunted, not in a friendly way but not arguing either.

'Just think,' said Sapho after a moment. 'We're here in a shitting tent. All right, we've got some half-decent wine, but we've frozen our balls off all winter. Soon, we'll be baking in summer heat. Suni, however, has probably been enjoying the spring sunshine in Carthage. Drinking in one of the inns near the Choma. Maybe he's even balling a whore right now, while we're stuck in the arsehole of Italy with nothing better to talk about than hunting. Have you thought about that?'

The wine coursed through Hanno's veins. He scowled at his brother. 'Suni's not doing any of those things.'

'Eh?' scoffed Sapho. 'Have you learned to divine the future, or to read men's minds from afar?'

'He's fucking dead!' shouted Hanno, his anger bubbling over again. 'He's rotting in a grave near Capua.'

'Dead? How can you be sure?'

'It doesn't matter. I just know.'

Sapho's eyes grew calculating. 'You can only have found that out when you left your men that time. My gods, did you go back to the estate where you'd been enslaved?'

Hanno stared at the glowing wood in the brazier and said nothing.

'You must have.'

'I talked to a slave there, yes. I wanted to find out if Suni had left safely. You remember that I told you he'd been injured.' Let him swallow that, Hanno thought. It wasn't so far from the truth.

Sapho's eyes studied his for a moment before they dropped away. 'You two were always thick as thieves. It's a damn shame that he's dead. What happened to him?'

'He'd been found in the woods – I don't know how – and taken in as a runaway. He played dumb, but for some reason the overseer became suspicious of him. The bastard accused Suni of stealing a knife from the kitchens,' lied Hanno. 'He was executed in punishment.'

'Fucking Romans. They're bloodthirsty savages.' Sapho drew a hand across his throat. 'This for them all.'

Except Aurelia. And Quintus. Even their parents weren't all bad. Hanno grunted in agreement, relieved that his brother appeared to have accepted his story. 'Forget about the Romans. There'll be time enough to think about them in the months to come. Tell me about this hunt. Have we any hounds?'

Sapho nodded happily. 'We're taking along a group of Gauls to use as beaters. Some of them have hunting dogs.'

'It looks to be a promising outing, then. We will be sure to find some game.'

'I haven't hunted since before we crossed the River Rhodanus.'

'And I since leaving Carthage!'

They grinned at one another, their argument forgotten – temporarily at least.

Spring was well under way, but the chill had been evident through Hanno's blankets nonetheless. It was nothing like the winter had been, however. He had grown used to extreme weather by now, but he was still glad that the worst of it had passed some time since. As he emerged from his tent, he smiled at the beauty of the dawn. Above, the rising sun had turned the sky every imaginable shade of red, orange and pink. The rock-hard ground glittered with dew; here and there it was possible to see lines of footprints made by men who had been up before the dawn. A layer of condensation coated every tent in sight. Plumes of exhaled breath meandered up from between them, marking the path of walking soldiers. Grey clouds of it hung over the cavalry's horse pens. Little trails of smoke rose from the cooking fires that had been lit.

Hanno stamped his feet, already glad that he had donned socks before lacing up his boots. Underneath his woollen cloak, he was wearing a thick tunic. Remembering the tale of Quintus' bear hunt, he had impulsively put on a mail shirt as well, cinching it at the waist with a belt. Hanno had seen the tusks on dead boars at Quintus' house. The risk might be small, but it wasn't worth taking. One thrust to the groin or the belly and a man's life was over. He put the macabre idea from his mind, offering up a quick prayer. Today would be about companionship and good sport, nothing else. He shook his limbs. It was time to find Mutt and make a quick circuit of his men's tents before shovelling down a bowl of porridge and meeting the others.

A couple of hours later and Hanno had almost forgotten that he was a soldier at war in a foreign land. The countryside was empty of life, its inhabitants long since fled to the safety of areas unoccupied by the Carthaginians. The nearest Roman forces lay to the north and west. With no need to worry about enemy troops, the camaraderie of the hunt had taken over. They travelled at an easy pace across the open farmland, a large group of men laughing and joking among themselves. At the rear, a dozen or more Gauls trotted along, armed with spears. In front of several of the warriors, big, rough-coated hounds strained at their leashes. Behind them came a handful of servants, leading mules laden down with small tents and provisions, insurance against a possible night outdoors.

Skins of wine were being handed around the horsemen, wagers made, boastful stories told. Mago rode in the centre, a lean, muscular figure who exuded energy. Naturally enough, most of the officers present wanted to share Hannibal's brother's company. They all clustered around him, but it was Sapho who sat on his horse to Mago's right. Currently, Cuttinus was on his left. Hanno had exchanged greetings with Mago, but he had no interest in currying favour, in hanging off the man's every word. He didn't care to admit it, but he was also wary of saying the wrong thing. He had been in hot water enough times with Hannibal not to want to risk it with Mago too. Therefore he rode with Bostar and Zamar a short distance behind the main body. In their company, it was hard not to feel carefree. 'This is just like home, eh, brother?' he commented happily. 'When we used to go hunting together outside Carthage.'

'It is,' cried Bostar, laughing.

Hanno turned to Zamar, whose only concession to the weather was a cloak over his open-necked, sleeveless tunic. 'Aren't you cold?'

A shrug. 'This is what it's like in winter in the mountains at home. It will warm up soon. That doesn't mean I wouldn't prefer the African sun on my face. But this is better than sitting on our arses in camp. It will clear out the cobwebs, and if the gods are with us, we'll have roast pork to fill our bellies tonight.'

Hanno's mouth watered at the thought.

By the time they had ridden to the foot of the huge mountainous promontory that jutted into the Adriatic, sent out the Gauls and the dogs to find scent, and spent hours trudging uphill, often on foot, leading their horses, Hanno was famished. His spirits were still high, however. The banter with Bostar and Zamar had been unending, and fresh meat was now a definite prospect. A middling-sized boar had been brought to bay by the dogs soon after they'd set off up the slope. Mago had dismounted and speared it through the chest. A couple of Gauls had remained behind with the body, their job to butcher it and to begin cooking the meat. By the time the hunters returned, the feast would be ready.

The rest had continued upwards; they were spread out through the trees in a long line: Mago in the middle, Sapho beside him, the others to either side. Hanno and Bostar rode to the far left of Mago; Zamar was just out of earshot to their right. The brothers spent the time poking at the vegetation with their spears, listening to the sounds of the Gauls and hounds to their front, and talking. It was as if the gods had answered Hanno's prayers. He had thought that when the army went into camp with the onset of winter there would be plenty of opportunities to seek out Bostar for such chats. Yet that had not been so. All the more reason to relish this, therefore. He had asked Bostar about Sapho once before, but had not got much out of him. Perhaps this was a better time, he thought. 'So Sapho is good friends with Mago now, eh?'

'He seems to be,' replied Bostar, trying not to sound irritated, but failing.

His brother's back had gone up already, Hanno judged, so things between them weren't good. He hadn't been sure that was the case, but it was no surprise. The pair's animosity had been clear from the moment he'd made it back to Hannibal's army. 'Has Sapho been spending much time with him?'

'Trying to, anyway. Mago's a busy man, but Sapho's been persistent. I'll give him that,' Bostar added.

'Always wants to be the best, doesn't he? Be the most popular. Yet it always seems to come back and bite him in the arse.'

'Until now,' added Bostar. 'Mago was impressed with us both at the Trebia, but it was Sapho who sought him out afterwards. He's been doing so ever since.'

'Why didn't you do the same?'

A *phhhh* of contempt. 'Not my way, brother, you know that.'

There was a chorus of barks and excited shouts from off to their right. The pair exchanged a look. 'That sounds promising,' said Hanno, grinning.

'It does, but we have to keep our place in the line, or anything that comes this way will get away.'

Hanno grimaced, because it was true. 'Will we see any damn game?'

'Trust in the gods, little brother,' advised Bostar, ducking under a low branch.

'Watch whom you call "little",' warned Hanno, but there was none of the anger in his voice that there would have been had it been Sapho who'd uttered the words. Somehow Bostar's affection for him always came through, whereas with his oldest brother there was a constant sense that Sapho wanted to dominate him. Why couldn't Sapho be more like Bostar? he wondered sadly.

They rode past a holm oak that had been struck by lightning. Its blackened trunk and branches were a stark contrast to the greenery of its companions all around. It reminded Hanno of a corpse left among the living. 'Do you trust Sapho?' he asked, before he could rein in the words.

Bostar's head turned. 'Do I trust Sapho?'

Shit, I should have kept my mouth shut, Hanno thought, but the words could not be unsaid. He decided to brazen it out, make light of it. 'Yes.'

'That's an odd question.'

Hanno was going to blurt that it was about a wager he'd won against Sapho, which his brother was refusing to pay, but he managed to stop himself. There was nothing like silence to give a man room to speak, indeed to put pressure on him to do so.

'Are you asking because you know he and I don't get on?'

'No,' replied Hanno, squirming a little beneath Bostar's gimlet stare. 'It's because of something that happened.'

'What?'

This wasn't how it was supposed to happen, Hanno thought angrily. He'd wanted Bostar to reveal his thoughts first. 'It was probably nothing,' he began.

A frenzy of barks and growls interrupted. Men roared excitedly; a horse whinnied. They heard the sound of something heavy thrashing off up the slope to their right. Curses followed it. A series of shouted conversations between those strung out along the line, and then they heard Zamar yell, 'Keep moving!'

'Whatever it was got away,' observed Bostar.

'There's hope for us yet,' said Hanno brightly, hoping that his brother would not enquire further.

No such luck.

'What happened then?' asked Bostar.

'When?' replied Hanno casually.

'Don't be all coy with me. You know exactly what I mean!'

Hanno could see by the cut of Bostar's jaw that he wouldn't be fobbed off. Praying that he hadn't made a big mistake, he related the tale of his passage across the swamps with Sapho, and of how he'd fallen into the pool. Bostar chortled a little at that, but the fierce concentration on his face didn't waver. 'Sapho's expression was so fleeting that I told myself I'd imagined it. I put it from my mind,' said Hanno. 'But I remembered it a few months ago, when I got back from patrol.'

'Why?'

Gods, he was going to have to reveal how he'd deserted his command. Hanno could feel his cheeks reddening, could sense Bostar's interest growing. He kneed his horse forward, avoiding his brother's gaze. 'I have no idea how, but he knew about me, em, leaving my unit for a short time.'

A heartbeat's shocked silence. Then: 'Leaving your unit?'

Hanno cast an embarrassed look at Bostar. 'I left Mutt in charge for three days while I travelled to Capua and back on my own.'

'In all the gods' names, why? Do you want Hannibal to have you executed?'

Hanno dared say nothing.

'What madness possessed you to do something so stupid?' Bostar glowered at him; again Hanno did not reply.

'You're no traitor, clearly. With other men, I'd have said the most likely reason was to find a woman for a night or two, but it's not in your nature to desert because of that.' Bostar's eyes narrowed. 'You were enslaved near Capua, weren't you?'

'Yes,' mumbled Hanno unwillingly.

'You went back to see someone you knew! Yet the man – Quintus? – whom you freed at the Trebia won't have been there. If he's not dead, he'll still be in the army. The same will apply to his father.' The shortest of pauses. 'His sister. You must have gone back to see his sister!'

Hanno shook his head in guilty agreement.

'You stupid bastard, Hanno. What if one of your men ratted you out on this? Did you not think of that?'

'Mutt was sure no one would say a word. I believed him.'

'Yet one must have spoken to Sapho, or we wouldn't be having this conversation.'

'You're right,' said Hanno miserably.

'Best make sure that you look after your soldiers in future. If Hannibal discovers that you've been consorting with the enemy, you'd be executed on the spot,' warned Bostar. He saw Hanno's expression. 'I suppose you know that already. What did Sapho say about it? Did he realise that you'd been to see Quintus' sister?'

'No. He thought I'd been off to find a whorehouse. I didn't persuade him otherwise.'

'A wise move.'

Hanno seized on the comment. 'So you *don't* trust him then?'

Bostar's eyes met his without wavering. 'No, I don't.'

Relief – and a little fear – suffused Hanno. 'Why not?'

'Finish your story first.'

'There's not much more to say. He went on about how dangerous what I'd done had been – the inference being that the danger wasn't just from the Romans, but Hannibal too. I challenged him, and he laughed it off as a joke. Yet it didn't damn well feel like one at the time. All I could remember was what happened when Hannibal found out that I'd let Quintus and his father go. Do you remember?'

'Of course,' replied Bostar grimly. 'Who could forget a man standing by while his two brothers were under threat of crucifixion?'

'He denied it at the time, and I believed him. But then there was the incident at the swamp. What Sapho said when I came back from patrol really made me wonder if he hates me. Why else would he even pretend to threaten that he'd tell Hannibal about what I'd done?' He eyed Bostar sidelong, and felt reassured by his thoughtful expression. 'That's everything.'

There was a prolonged silence, which Hanno did not attempt to break.

Finally, Bostar let out a long sigh. 'I never thought I would ever tell a living soul about what passed between me and him in the Alps. Now it seems I must.'

'Was it something like me falling into the swamp pool?'

'It was even worse than that. I was blown over a precipice in a storm.

Luckily, I broke my fall by grabbing a jutting branch just below the cliff edge. Sapho saw what happened. He didn't rush to my aid, even though the branch was about to give way. When it did, I tried to jump up to safety. He grabbed me then, which saved my life.'

'Gods above!' cried Hanno, horrified. 'Why did he not act before?'

'I don't know. When he did, it was out of instinct,' replied Bostar. 'Yet I'm certain that if I'd fallen a few heartbeats earlier, he would have just watched me go. The dog couldn't say why he hadn't moved the instant I fell. He didn't have an answer either when I accused him of being glad that you'd vanished.'

'Why would he have felt like that? Apart from the fact that we always argued, I mean.'

'I was in Iberia at the time. With you gone too, he'd had Father's attention all to himself.'

A deep sadness flowed through Hanno. The conversation had made him remember Mutt's unhappiness with Sapho's refusal to let him recross the river during their combined patrol. Maybe he hadn't just been following Hannibal's orders to the letter? Maybe he'd been pleased that Hanno was presumed dead?

'What is it?'

In a low voice, he told Bostar, who shook his head sadly. 'You or I would have acted in the same way, but our anguish would have been plain to Mutt. I think that Sapho's reaction intimates that he felt differently.'

Bostar's logic was hard to argue with. Hanno let out a heavy sigh. 'What has he become?'

'A man driven by fierce ambition. That's the only thing that makes sense to me.'

Hanno nodded in agreement. 'What did you say after he'd rescued you?'

'That I would repay the debt. From that moment onwards, however, he'd be dead to me. I swore not to tell Father. I've kept my word too.' A smile quirked Bostar's lips. 'But I said nothing about not telling you.'

'You should have told me sooner!'

'I could say the same to you. Naïvely, I thought it was possible that you and he could have a better relationship – as long as he didn't try the same shit with you as he did with me.' A cloud passed over Bostar's face. 'I should have known that he was capable of it after the ambush at the Trebia.'

'No man likes to think that his brother is capable of such things,' said Hanno. 'I was ashamed even to contemplate it.'

'What if Sapho had let you die in the swamp?' Bostar's tone was anguished.

'He didn't. And, like you, I won't ever let something like that happen again,' replied Hanno firmly, trying to ignore the sorrow welling in his heart. 'I'll always be on the alert from now on.'

'Who'd have thought it, eh?' Bostar's face mirrored Hanno's unhappiness. 'That we'd have a brother so treacherous?'

'I never imagined it could come to this. What if we went to Father?'

'There's no point. Father loves him, as he does us. I don't think he'd really hear what we had to say, especially without evidence. If he was challenged, Sapho would deny everything.'

'It would be our word against his,' mused Hanno. 'With neither side able to prove the other wrong.'

They digested the bitter reality of the situation in silence.

'And you're sure it's ambition that makes him do it?' asked Hanno, still trying to understand.

'Yes. From when we were small, Sapho always wanted to be the best. Being the oldest, he *was* better at everything – at least until we both reached manhood. I can remember how angry he was the first time I beat him in a foot race. It was a one-off, he said, but then I did it again. Not long after, I began to do better than him during our officer training. He grew so jealous then; in retrospect, I wonder if that was the time he began to be harder on you.'

'Maybe. I can scarcely remember a time from my childhood when he didn't lord it over me.'

'Once the war started, I think he transferred his need for approval from Father on to Hannibal. During the siege of Saguntum, I happened to save our general's life quite by chance. It felt as if Sapho hated me for that. I think his need to be recognised is what's driven him since. Getting close to Mago is just another way to try and win Hannibal's approval.'

'Do we mean nothing to him then?' growled Hanno. 'Or does he just tolerate us as long as we don't block his path to glory?'

'I don't know how his mind works,' said Bostar heavily. 'But I suspect the latter. Whatever the reason, neither of us can trust him. We must watch our backs; keep our mouths shut; obey our orders. There must be no more foolhardy escapades to Capua. If your actions became public knowledge, Hannibal would have to make an example of you – and he *would*. I doubt that he'd like the fact that Sapho had been the one to inform on his brother, but that wouldn't stop him.'

They exchanged a grim look.

Real grief gripped Hanno, but not just because of Sapho. It felt as if his chances of ever seeing Aurelia again had just slid off a cliff edge into oblivion. He'd known his dream of being reunited was a fantasy, yet, for all that, it had given him some succour. No longer. 'Very well,' he said firmly. 'I will not try to visit Capua again.'

'Good.' Bostar seemed relieved. He aimed his spear up the slope. 'Let's find ourselves some game to kill. I don't know about you, but I've had enough misery for today. It's time for some sport.'

'Agreed.' Yet as Hanno kneed his horse onwards, there was no denying the feeling of loss in his heart. It was as if he now had only one brother, not two. It wasn't a true bereavement, but it felt similar to one. So too did the pain of knowing once and for all that he and his life were totally incompatible with Aurelia and hers. The best he could do, Hanno thought with a fond glance at Bostar, was to appreciate the relationships that he had. He offered up an ardent prayer to Baal Hammon, Tanit and Eshmoun. Watch over my brother and father, I beg you. Keep them safe. They are all I have.

He left out Sapho.

Chapter XVI

North of Capua, two months later . . .

'I'm not sure that this is a good idea.' Lucius' voice came from outside the litter.

Aurelia's stomach twisted, but all he saw was her widest smile as she lifted the drapes. 'You promised me!'

'In a moment of weakness. It's midsummer now; you yourself complain about how hot it is in the middle of the day.'

'That's why we're setting out now, before dawn,' she replied sweetly. 'We'll reach Capua not long after midday. I can take a rest the instant we arrive.'

'A city is the last kind of place for a woman in your state to visit,' he grumbled. 'Open drains. Disease. Rats. Bad vapours.'

'I'll keep away from all of those. I'm not an invalid! I'm well able to walk around, you know that. There's so much I need to buy before the baby comes.'

'A slave could do it.'

'They'd forget half of it, or purchase the wrong thing. It's far easier for me to do it. And don't forget my mother. She will have come to Capua to see me, probably for the last time before the baby is born.'

'I don't know. Maybe you should stay behind. Your mother can always travel here. What if your labour starts early?'

'That won't happen,' Aurelia said with a confidence she didn't totally feel. 'Even if it did, Capua is full of surgeons and midwives, each of whom will be as experienced as the woman who lives nearby. What better place could there be to give birth?'

'It's asking for trouble to make light of it,' he said irritably, shifting on his horse's back. 'Don't you know how many babies and women die during childbirth?'

He can't help himself, mentioning the child before me, thought Aurelia, fighting back bitterness. Since she had told him of her pregnancy, his attitude towards her had utterly changed. True, she no longer had to endure his advances – her mother had been right about that – but much of the time, it was as if Lucius now viewed her as nothing more than a vehicle to carry his son to term. To bring that up, however, would be pointless and might further endanger her chances of winning this argument. 'Yes, husband. I meant no disrespect,' she said meekly. 'But I offered a lamb to Ceres yesterday. The soothsayer could find no reason in the entrails for me not to go to Capua.'

Defeated by the divine, Lucius gave a reluctant nod. 'Very well. We had best leave now then. I want to be far down the road when the sun comes up.'

'Of course, husband.' Aurelia concealed her satisfaction until the drape had fallen back into place. Without doubt, this would be her last chance before the birth to enjoy the sights of Capua. A long period of time on Lucius' family estate had given her an even greater appreciation of the city's attractions. Its baths, theatres and good shops beckoned in her mind. There was the prospect of seeing her mother away from her new home; of calling on Martialis; there was a possibility, albeit remote, of seeing Gaius there. The list of things she wanted to do was endless. Once the baby was born, all chance of doing such things would vanish for many months. It was worrying how close the door of opportunity had come to closing. Aurelia gave thanks to Fides for making Lucius keep his word.

As the litter was lifted into the air by a quartet of Lucius' strongest slaves, she settled back on to the soft cushions and made herself as comfortable as possible. Rising so early didn't suit her in her current condition. She had grown used to dozing until midmorning. A nap now would help to prevent her feeling too fatigued later. Rocked by the swaying motion of the litter and the murmur of conversation between Lucius and Statilius, it wasn't long before her eyelids began to droop. Phanes' image briefly crossed her mind, but she was able to push it away. Lucius' tactic had worked. Her mother's most recent letter mentioned how the moneylender had unexpectedly reduced the amount demanded each month. Atia had no idea why, but things were much easier as a result. Content that all was well, Aurelia fell into a deep, dreamless sleep.

Apart from a brief stop to eat a little food, the party – Lucius, Aurelia, Elira, Statilius and a dozen other slaves – travelled without pause, reaching Capua not long after the sun had reached its zenith. The loud churring of the cicadas that had accompanied them all the way was finally drowned out as they passed beneath one of the six stone gateways that gave access to the city. Inside the walls, the air was still and hot. Here the sun could concentrate its attention on the narrow streets that were lined on either side by buildings several storeys high. The temperature in the litter, which had been increasing steadily, rose to unbearable levels. Aurelia was glad to reach Lucius' city house, a spacious affair with a grand courtyard full of shade and pattering fountains. While he met with clients who wanted his patronage, she spent the rest of the afternoon reclining there, fanned by two slaves with palm branches and sipping cool juices brought to her by Elira.

In the early evening, Aurelia determined to go out. The dreadful heat had begun at last to abate, and she wanted to make a start on her shopping list, which, thanks to the advice of the local midwife, was quite extensive. Lucius was still busy. Apart from recommending she take a slave as protection and authorising Statilius to give her a purse of coin, he barely looked up from his desk when she stuck her head inside his office door. His lack of attention didn't surprise her. It took something monumental to drag him from his estates' accounts. Not that she minded. After his earlier outburst, she wanted to escape before he also reconsidered her outing.

Stepping from the cool of the house into the baking warmth of the street was like being slapped in the face. Despite the umbrella wielded by Elira, which shielded her from the unforgiving sun, instant beads of sweat prickled on Aurelia's scalp, forehead and swollen belly. Her dress stuck to her back. The insides of her thighs rubbed together. Perhaps coming to the city *had* been rash? Dismissing the notion, she pictured the items on her list: a cradle, swaddling cloths, squares of linen to wash and dry the baby, scented oils to use when bathing. If she could find it, Aurelia had also resolved to buy some expensive perfume as a treat. After that, a visit had to be paid to the stall in the forum that sold spiced sausages. She had been craving them for months. The cook in Lucius' house had tried to follow her instructions in recreating them, but his version wasn't a patch on the real thing. Perhaps the stallholder would part with his recipe if she slipped him a few coins. That happy thought helped carry her from Lucius' house down the quiet residential street to the main avenue that led to the forum.

A strapping farm slave armed with a short cudgel dogged their footsteps. Aurelia soon noticed that more often than not his gaze was directed at Elira's shapely rear; a sharp reprimand redirected his attentions to their surroundings. With the threat of Phanes removed, there was little risk in being abroad at this hour, she thought, but that didn't mean there weren't cutpurses about. The purse Statilius had given her weighed heavily around her neck. A shawl might have covered it from prying eyes, but there was no way Aurelia could have borne the extra layer of clothing. As it was, she was already dreaming about peeling off her wool dress when they got back.

Although the crowds frequenting the streets and the forum added to the heat and the feeling of claustrophobia, the expedition began well. Aurelia spent time in a cloth merchant's shop, admiring the wide variety and colours of fabrics on offer. She handled a piece of silk for the first time and was amazed by its gossamer appearance and the way it slipped through her fingers. The price was no less stunning: a hundred didrachms for a short length that would serve only as a lady's scarf. 'You've got to understand, mistress,' the sweating shopkeeper explained, 'it's come thousands of miles just to get here. Far to the east of Greece and Asia Minor. Past Judaea and Syria. Months of journeying beyond Persia, even. It comes from the land of the Seres, a yellow-skinned people with black hair and slanted eyes.' Aurelia had laughed, disbelieving, and settled instead for a score of linen squares and two sets of swaddling cloths.

Drawn by the alluring smells, she next ventured into a perfumer's. The proprietor, a Judaean with twinkling eyes, insisted on giving her a tour of his premises. Aurelia's curiosity got the better of her. There were benefits to being a Roman matron, she thought. Some doors that had previously been closed to her now opened with ease. The Judaean seemed trustworthy, and she had little compunction about leaving the male slave outside. Elira came with her. As Aurelia's eyes grew used to the dim light, she gazed with fascination at the benches lined with little glass flasks and vials, the mixing bowls and the copper alembics in which the perfumes were prepared. A dizzying mix of smells assailed her nostrils, among them coriander and myrtle. Urged by the Judaean, she dabbed essence of almonds and lilies on her wrists and neck. Countless others were offered to try. After a while, she lost count. 'I love them,' she said, refusing yet another bottle, 'but there are too many to choose from.'

'You must have a favourite, mistress.' The Judaean smiled, all brown teeth and reddened gums. 'The rosewater, maybe? Or the lily? Choose one. I'll give you the best price in Capua, and because you're so beautiful, you can have a second vial at half price.'

Aurelia laughed. The shopkeeper was a rogue, of that there was no doubt, but he was charming and friendly. She wanted to give him custom. 'It has to be the lilies.'

'I knew it!' He clapped his hands, and one of the slaves working at the benches padded to his side. 'Prepare two bottles of essence of lilies from the latest batch. Quickly!' As the slave hurried off, he bowed to Aurelia. 'Would the lady like a cup of wine? I have a fine vintage from Sicily, and another from our own Campania.'

Aurelia mock-frowned at him. 'You haven't mentioned the price yet.'

'It will be a fair one, I swear to you, on my father's honour.'

'So what is it?' she asked, growing a little suspicious.

A greasy smile. 'Ten didrachms for the first bottle, five for the second.'

Even without Elira's gasp, Aurelia knew the demand was exorbitant. 'A fair price, you say? Ha!' She turned, as if to go.

'My lady, wait! We can negotiate.'

'Your perfumes are incredible,' she said, ignoring his pleased nod, 'but I couldn't pay any more than one didrachm for a bottle of the lily.'

The Judaean wrung his hands together. 'That would not even cover my costs. Do you know how many flowers have to be used to make just one vial? More than two hundred! Then there's the labour that goes into its preparation.'

'All work that is done by your slaves,' said Aurelia tartly. 'Whom you don't pay.'

He was unabashed. 'The flowers have to be bought; the running costs of my workshop are high indeed. I couldn't take less than eight didrachms for the first bottle. Twelve for the two.'

Aurelia walked away without a word. She'd gone no more than three steps before the Judaean spoke again. 'Ten didrachms!'

She kept walking. 'I'll give you three.'

'Mistress, you are trying to ruin me!' he wailed.

She stopped.

'Eight,' he ventured.

At last she turned to look at him. 'Five.'

'Let us split the difference, as friends would. Six and a half didrachms.'

'Six,' declared Aurelia, knowing she had him.

He let out a long sigh. 'Very well, mistress. I, a poor ignorant trader, give you this price because of your outstanding beauty and charm.'

Despite herself, she smiled. 'Here.' The coins were gone from her hand in the blink of an eye. More bowing and scraping from the Judaean. The perfume arrived a moment later; Aurelia gestured Elira to take the long-necked vials.

'Some wine?' he asked again.

'Thank you, but no,' replied Aurelia, suddenly overcome by the intense heat radiating from the workshop's low tile roof. The Judaean didn't protest, which pleased her. She must have fought him down to a good price.

'Please come back when the baby is born, and try some more of my products,' he urged. 'I have scents to drive a husband wild with desire.'

'I will.' Aurelia made her way towards the front of the shop. Intent on getting out into the fresh air, she didn't see the masked figure slip out from behind a set of shelves. The first thing she knew was the prick of a knife at the base of her spine. Her right arm was wrenched up behind her back. A low voice growled in her ear, 'Over here, bitch.' She felt herself being propelled over to the far wall. Elira cried out, and the Judaean spluttered in dismay. 'Nobody move, or I'll cut the whore's throat,' barked the man.

'Who are you? What do you want?' She fumbled for her purse with her free hand. 'Take this.' It was snatched from her grasp. Relief turned to terror a heartbeat later, however, when Aurelia felt the back of her dress being lifted up. She opened her mouth to scream, but a sharp poke from the knife reduced her cry to a whimper.

'Unless you'd like me to gut you as well, stay fucking still.'

'I'm pregnant.' Aurelia began to cry. She tried to turn around and look at her attacker, but was stopped by a slap to her face. 'Please, don't do this. I'll lose my baby.'

A cruel laugh. 'That's none of my concern. Next time, you might think twice before having an honest businessman threatened.'

Aurelia's distress was so great that his words didn't register. Nausea washed over her as he released her arm to rip at her undergarment. Feeling faint, she reached out to hold on to the bench in front of her. Great Ceres, she prayed, do not let my baby come to any harm. Please.

There was a grunt of satisfaction as he succeeded in baring her rear; a pause as he tugged at his own clothing. 'I'm going to enjoy this.'

This was her only chance, thought Aurelia. Her eyes fixed on a large glass bottle full of liquid. If she could just grab that, wheel and smash it on his head, she might escape. Little by little, she eased her fingers over the work surface. There was no reaction from behind her, just the hideous feeling of something stiff pushing against the tops of her thighs. Terrorised, Aurelia lost all control and lunged for the bottle. A muttered curse; a blinding pain in her lower back. In slow motion, the vessel slid over the edge and fell to the floor, where it shattered into a thousand fragments. A warm liquid ran down on to Aurelia's buttocks. She knew it for blood. Waves of agony rippled out from where the blade had opened her flesh. Why hadn't he stabbed her? she wondered dazedly.

He cuffed her heavily across the back of her head; only her outstretched hands prevented her face smashing off the bench. 'Try another trick like that, bitch, and it will be your last.' His erection probed forward again, searching for a way into her.

Her eyes hunted for another object to fight with. Nothing lay within reach. She lifted her legs one by one, tried to twist away from him, but he just slapped her buttocks and laughed. 'I love it when a woman fights back!'

Her despair mushroomed. Aurelia could feel her ability to resist ebbing away with the blood running down her legs. Let him do it, she thought wearily. If coupling with Lucius doesn't harm the baby, this won't either. It's better to survive. Better that my child lives rather than dies.

The sound of rushing feet in her ears made no sense. It was followed a heartbeat later by a loud cracking sound and a cry of pain. Aurelia was still struggling to understand what had happened when a hand grabbed hers. 'Come on, mistress! Run!'

Aurelia lurched upright, took in her attacker reeling backwards, clutching his head. An alembic rolled in circles at his feet, the large dent in its surface evidence of what Elira had done. Panic flared in her belly – he was still conscious and still armed. When Elira tugged at her arm again, Aurelia ran for the door after her slave. A roar of anger gave her extra speed, but it was too little, too late. There was no way that she could outrun a big man in her state.

That was until the Judaean, who had appeared from nowhere, emptied a flagon of scented oil over the floor between them. There was a strangled cry and a thump as the man's feet went from under him. Aurelia dared to hope for the first time. Few people would help but outside they could blend into the crowd while her slave slowed down or stopped the attacker.

'I'm coming for you, you whore!'

Near the shop's entrance, she risked a glance behind her. To her horror, her attacker had scrambled to his feet. The Judaean approached him, but retreated before the savage thrusts of the man's blade. 'Out of my way, greybeard, or you'll be picking up your own guts!'

'Mistress!' Elira was beckoning urgently.

Aurelia urged her tired legs onwards and burst out into the golden light of the setting sun. Lucius' slave regarded her with open mouth. She must look a sight, thought Aurelia, with blood all down her back, but there was no time to consider that. 'I was attacked inside. Stop the man who's chasing us. He's masked. He has a knife!'

'Y-yes, mistress.' Looking scared, he raised his cudgel.

She shoved past without another word. Whether he survived or not was none of her concern. What mattered was that she got away. The street was busier than ever. Women, men, children, carts pulled by oxen, mules laden down with merchandise. Residents of the city, visitors, slaves and merchants: they were all out at this, the best time of day to do business. The press, the reek of unwashed humanity made Aurelia begin to panic. 'Which way is Lucius' house?' she hissed at Elira.

The Illyrian's hand stabbed to their left. Aurelia's heart sank. A large wagon was nearing them from that direction. It was loaded so heavily that there was almost no room to pass on either side. Under normal circumstances she could have squeezed through, but not now. If they went the other way, however, they risked getting lost. The pounding of feet close behind made her mind up. It was go right, or die. 'The other way!' She pushed Elira forward. 'Quickly!'

They shoved into the crowd, ignoring the protests and cries of indignation that met their entry. It was hard to follow Elira, but Aurelia did her best. She dodged under the outstretched arm of a beggar who was harassing a portly, well-dressed man; she muttered an apology as she edged past a woman who was berating a small child for not holding her hand. Her feet dragged with every step and her belly felt as if it had doubled in size. The pain from her back was excruciating, but she pressed on regardless. Perhaps twenty paces into the mass of slowly moving people, she risked a look over her shoulder. At first, she thought they had escaped. There was no sign of her attacker. Maybe the slave had restrained him? Another scan changed her mind. Not far behind, a hooded man was wading through the throng; his elbows moved right and left like clubs, clearing the path before him. One of his victims, a merchant, began to protest. A heartbeat later, he had collapsed out of sight, levelled by a punch to his considerable paunch.

'Oh gods,' whispered Aurelia, fighting exhaustion and resignation. All at once, the exertions of the day, the heat, her gravid condition were overwhelming her. She wouldn't be able to go much further. Why had she been so foolish? She should have taken Lucius' advice and stayed at home.

She wasn't expecting the crowd to part. When it did so quite suddenly, Aurelia stumbled and almost fell. A few steps ahead of her, Elira had just collided with a strapping man whom she did not recognise. Even as the Illyrian was being cursed for being a stupid slave, Aurelia took in the toga-clad figure behind the man. Grey-haired, distinguished-looking, he had to be one of the magistrates who ruled Capua. His companion, whose presence had been clearing the way, was his bodyguard. She rushed forward. 'Your pardon, good sir.' She clutched at the guard's hand, gave his master a beseeching look. 'Help us, please!'

The big man's brows lowered in suspicion, but before he could say a word, the magistrate spoke. 'Stand back. By her dress, she is clearly of good standing. Can't you see she's hurt?'

'I'm all right,' replied Aurelia stoically.

'What has happened, my lady?' asked the magistrate, his tone concerned.

'I was attacked in a perfume shop down the street. My assailant is still after us.'

'This is an outrage. Lay your hand to your sword, Marcus.'

Tears of relief sprang to Aurelia's eyes as the bodyguard stepped forward. 'What does he look like?'

'You'll see him any moment. He was just behind us. I didn't see his face, but he's big, and wearing a hooded cloak.'

Marcus grunted; his sword snickered from its scabbard.

Aurelia's gaze followed his, left to right, right to left at the semicircle of people regarding them. There were men and women, young and old, tall, thin, short and fat. They had skin as white as alabaster, black as charcoal and every shade of brown under the sun. She could see no mask or raised hood, however, no familiar bulky figure.

They waited. And waited. There was no sign of her attacker. No one dared to push past the magistrate from either direction, but eventually people began complaining. Aurelia began to grow self-conscious. She was almost grateful for the wound on her back: proof that she was no madwoman. 'He must have seen you,' she said lamely.

'Most likely,' agreed the magistrate. 'Hannibal himself would think twice before tackling Marcus here. Best forget him. You need urgent attention from a surgeon.'

'I want to find him,' protested Aurelia, although she knew that the magistrate was right. There was no chance of finding the man who had nearly raped her. He would be long gone.

'Your slave can help Marcus to search for him,' said the magistrate kindly. 'You, on the other hand, are returning with me to your house. But first, a message to the surgeon, with all possible speed. Who is your husband? We should also send word to him.'

'His name is Lucius Vibius Melito,' said Aurelia. Her vision blurred for a moment. She could feel herself swaying.

'Melito?' His voice was at her elbow, his grip supporting her, for which she was very grateful. 'Why didn't you say before? I know him and his father well. No need to tell me where his house is. Come.'

Aurelia's legs would not obey her any longer. As her knees buckled and she crumpled to the ground, she was dimly aware of raised voices around her. It was the last thing she remembered.

She was woken by the baby kicking in her belly. Aurelia's eyes opened, adjusting slowly to the dim light. She was in a bed, lying on her side, facing the wall. Relief bathed her as she recognised the decorated plaster. It was the main bedroom of Lucius' house in Capua. Her back ached, but not as badly as she would have expected. Nor were there any signs that she was in labour, another cause for relief. With difficulty, she rolled over on to her back. Pain stabbed through her, and Aurelia moved on to her other side as swiftly as she could. To her surprise, Lucius was sitting right beside her on a stool. His face twisted with emotion – anger, relief, sadness – she wasn't sure. 'How are you feeling?'

'Sore.' Maybe she had been hasty in deciding that her wound was minor. 'My back. Is it——?'

'The surgeon attended to it. A long cut, but not deep. He's stitched it up. It will heal in two to three weeks, he says.'

Aurelia's head felt heavy as she nodded. 'How can I be so tired? I've only just woken up.'

'You lost quite a lot of blood,' chided Lucius. 'Fortunately it was Calavius, the chief magistrate himself, who came to your aid. Thanks to him, the surgeon arrived soon after you did.'

It took a moment for that to register. 'I see.'

'It's a wonder that the baby didn't come early.'

She touched her stomach, reassuring herself. 'How long have I been asleep?'

'A day and a night.'

'Gods above,' she muttered.

'What were you thinking to go out as you did?' he asked, his anger spilling forth again.

'You did not protest when I told you I was going.'

He didn't acknowledge her words. 'You should have taken more slaves with you.'

Why is he being like this? she wondered. 'That would not have stopped what happened. I went into the shop alone apart from Elira, as I always would. The man followed me inside. Did Elira not tell you?'

'What if you had lost the baby?' His voice was accusing.

Ah, that's why he is so upset, she thought bitterly. The child is more important than I am. 'I didn't.'

'But you could have.'

'I didn't,' she repeated, angry now. 'But if Elira hadn't intervened, I would have been raped.'

That seemed to bring him to his senses. A heavy sigh. 'Thank all the gods that that didn't happen. What I can't understand is why someone would pick you out like that.'

'There are men like that everywhere. It was just my bad luck to catch his attention,' said Aurelia with a shudder.

'It wasn't one of Phanes' apes, was it?'

The name triggered something in Aurelia's memory. 'Maybe. He said something about thinking twice before having an honest businessman threatened.' Lucius looked at her blankly, so she told him about the attack on Phanes in the temple.

'Who in Hades ordered that – your mother?'

'No! She came to me, asking if I knew who it could have been.' Don't let him ask any more questions, she prayed. It was better if Lucius didn't even know of Hanno's existence.

To her relief, he let it go. He was silent for a time, tapping a finger off his lips in thought. 'Phanes has to be the most likely culprit. I will have my men pay him a *visit*. It doesn't do any harm to let sewer rats know their place from time to time.'

The way he said 'visit' made Aurelia smile. She could no longer control her drowsiness, however. Her eyes closed. All she wanted to do was sleep.

'The surgeon says it would be best if you stayed here until your time arrives.'

She roused herself with an effort. 'Why?'

'He thinks that another journey in this heat might bring on your labour prematurely. Staying here will be more relaxing for you.' Lucius seemed content with this notion.

Aurelia was also pleased. Although she was unused to the house, Capua was very familiar to her. 'That's fine,' she murmured. 'The baby will be born here.' Her eyelids closed again. It might have been her imagination, but she fancied that she could feel Lucius stroking her hair as she slipped away into oblivion.

In the event, staying in Capua proved to be a blessing in disguise. Atia could visit much more easily than before; indeed once she knew Aurelia's intentions, she moved into the house for the duration. Having her mother on hand proved a great comfort to Aurelia, for her nervousness about the birth was growing as it drew ever closer. Her anxiety wasn't helped by her worries over her father and Quintus. Everyone was obsessed with the impending battle against Hannibal – no, the impending victory over him – that surely must come soon. Two weeks after the attack in the perfumer's, the two new consuls passed Capua on their way south. Forty thousand troops, citizens and socii, marched and rode with them. The populace turned out in droves to witness the spectacle.

Aurelia's wound had healed well enough for her to travel by litter with Lucius to the city ramparts, the best local vantage point. She would remember the sight to her dying day. The massively long column that extended from north to south as far as the eye could see. (By all accounts, it had been passing Capua since daybreak; men said that the tail wouldn't go by until mid-afternoon.) The sound of thousands of studded sandals striking the ground in unison, which filled the air with an ominous thunder. The soldiers' rhythmic chanting. Winding through the din, the blaring of trumpets. Sunlight flashing off the metal standards that marked out each legion, maniple and century. The trails of dust rising from the cavalry units, which were dwarfed by the orange-brown clouds that hung in the air over the entire host. Marching through the dirt sent up by the men in front must be horrific, she thought, especially in addition to the incredible heat and the mass of heavy armour and weapons that each man carried.

Aurelia had seen her father dressed in his uniform before; had wept as he rode away. She'd done the same when first Quintus, and then Gaius, had left. Yet seeing the army brought home the hideous reality of war in a way that truly unnerved her. Hannibal's host was nowhere near as large as the Roman one would be when the consuls reached the other legions. But there was no avoiding the fact that when battle was joined, many thousands of men would die. More even than at the Trebia or at Trasimene. If that was the case, what chance had her father and brother of surviving? A dark gloom cast its shadow over her. Lucius' excited comment about perhaps joining the army hadn't helped. Aurelia hoped that her protestations had convinced him not to pursue the idea, that his father would disabuse him of the notion. For all that she didn't love him, he was a decent man and her future lay with him. He must not go to war too.

She'd had enough of watching the martial display. 'I want to go back to the house,' she said, touching Lucius' arm.

'Soon.' His eyes roamed eagerly over the column. 'Look, there's another legion standard. A minotaur, I think.'

Aurelia resolved to ask him again in a moment. After what had happened, she didn't want to return to the house alone. She also wanted his arm to lean on when negotiating the steps to street level. By now, her stomach was so large that she waddled rather than walked. Physical activity of *any* kind was uncomfortable. How much longer will it be? she wondered, rubbing her belly. Her discomfort now outweighed her fear – just. It would do no harm to call in to the temple of Bona Dea on the way back, she decided. Her offerings to the goddess of fertility and childbirth had been frequent, but there was no harm in making another.

'You're hot.' Lucius wiped a bead of sweat from her brow. 'My pardon. You mustn't stay out for long in these temperatures. Let's return to the house.'

Aurelia gratefully took his arm. They walked the short distance to the staircase that they'd ascended. A sentry saluted; a friend of Lucius' called out a greeting. The wife of another wished Aurelia well, and subjected her to a barrage of advice. Her smile of acknowledgement faltered as an intense pain radiated from her lower belly. It passed within a few heartbeats; the other woman did not notice. Muttering a goodbye, Aurelia walked a few more steps. Another wave hit her then, and she stopped dead, taking deep breaths to try and move through the agony.

'Are you all right?' asked Lucius.

'It's nothing. I'm fine.' She tried to straighten, but another contraction – she recognised it as that this time – surged in and she gasped.

'Is it the baby? Is the baby coming?'

'Maybe,' she admitted.

To his credit, Lucius remained very calm. His friend's wife was called over and asked to wait with Aurelia. He hastened down the steps, returning with two of his slaves, who helped her down to the waiting litter. The midwife was sent for. He held her hand and whispered soothing words all the way back to the house. Surrendering her to the care of her mother and Elira, he went to offer prayers at the lararium.

Aurelia remembered only fragments of the hours that followed; it was terribly hot and humid in the bedroom, and the sheets beneath her were drenched in sweat, making the hard bed she lay on feel even harder. Bizarrely, the bladders filled with warm oil at her sides felt comforting. Atia sat close by, rubbing creams on her belly and talking to her. Between regular internal examinations on Aurelia, the midwife busied herself by praying and readying her supplies on a table: olive oil to use as a lubricant, sea sponges, strips of cloth and wool, tinctures of herbs and pots of ointment. As time passed, Aurelia's contractions grew closer and closer together, exhausting her. She was aware of crying out with each wave of pain. At one stage, she heard an anxious Lucius at the door; he was banished by Atia.

At last the midwife's examination revealed that Aurelia's cervix was sufficiently dilated. She and Atia helped her to the birthing chair. This had armrests for her to grip on to; it supported her thighs and bottom, leaving a 'U' shaped gap between her legs, access for the midwife. Aurelia's fear reached new heights as she eased on to it, but Atia's encouragement and the urgent cries from the midwife, who was crouched on a stool before her, helped her to go on. To keep breathing; to push when she was told to.

In the end, the baby emerged with less difficulty than she'd imagined. It came in a rush. Mucus, blood and urine spattered on the floor. The midwife gave a happy cry; so too did Atia. Aurelia opened her eyes to see a purple-red bundle topped by a thatch of spiky black hair being lifted to her breast. 'Is it alive?' she gasped. 'Is it healthy?'

A mewling cry answered, and her heart filled. 'My baby,' she whispered as the midwife placed him on her chest.

'It's a boy,' said Atia. 'Praise be to Bona Dea, Juno and Ceres!'

'A boy,' whispered Aurelia, filled with elation. She had done her job, in part at least. She kissed the top of his downy head. 'Welcome, Publius. Your father is looking forward to meeting you.'

'Well done, daughter,' said Atia, her tone warmer and gentler than usual. 'You've done a fine job.'

After a little while, the midwife tied off and cut the cord. With some help, Aurelia walked the few steps to the second, softer bed where she lay down to rest and to feed Publius. It was strange that she'd had doubts about being pregnant, she thought, gazing adoringly at her son. The discomfort of the previous few weeks and the pain of her labour were already dimming in her mind. It all seemed worthwhile now. Lucius in particular would be ecstatic. As long as Publius thrived, his family bloodline had been secured.

As sleep took her, Aurelia felt more content than she had done in an age. She didn't think about Hanno.

Chapter XVII

Cannae, Apulia

Urceus cleared his throat and spat. The glob of moisture vanished in the dust before their feet. He wiped sweat from his brow. 'Gods, but it's so hot. So dry. There isn't a fucking blade of grass left in the entire camp.'

'Hardly surprising. It hasn't rained for weeks,' said Quintus with a wink, 'and sixty thousand soldiers tramping the whole area every day don't help either.'

Urceus threw him a baleful glare. 'Smart arse. I'd ask for wind, but the damn breezes here only cause dust storms. I never thought I'd say it, but the sooner autumn comes, the better.'

'It won't be for a while yet.'

'All the better that matters will come to a head soon.'

'They didn't today, though,' mused Quintus. Their encampment was no more than a mile from that of Hannibal. They and upwards of ten thousand other soldiers had only just returned from several hours spent in the hot sun, arrayed in battle lines before their own ramparts, the consul's response to Hannibal's entire army being ready for a full battle. The initial tension had been unbearable. Prayers had been audible throughout the ranks, men had joked in over-loud voices or found none too plausible reasons to piss where they stood. Once it had become apparent that the enemy was not going to attack them and that Paullus wasn't going to mobilise all the legions, an air close to euphoria had descended. Suddenly, their thirst and the strength-sapping heat were the only things that had mattered. The order to return to camp had been greeted with universal delight.

'How come Paullus didn't accept Hannibal's offer of battle?' muttered Urceus, before sucking at his water carrier like a babe that hasn't been fed for a day.

'No one likes to have the ground chosen for him,' replied Quintus. 'A lot of posturing goes on before battles. Moving camps, marching one's army close to the enemy, setting ambushes. They're all designed to provoke a response.'

'Quite the veteran, eh?' Urceus' voice was half sarcastic and Quintus wished he'd kept his mouth shut. Talking knowledgeably about tactics – a topic he'd studied with his father – was a sure way to rouse suspicion about his true identity. He breathed a sigh of relief as Urceus went on, 'Been listening to Corax, have you?'

He pulled a sheepish grin. 'Yes.'

'Corax is probably right. It's not as if we can just march away after spending this much time within striking distance of the guggas. That would be catastrophic for the army's morale. We'd be the laughing stock of Italy, the consuls know that. Fabius' stalemates were fine for a time, until enough legions had been raised and our defeats forgotten a little. But now the Republic needs a victory, and an emphatic one at that.' He eyed Quintus speculatively. 'Hannibal's as keen for a fight as we are, though. He's not afraid.'

Quintus thought of Hanno, whose passion to fight against Rome had been palpable from the moment he'd felt it safe to reveal it to Quintus. The desire of Hannibal, a general who had led his troops on an epic journey to Italy, had to be even more overwhelming. If Rome had been roundly defeated in that war, been forced to pay vast reparations and had also lost a huge chunk of its territory to Carthage, I would probably feel the same way, he decided. 'This is what Hannibal has been wanting since Lake Trasimene,' he said, ignoring the tickle of fear that caressed his spine. 'His army has been waiting for us these past two months. That's why he moved his camp from Cannae to this side of the River Aufidius, and offered battle today. Refusing to play his game shows him that he can't have it all his way.'

'I suppose,' said Urceus. 'Things might be different tomorrow with Varro in charge, though.'

The tradition that each consul led the army on alternate days was as old as Rome itself, but when the two men were very different characters, problems could arise. Quintus asked that that would not happen during this campaign. 'He does seem more fiery than Paullus,' he admitted.

'The clash with the gugga cavalry and infantry when we were marching south proved that,' Urceus added. 'The only reason Varro ordered the withdrawal was because the sun was about to set. I can't see Paullus acting like that.'

Quintus grinned at the memory. The enemy ambush had seen some fierce fighting. Although it had been inconclusive, it had given the men of Corax's and Pullo's maniple a real hunger for victory. The same attitude appeared prevalent throughout the whole army. 'He's just a little more cautious than Varro, that's all. After what happened at the Trebia and Trasimene, there's nothing wrong with that. I've heard it said that Hannibal's supplies will run out in a couple of days. If we do nothing, he'll have to break camp, which could grant us an opportunity to attack. Paullus is probably just waiting for that.'

'But there's no need to wait! We've got an army nearly twice the size of Hannibal's now! More than fifty thousand legionaries can't go wrong, my friend. Our men broke through the enemy lines at both the Trebia and Trasimene, remember? As long as neither consul does anything stupid, we'll simply flatten the guggas when it comes to a fight.'

Quintus relaxed a little. It was impossible not to agree with Urceus. Everyone was of the same opinion. As Calatinus had told him, they might have slightly fewer horse than the Carthaginians, but the task facing their cavalry was simple. The enemy horse had to be contained, that was all, while the infantry smashed a great hole in Hannibal's main line. Once that was done, the cavalry battle would largely become superfluous. 'We can sit back and just watch you lot sweating in the sun,' Calatinus had joked. It was easy enough to picture the legionaries wheeling to complete the massacre of the Carthaginian foot soldiers. Even if by that stage Hannibal's riders had gained the upper hand in their clash with the Roman horse, thought Quintus, they would be able to do little more than harass the legionaries. 'Victory will be ours!' he said, feeling the certainty in his belly grow.

'Victory will be ours,' repeated Urceus. 'And it could well be tomorrow.'

* * *

Hanno's muscles were weary as he followed the messenger to Hannibal's tent. Although there had been no battle, it had taken most of the day to leave their position and form up opposite the Roman encampment; to wait there, their challenge unanswered; and then to return whence they had come. He questioned the messenger, one of Hannibal's scutarii, but the man claimed not to know why their general had summoned him. His tiredness fell away as they neared Hannibal's great pavilion at the centre of the camp. A crowd stood before it, perhaps thirty-five men from all sections of the army. There were Numidian officers, Gaulish, Balearic and Iberian chieftains. With a thrill of excitement, Hanno recognised Hannibal's brother Mago, and his cavalry commanders Maharbal and Hasdrubal. His father was present too, with Bostar, Sapho and the other phalanx commanders.

Gods, I'm not the last one here, am I? Hanno's face reddened as they joined the group. His discomfiture soared when Hannibal, clad in a simple purple tunic, saw him amidst the throng.

'Welcome, son of Malchus,' said Hannibal. 'One of the men who has kept this army fed of late.'

Appreciative murmurs met his words.

Embarrassed now, and delighted by this public recognition, Hanno grinned like a fool. When Sapho winked at him, he was able to return the gesture without effort.

'To business,' declared Hannibal, indicating the table before him, upon which sat little piles of black, and white, stones. 'The Romans did not accept my offer of battle today.'

'Worse luck, sir!' called Sapho.

'Damn right,' added a Gaulish chieftain. 'My men are still complaining!'

A burst of laughter.

Hannibal smiled. 'There will be a fight soon, never fear. It may well be tomorrow.'

In a heartbeat, the atmosphere had changed. Tension creased every man's face.

'Most of us were standing near the Roman camp today, but not all. Zamar' – he indicated the Numidian – 'and a few of his best men were lying on top of the hill at Cannae. Would you like to hear what they saw?'

A chorus of loud growls, of 'Yes, sir!'

'It wasn't that much, at first glance. A party of enemy officers, on the other side of the river. Zamar watched long enough, however, to recognise that the Romans were scouting out the ground.' He let them suck on the bones of that.

Malchus' gravelly voice broke the silence. 'You think that the consul who's in charge tomorrow is going to march the legions over there, sir?'

'I do. Come and see the plan that we shall follow should I be right.' Hannibal's teeth flashed from the depths of his dark beard, and he tapped the table top.

There was a rush to join him. Hanno did not dare to stand at the front, but thanks to his height, he still had a good view over his father's shoulder.

'These are the hills upon which Cannae sits.' Hannibal's fingers trailed over a line of large pebbles, before moving on to a thin strip of leather that ran roughly parallel to the stones. 'And this is the River Aufidius.' He glanced up. 'Everyone clear?'

'Yes, sir.'

With swift motions of his hands, Hannibal arranged a score or more black stones in three lines, forming a great rectangle. He placed the shape's long sides so that they ran parallel to the hills and the far side of the river. 'The legions' three lines.' On either side of the 'legions', he laid a thin row of more black stones. 'The enemy cavalry.' A disordered pattern of tiny pebbles in front of the rectangle. 'The enemy skirmishers.' Again Hannibal let silence fill the air, let his officers make sense of what he'd done. After a few moments, he continued, 'If the Romans intend to fight on this ground, they will have to do so like this. With a narrow frontage and a much deeper formation than normal. It seems sensible to do that. Half their men are new recruits. Marching them into battle like this will keep them in position and prevent them from panicking. Thanks to the hills and the river, it also restricts the area available for cavalry combat, which they know we are likely to win.'

His hands moved again, assembling the white stones opposite the black.

Hanno stared, but could not make sense of what he was seeing. He looked around, saw the same incomprehension on other faces.

'Ha!' Hannibal chuckled. 'Can any of you tell me what my idea is?'

'These are our cavalry,' said Hasdrubal with a little smile, pointing at the lines of stones on either side of the central pattern.

'Smart arse!' Hannibal gave him a good-natured clout. 'You're right, of course. I want you on the left, near the river, with the Iberian and Gaulish horse. Maharbal, you're to take the right flank with the Numidians. When the fighting starts, I want you both to advance. Hasdrubal, you're to drive off the citizen cavalry. Maharbal, engage the socii horsemen, but do not close with them. Hasdrubal, keep your men on a tight rein. The instant your objective has been achieved, you're to turn and come to Maharbal's aid.'

'Yes, sir,' replied the cavalry commander.

'This looks a little like a house lying on its side, does it not?' Hannibal's fingers traced the outline of the stones that lay between the cavalry wings. 'Two walls, and a slightly domed roof. And rain falling on top of it.'

'Put us out of our misery, sir,' demanded Malchus. Hanno's emphatic murmur of agreement was repeated by many others. What would their general's latest stroke of genius be?

'Very well. The "rain drops" are our skirmishers, the house is our centre, clearly. It's to be made up of Gauls and Iberians, and I will command it with you, Mago.' His brother looked pleased.

The Gaulish chieftain who had complained about his men leaned forward and jabbed at the stones with a thick forefinger. 'Is great honour to stand in centre, with you as leader,' he said in poor Carthaginian. 'But why bow the line forward like this? Is stupid!'

Some officers looked shocked at the Gaul's abruptness, but Hannibal just smiled. 'Think,' he said gently and tapped the black rectangle. 'Eighty thousand legionaries cannot be stopped, even if half of them are inexperienced. No one could do it, not even you and all your fine warriors.' His respectful gaze found the Gaulish and Iberian chieftains one by one. They gave him grudging nods in return.

'So, Romans push us back, and back?' asked the chief.

'Yes.' Hannibal moved the 'roof' until it had flattened into a straight line. 'To here. Naturally, the Romans won't stop at that stage.' He nudged the white stones until they bowed inwards. Then he parted a few of them. 'Our lines might even break.'

The Gauls and Iberians looked unhappy, but none of them protested.

What the hell is he playing at? Hanno wondered, shifting uneasily from foot to foot.

His father turned. 'Trust in Hannibal,' he whispered. 'He knows what to do.'

I damn well hope so, thought Hanno. He took a deep breath, let it out slowly. Hannibal always had a plan.

'The moment that that happens is when you' – here Hannibal caught Hanno's eye – 'and the other phalanx commanders come in . . .'

Like most of the infantry, Quintus had taken to lying on his blankets outside. The temperatures over the preceding weeks meant that sleep was impossible inside their eight-man tents. Even under the stars, however, there was little comfort to be had for hours after the sun had set. Men remained awake for some time before managing to fall asleep.

Thanks to the manoeuvrings of the previous day, which had been one of the hottest since the summer began, Quintus had heard not just the second watch being sounded, but the third. Being woken by the trumpets while it was still dark did not therefore improve his mood. 'Varro has his mind made up then,' he grumbled to Urceus.

The jug-eared man sat up, rubbing his eyes. 'Seems like it. The gods be with us.'

Quintus was not alone in muttering in agreement. More than one man reached for the lucky amulet that hung around their necks.

'I won't have a tongue as thick as a plank today.' Urceus kicked at the two bulging water bags by his feet.

'Me neither.' Quintus had been quick to copy his friend; Corax had told the entire maniple to do the same. Unless they were fools, every soldier in the army would carry plenty of water into battle. Dropping from thirst was a more stupid way to die than many.

'Up! Up, you maggots!' Corax came striding down the tent lines, already in his full uniform. His vine cane thwacked down on any man who had not got to his feet. Quintus stood at once; Urceus did likewise.

'Today's the day, my boys, today's the big day! Have a piss, have a shit if you need it. Have one even if you don't need it, because my bet is that you won't get another chance later.' Striding on, Corax smiled at the slightly nervous laughs that followed his comment. 'I want no loose studs on the soles of anyone's sandals, so check that before you put them on. Don your armour! Sit it comfortably, with your belt taking the weight of your mail, if you wear it. Walk around a bit, to ensure that you've got it right. Get a mate to check your straps – all of them: caligae, breastplate, helmet, shield. Check that your sword's loose in its scabbard, that there are no splinters on the shafts of your javelins. Make an offering to the gods, if you're of a mind. Do not forget to check that your water bags are full. Then, and only then, pack up a loaf of bread, and a piece of cheese, if you're lucky enough to have that too. This could be a long day, and a bite of food when a man's belly's stuck to his backbone with hunger can give him the energy he needs to go on.'

Corax walked on, repeating himself at regular intervals, doling out gruff encouragements and blows from his vine cane in equal measure.

Quintus watched him admiringly before he began to follow his orders. For a time, there was no chance of brooding about what might happen that day. They were all far too busy preparing themselves and then forming up. Through the gaps in the tents, he saw the legionaries of other maniples doing the same. He wished he could take wing and observe the vast camp from above. What a sight it would make: tens of thousands of soldiers leaving their tent lines, assembling on the camp's main avenues and on the open ground inside the fortifications. Preceded by their standards and trumpeters, they would tramp out of the four gates, there to join up and assume a marching formation.

Dawn had broken by the time they had reached their allotted place in the column. Dust rose in great clouds, coating everyone in a fine layer of brown, making men cough and curse. The heat was mounting steadily; the sun's rays beat down on the army, baking the soldiers in their armour. Quintus was sweating heavily just from standing where he was. When the order came from the nearest tribune to move off, he breathed a sigh of relief. Any movement of air at all across his face was welcome.

'Thank the gods that we're relatively near the front, eh?' Urceus jerked a thumb to their rear. 'I pity the poor bastards who have to eat our dust all the way to wherever we're going.'

'The cavalry have the best of it,' said Quintus, scanning a party of horsemen who were riding alongside their maniple for a sign of Calatinus. 'They don't send up half the amount of dust that infantry do.'

'Their job's easier too,' grumbled a man in the rank behind. 'Fucking pretty boys.'

Urceus snorted with amusement. 'They'll be sitting around fanning themselves much of the time while we're grinding ourselves against the guggas like a file off a knife.'

Quintus had to rein in his instinctive reaction, which would have been to defend, heatedly, the men with whom he had previously fought. Much as he hated to admit it, though, his comrades did have a point. Their cavalry had not performed well thus far against Hannibal. 'I don't think it'll be quite that easy for them.' He thought of his father and Calatinus, and begged Mars, the god of war, to protect them both. 'No doubt that we'll have it harder, though.' His stomach twisted, and he added a prayer for himself and all the men around him – except for Macerio. *Curse him!* The blond-haired man was two ranks back and a few steps off to his left, and Quintus asked that whatever happened, he didn't end up with Macerio right behind him. In the chaos of a fight, no one would notice the direction from which a man was slain.

Dying like that was an even less attractive prospect than dying from thirst, or a Carthaginian blade.

Quintus knew that the uncontrollable waves that swept men about during battle might also mean that Macerio's back could be presented to him instead of the other way round. He would have preferred to end his feud with the blond-haired man face-to-face, but Rutilus had lain unavenged for too long. If the opportunity presented itself, he would take it.

'Hades, why are we forming up with such a narrow frontage?' complained Quintus, who was standing in the seventh rank with Urceus, Severus and three more of his tent mates. 'Six men wide per maniple? It doesn't make sense. At this rate, none of us will get to do any fighting.'

Urceus shrugged his broad shoulders. 'We've a better chance of being alive come sundown, though,' he whispered.

It was as if Corax, who was in the front rank, had supernatural hearing. His head twisted. 'Who's that whining?'

Quintus buttoned his lip and stared straight ahead at the back of the helmet of the man in front.

'We form up as ordered, you miserable lowlifes! Is that clear?'

'Yes, sir,' they all answered.

Corax's scowl eased. 'I know it's fucking uncomfortable standing here, waiting to move forward. I know how hot it is, how the dust is getting into your eyes, your mouth, your arse crack. You want to get it all over with. But Varro knows what he's at. So do Paullus and Servilius. The tribunes are following their orders, see? This is where we'll fight because here we have our flanks protected.'

Quintus' eyes shot to the left. Through the swirling dust, he could see a line of low hills and the fortified walls of Cannae, where Hannibal's camp had been until a couple of days before. Somewhere at the foot of the slope, Varro was positioned with the allied cavalry. Out of sight to his right lay the River Aufidius, which they had forded to reach this spot. There his father and Calatinus would be, under Paullus' command. He prayed that they would fight bravely, and live to see victory. Corax was still talking, and Quintus quickly focused in again.

'We move when Servilius says so, not a fucking moment before!' yelled the centurion. 'Not every soldier here today is as well trained as you lot. The four legions that just joined us are mostly made up of wet-behind-the-ears lads who haven't yet shaved, let alone faced the guggas. Forming them up narrow and deep takes time, and we're doing it because then it's far easier for their officers to maintain formation as we advance. And in case you hadn't got it through your thick skulls yet, keeping our formation is all-important today! We've got to hit those Carthaginian whoresons so hard that they never recover from the shock of it. Twenty-four ranks of us should make sure of that, eh?'

Everyone within earshot cheered.

Corax looked satisfied; he turned away. Although the centurion hadn't identified him as the one who'd spoken, Quintus breathed a sigh of relief. 'At least we'll be able to throw our javelins. The men three ranks behind us won't even be able to do that,' he muttered to Urceus. 'We might not even get to draw our swords if the Carthaginians break quickly.'

'Don't be so sure,' came the solemn reply. 'The cogs of war are relentless once they begin to turn. They could well grind enough men up to ensure that our swords get blooded this day.'

The allusion was grim enough to dampen Quintus' enthusiasm a little. This was where he wanted to be, however. Becoming an infantryman was what he'd wanted, and what he had finally achieved. It was a world away from what he had known as a cavalryman, and his skills were very different, too, to those he had learned as a veles. No longer would he be able to charge his horse, to wheel and ride away from the enemy if needs be. Nor would there be any running charge at the Carthaginian lines, no exchange of spears with the opposing skirmishers and the possibility of retreating to the relative safety of his own forces. Instead he would march, pressed up against thousands of his fellows, straight at Hannibal's men. And it would happen this morning. Hundreds of paces to their front, the enemy army was forming up. Quintus could hear the Gaulish carnyxes being blown. *Parr-parr-parr. Zẓeyrrp. Parr-parr-parr. Zẓeyrrp. Booooooooo.* He didn't like hearing them again. As at Trasimene, they promised bloodshed, violent, vicious bloodshed. Unlike the previous day, there would be no getaway, no option of withdrawing to the safety of their camp. In the confined area between the hills and the river, a battle on the grandest scale was about to start. Whichever set of infantry prevailed would win the day, of that he had no doubt. The contest would be bitter, right to the end. Countless men would fall, on both sides. The doors to the underworld probably lay open already in anticipation.

Quintus swallowed hard, tried to ignore the urge to piss. How could his bladder be full again? he wondered. He'd emptied out every last drop before they marched out of the camp. A moment later, he was pleased when Urceus balanced his scutum on one hip and freed himself from his undergarment with his other hand. Quickly, he copied his friend. Their actions set off a rash of men doing the same. 'Don't piss on the back of my legs!' protested a number of soldiers. A wave of nervous but relieved laughter rippled through the maniple.

I'm not the only one who's scared, thought Quintus, oddly reassured. Macerio didn't look too happy either, which pleased him.

Parr-parr-parr. Zẓẓeyrrp. Parr-parr-parr. Zẓẓeyrrp. Booooooooo. Even at a distance, the carnyxes' unearthly sound could compete with the Roman trumpets and the officers' shouts.

'Fucking savages! That's the mating call of the Gaul! Anyone seen some dog-ugly women about, lads?' Corax had seen what was happening. He broke ranks and moved to stand where he could see them better, cupping a hand to his mouth. 'Most Gaulish "women" have worse beards than Hercules himself. I should know, I've seen them! They're broad in the beam too, with hips like a suckler cow. If you see any of the bitches, keep them at javelin length, or you'll catch a bout of pox that will knock you on your arse for a month.'

The mood lifted. Men winked at each other and chuckled.

'There's nothing like the prospect of battle to make men want to urinate. It happens to me too,' Corax said in a loud voice. 'Some of you might also need a shit. Don't stand on ceremony. I advise you do it while you can. Better your comrades' laughter than to have it run down your leg when a gugga is busy trying to gut you. If you're feeling sick, there's no shame in puking either. Empty your guts now, and you won't have to when to do so will mean your death.'

Silence. A few soldiers cast embarrassed looks at one another. There was a little stifled laughter.

'I'm fucking serious, lads!' bellowed Corax. 'If your body needs rid of something, let it out now! If you don't, you'll regret it later.'

Quintus was mightily relieved that he'd used the latrine trench earlier. He glanced at Urceus, who smirked. 'I had a good shit before we left the camp, don't worry.' One of their tent mates wasn't so lucky, however. A chorus of lewd jokes and complaints about the smell rained down on him as, red-faced, he squatted where he was and emptied his bowels. Hoots of amusement and insults rose from elsewhere in the maniple as other soldiers did the same, or were sick.

Corax waited, hands on hips, until the ranks had settled again. 'All done?'

A few muted voices answered, 'Yes, sir.'

'Fine. You'll feel better having shed that weight.'

Titters of laughter.

'Have a drink. Just a mouthful or two. Save the rest for later.'

Throughout the maniple, men slurped from their water carriers. Quintus longed to fill his belly, but he did as the centurion had ordered. His nerves were still at him. The last thing he wanted to do was vomit it all up again.

'How bad is the smell, lads?' asked Corax.

'Fucking terrible, sir!' shouted a voice.

He leered. 'That's what I like to hear. It'll keep you from falling asleep while we wait. Why don't you smear a bit on the tips of your pila? There's nothing like a coating of shit or puke to cause a wound to fester. Think of that when your javelin sinks into the flesh of a stinking Gaul!'

The legionaries liked that. Their lines rippled a little as men shifted to follow Corax's suggestion.

'The order to advance won't be long coming,' cried the centurion. He pointed to left and right. 'The velites are ready. The cavalry's in position. Most of our front rank is in place. The principes and triarii are right behind us. The velites will commence hostilities, but it won't be long until our moment of glory is here! Our chance to balance the scales after what happened at the Trebia and Trasimene. I want the ground to run with Gaulish blood! Gugga blood! The blood of every filthy son of a whore who follows Hannibal!'

There was a loud rumble of agreement as they digested that. There was still a tinge of nervousness in the air, but the general mood was calm, determined. The carnyxes had been forgotten for the moment. Corax's jokes about shit and piss had lifted men's spirits, thought Quintus admiringly. The centurion had allowed his soldiers to feel scared, without panicking them. It had been skilfully done.

'Are you ready to give Hannibal's rabble the hiding of their lives, boys?' called Corax.

Quintus licked his lips, gripped his pilum shaft, gave Urceus a tight nod. 'YES, SIR!' they both roared.

So too did every man in the maniple.

Hanno scratched at the base of his neck again, frustrated, hot and irritable. He couldn't see the skirmishers: Balearic slingers, Libyan javelin men and

Iberian *caetrati*, but the air was full of their yips, cries and shouts. The sounds competed with the whirr of thousands of sling stones flying at the enemy, and the incessant braying of the Gauls' carnyxes nearer to hand. *Parr-parr-parr. Zʒʒeyrrp. Parr-parr-parr. Zʒʒeyrrp. Booooooooo.* Hanno hated the instruments' din, which had given him a headache. A sour grin creased his face. If it was this bad for his side, he could only imagine the effect it would be having on the Romans, plenty of whom would remember the carnyxes from the Trebia and Lake Trasimene. Let the miserable dogs tremble! he thought. We are coming for them. He longed for the fighting to start. Standing here in the summer sun, temples pounding, was torture. Not torture, he thought, touching his scar. Fucking hot and a pain in my head, that's all. He fought his impatience. The infantry and cavalry wouldn't clash for a while yet, and he and the other phalanxes would not have any role to play until after *that*.

The Libyans had been divided up between the army's flanks. Hanno's unit was standing in a narrow but deep formation, behind the left edge of the Gauls and Iberians, and facing forward. It was part of a line of phalanxes, perhaps five thousand men in total, one that had been replicated on the opposite flank. Both groupings were out of sight of the Romans, which meant that Hanno and his men could see nothing at all of the ground between the armies, and that made the tension unbearable. We stay where we are. Hannibal gave us our orders, he told himself. We will follow them exactly. Everything depends on us. His flesh itched again, and he tugged at his cuirass: a pointless exercise. It settled back against his chest the instant he released it.

'Something wrong, sir?' asked Mutt.

'Eh? Nothing much. There's a rough spot on the inside of the top rim of my breastplate. I should have sanded it down last night.'

'You'll be sore by the end of the day, sir,' observed Mutt dryly.

'Yes, I know,' Hanno snapped.

'Take it off, sir.' Mutt rummaged in a pouch that hung from a thong around his neck and, with a satisfied smile, produced a small file. 'I'll sort it out for you in a moment.'

'I can't.' Hanno gestured at the files of men to their left and right, at the squadrons of cavalry that waited opposite, ready for the order to advance. 'Something might happen.'

'We won't have to do anything for a good while yet, sir,' said Mutt patiently. 'Do it now, while you can.'

Mutt was right, thought Hanno. Their skirmishers had deployed only a short time before. The real fighting wouldn't start for hours, but by sunset, he would have a raw, oozing wound on his chest. *If I survive* . . . 'Very well.' He stepped out of line and laid his shield on the hot earth. His helmet and sword were next. Mutt moved to his side, undoing the straps that held the front and back of his cuirass together. Hanno eased off the heavy metal, letting out a sigh of pleasure as warm air moved over his sweat-sodden tunic. 'Gods, but that feels good.' He handed the cuirass to Mutt, who found the protruding edge with a finger and got to work at once. Hanno took the opportunity to walk along his men's lines, chatting and making jokes.

'Can we take off our mail shirts too, sir?' asked one grinning soldier.

A rumble of laughter passed up and down the phalanx.

'I wish you could,' replied Hanno. 'Hannibal might have something to say if he saw you, though. Standing here without your helmets on is as much as I can allow, I'm afraid.'

The man pulled a rueful face.

'Have some water, or a bite of food if you've got it,' Hanno advised and moved on.

'Taking it easy, brother?' As ever, Sapho's tone was mocking.

With gritted teeth, Hanno turned. Bostar and his father – who was in command – were on the opposite flank. Cuttinus, who was leading their side, had his phalanx positioned some units to Hanno's left. His was the closest to the enemy, whereas Sapho's phalanx was the next one along to Hanno's. It wasn't surprising that he had turned up. 'I could say the same thing about you, leaving your position.'

Sapho ignored his comment. 'You look as if you're taking a stroll along the Choma. Where's your breastplate? Your sword?'

Hanno barked, 'None of your business.'

'Tetchy! Is the heat getting to you?'

Hanno bit back a curse. 'Sapho, a word.' He stalked away from his men, towards the lines of cavalry. His brother followed, eyebrows raised. 'I won't take shit like this,' Hanno growled. 'Like it or not, friendship with

Mago or not, you and I are the same rank. It's not as if we haven't had this conversation before either. I'm no longer a boy, so don't patronise me. And I do not take kindly to you making sarcastic remarks in front of my men.'

A short silence.

'Fair enough,' said Sapho. 'I'm sorry.'

Surprised and not a little suspicious at this reaction, Hanno scanned his brother's face for signs of duplicity. He could see none. 'Fine.' He offered his hand. Sapho took it, and they shook. Hanno suddenly felt the need to explain. 'There was a rough edge on the inside of my cuirass. It was rubbing. Mutt's filing it down for me.'

'Good idea. A thing like that can distract a man in the midst of a fight. It'd be a stupid way to die, wouldn't it? Stuck by a legionary because you were scratching an itch?'

They both laughed, and the tension eased further. 'Are your men ready?' asked Hanno.

'Yes. They're lean and hungry. Impatient, like me. But the wait will be worth it.'

Hanno latched on to the conviction in Sapho's voice. He leaned close and muttered, 'You think we'll win?'

'Of course!'

'It's not that certain, brother. Many of the Romans might be inexperienced, but they outnumber us nearly two to one. I know that we have more cavalry, but there's little room for them to manoeuvre. If the legionaries punch through the centre of our line, what we do mightn't make any difference.'

'Now you listen to me.' Sapho's tone was firm and unusually kind. 'I've been following Hannibal for a lot longer than you. Saguntum seemed impossible to take, but he did it. Only a madman could have thought that tens of thousands of soldiers could march from Iberia to Gaul and over the Alps into Italy, but Hannibal did it. Our army was in pieces after the crossing of the mountains, but he still defeated the Romans at the Ticinus – and the Trebia. You saw what he's capable of there, and at Trasimene. Our general is intelligent, determined and a great tactician. In my opinion, he's also a genius.'

'True,' said Hanno. 'He always knows what to do.'

'By the end of today, Hannibal will have won a victory that will go down in history alongside the exploits of Alexander. And you, Father, Bostar and I will be there to celebrate it.'

The image – and a memory – made a slow smile spread across Hanno's face. 'As we did after the Trebia?'

'Exactly. Rome must pay for all the wrongs it has done to Carthage.' Sapho raised his fist. 'In blood.'

'In blood!' repeated Hanno.

The sun hadn't quite reached its zenith, and the heat was incredible. Hanno had had to stop himself supping from his water bag, which was already half empty. He wasn't as used to not drinking as his men, few of whom he had seen touch their carriers. How long had it been since Hasdrubal had led the Iberian and Gaulish cavalry charge? Hanno had no idea, but his heart felt as if it had been in his mouth since that moment. He'd spent his time craning his head and trying to peer around the back edge of their front line. Even if he had been able to view what lay beyond the massed ranks of soldiers, which he hadn't, the great dust clouds sent up by the horses' hooves would have prevented him from seeing a thing. The knowledge hadn't stopped him, however. It was something to do, something to while away the time, which was moving at the pace of a tortoise.

He eyed Mutt, who was standing beside him. 'What in hell is happening, do you think?'

A doleful shrug. 'Who can say, sir?'

Frustration made Hanno want to shake his second-in-command, but there was no point. 'Don't you care?'

A solemn look. 'Course I do, sir, but I can't help Hasdrubal or the skirmishers, can I? Except by praying, which I've done. The best thing to do is to wait, and not think about it. When it's our turn, then I'll show you how much I care.'

'I know you will,' said Hanno, feeling a little embarrassed. He took a step out of line and peered after the cavalry. 'Hasdrubal's men must be containing the Roman horse at the very least, because there's been no sign of them.'

'Very true, sir.'

'Baal Hammon grant that they drive the Romans from the field as Hannibal wanted.' Whoops and cheers to their right made Hanno twist his head. He made out slingers and javelin men spilling into view from the ranks of the Gauls and Iberians. Muttering to one another, his soldiers shifted with excitement. 'The skirmishers are coming back!' cried Hanno.

'So they are, sir,' said Mutt, with more signs of life. 'It'll be the infantry's turn next.'

Mutt was right. It took a while for all of the lightly armed soldiers to return, shouting and exhilarated that they had taken on a far superior number of Roman velites and lived to tell the tale. A little time went by, and nothing happened. The tension rose as the temperatures had, almost to boiling point. A great sigh went up when the enemy trumpets sounded a repetitive set of notes, over and over. It was the signal to advance. The wait was over.

Hanno actually felt relief; he saw the same emotion in more than one man's face.

TRAMP. TRAMP. TRAMP. The noise of more than eighty thousand legionaries walking in unison was incredible. The ground beneath Hanno's feet was reverberating from the impact. His stomach twisted with fear. In all of his life, he had never thought to hear or feel such a sound. At the Trebia, the sound had been impressive, but it had been diminished by the biting wind. At Trasimene, the Romans had never had the opportunity to move forward as one mass. He wished that he could stand in the front line, just for a moment, to witness the sight. I might shit myself, he thought with a touch of black humour, but it would be incredible to behold. So too would the spectacle of the Gaulish and Iberian warriors outdoing themselves to impress their fellows, and Hannibal. And the clash when the two sides met. Gods, what would that be like? Hanno took a deep breath; he let it out slowly. Stay calm. Our turn will come. Our turn to shine will come. Hannibal will be proud of us. *Carthage* will be proud of us. And I shall have my revenge for what was done to me at Victumulae – if not on Pera, then on every Roman who comes within range of my blade.

* * *

After perhaps an hour of skirmishing with their Carthaginian counterparts, the twenty thousand velites had been recalled. They had come spilling back into the narrow gaps between the maniples, shouting encouragement at the hastati and boasting of how many casualties they had caused. Fortunately, they had lost few of their own number. An air of even greater excitement, mixed with nervous anticipation, descended on the legionaries. Prayers were uttered, bargains made with the gods, throats cleared of phlegm. More men took a piss; a few puked up the water that they'd drunk. There were few jokes, fewer smiles. Matters had become serious.

The order to advance came the moment that the last of the velites had pulled back. A spontaneous, almighty cheer had gone up. No one had needed to be told to start clashing his pilum off his shield. The din had been incredible, and had gone on for some time. Corax and the other officers had had to resort to hand signals to get their soldiers to close up the gaps and to start moving. It was a good distance towards the enemy, however, and it wasn't long before the noise abated. Men needed to save their strength for the walk under the burning midday sun. Standing in such close proximity to each other for more than two hours had been soul-sapping, like being in a crowded, overheated caldarium. Temperatures had risen to the point that the soles of Quintus' sandals were hot to the touch. Any visible portions of his tunic were dark with perspiration. His felt helmet liner was saturated. Runnels of sweat ran down his forehead and into his eyebrows. Hands full of shield and javelins, he blinked the salty sting of it from his eyes.

'How far have we come, sir?' Urceus called out.

Corax didn't even turn his head. 'By my count, six hundred paces. Perhaps two hundred to go until we reach the guggas. Are you with me, lads?'

'YES, SIR!' they roared from their parched throats.

'Onwards!' Corax levelled his pilum at the enemy.

TRAMP. TRAMP. TRAMP. The noise of eighty thousand soldiers advancing shook the ground.

Quintus peered around the heads of the men in front. Gusts of air were throwing up clouds of dust between the armies, but the Carthaginian lines were clearly visible now. 'That's odd.'

'What?' demanded Urceus, craning to see.

'The centre of the enemy line is further forward than the sides. It's curved forward, like a drawn bow.'

'It's just their lack of discipline. The damn fool Gauls in the centre want to start fighting first!' said Urceus dismissively.

Severus sniggered. 'They'll soon change their minds.'

Severus was probably right, thought Quintus. Gauls were notoriously ill disciplined.

They walked on another twenty paces. Still the legionaries remained silent, conserving their energy. Thirty paces. Forty. Then it was sixty. Eighty. The carnyxes continued their hideous cacophony – as they had since the enemy host had formed up. *Parr-parr-parr. Zzzeyrrp. Parr-parr-parr. Zzzeyrrp. Booooooooo.* The Gauls blowing them must have enormous bloody lungs, thought Quintus wearily, wishing they would just shut up. Darting movement to the front attracted his attention. As if to accompany the carnyxes' weird sound, dozens of individual warriors had just broken ranks and were prancing up and down before their comrades, bare-chested, waving their weapons and roaring abuse at the Romans. There were even a few who looked as if they had stripped naked. Quintus couldn't help but feel a tremor of fear. *They're fucking crazy.* He shook his head. Without armour, such men would be easily killed. The volleys of javelins would probably see to most of them. And as for the rest, he thought, well, all the hastati at the front had to do was hold steady, keep their shields together and thrust with their swords, not hack. 'Hold steady,' he whispered. 'Hold steady.'

Urceus' jaw was white with tension, but at Quintus' words, he let out a chuckle. 'We'll do it, by Jupiter's cock. There are far too many of us for the sewer rats to stand against.'

Quintus pulled his lips up into a smile of agreement, prayed that they lived to see the inevitable victory. Twisting his head, he searched for Macerio's among those to his rear. The blond-haired man seemed as scared as ever. *Good. I hope the fucker shits himself when it starts.*

'A hundred paces, lads,' shouted Corax. 'Take a pull of water if you need it. Take a look at your comrades to left and right. Remember that those men are who you're fighting for.'

Quintus glanced at first Severus and then Urceus; he gave them both a stare that said, 'Whatever happens, I'll be watching out for you.' His heart swelled, because they did the same to him. He couldn't ask for better men to stand with.

'At sixty, I want you to start making a right racket,' cried Corax. 'Clear?'

'Yes, sir,' the hastati replied.

'LOUDER!' bawled Corax. 'Those fuckers opposite aren't here to play games with.'

'YES, SIR!' There was more enthusiasm this time.

'Good. Seventy-five paces.'

Quintus' lips moved, counting each step he took. Without looking, he knew that every man in the maniple was doing the same. Mars, watch over me, he prayed. Grant us victory. Protect my comrades.

Clash! Clash! Clash! Other legionaries began to renew their clamour.

'Sixty paces, boys!'

Quintus struck his iron pilum shaft off the metal rim of his scutum. *Clash!*

In no time, the 150-odd men of the maniple were making the same noise. So too were twenty thousand other hastati. *CLASH! CLASH! CLASH!* Quintus' ears rang with the reassuring sound.

Corax kept them walking at the same slow pace. Now they could discern the faces of individual enemy warriors. Gauls with flowing moustaches and braided hair, wearing pointed iron helmets similar to their own. Big men for the most part, bare-chested, wearing colourful tunics and the occasional metal pectoral plate. They were armed with big, painted shields with iron bosses, long spears and straight swords. It was easy to spot the chieftains with golden torcs around their necks, mail shirts and ornate designs on their shields. There were also groups of Iberians, smaller men in crested and feathered helmets, and crimson-bordered cream tunics. Their shields were small and round, or flat and rectangular; they were armed with long, all-iron javelins, and swords, both curved and straight.

Every single one appeared to be screaming his contempt at the Romans.

Quintus felt his own anger rise. 'We're coming, you bastards!' he bellowed.

'Prepare to die!' added Urceus. Around them, his comrades were roaring their own insults.

Many of the enemy soldiers began throwing their javelins, which rose into the blue sky in threes and fours. The hastati responded with jeers; one of Quintus' tent mates hurled one of his pila. Nearby, other men struck by nerves loosed early as well.

'HOLD, YOU MAGGOTS!' shouted Corax. 'HOLD!' roared other officers. Corax tramped on. 'Fifty paces!'

Few of the enemy missiles had the range to reach the legionaries, but that didn't stop the Carthaginian soldiers. More and more of them cocked back their right arms and threw. They're scared too, thought Quintus. Launching their javelins helps to combat their terror, shows their comrades that they're prepared to fight. He wanted to do the same. Anything was better than just walking in the maw of death.

'Forty paces! Halt. Front eight ranks, take aim. RELEASE!' Corax's right arm jerked forward, and his sword tip pointed directly at the enemy.

All along the Roman formation, the same order was being repeated. 'RELEASE!'

Quintus had never seen so many pila in the air at once. They flew up in graceful shoals, tens of thousands of them. It was an unforgettable sight. As his eyes rose, he saw an eagle far above, aloof, regal. Under normal circumstances, seeing such a bird would have signified good luck. Yet scores of vultures also hung on the warm currents, waiting patiently for the feast that would follow. Their presence was far more ominous. He blinked. Off to his right, a huge dust cloud was trailing upwards from the battlefield. The cavalry on Hannibal's left flank was charging the horsemen on the Roman right. His head turned. A similar bank of dust was rising from his left. Now Quintus felt nauseated. That was when he saw the hundreds and hundreds of enemy javelins that were scudding back in response to their volley. This is it, he thought, heart hammering in his chest. This is when it begins.

'SECOND PILUM! TAKE AIM. RELEASE!'

In reflex, Quintus bent his right arm and flung his javelin with all his strength. With so many ranks in front of him, there was no way *he* could aim. He lobbed it as high as possible, to give it the best chance of landing among the enemy.

'SHIELDS UP!'

The enemy missiles were already landing. With a soft choking noise, a hastatus two ranks in front of Quintus went down, a spear through his neck. Cries of pain rang out from Quintus' left, his right, before him and behind. He ducked down with his scutum over his head. Waited, panting, sweating, full of dread, for an impact. All around him, he heard other shields being struck. The loud thumps were in stark contrast to the softer noises of javelins running into men's flesh and the screams that followed. His gaze crossed with that of Urceus, whose teeth were gritted. Neither spoke. What was there to say?

'LOWER SHIELDS! DRAW SWORDS!' Corax was about twenty paces away, but the din was already so loud that his words were barely distinguishable. 'FORWARD!'

Quintus glanced to either side. The officers in other maniples were also encouraging their men to advance, but the missile barrage had caused gaps to develop between the units. Some were now a few steps in front of his maniple, others ten or more behind. Gone was the uniform line that had existed as they began their walk towards the enemy.

CLASH! CLASH! CLASH! The hastati began to beat their swords off their scuta. Quintus did the same. He covered the remaining distance in a dream. Men close by were praying, cursing, muttering to themselves. The smell of piss grew strong, and with it, Quintus' fear. But there was no going back. He was surrounded on all sides, pushed onwards by the inexorable weight of tens of thousands of his fellows. He drew deep on his reserves, gripped his gladius hilt until his knuckles went white. Jupiter, Greatest and Best, protect me, he asked. Mars, god of war, hold your shield over me. That helped. A little.

'TWENTY PACES, LADS!' Corax bawled. 'FIFTEEN. STEADY!'

They're not even making us charge the last bit, thought Quintus. It must be because there are so many new recruits. If they ran, too many individuals would lose their balance and fall when the two sides struck. His guts roiled at the idea. Fourteen paces. Thirteen. Twelve. Eleven. The clashing noise stopped as men prepared to fight. Both sets of soldiers continued to shout abuse at each other.

Incredibly, this was the moment that three Gaulish warriors chose to attack the Roman lines – on their own. Quintus stared in shock as, yelling like madmen, they swarmed forward. Curses rang out; he heard the impact of metal on metal; shouts; a strangled cry, followed by another.

'What the hell's happening?' asked Urceus. Shorter than Quintus, he could not see much more than the rank in front.

Two figures broke away and ran back towards the Carthaginian front rank. Both were waving bloody swords. An immense roar of triumph greeted their arrival.

'First blood has been spilt,' replied Quintus grimly. 'Two of our men; one Gaul.'

Urceus spat his contempt on to the dusty ground. 'Bring the rest of the whoresons on.'

Quintus wanted to agree. Yet the audacity of the Gauls' assault and the fact that two of them had each managed to kill a legionary was further harsh evidence that this would be no easy struggle. *May the gods be with us.*

'ONWARDS!' roared Corax.

Because of its position near the enemy 'bulge', Corax's maniple was among the first to hit the Carthaginians. Despite the fact that one side was static and the other only walking, the impact when the two met was considerable. It couldn't fail to be, thought Quintus, steadying the soldier in front with his scutum, feeling the man to his rear do the same to him. The legions' frontage extended for more than fifty score paces, which meant that it took a little time for all the legionaries to engage the enemy but in the following few moments, the remainder collided with the Carthaginian troops. *Crash. Thump. Crash. Thump.* Countless shields battered into one another and, as they'd been trained, thousands of legionaries strained with all their power to unbalance their opponents.

Shouts of encouragement from the officers; war cries from the Gauls. Trumpets blaring from their rear; the incessant noise of the carnyxes. Cries of anger, of pain, of anguish. Then the screaming began. It started with a hastatus in the first rank somewhere off to Quintus' right, but was quickly joined by another voice and another – and another. Soon it was coming from everywhere to his front. He could hear nothing but the sound of men roaring their agony to an uncaring world, the jarring clamour of opposing sets of musical instruments and the repetitive clash of weapons. His mouth was as dry as the dust beneath his feet. The temperature, which had been rising steadily during the morning, was now intolerable. Quintus felt as if he was going to fry, like a piece of meat in a pan. What insanity had driven him to join the infantry?

'This is fucking torment,' shouted Urceus in his ear. 'What shall we do?'

'We wait,' said Quintus dully. 'When enough men have been slain, our turn will come.'

Urceus' eyes held his for a moment and then flickered away.

Give me strength, O Great Mars, Quintus prayed. For today I shall need it.

Repeated clashes with the enemy front line had caused a further fracturing of the Roman formation. In some places it had been pushed back; in others, it had advanced a little. With the sun almost overhead, Quintus would have lost all sense of direction but for the range of hills to one side of the battlefield that were occasionally visible through the dust clouds. Nothing had gone as he had imagined it. All was confusion. All was chaos. Gone was the uniform line that had begun the advance. The tide of battle ebbed and flowed. Soldiers clashed, over and over. Some were wounded, some died and then, hurling abuse, the rest broke away from each other. Units lost contact with one another, failed to keep in line as they were supposed to. It was impossible for anyone to know what was going on further than perhaps twenty paces away from where they stood. It was natural, therefore, that groups of soldiers tended to bunch up close to their officers, or around the braver individuals among their comrades. The Carthaginian troops had done the same, turning the battle into a seething mass of large but separate contests.

Unsurprisingly, the hastati in Quintus' unit clustered around their remaining centurion. Pullo had fallen early on, leaving Corax as the only senior officer. Amidst the mayhem, he was like a bulwark against the storm. Quintus had never been more glad to have such a charismatic, brave leader. Casualties had not been heavy initially, but as time passed, men grew tired. That was when they began to make mistakes – and men who did that died or were severely wounded. Since the maniple to their right had lost both of its centurions, scores of its hastati had been cut down. Without Corax, the same could well have happened to him and his comrades. But it hadn't. Yet. Quintus had the additional worry of having to watch out for Macerio, in case the whoreson tried to stab him in the back. Fortunately, Urceus was also on the lookout. Thus far, nothing had happened.

A few moments earlier, the two sides had pulled back from one another. This was happening regularly, when each set of soldiers grew too tired to fight on without respite. Quintus' rank had immediately been summoned by Corax from the mass of hastati who had not yet taken part in the combat. He, Urceus, Severus and the others had shuffled forward to their centurion, who was bleeding from a cut to his cheek. He was unhurt otherwise, however, and there was a terrible gleam in his eyes. 'Ready to do your bit, lads?' he asked.

'Yes, sir,' they answered, regarding the Carthaginians and the ground between them with a mixture of horror and fascination. Quintus had seen battlefields before, but, as a cavalryman, he had never been thrown into the midst of the carnage like this. It was appalling. Great patches of the dusty earth had been turned scarlet. The area was coated – literally – with the bloody bodies of the dead and injured. Severed limbs were scattered here and there. Discarded helmets, shields and swords added to the detritus. Moving forward had now become an exercise in trying not to trip up before reaching the enemy. It was accompanied by a never-ending din of shrieks. Many of the wounded had been dragged back by their comrades, but plenty more remained in no man's land, where they wailed their agony while enough strength remained in their lungs.

'It's not pretty, and it will get worse,' said Corax in a harsh voice. 'Those fucking Gauls are tough, I'll give them that.'

'What's next, sir?' asked Urceus.

'We drink some water. Have another piss. Rest for a little bit. Then we'll go at them again.' Corax eyed them each in turn. 'And we'll keep doing that until the scum break. You with me?'

The hastati who had been fighting already let out a ragged cheer. Quintus and the others hurriedly joined in, keen not to be seen as unwilling. Corax nodded at them, pleased. 'Rest now, boys,' he commanded. 'You'll need all your energy in the hours to come.'

Quintus did a quick check of his sandal straps and the strips of leather that ran under his chin to hold his helmet in place. Satisfied that they were tight, he wiped his hands clean of sweat, ensured that he had a firm grip on his sword hilt. He glanced at Urceus, who was guzzling water from his carrier. 'Ready for this?'

Urceus lowered the bag and scowled. 'As I'll ever be. You?'

'The only way to victory is through those damn Gauls and out the other side. I'm not going to stop until I get there,' replied Quintus, hoping he sounded bolder than he felt.

'That's the spirit,' said Corax, clapping him on the shoulder. 'You might make a princeps yet.'

Quintus grinned, but his new confidence wavered when the Gauls opposite their position began a new chorus of war cries. Corax's reaction was instant. 'Close order! They're coming at us again.'

They moved to stand side by side, perhaps fifteen men wide and three deep. Quintus found himself in the front rank, with Urceus to one side and Corax on the other. He had only just had a drink, but his mouth was parched. Forget your damn thirst, he thought, forget your fear. Concentrate. Watch your footing. Keep your shield high and your face protected.

'Forward, lads,' shouted Corax. 'Slowly. No point rushing – we've got all day to beat these motherless gugga bastards!'

A ripple of laughter through the ranks, and Quintus' spirits rose. Morale must still be high if men could find humour in their situation.

Parr-parr-parr. Zzzeyrrp. Parr-parr-parr. Zzzeyrrp. Booooooooo. The Gauls playing their carnyxes gave fierce encouragement to their fellows. On they came, a bunched mass of warriors perhaps fifty strong. They were led by a stocky, middle-aged man in a mail shirt and ornate helmet. Two gold torcs around his neck further proclaimed his status. This is a tribal war band, thought Quintus. Slay the chieftain and the others will flee. That would prove no easy task, however. A pair of burly men, similarly armoured, flanked the leader. Their size and polished weapons were proof of their abilities.

Corax had come to the same realisation; the chieftain had to be killed. 'Here, you stinking, flea-bitten whoreson!' he roared, pointing his sword. 'HERE!'

The Gaul saw Corax's crested helmet and the phalerae on his chest and recognised that he was the best foe to attack. With a loud growl, he broke into a trot. His men followed at his heels. Quintus fought the panic that came bubbling up his throat.

'Ready, lads?' shouted Corax. 'Here they come!'

With the chieftain aiming for Corax, Quintus was going to face one of his bodyguards, a hulk carrying a lethal-looking sword and a long, oval shield adorned with a swirling snake. This was a fearsome adversary, but he couldn't let his centurion down. Quintus shuffled his left leg forward, made sure that it was on a stable footing and bent his knee to brace his shield. Leaning into the curve of the scutum, he stooped so that the only visible part of him was his eyes and the top of his helmet. The warriors were upon them. Quintus' vision was full of charging, screaming Gauls. His opponent was already swinging a massive overhead blow at him.

He dropped his head, letting the metal rim of his shield take the impact. *THWACK!* His scutum was nearly ripped from his hand. Quintus thrust forward with his gladius, felt it strike the warrior's shield. *Damn it!* He tugged it free, risked a glance over his scutum, had to duck down to avoid being brained by another mighty swing. Again his left arm was wrenched downward. Panic tore at him. A few more blows like that and he wouldn't be able to defend himself any longer. Quintus peeked around the side of his shield, stabbing intuitively at the warrior's left foot. His blade connected, sliced into flesh.

With a roar of pain, the warrior staggered backwards. Quintus took another look. Blood was pouring from the man's foot. It wasn't a mortal wound by any means, but it had granted him a breather. To his left, Urceus was trading blows with a red-haired Gaul. Corax was fighting the chieftain. Neither bout had been decided as yet. Quintus' heart leaped into his mouth. Maybe he could help Corax? There would only be the briefest of opportunities before his own opponent renewed his attack. That made up his mind. As the chieftain thrust at Corax, Quintus rammed his gladius at the man's armpit. *Mars, guide my blade!* The links in the chieftain's mail shirt gave way beneath the force of Quintus' thrust and the iron slid deep into his chest. The chieftain's eyes bulged in shock; a choking cry left his mouth – and Corax stabbed him through the right eye. Aqueous fluid spattered everywhere. Gouts of blood followed the watery liquid as Quintus pulled *his* weapon free. The man dropped to the ground like a sack of wheat.

'Well done,' muttered Corax. 'Shout as loud as you can now, and advance with me.'

Quintus let out the most ferocious scream and took a step forward. Beside him, Corax stepped over the dead chieftain. 'Your leader is dead, you scum!' he yelled. 'The same's going to happen to you!'

The warrior whom Quintus had been fighting looked dismayed. Encouraged, Quintus clattered his sword off his shield and bellowed insults at him. The Gaul glanced uncertainly at his comrades. Moved back a pace. Then another.

'CHARGE!' Corax sprang forward like a hound let off the leash.

Quintus followed him out of instinct. From the corner of his eye, he sensed Urceus scrambling to join them. *Thank all the gods.*

The nearest Gauls broke and ran. From that moment, it was like watching the tide beginning to turn. Dismayed by their comrades' about-face, the entire group of warriors turned and fled for the main body of Carthaginian troops. Eager to press home their advantage, the hastati pursued them, hacking down a good number before they reached safety. Quintus stabbed one warrior in the back, his blade grating off the man's spine and dropping him like a puppet with cut strings. His victim's shrieks were piteous, and he slowed to give him the death stroke.

'Back! Back!' roared Corax.

Quintus raised his arm. He had time.

'Pull back, I said.' Corax grabbed his right arm, pinning him with his gaze.

'I was going to finish this one off, sir.'

'Leave him.'

'Sir, I—'

'He wouldn't do the same for you. Besides, his screams will put off his comrades. Come on.'

There was no gainsaying his centurion. Asking Pluto to take the man quickly, Quintus trotted back to their original position. Corax moved about, bellowing at men to withdraw, slapping them on the back with the flat of

his sword if they didn't hear or immediately obey. 'Re-form the line,' he
shouted over and over.

It wasn't long before they had regrouped. The hastati had lost three
men, but more than a dozen Gauls lay on the ground, dead or with grievous
wounds that would see them to the underworld. Exhilarated by their success,
the legionaries grinned at one another, boasted about what they'd done,
gave thanks to their favourite gods. Quintus felt proud of the way he'd
fought. He looked for the warrior he'd injured in the charge and was
relieved that he seemed to have stopped moving. The big man whose foot
he'd cut was also visible, in the lines opposite. Seeing him, Quintus made
an obscene gesture, which was returned, but with less gusto than his. His
confidence swelled. 'I'll kill him next time.'

'Who?' Urceus' voice.

'The big fucker who was with the chieftain. I only wounded him just
now.'

'Suddenly keen, aren't you?' Urceus thumped the side of his scutum
off that of Quintus.

'It feels good to have driven some of them back.'

'And we'll do it again,' interrupted Corax. He gave Quintus an approving
nod. 'My thanks for skewering that chieftain. That's what broke them.'

Quintus grinned self-consciously. 'I did my bit, sir.'

'Keep doing that.' Corax was about to say more, when he saw something
over Quintus' shoulder. He stiffened to attention. 'Sir!'

'At ease, centurion,' said a voice. 'No one is to salute. I don't want the
enemy to see me just yet.'

Quintus turned, catching a hate-filled stare from Macerio. He ignored
it, mainly because he was stunned by the sight of an officer clad in a
general's red cloak approaching through the ranks. It was the proconsul
Servilius Geminus, the commander of their entire centre. A score of hard-
faced triarii, his guards, stood a little distance back. 'Sir!' Quintus said in
a low voice. Urceus and their companions were quick to echo him.

Servilius smiled as he passed by. 'You are Centurion . . .?'

'Corax, sir, centurion of hastati in what was Longus' First Legion.'

'What's the situation here?'

Corax explained. Servilius looked pleased. 'I've been looking for a place to lead a full-frontal attack. The two maniples to your left have also done well. If we join together, the rest of the front line will follow. One big push, and I think the Gauls will break. Are your men ready to help achieve that, do you think?'

'Of course, sir!' growled Corax.

'Good. Make your preparations. I'm returning to what will be our centre. That's where the maniple to your immediate left is positioned. When I'm in place, I'll give you the signal.'

'Very well, sir.' Corax's smile was lean and hungry. The instant that Servilius had slipped away, he rounded on the hastati. 'You heard the general. You've fought bravely thus far, lads, but this is our chance! No one will forget the soldiers who turned the guggas at Cannae. Who began the rout that saw Hannibal defeated once and for all.'

'We're with you, sir,' said Quintus eagerly.

'All of us,' added Urceus.

A rumble of acknowledgement from the rest, and Corax nodded with satisfaction. 'In that case, be ready for Servilius' signal. At his command, unleash hell!'

They *would* smash the Gauls, thought Quintus. After what they'd just done, he felt sure of it. He prayed that his father and Calatinus were faring as well on the right flank, and that if Gaius were here, that he was playing his part on the left flank. The enemy cavalry *had* to be contained.

As long as that happened, he and the rest of the infantry could do the rest.

Chapter XVIII

T he fighting had been going on for a long time before it became
evident that the centre of the Carthaginian line was going to
crumble and break. Immense credit was due to the Gauls and
Iberians, thought Hanno. They must have been dying in their hundreds
since battle was joined, yet they had held and held when, normally, they
might have cracked. Hannibal and Mago's presence must have helped, but
their accomplishment had also involved considerable bravery. Eventually,
however, the pressure of so many legionaries pressing forward began to
take its toll. Hanno was scrutinising the proceedings like a hawk and spotted
the warriors in the rear ranks some distance away beginning to waver. The
men nearer to hand remained where they were, chanting and hammering
their weapons off their shields, but not those in the centre, upon whom
the burden of the enemy attack would fall when their fellows in front
entirely gave way. Even as he watched, a handful of Gauls backed ten steps
or so from the main body of soldiers. They stood, faces uncertain and a
little ashamed, but almost at once they were joined by half a dozen more
men. A heartbeat later, another larger group left the rear ranks, which
doubled their numbers in one go.

'Look,' Hanno said to Mutt.

'I see them, sir.'

It was like watching sheep trying to get away from the shepherd, thought
Hanno. No one individual will make a move until it sees that another will
do the same. A group forms; they look about to see which way is best.
They dither for a bit, and then some of them make a run for it. The instant
that happens, the whole flock joins in and the process becomes a stampede.
In the time it had taken him and Mutt to exchange two sentences, a score

more warriors had retreated. Hanno's fear that the Romans would break through vied with a frisson of exhilaration that, crazy as it was, Hannibal's plan appeared to be working. 'At least they're not running,' he observed. 'We'd best be ready all the same. Cuttinus will be giving us the signal to move any moment. Have the men turn to our right and face inward.'

'Very good, sir.' Mutt turned around so that the soldiers nearby could hear and cupped a hand to his lips. 'On my command, turn to the right!' He scurried off down the side of the phalanx, spreading the word. By the time he had returned, which wasn't long, hundreds of Gauls and Iberians were walking – fast and backwards – away from the centre of the line. Mutt cast a glance at Hanno, who nodded. 'TURN!' roared Mutt. 'TURN!'

It was as if they had read Cuttinus' mind. A sharp set of notes from his musicians signalled that the phalanxes should wheel as Hannibal had told them to do. Some of Hanno's soldiers took an eager step forward as they faced towards the men who were retreating. An angry roar from Hanno saw them shuffle back into line. He was rigid with tension now. Even the Iberians and Gauls near them – the men at the leftmost edge of the line – were pulling back. They were doing so slowly and in good order, facing to the front with their swords and shields raised high. If the order came, they could stop and immediately begin to fight. He corrected himself. When the order came. Because the only reason that so many warriors were withdrawing was because those at the very front were no longer able to hold back the Romans. Any moment now, a tide of legionaries would come pouring through what had been the centre of their battle line.

Another set of notes from Cuttinus.

'CLOSE ORDER!' shouted Hanno. He broke formation to watch his men move shoulder to shoulder, shield resting against shield, as they'd been trained these past months. Pride filled him at how fast they did it. There were perhaps forty men fewer than had been in the unit when he'd taken command of it, just before the Trebia. He might not have been with them since Iberia, but Hanno felt bonded to them now. A mad notion took him. There was probably just enough time, if he moved fast. He dragged out his sword and walked to the soldier at the left-hand edge of the phalanx. It pleased him to see that it was the older man who'd been with him the night that he'd been captured at Victumulae. A steady pair of hands where it counted, he thought, giving the veteran an approving nod. The gesture was returned, which prompted a warm feeling in Hanno's belly.

'You've all been through a lot since you sailed from Carthage to join Hannibal in Iberia,' he called. 'You've fought and marched all the way to Italy!' The Libyans cheered him then, and he began to walk slowly along the front rank, clattering his sword tip off the metal rims of their scuta. 'From Carthage to Iberia to Gaul to Italy! And never beaten! Be proud of yourselves!' *Clatter. Clatter. Clatter.* Their roars of approval, fierce grins and eyes bright with determination told him to continue. 'Today, Hannibal needs you more than ever. As he has never needed you before!' Hanno was about halfway along the front rank. Everyone in the phalanx could hear him here. He turned and pointed dramatically with his sword. His guts twisted. The Gauls and Iberians were running now. They had broken. 'The bastard Romans are going to appear there any instant. What are we going to do to them?'

'Kill the fuckers!' screamed Mutt with more energy than Hanno had ever seen him display. He was standing at the far right of the front of the phalanx, where it abutted the next unit.

'KILL! KILL! KILL!' shouted the men, hitting their shields with their gladii.

The Libyans in the next phalanx took up the chant at once. 'KILL! KILL! KILL!'

Soon it was echoing all along the line, drowning out the retreating warriors' shouts of dismay.

Satisfied, Hanno resumed his place in the front rank.

Cuttinus' musicians sounded the advance.

Heart pounding, Hanno popped his sword under his left armpit and gave his right hand a last wipe on the bottom of his tunic. He repeated the process with his other hand. 'FORWARD, AT THE WALK! HOLD THE LINE! PASS THE WORD ON.' Mutt would keep the phalanx close to the one to their right.

They had gone about twenty paces when Hanno saw his first legionary. Some fifty steps to his front, the Roman was pursuing an Iberian who had flung away his shield. A savage, arcing cut from the legionary's sword opened the Iberian's flesh from shoulder to waist. Blood sprayed; he fell to the ground, letting out a high-pitched shriek. The legionary hardly paused. He ran on, trampling the body, not even seeing the phalanxes of Libyans. Nor did his comrades, a dozen or more of whom came tearing on behind him. Excitement thrilled through Hanno. We look like them, he thought. He would wager that Hannibal had even thought of this little detail.

The sudden signal to halt came as a surprise, but Hanno obeyed it nonetheless. 'HALT! Stay where you are,' he bellowed.

'Why, sir?' asked the man to his left. 'There they are!'

Unasked, it came to him. 'We let as many of the dogs go past as possible, because that way, more of them will be trapped.'

The soldier bared his teeth. 'Ah, I see, sir. A good plan.'

'Not a word now. No shouting, no cheering. Stay quiet. Pass it on.'

With a grin, the soldier did as he was told. Hanno ordered the man to his right to do the same. Then they waited, knuckles white on the grips of their weapons, as they hid in plain sight of the Romans. The numbers of Carthaginian troops retreating had slowed to a trickle, and with each of Hanno's rapid heartbeats, scores upon scores of legionaries charged into view. Soon it was hundreds. More men than he could count. Cheering. Shouting insults. Encouraged by officers. So eager to kill the enemy that all semblance of order, of maintaining formation, had been lost. They did not even see the Libyans waiting to their right, not a javelin shot away. There were a few cursory glances thrown in their direction, but no one registered that these were not just other Romans. After all, the enemy had broken!

Gods, thought Hanno. This can't go on. They will see us. Eventually, they have to.

His heart thumped out another dozen beats. Hundreds more Romans flooded past them. So many were advancing into the gap now that some of the men were coming within spitting distance of the Libyans' lines. 'Hold,' hissed Hanno. 'Hold!' Come on, Cuttinus, he screamed silently. Give us the fucking order!

And then it came. Strident. Piercing. Definitive.

'FORWARD!' screamed Hanno. 'KILL!'

'KILL! KILL! KILL!' yelled his men.

They'd gone ten paces before the first Roman faces turned and saw them. Even then, with death approaching, it didn't register. Only when

Hanno was so close that he could see the pockmarks on the nearest Roman's face did he observe the first signs of fear among them. He saw jaws drop, panic flare in eyes, heard shouts of 'Stop! Stop! They're not our men!' and 'Turn, lads, turn!'

But it was too late. The Libyans swept in on the undefended Roman flank like avenging demons. Hanno's fear was swept away by a red mist of battle rage. He saw Pera in every Roman face. He would slay them all.

'KILL! KILL! KILL!'

'At this rate, we'll run the bastards all the way to the west coast,' shouted Urceus, slowing up. He wiped his brow with the back of his sword arm. The movement left smears of blood across his face, turning him into a wild-eyed maniac.

I probably look like that too, thought Quintus. He didn't care. Nothing mattered any longer except moving forward – and trying to stay alive. He stared at the fleeing Gauls and Iberians, still not believing his eyes. Servilius' charge had worked like a dream. They had smashed into the mass of Gauls with the long spears of the triarii at the point of the wedge. Surprised by their enemies' ferocity, the tribesmen had fallen back. That had been enough encouragement for a large number of other hastati to come barrelling forward again. The fighting had been intense, more savage than what had gone before, and the Gauls had not given up without a hard struggle. They had retreated, but had continued to face the Romans and to fight. Slowly but surely, though, the legionaries had pushed on, one bloody step at a time. In Quintus' section of the line, they had pushed the Gauls back a couple of hundred paces at least. A few heartbeats prior, however, things had changed. He didn't know what had been the final straw, but many of the warriors had begun to flee. It was odd how fast panic spread once it took hold, he thought. It wasn't dissimilar to watching a spark take hold in a bundle of dry kindling, the way the flames licked and wrapped them- selves around the next piece of wood with fearful speed. Before you knew it, you had a proper fire going.

'Crespo? You hurt?' Urceus' voice.

Quintus came back to the present. 'Huh? No.'

'Damn glad to hear it.' A water bag was thrust in his face.

Quintus took a long swig, and then another. The liquid tasted of waxed leather and was blood-warm, but he was so parched that he didn't care.

'On, lads, on! Keep the line formed. The principes and triarii will be on our heels.' Corax was talking to other soldiers, but the effect was the same. Quintus tossed the carrier back to Urceus, who stoppered it and hung it over his shoulder again. Then, exchanging a determined look, they moved off.

The three maniples led by Servilius and Corax continued to press forward as one bloc. It was inevitable that their close-order formation broke up as the legionaries' hunting instincts – and bloodlust – took over. There were few commanders in the world who could keep their men tightly together in such situations. This was the easiest time to cut down the enemy, the time when defeated armies suffered most of their casualties. Men who were running did not defend themselves. They were often unarmed, having discarded weapons and shields so that they could get away faster. The Romans' speed picked up even further. The air filled with bloodcurdling shouts.

Quintus' fear had been replaced by a mad exhilaration, and a desire to kill. He wanted revenge for all his comrades who had died at the Trebia and at Lake Trasimene. For the innocent civilians of Campania and other areas who had died at Carthaginian hands. He slashed and cut, hacked and thrust. Hamstrung men, split open their ribs, opened their bellies. Decapitated one warrior; chopped an arm off two others. Blood spattered over his shield, his face, his sword arm. Quintus didn't care. There was so much gore, piss and shit on the ground that his feet squelched as he walked. He barely saw it. There was no sport, no skill in stabbing men in the back, but that didn't matter either. He slew until his gladius was blunt and his muscles ached from the repetitive action of using it.

Eventually, their advance began to peter out. Exhaustion had taken hold. They had been beneath the summer sun since it had climbed over the horizon. Marching. Fording rivers. Advancing. Throwing javelins. Engaging in close combat. Even killing defenceless men used up energy. Finally, though, the Gauls and Iberians began to outstrip the hastati. Their fear gave them a fraction more speed. Deprived of victims, lacking the strength to increase their pace yet again, Corax's legionaries slowed to a walk. As ever, the centurion seized command. 'You're doing fine, boys. Time for a breather. Have a drink. Fill your lungs.'

To Quintus, Corax's words were muffled, as if they were standing in dense fog. He felt as though he were outside his body, watching himself mumble a few words to Urceus, gulp down some water, wipe the worst of the blood off his blade, stare unseeing at the mutilated corpse at his feet. His gaze wandered to their left, registered something that didn't make sense. He blinked, looked again, came back to earth. 'Those Gauls aren't retreating.'

'Eh? The mangy sheep-fuckers I can see are running as fast as their legs will carry them,' said Urceus with a laugh.

'Not those ones. Those – over there.' Quintus pointed.

Urceus looked, scowled. 'Ha! What of them? It won't be long before they also panic and flee. We're unstoppable now.' He jerked a thumb to their rear, to the great mass of soldiers advancing towards them. There was little order visible, but no one could deny its huge momentum. The ground trembled with the tread of so many thousands of feet.

Quintus shrugged. Urceus was right. Who could stand before so many soldiers? There were twenty thousand hastati in the army's first line, the same number of principes in the second and about ten thousand triarii in the third. Mix the thousands of velites in amongst that and it made an unbeatable force. Hannibal's host was nowhere near as large. 'Victory will be ours,' he muttered, feeling the surety of it in his bones.

'Of course it will,' replied Urceus. 'Let's keep moving.'

They had gone no more than a dozen steps when rousing cheers began to rise from their left. A heartbeat later, the same shouts could be dimly heard far to their right. Engaged with a Gaul who was still prepared to fight, Quintus ignored it. Urceus came to his aid and they swiftly put the warrior down into the crimson mud. Panting, Quintus gave his friend a nod of thanks. The noise was louder now, originating from all along their left side. Mixed with the shouts, Quintus thought he could hear cries of dismay. Of fear. Of panic. The first tickle of unease licked at his spine. 'What's happening?'

'I've got no fucking idea.' Urceus also looked a little nervous.

CRASH. A shocked silence, then the booming sound was repeated from their right. Quintus wanted to puke. The force of the impacts was such that it could mean only one thing. 'Hannibal must have wheeled part of his line. To take us in the sides.'

Urceus' face twisted in disbelief. 'How?'

'Jupiter, I don't know!'

'No, that can't be it. Besides, his centre is smashed to smithereens! What's to stop us from driving on through the lot of them?'

'You're right,' said Quintus, flushing.

Corax was frowning, but that didn't stop him ordering them forward again. They advanced at the walk this time, secure in the knowledge that with so many soldiers behind them, they could not be stopped. As at the Trebia and Trasimene, the might of the infantry would prevail. Except that on this occasion, their cavalry would, gods willing, have held the enemy horse. When they had entirely broken through, they could turn to either side and fall on the Carthaginian rear. That was how Corax had explained it to them anyway, thought Quintus, struggling against waves of tiredness. He was beyond questioning what they would do.

'Shitting hell! Look.'

The urgency in Urceus' voice broke through Quintus' fatigue. His eyes followed those of Urceus, towards their front. 'No.' *It's a living nightmare.*

What he saw defied belief. Once an army broke, it was unheard of for it to halt and begin fighting again. Yet some hundred paces away, some of the fleeing Gauls and Iberians had come to a standstill. A few had already turned, and were roaring at their comrades to stop running.

The realisation struck Quintus like a punch to the solar plexus. 'That's why the centre of his line was bowed forward to meet us. It was a trap. It was all a trap,' he said, feeling the fear uncoil afresh in his guts. 'Sir! Do you see this?'

'Aye,' snarled Corax. 'Hannibal is even smarter than we gave him credit for. Form a line, boys! The fighting isn't over yet. We'll have to teach those gugga dogs another lesson before they put their tails between their legs and run away for good. But do it we will. *Roma victrix!*'

The hastati raised a cracked cheer by way of answer, but their throats were too dry to continue it for long. A moment later, as if prompted to give the lie to the centurion's bold words, a number of carnyxes started up their terrifying clamour again. Some men's shoulders visibly slumped at their hideous sounds. Quintus gritted his teeth. He had come to loathe the instruments – and fear them. *Parr-parr-parr. Zʒʒeyrrp. Parr-parr-parr. Zʒʒeyrrp. Booooooooo.* The carnyxes' tune was not going to go unaccompanied either. Incredibly, a handful of Gauls who had stripped naked emerged from amidst their comrades and repeated the threatening performances they'd put on before the battle began: beating their chests, waving their swords and cupping their genitalia at the legionaries. Their shouted insults were unintelligible but very clear. Moments before, they had been retreating. Now they were keen to renew hostilities. The display had a marked effect on the men who were still running. Quintus saw a number stop, twist their heads to look, and then make an about-face. At first it was a handful, but with each thud of his pounding heart, more warriors joined them. His eyes closed briefly as he tried to take it in.

The Gaulish retreat hadn't just stopped. It had turned around. It was an attack again.

Quintus felt more weary than he had ever been in his life. Pure fantasy though it was, he wished that the Gauls would vanish. He longed just to lie down, to take the weight off his aching feet, to get out of the damn sun, even to sleep. But there was no chance of that. Deep in his belly, he knew the fighting that had gone before would be as nothing compared to what was to come. The troops that had attacked their flanks – quite possibly the Libyans, and among them Hanno? – would be rested. Fresh. Eager to fight. Quintus' mind was full of new, unsettling doubts. He gave the sun a baleful glare, wishing it were nearer the horizon. How many thousand Romans would die before it set? Would he and his comrades be among them? Would his father? Gaius? Calatinus? And, more crucially, was victory as certain as it had seemed that morning?

Quintus was no longer sure. About any of it.

Hanno had never imagined that Hannibal's plan could work quite so well. Yet it had, causing his admiration for his general to grow even further. The Romans had taken Hannibal's bait and swallowed it in one great gulp. The consequence was that their advance had come to a complete halt.

The legionaries within sight looked terrified, exhausted, demoralised to a man. Hanno could only imagine that the same was true of the men facing his father's Libyans, on the other flank. It seemed that the Gauls and Iberians had re-formed too, because he could hear the sounds of fighting coming from off to his right, where the warriors had retreated. The Romans must be hemmed in to their rear as well, he thought elatedly, or they'd be running that way by now. That meant that Hasdrubal and Maharbal had been victorious in the cavalry battle, which in turn signified that their horsemen were at this moment harassing the back of the Roman host. Hanno's heart lifted even further at that thought. Nothing terrified infantry more than a disciplined cavalry charge. From the corner of his eye, he caught men starting to shift from foot to foot, which pleased him. He'd only pulled them back a short time before, to rest and to drink some water. It made sense: the Romans were going nowhere. Yet his soldiers already wanted to renew the fight. It boded well.

The legionaries opposite had no javelins, and their discipline was fading fast. Each time Hanno led his phalanx forward, most of them panicked and tried to flee. It wasn't combat any longer. Cutting down men who had their backs turned was butchery, nothing more. But it had to be done, thought Hanno grimly. Rome did not understand diplomacy. Brute force was the only thing that would drive the lesson home. Besides, not every legionary had given up. The sounds of fierce fighting could yet be heard from other parts of the battlefield. If their fellows here took heart from that, or were rallied by an officer, they might still pose a threat. They therefore needed to be crushed. Utterly.

'Ready to send some more Romans to hell, boys?' Hanno cried.

His soldiers roared their bloodlust back at him, and together they advanced. Scuta high, only their helmets and their eyes showing, reddened gladii protruding from the shield wall like the poisonous barbs on a stone-fish. The Romans wailed at their approach, and Hanno's troops picked up speed. 'Slowly,' he shouted. 'Reserve your strength for killing. We're going to be at it for the rest of the day.'

The men who heard him laughed like madmen then, and fresh terror bloomed on the faces of the nearest legionaries. Those at the front pushed and shoved at their comrades behind, trying to put bodies between them and the enemy. The entire mass of legionaries swayed and moved back several steps.

The red mist began to descend on Hanno. Weirdly, the scar on his neck began to itch too. 'Where are you, Pera?' he roared. 'Pera! Come out so I can gut you like the coward you are!'

No one answered, but one legionary suddenly charged straight at them. Shieldless, wounded, spittle flying from his lips, he had clearly lost all reason. He looked nothing like Pera, but Hanno longed for the man to attack him. Instead he slammed into the shield of a Libyan ten paces away. A pair of gladii ran him through before he could use his own blade, spitting him through his unarmoured abdomen. 'Stupid bastard,' said one of the Libyans as he shoved the dying Roman backwards with his scutum.

They were only half a dozen steps from the legionaries now. A handful of men prepared to fight, but the majority were crying like children. Many had dropped their shields and swords and, with their backs to the Libyans, were ripping at those in their way with their bare hands. Four steps. Two.

'Pera? I'm coming for you, you arse-humping piece of shit!' Hanno picked his target, a legionary with a similar build to Pera. Rammed his sword into the right side of the man's back, just below his small iron back plate. Resistance, easy push, shove – and he felt it come out of the legionary's belly. An ear-splitting shriek of pain. Hanno twisted the blade for good measure, ripped it free and watched in fascination as a tide of blood followed it out. The man's knees were already folding. Hanno shoved him on to the ground with his shield boss and barged into the mass of enemy soldiers. Even with their level of panic, it was a dangerous move. He had no one to protect his sides, but he had gone beyond sense. He was back in the cell in Victumulae, dangling by his wrists. Pera stood before him in his mind's eye, a hot iron raised towards his face.

Next in his path was a terrified young legionary who raised his hands towards Hanno, palms out. 'I surrender! I surrender!'

'Fuck you.' Hanno stabbed him through the stomach, the easiest way to finish a man for good, and, pulling the blade out, cut down the man next to him with a backhanded slash to the side. He felt a body shoving in behind him and, cursing, tried to turn and kill whoever it was. The mist parted long enough for him to recognise Mutt and to stay his arm. They fought side by side for a time, savagely, efficiently, killing and wounding a dozen or more Romans. There was no resistance. It was like slaughtering spring lambs. The pair only stopped when the legionaries before them managed to break away and flee. Hanno made to pursue them, but Mutt blocked his path.

'Out of my way!' Hanno snarled.

Mutt didn't move. 'You'll get killed, sir.'

The certainty in Mutt's voice sank home. Hanno blinked.

'You want to defeat the Romans entirely, don't you, sir?'

'You know I do!'

'Then don't throw your life away. Stay calm, sir. Keep the lads in check. Attack, withdraw, attack again. Just as we've been doing. It's simple, and it works.' Mutt stood aside.

'You're right.' Hanno took a deep breath, regained a little control, felt his muscles trembling with weariness. 'Tell the men to halt. They'll need a drink and another break.'

Mutt gave him an approving look. 'Yes, sir.'

And so it went on, for hours. It became a bizarre routine. Apart from the phalanx to either side of his own, Hanno couldn't see what the other units were doing. He assumed it was much the same. Pull back, regroup, tend the wounded. Share out the water and wine that remained. Rest. Some men produced food that they'd stashed inside their tunics; it was passed around and devoured. It also became necessary to sharpen their sword blades regularly; they were blunt from being shoved into human flesh.

On one occasion, a senior officer of some type, perhaps a tribune, tried to lead an attack while Hanno and his men were resting, but it was a half-hearted affair that swiftly ended when Mutt slew the officer. The rest of the time, the Romans in his section of the line seemed content to do nothing but emulate the Libyans' behaviour. It wasn't surprising, thought Hanno as he watched them during one rest period, for these were the only times when they weren't being killed. Some of the legionaries still fought back when he and his men attacked. Once or twice, he and his Libyans were even driven back a little way. For the most part, however, the Romans had given up resisting. Dull-eyed, catatonic, sunburned, they were just waiting for death to take them — like cattle or sheep in pens outside a butcher's shop. It had not occurred to Hanno before, but he wondered if his men – if the army – would be able to dispatch every single legionary on the field before darkness, or before their exhaustion got the better of them.

After the uncertainty with which the day had begun, it scarcely seemed possible that he could be contemplating the annihilation of such an enormous Roman host. Hanno gave thanks to his favourite gods, but he was careful to dampen down his feelings of triumph. Plenty of the enemy were continuing to fight. The battle was not over, and would not be until the sun had set. He would reserve judgement until then. Before that, he and his men still had a job to do.

To kill yet more Romans.

It was as if the Gauls and Iberians facing them were different men to those who'd broken and run earlier, thought Quintus. In spite of the heat, the dust, the sun, the tribesmen had a new enthusiasm for the fight. It had re-emerged since the Carthaginian attacks had fallen on their flanks. Thanks to this enemy effort, the Roman advance had wholly stalled. The warriors' attacks on the legionaries' front did not last for long, but they were deadly nonetheless. Despite Servilius' and Corax's efforts, every single one ended with dead hastati. Sometimes just a few, but more often than not it was ten or more. Roman morale slipped with every successive assault. The cries of their wounded, who lay before them – they had given up dragging men who were going to die back to their lines – as well as to their rear, didn't help. One hastatus had been whimpering about his mother for so long that Quintus would have ended his suffering himself if the unfortunate hadn't been lying so close to the enemy.

It was as well that the Gauls tended to pull back quickly, or the legionaries might have broken already. The enemy were bone tired now too, which meant that they could not press home their advantage as no doubt their leaders would have wished. That was of little solace to Quintus or his comrades, of whom perhaps ninety remained. Typically, Macerio was one of them. It didn't matter that the Carthaginian troops had to break for regular rests. The Romans were surrounded, like a vast shoal of fish in a net. And slowly but surely, the net was being tightened, pulled on to the fisherman's boat. Quintus had lost all concept of time, but it had to be the middle of the afternoon. The malevolent yellow orb that was the sun still hung high in the sky, which meant that the fighting had been going on for six, maybe more, hours. The cavalry battle had been won by Hannibal's horsemen – it had to have been, or the Carthaginian rear would have been under attack by now. There would be no relief from their ordeal. It was a case of breaking through the enemy lines, or dying. Gazing around him, Quintus knew that many of his comrades would be doing the latter. So would he and Urceus, if something didn't change. He wondered vaguely where on the battlefield Hanno might be, and if he too would still be alive by the end of the day. It seemed a lot more likely than his own survival.

'Here they come again,' croaked Urceus.

A chorus of curses from their comrades. More than one started to pray. Incredibly, after all the sweat that they'd each shed, one hastatus began to have a quick piss.

'Where's Corax?' asked a voice. No one answered, and an unhappy air settled over the group.

Quintus scowled, hefted his battered scutum, tried to ignore the trembling in his sword arm. 'Have you seen him?' he hissed at Urceus.

'Not for a while. He'll be back.'

'He'd fucking better,' Severus responded.

Someone's got to take command, thought Quintus grimly. Fast. 'Close order!' he shouted. 'Anyone with a javelin, prepare to loose on my command.' He was relieved that no one questioned him. They did as he said, glad no doubt to be given orders.

The Gauls no longer ran at the hastati. They just walked. Some shouted war cries, but most remained quiet. Their throats had to be as dry as the Romans' were. Even the men with the carnyxes had given up. The clamour of battle rang from all around them, but in their odd oasis, there was little noise. It was worse facing the tribesmen when they were quiet, Quintus decided. They always attacked while screaming at the top of their lungs; in contrast, the silence was even more ominous.

'How far away are they?' he muttered to Urceus.

'Fifty paces or so.'

Quintus agreed. He began to count in his head. At thirty paces, he glanced to either side. Following Corax's orders, they had continually picked up discarded pila, but as the day had gone on, fewer and fewer were reusable. Fewer than a dozen men had javelins, he saw, but it was still worth a volley. Every Gaul who lost his shield was an enemy who was more easily killed. 'Steady now! Let the whoresons come! Do not loose yet.'

He was shocked when the Gauls suddenly began to run. That was when he noticed the band of soldiers in the middle of their formation. These were no tribesmen. Every man among them sported a mail shirt and a black cloak; all were carrying scuta and swords. A few others were wearing muscled cuirasses and Hellenistic helmets. Could they be Carthaginian officers? Sweat sluiced down Quintus' back when he saw that one man had a purple tunic. The patch of similar-coloured fabric over one eye confirmed his suspicions. He couldn't help himself. 'It's fucking Hannibal!'

'What's he doing here?' Urceus snarled, but the fear was palpable in his voice.

A wail of dismay left Severus' throat.

'We're all going to die!' cried someone who sounded just like Macerio.

'Shut your mouths!' cried Quintus, but it was too late. Fear raged through the ranks – he could practically see it, ravening, tearing away the last of the men's courage. 'Take aim. LOOSE!' he roared.

Most of the javelins went up, but the volley was ragged. The rest of the hastati with pila stood transfixed with fear. The Carthaginian charge drew nearer. The Roman lines wavered. Steadied again. 'Throw the damn things, or drop them,' bellowed Quintus. 'Draw swords!' He didn't even see if the javelins got thrown. The enemy were too close.

Eager to impress their general, the Gauls fought like men possessed. They swarmed in, hacking savage overhead blows at the heads of the hastati, wrenching at their scuta and stabbing them in the neck. Throwing themselves, uncaring, into any gaps that appeared, the warriors broke apart the maniple's shrunken ranks within a matter of moments. Quintus and Urceus fought like twins joined at the hip, holding their own, but Severus soon went down beneath the blade of one of the black-cloaked enemy soldiers, clearly one of Hannibal's bodyguard. The hastatus to Severus' left lost his sword arm and then his head. Two scarlet fountains from his wounds pumped blood everywhere as he fell on top of Severus' body. The few men who were left beyond that were surrounded a heart-beat later. With their left flank exposed, Quintus and Urceus fell back, still fighting. The men to their rear saw what was happening and gave way too.

The general was only half a dozen steps from them by this stage, but he could as well have been on the moon. There were three burly bodyguards between them, men who looked fresh, eager and very dangerous. It was bizarre being so close to the individual who was responsible for the tumult of the previous twenty months and more, and being helpless to do a thing about it. Fascinated, Quintus' gaze kept flicking back to him. Despite the rumours, Hannibal was not a giant or a monster. He was a brown-skinned, one-eyed, bearded man of medium height. Unremarkable. By all the gods, he must be charismatic, Quintus thought.

And then, like an autumn wind that carries leaves off the ground and into the ether, the fighting swirled them apart. Quintus and Urceus were driven back twenty more steps. They sensed rather than saw the hastati behind them turn to run, and cursed them for cowards. There were perhaps forty-five of them bunched up together, still facing the enemy, who had halted to draw breath little more than ten paces away. To his credit, Macerio was still with them. Hannibal was moving among his men, talking and gesturing towards the hastati. 'So this is how it ends,' said Quintus, letting out a long breath.

'I suppose we should be grateful that we're going to die fighting Hannibal himself,' replied Urceus sourly.

Quintus managed a chuckle, but there was no humour in it. 'Who knows? If Fortuna is kind to us, we might even manage to kill him before the end.'

'A man can dream,' retorted Urceus. He eyed Quintus sidelong. 'It's been good knowing you, Crespo.'

There was a lump in Quintus' throat. I'm not called Crespo, he wanted to say, but all that came out was, 'You too, my friend.'

The Gauls and black-cloaked soldiers began to clatter their weapons off their shields. 'HANN-I-BAL!' they shouted. 'HANN-I-BAL!'

A frisson of fear rippled through the hastati. Quintus knew in his gut that after everything they had been through, this was too much. 'Steady, boys,' he cried, fighting his own creeping dread. 'STEADY!'

'What in Hades is going on here?' Miraculously, Corax's voice was by Quintus' ear. He could have wept with gladness.

'It's Hannibal, sir. He's here, with some of his bodyguards. The Gauls, they . . . Our lads are so tired, sir. They can't . . .'

Corax's eyes bored into his and saw the utter exhaustion. He scanned the enemy lines opposite, spat a curse at Hannibal, assessed the situation for what it was. 'Shit. If we stay here, we're all fucked. Pull back.'

Quintus blinked. 'Sir?'

'You heard me, hastatus.' Corax's voice cracked like a whip. 'Pull back, boys. Keep your formation. Walk back slowly, a step at a time. Do it!'

The hastati didn't need any encouragement. With fearful eyes on the enemy, they shuffled back five, ten, fifteen paces. They had to walk over their own wounded to do so, which was heart-rending, and sickening. Bloody hands reached up to them. Pleading voices filled their ears. 'Don't leave me here, please! Please . . .' 'Mother. I want Mother. Mother!' 'It hurts. It hurts so bad. Please make it stop.' Quintus saw more than one man thrust down quickly with his gladius. He did the same himself, but was unable to meet the terror-filled eyes of the hastatus whose life he ended. When they had retreated for perhaps two score paces, Corax had them halt.

'They're not going to come after us,' said Quintus, eyeing the enemy and daring to hope.

'No. Hannibal has gone, look. He's got to keep moving among his men, keep them fired up so that they continue to press home their assault.' It was the first time that Quintus had ever heard weariness in Corax's voice. Panic flared in his belly, but it was replaced by relief when he glanced around. There was still a determined set to his centurion's jaw.

'You did well back there.'

'Sir?'

'I was on my way back, but too far away to do anything when I saw that the enemy were about to attack. Our lines were wavering until you took control. Well done.'

Quintus' face, red from physical exertion and the sun, turned an even deeper colour. 'Thank you, sir.'

A tight nod. 'I went to talk to Servilius, to see if we could make a counter-attack, but I found him dying. His lines have collapsed entirely. I was lucky to get away.' Corax's voice was flat and hard.

Quintus made himself ask. 'The battle's lost, isn't it, sir?'

A silence, which spoke volumes.

'Yes, it is,' said Corax at length. 'Hannibal is a genius to do what he's done here today. Damn his eyes! Only the gods know how many men will lie here by nightfall.'

Quintus glanced at Urceus and saw the same hopelessness in his face that he felt in his heart. Escape from the Gauls meant little when they were still surrounded. 'What shall we do, sir?'

'Avoid fighting the enemy for the moment. Rally a few more men together. Then we're to search out a weak spot in the enemy's formation and smash a fucking great hole in it. We'll head for the river, and our camp. If that can't be held, we'll retreat to the north.'

The task that Corax had just set them sounded harder than scaling the highest peak in the Alps in midwinter, but Quintus found himself agreeing. He heard Urceus doing the same. As Corax told the other hastati of his plan, no one argued, least of all Macerio. Quintus wasn't surprised. The centurion had won their trust a long time before, not least at Lake Trasimene, when he had led them through the Libyan phalanxes, but also in the subsequent trials and tribulations. It wasn't as if they had many other options anyway, other than waiting to be killed by the Carthaginians. From the dazed expressions on the faces of the legionaries around their position, that was what would happen to many, but in Quintus' mind, that was no choice at all. I might be tired, he thought. I might be beaten. But I'm not a fucking sheep who just stands and waits for its throat to be cut.

Hanno's hunch that his men might grow too weary to kill proved accurate. By the time the sky had turned every possible shade of pink and red, presaging a stunning sunset, most of his Libyans were like drunk men. They staggered as he ordered them to advance, and were barely capable of lifting their shields and swords, let alone killing yet more Romans. During one of their most recent assaults, Hanno had lost a few soldiers when some desperate legionaries had seen their exhaustion and turned on them. It was pointless losing valuable men like that, and he was forced to withdraw more than half of his phalanx from the fighting. That move left a gaping hole in his section of the line, and after that, it was inevitable that legionaries began to escape. They broke away in ones and twos, in small groups and sometimes in large. Weaponless, shieldless, cowed and broken, they skulked off into the darkening air like whipped curs. The Libyans watched them go, unable to prevent them. When the largest number yet began to retreat, Hanno spat on the ground with frustration. He considered chasing them, but knew that it would be too much for his exhausted men. Besides, easier targets – the legionaries who had not run – yet remained close by.

Even those now presented a problem. The light was leaching fast from the sky. The birds of prey that had hung over the battlefield all day had gone. Even the wind had calmed, allowing the swirling dust to settle some-what. Before long, it would be too dark to do anything other than withdraw from the field. The sounds of combat had diminished. The predominant sound was the screams of the injured and dying. Hanno had never felt more tired: he too was only capable of fighting for a short time before having to rest. Yet despite all this, the battle madness still controlled him. They could manage one or two more assaults on the nearest legionaries, he told himself. They could kill more of them. Pera might be among their number.

Hanno prowled along his soldiers' lines, exhorting them to another mighty effort. They groaned, they grumbled; he heard a few muttered curses. But they got to their feet again, formed a ragged line. There were perhaps seventy of them; the rest were sprawled, uncaring, on the blood-sodden ground to their rear. Hanno noted, as if for the first time, that every single man's right arm was red to the elbow with a mixture of fresh and clotted blood. Their shields looked as if they had been dipped in a vat of scarlet dye. Their faces and helmets were spattered with flecks of red; so too were their feet and sandals. They were literally covered in blood from head to toe. Scarlet demons. Creatures of the underworld. I must look the same, Hanno thought, feeling a trace of revulsion. It was no wonder that the Romans wailed when they approached.

'Will this be the last attack, sir?' Mutt's voice was low.

Hanno gave him an irritated look. 'I hadn't planned on it, no.'

'I don't think many of the lads can take much more, sir. Look at them.'

Unwillingly, Hanno studied his soldiers again. He was shocked to see that some of them were using their scuta to prop themselves up. More than one had laid his head on a forearm resting on the iron shield rim. Could that man be snoring? he wondered. His gaze wandered to the nearest Romans, a huddled mass of perhaps a hundred legionaries under the command of a wounded centurion. 'I'm not just letting that lot escape,' he said stubbornly. 'No way.'

'One last attack, sir. Any more than that and you'll start killing our own.'

Hanno didn't want to admit it, but Mutt was right. Even he, his second-in-command, who could march all day without breaking a sweat, looked spent. If that was the case, even Hannibal would not think worse of him for calling a halt at this stage. 'Very well. But I want that centurion dead before we pull back. They'll break once he's down.'

'Yes, sir. I think we can manage that much.' Mutt's teeth flashed white amid the red that coated his face. 'After that, I think it'll be safe to venture that we've won, eh?'

'I'd say so, Mutt. Even the fucking Romans will have to admit defeat after this. Their army has almost been wiped out.'

'Hearing that out loud feels damn good, sir.'

'It does.' For the first time, Hanno allowed himself to savour the feeling of triumph. All that was required to make the day an unmitigated success was that his father and brothers – even Sapho – had survived. It was unlikely that he'd find them this night, but he could search for them in the morning. Gods willing, they could all celebrate Hannibal's victory together then.

'Ready, sir?' asked Mutt.

'Yes.' Hanno watched as Mutt rallied the Libyans, getting them to form up in close order. 'One last bout before we're done, boys,' he croaked. 'A gold piece to the man who hands me that centurion's helmet.'

His soldiers' throats were parched, but they growled their appreciation at him. One even found the energy to start beating his sword off his shield again. The rhythm was infectious. Several men joined in, and Hanno laughed as the Roman line, such as it was, visibly backed up a step. He could see the centurion, who was at the front, roaring abuse at soldiers who must have been pulling away from the rear of their formation. 'They're wavering! One good strike and they'll break! You hear me?'

Incredibly, there was a cracked cheer. 'HANN-I-BAL!' yelled Mutt.

'HANN-I-BAL!' shouted a number of men.

The Romans retreated again.

'Again,' Hanno hissed.

Mutt repeated his cry. 'HANN-I-BAL!'

This time, not even the centurion could hold the legionaries. They turned and fled.

Howling like wolves, Hanno and his soldiers chased them into the night.

Corax had taken one look at the soldiers in the main camp and made his men turn on their heels. There had been a few protests. It was nearly dark. After a short but brutal assault, they had escaped the ring of Carthaginians who even now were butchering their comrades. After that, they had forded the Aufidius and straggled back to their encampment through the darkening air. 'We've done enough, sir,' said one man. 'We're dead on our feet, sir,' added another. 'The guggas won't come after us tonight, sir,' Urceus chipped in. Quintus, who was swaying to and fro with exhaustion, was about to agree. He was stunned into silence by Corax's response.

'Stay here if you wish, you maggots, but don't be surprised when the gugga cavalry arrives in the morning. Don't think they won't! Hannibal will want to secure the entire area. If we keep going now, we can be miles away by dawn, beyond the enemy's reach. You can rest then. Sleep in the knowledge that you won't wake with an enemy spear through your guts.'

The centurion had gathered some food and then set off without even looking to see who followed. Quintus and Urceus had exchanged a resigned glance and then set off after him. Corax's words had the ring of truth to them. What was a couple of hours' marching compared to death? All but six men had joined them, giving them a total of just over thirty hastati. To Quintus' frustration, Macerio was not one of those who stayed behind. The blond-haired man had come through the battle unscathed, and it seemed nothing could rid them of his company.

Despite Macerio's presence, the moonlit walk might have been pleasant:

the visibility was good, and the temperature was now balmy. Yet, terri-fied that they would be pursued, the majority of the party started at every night sound, every rustle of wind through the trees, saw Carthaginian soldiers behind each bush. Everyone was bone-weary. Sunburned. Famished – the brief moments granted them by Corax had allowed them only to find a few mouthfuls of food. Most of all, the legionaries were in complete shock at what had befallen them and their army. The impossible had happened. Hannibal and his soldiers had defeated – more likely massacred – eight legions, their cavalry and their attendant socii. Almost the entire military force of the Republic had been wiped from the face of the earth in one day, and by a host that was significantly smaller in size.

There was no conversation. Men were grieving for their fallen comrades. Quintus was sorry that Severus and so many others in his unit had been slain, but his prayers for them were brief. Instead he pleaded with the gods that his father, Calatinus, and Gaius – if he'd been present – had all survived. It was too much to ask for, he knew, yet he couldn't bring himself to ask that one live in preference to the others. The day had been cruel enough without having to make another black-and-white choice.

Hours passed before Corax was satisfied that they'd travelled far enough from the battlefield. Using the stars as a guide, he had led them northwest, towards the low hills upon which lay the town of Canusium. They didn't reach the settlement itself, but as the centurion said, it couldn't be much further. The group would gain the nominal safety of its walls the next morning. 'Get some sleep now, boys. You deserve it,' Corax said solemnly. 'I'm proud of the way you fought today.' Quintus lifted an eyebrow at Urceus, who grinned. The centurion's words lifted the other men's spirits a little too. His praise came so rarely that it was to be savoured.

Putting himself up for the first watch, Corax settled on a nearby rock, his sword and shield to hand. The drained hastati literally dropped where they stood, uncaring of the rough ground and the fact that they had no blankets. Quintus and Urceus lay down beside one another, under the branches of a large holly-oak tree. They were asleep the instant that their heads hit the warm earth.

Quintus dreamed of blood. A plain soaked, covered in it, with a line of hills on one side, similar to the site where they had fought that day. Myriads of small islands dotted the terrible crimson sea. To his disgust and horror, he saw they were not soil or rock, but corpses. Some were clearly Gauls, Iberians or Numidians, but the vast majority were legionaries. Men who had died a violent death. Mutilated, often with glistening loops of gut hanging from their bellies. Gaping cuts showed in their flesh from the top of their heads to their toes: injuries that would have given a man a lingering, painful death. The bodies' lips lay slackly parted, purple tongues bloated and protruding. Every cavity was full of maggots: eye sockets, mouths, wounds; yet the faces' expressions were clear. They were scornful, accusatory, full of hate. How did you survive when we did not? they seemed to ask. I don't know, Quintus screamed back. I should have died, a dozen times over.

Sweating, heart thudding, he came to with a start.

The movement saved his life. A hand clamped over his mouth, but the dagger that would have buried itself in his throat hissed by his ear instead and rammed into the earth. His eyes flicked upwards, to his attacker. Macerio: crouched alongside, his lips twisted in a snarl of hatred. Who else? Quintus thought bitterly. The blond-haired man tugged on his blade, dragging it free of the soil. Up it rose again. Suddenly wide awake, Quintus grabbed Macerio's forearm. They grappled for control of the dagger, one trying to hold it where it was, the other attempting to bring it down into his enemy's flesh. For a few heartbeats, there was stalemate. Quintus did his best to bite Macerio's other hand, but his teeth could gain no purchase on his enemy's palm. He swung his legs around, trying to wriggle beyond Macerio's reach, but the blond-haired man simply leaned more of his upper body weight on to his arms, effectively pinning Quintus where he was. 'I should have finished you long ago. I thought you'd be killed today,' he whispered. 'Better late than never, though.' Despite Quintus' best efforts, Macerio's arm began to descend slowly towards his face.

How can it come to this? Quintus wanted to scream. I lived through the battle, only to die like a dog? His legs kicked out again, and connected with something. Someone. Urceus! He kicked out, over and over. There was an angry grunt by way of reply, and then a muttered question. Quintus lashed out one last time before concentrating all of his energy on preventing

Macerio's blade coming even closer to his flesh. It was already less than two hands' width from the base of his throat, and pressing closer with each frantic breath he took in through his nostrils. Quintus could feel his arm weakening. It had never fully regained all of its previous strength after the arrow wound he'd sustained. Fuck you, Macerio! he thought. I'll see you in Hades.

There was a meaty thump. Macerio's eyes went wide; his body stiffened; his knife point wavered, and then Quintus suddenly had control of his enemy's arm. Macerio's other hand slipped off Quintus' mouth. A sucking sound, such as a blade makes when it leaves a man's flesh, and then another heavy impact. Making a low, groaning sound, Macerio toppled to lie beside him, face down. Quintus gaped. Urceus was standing over them, his fist tight on the hilt of a gladius – which was protruding from Macerio's back. He tugged it free and stuck the blond-haired man again for good measure. 'Go to Hades, you piece of filth.' He spat on Macerio's body.

Quintus sat up, trembling with relief. 'You saved my life. Thank you.'

'I just wanted you to stop kicking me,' said Urceus with a grin. His face grew serious in the starlight. 'No, you're my friend. What else could I do?'

Quintus thumped him on the shoulder. Other men, woken by the noise, were calling out now. Corax was tramping over, demanding to know what was going on, threatening to castrate anyone he caught fighting. In that moment, it didn't matter. None of it mattered, not even the battle. He was alive. So was Urceus. Macerio would never trouble him again. Quintus would have preferred to have killed his enemy himself, but he'd settle for this. Urceus had also been a friend to Rutilus. Rest in peace, he thought. Your murder has been avenged.

It was a small piece of solace at the end of the most horrendous day of his life.

Hanno stirred when the sun's heat on his body became too much. He groaned, and tried to go back to sleep. He couldn't. Mixed with the buzz of a million flies above him was a low, moaning sound. Gods, he thought, that's the wounded. With that, he was awake. There was a tacky feeling in his mouth that he recognised as dehydration, and his eyelids were gummed shut with sleep. Every part of his body ached, but he was alive, and that was more than could be said for the thousands who had fallen in the battle, and those who would have died overnight. Hanno opened his eyes. The first thing he saw was the outline of wings. Scores of sets of wings, far above. *Shit.* The sky was filled with vultures, more than he had ever seen before. He dragged himself to his feet. Around him, his soldiers still lay sleeping. They were yet in the midst of the battlefield, because by the time they had finished with the last of the Romans the previous night, there had been little point trying to pick their way through the confusion of bodies and weapons to their camp. Dawn was only six hours away. Hanno had had his men clear enough space to lie down, set a few sentries, and let the rest collapse in a heap. Now he stared beyond their recumbent forms to where the carnage began. Even though he knew what to expect, now the mania of combat had left him, the sight was indescribably shocking. The proof of their remarkable victory – of Hannibal's extraordinary triumph – could not have been more graphic.

Bodies, thousands and thousands of bodies, as far as he could see in every direction. They lay singly, together, in piles, every race and colour under the sun, locked together in the dispassionate embrace of death. Libyans. Gauls. Iberians. Balearic and Ligurian tribesmen. Romans and socii, united as they had been in life. All, all of them were covered in blood. It coated everything: men, weapons, helmets, standards. Even the earth was bloody, as if the gods themselves had come down in the night and painted it scarlet. Hanno's eyes roamed over the nearest bodies in morbid fascination. They were stabbed through, hacked open, disembowelled. Armless. Legless. In a few cases, decapitated. Lying with their faces in the red-stained earth, on their sides, or on their backs, gaping mouths open to the swarms of flies that hung everywhere. The stench of shit and piss filled his nostrils. Mixed with that was the coppery tang of blood; already there was a whiff of gas from the bodies that had begun to rot. What it would smell like by the day's end, he could only imagine.

In the distance, Hanno could make out the corpses of horses, where some of the cavalry battle must have taken place. If he strained his ears, he could hear whinnies from some beasts yet living. Distaste filled him. They would need to be slain, and the day would be spent scouring the area for soldiers of their own who lived, and dispatching those of the enemy who hadn't yet gone to Hades.

He heard a shriek, suddenly cut off. His attention was drawn to figures moving among the bodies off to his left. They were Gaulish women, killing Roman wounded as they searched for their men. Father! he thought. Bostar. Sapho.

Waking Mutt, Hanno issued orders to fetch water from the river and whatever food could be found. 'Once you've done that, start looking for men of ours who are alive. Carry them here and do what you can for them. We'll get them back to the camp later.'

'And the Romans we find still breathing?' asked Mutt.

'You know what to do with them.'

'Aye, sir.' Mutt's expression became shrewd. 'You going to search for your family?'

'Yes.'

'The gods grant that they all made it, sir.'

Hanno threw Mutt a grateful look and left him to it. Sapho had been closest to them during the battle, so he made for his position first. He found his brother sitting propped up against a pile of Roman corpses, setting his men similar tasks to Hanno's. A bloody bandage around his right calf explained why he was seated.

'Hanno!' A broad smile creased Sapho's face as he approached. 'You're alive!'

'It's good to see you, brother!' Despite all that had passed between them, Hanno felt his heart swell with happiness. He knelt by Sapho and they embraced. 'You're hurt. Is it serious?'

'It's not too bad.' Sapho scowled. 'The last fucking Roman I killed got me as he went down. It shouldn't have happened, but I was tired.'

'We all were by the end of it,' said Hanno. 'What a day, eh?'

'Hannibal's name will go down in history for this,' said Sapho.

'Without doubt,' agreed Hanno. Hannibal could now do no wrong in his eyes.

They savoured that thought for a moment.

'Have you seen Father and Bostar?' asked Hanno.

'Not yet, but I've sent a soldier to search for them.'

Hanno rose. 'I'm going too.'

'Eshmoun guide you to their sides. Bring me word as soon as you can.'

'I will.'

Using the line of hills as a reference point, Hanno slowly made his way across the battlefield. The area he crossed was where the main body of legionaries had fought – and died. For every Carthaginian soldier's body, he counted at least half a dozen Roman. Plenty of men from both sides were alive. Many, even the Romans, raised their hands in supplication to him, pleading for water, or an end to their suffering. Hardening his heart, Hanno stalked by without a second glance. The Roman corpses made him think of Quintus and Fabricius. He hoped for Aurelia's sake, and the friendship that had once existed between him and Quintus, that both men had survived. There were groups of Iberians and Gauls everywhere, men who must also have spent the night in the field. Now they were scouring the dead for valuables. From the cries of pain that rose regularly, they were also indulging in a little torment of any living enemies whom they encountered. Hanno didn't really approve, but such behaviour was the norm, so he shut his ears and averted his gaze and walked on.

He found where the Libyans had stood on the opposite flank a short time later. Clusters of weary-faced soldiers stood around, sharing water skins and talking in low voices amongst themselves. Hanno practically ran up to the first group. 'I'm looking for Malchus,' he said, butting in. 'Or Bostar, who commanded a phalanx.'

'You must be another of Malchus' sons, sir,' said one of the Libyans, a bearded man with a hooked nose.

'Yes, yes, I am Hanno. Well?'

'I haven't seen Malchus since yesterday, sir, but Bostar's been here, talking to our commanding officer.'

Hanno's heart leaped with joy. 'Where is he?'

'Last I saw of him, sir, he was walking that way.' The soldier pointed off to his left. 'That was where Malchus' phalanx was positioned. About a hundred paces away.'

Hanno grinned. He would be reunited with his father and brother at the same time. 'My thanks.' He hurried off as fast as his tired limbs would take him. Gods, but he was looking forward to getting drunk with Bostar that night. Sapho too. He grinned. After such a momentous day, their father might even shed his normal reserve and join them.

The happy thought vanished as he recognised Bostar's outline. His brother was kneeling with his back to Hanno. A body lay on the ground before him. Bostar's slumped shoulders told Hanno everything he needed to know. 'No. Please. Father!' He covered the distance between them in a heartbeat. His stomach lurched as he took in the bloodied shape of his father. He was clearly dead. Hanno froze, and a great wave of anguish washed over him.

Bostar's head turned. Tears had run tracks through the blood that coated his grief-stricken face. But the corners of his lips turned up at the sight of Hanno, and he stood. 'Brother!'

Hanno tore his eyes from his father's corpse, stared at Bostar, felt tears run down his own cheeks. They wrapped their arms around one another and held on for dear life. Both men wept unashamedly. 'Sapho is alive,' murmured Hanno after a little while. Bostar stiffened, before answering, 'That is good.' There was no need to say any more.

It was a long time before either released his grip. When they did, the pair turned instinctively to look down on their father. Despite a number of fearsome injuries, all of which were to his front, Malchus' face was serene. He looked years younger than his age.

'He wouldn't have wanted to go any other way,' said Hanno, proud but sad.

'I agree. His men told me that the Romans in this section had already broken when he took his mortal wound. So he knew that we had won.'

'Maybe that's why he looks so peaceful,' said Hanno in wonderment.

'I think that's exactly why. Once he knew that Hannibal's plan had worked, death would have been a release for him. Father would never have admitted it, but all he really wanted after Mother died was to be with her once more. Remember how he changed when she was gone?'

'I do,' murmured Hanno. Arishat, their mother, had been the light of their father's life. 'I always felt that something in him died with her.'

'Now they can be together again.'

'It's good to think of them like that.' Hanno felt his grief ease a little. *Farewell, Father. Greetings, Mother. Look after one another.*

'They can watch over us as we march on to victory over Rome,' added Bostar, throwing an arm over Hanno's shoulders.

Hanno liked that image. It seemed fitting, somehow. 'You think that will be Hannibal's next move?'

'I'm not sure. To be honest, brother, I don't care that much at this very moment. After what we did yesterday, every Roman will be shitting themselves about what we do next. For now, let's remember Father and the rest of our dead, and celebrate our achievement.'

'Aye. I think Father would have wanted us to rejoice over this victory,' said Hanno. 'Before I found you, I had hoped he might join us in a drink tonight.'

Bostar chuckled. 'You know, I think he would have, just this once. We'll keep a brimming cup for him this evening, eh?'

Swallowing the lump in his throat, Hanno nodded. Their father would never be forgotten – and nor would their victory here, on the fields of blood.

Chapter XIX

Capua, two days later . . .

The wailing started just after dawn. It began as a few isolated cries of dismay, like those of a family discovering the death of a loved one. It wasn't long, however, before other voices joined in: scores, and then hundreds of them. Aurelia was already awake, nursing Publius. Unsettled, she carried him – still on the breast – out into the courtyard. Here the volume was far louder, even more disconcerting, and Publius became distressed. As she tried to soothe him, Lucius emerged half-dressed from his bedroom, looking angry and alarmed. Almost every slave in the household was lurking by the doors to the kitchen, whispering, pointing, muttering prayers. Yet more voices joined the clamour and a cold knot of apprehension formed in Aurelia's gut. 'What's going on?'

'I'm not sure,' Lucius replied curtly.

He was being evasive. Aurelia had an idea what it might be, but like her husband she was not prepared to say what she feared.

An enormous *boom* sounded overhead; their heads lifted. Banks of black cloud were sweeping in from the west, brought in by a wind that had suddenly picked up. Light flickered within the clouds, presaging lightning. Another crackle of thunder. They shared a worried look. This was a bad omen. Added to the racket, it felt even more menacing. A few of the slaves began to weep.

'Be silent!' roared Lucius. 'Out of my sight. Get back to work.' The slaves scurried from view, urged on by Statilius. 'I'm going to find out what's causing the alarm,' said Lucius, his face grim.

Aurelia felt a lurch of panic. 'Send Statilius instead.'

He didn't respond. 'Bar the doors when I am gone. Let no one in until I return.'

She didn't argue. Rarely had she seen him so set upon a purpose. 'Be safe, husband,' she whispered.

A short smile and he vanished into the tablinum, shouting for his sword. She watched him go, feeling sick at the thought of what he might discover.

Waiting for Lucius to return was hellish. The noise outside continued to increase in volume. It was audible even with the rumbling of thunder that accompanied it. In it, Aurelia heard women's screams, men shouting angrily, the crying of babies and the braying of mules. Even when the rain began to fall, the unearthly sound did not stop. It was what Aurelia imagined Hades might sound like. Gooseflesh erupted all over her body; she could not settle Publius, no matter how hard she tried. He didn't want to feed; his usual lullabies made no difference. All he would do was cry. In the end, she walked him around the colonnaded walkway that enclosed the courtyard. That helped a little.

A barrage of hammering on the front door nearly made her jump out of her skin. Lucius' voice demanding entry reassured her that it wasn't a demon come to claim them, but her stomach still roiled as Statilius ran to let his master in. Lucius appeared a moment later. He was soaked to the skin and his cheeks were haggard, as if he'd been out in the weather all day.

Aurelia walked to meet him, cradling Publius, who mercifully fell silent. Nausea clawed the back of her throat, but she fought it away. Neither husband nor wife said a word as they neared one another. Close up, Aurelia saw that Lucius had been crying. His face was stricken. 'They lost, didn't they?' she said, uttering the unthinkable, which had been in her mind since the commotion began. 'Hannibal won.'

His nod was mechanical, as if he'd been drugged.

If Aurelia hadn't been holding Publius, she would have fallen. Calm. You must stay calm, she thought. 'Tell me.'

'Two messengers presented themselves at the gates just after sunrise, demanding an audience with the magistrates. An announcement was made in the forum after that meeting. All kinds of rumours are flying about, but

I managed to speak with an official whom I know. He's level-headed, so his account is as reliable as can be expected. Two days ago, it was Varro's turn to lead the army. He was determined to start a battle, even though Paullus wanted to wait until a better location could be found.' Lucius spoke in a monotone. 'Varro crossed the River Aufidius and drew up the legions in one great bloc. Hannibal's army followed and formed up opposite. Our soldiers advanced on the middle of the enemy line, with the cavalry in support on the wings. Varro's intention was to smash the guggas apart with one decisive blow, before annihilating their broken remnants. Our horse had to hold the flanks. Except everything went wrong. Hannibal's horsemen attacked on both sides. They put the citizen cavalry to flight almost at once, while the socii riders were bogged down by his infernal Numidians. We had such superiority of numbers of infantry that that shouldn't have mattered – in theory. The trouble was, Hannibal had a master plan that Varro didn't see. His weakest troops were standing in his centre and in a formation slightly bowed towards our soldiers. When the fighting began, the enemy was driven back slowly. But as the legionaries drew level with the rest of his men, Hannibal had his wings – which were made up of his Libyan veterans – swing around to attack the legions' sides. Much of his cavalry fell upon our rear at the same time.'

Aurelia felt cold all over. 'Where were our horsemen by this time? The citizens, especially?'

'Driven off, or killed.' His eyes caught hers. 'I'm sorry, Aurelia.'

Father! Gaius! She had to lean against a pillar to hold herself upright. Lucius' gaze was steady and it helped her to gain control. 'Go on. I want to know everything. How many dead?'

'No one knows for sure. One of the tribunes sent a group of riders to inform the Senate as the sun fell. Apparently, Varro escaped to Venusia with a few thousand men. More still fled to Canusium. There were stragglers all over the countryside. It will take days to calculate the losses.'

'How many?' she demanded again.

'Thirty thousand, perhaps more,' he said quietly. 'That's what the messengers think.'

Aurelia reeled. It felt as if someone had punched her in the solar plexus. 'Quintus is dead too, then.' She could control her emotions no longer.

Clutching Publius to her as if he'd be stolen too, she let the sobs come. Alarmed, he also began to wail. Lucius moved towards her, but she waved him away. 'How can the gods do this to me?' she screamed. 'Take three of the most important men in my life in one sweep? Curse them for being faithless! Curse them for never listening to our pleas!'

'Aurelia! You cannot say such things! It will bring misfortune upon us.' Lucius was appalled.

'Misfortune?' she shrieked. 'How could anything be worse than what you've just told me? This for the gods!' She hawked and spat on the floor. Even as she did it, Aurelia regretted it. But it was too late.

'Be silent, wife! Control yourself, or I shall be forced to do so for you.' The veins on Lucius' neck stood out like purple ropes. 'Is that clear?'

Aurelia was stunned by the level of his anger. 'Yes,' she whispered.

'To your room! Attend to my son. That is your damn job, not calling down the anger of the gods on this family, this house.'

Weeping, Aurelia fled before his fury. What madness had possessed her to speak as she had? She was but a mere human, condemned to accept whatever was handed out to her, good or bad, by the all-powerful deities. Defying them would make no difference, and would in all likelihood make things worse. Yet part of her could not help thinking: How could things be any worse? Father is dead. Quintus is dead. Gaius is dead. Our army has been destroyed. She would never know, but no doubt Hanno had also been slain. Hannibal and his army could now visit whatever fate they wished upon the Republic.

Publius stirred in her arms, and her heart lurched her back into reality. Here he was, more precious than any of the other people or things in her life. She began silently to beg forgiveness of the gods. Do not take my child from me, please. Forgive my transgression, which was made in the depths of despair. Such words will never pass my lips again. I shall make generous sacrifices in expiation. Aurelia prayed long and hard and as earnestly as she had ever done in her life.

It was only when she had finished and settled a sleeping Publius in his cot that Aurelia dared to allow her grief to resurface. She lay on her bed and sobbed into the pillow, wishing that Lucius would come to comfort her. It was a faint hope, which disappeared as the hours passed. Elira crept in at one point, but Aurelia, angry that it was not Lucius, shouted at her to get out and not come back. Thoughts of Hanno did not help either. He was a fantasy figure, whom she would never meet again, let alone conjure into an appearance here.

Eventually her tears dried up, not because she felt any better but because she had none left to shed. When she emerged, red-eyed and exhausted, Statilius informed her that Lucius had gone to find out more news. The sounds of distress from the streets had eased, but only a fraction. Aurelia expressed an interest in going to the forum, but the major domo regretfully told her that the master had left orders that no one should leave the house before his return.

She had no energy left to defy Lucius' command, no strength to ask for Elira or that a messenger be sent to her mother, no capacity to do anything other than retire to her room. There Publius was beginning to cry again. Sinking even deeper into misery, Aurelia tended to him as best she could. Somewhere in her consciousness, she was aware that caring for her baby would provide a way through the pain, but it was of scant comfort in that dark moment. Utterly drained, she fell asleep some time later, fully clothed, on her bed.

During the evening, the sound of Lucius' arrival roused her from her torpor but she did not dare go out. Ears pricked, hopeful, she fed the baby and waited for her husband to come to check on her. He didn't. The snub shouldn't have hurt, Aurelia reasoned. After all, she didn't love him. Yet the gesture cut as sharply as a knife. He was her husband. An ally, when she had so few. Fresh tears flowed. The last thing that Aurelia thought before falling asleep again was that it would be a relief never to wake up.

There was to be no such blessing. Publius woke not long after with colic. She spent the rest of the night in a semi-catatonic state, nursing him, walking him and snatching a few moments of rest whenever he closed his eyes.

Aurelia had never entrusted her baby to Elira's care for long before, but she did that day. 'Wake me only when he needs to feed,' she ordered. Agonisingly, however, she found no rest even when Publius was out of earshot. All she could think about was the slaughter that had just taken place and how she would never see her father, Quintus or Gaius again.

This was to become the pattern of Aurelia's life for the next few days. Her mother's arrival meant that she had more help with Publius, but when Atia tried to start talking about the battle, Aurelia walked away. She was too distraught to open up to anyone. Lucius came and went, checking on the baby in the daytime but barely bothering with her. He was still angry with her for defying the gods. Aurelia heard from Statilius that the mood in the city was one of open fear, which did nothing to help her state of mind. In the end she had the major domo send a slave to an apothecary's, there to buy a flagon of *papaverum*. Having downed several large mouthfuls of the bitter liquid, Aurelia was relieved to feel herself succumbing to unconsciousness. Over the course of the following days, she found constant respite in its embrace. Soon she could not sleep without it, nor even get through daylight hours without a few nips to keep her going. Atia appeared not to notice; Elira cast worried looks at her, but Aurelia was oblivious. It dulled her feelings, blunted her agony. *That* was a blessing. It made life bearable. Just.

Aurelia was aware of the door opening and someone entering. The papaverum that she'd consumed not long since was just starting to take effect, enfolding her in its warm cocoon. It was too much effort to open her eyes. Whoever it was – Elira, probably – would see that she was asleep and leave her alone. Even if the baby needed a feed, it could wait.

'This has to stop, wife.'

Lucius. It was Lucius, she thought, dragging her eyelids open. He was standing over her, a disapproving frown on his face.

'Your mother tells me you're drinking this.' He waved the flagon that now lived by her bed.

So her mother had noticed, thought Aurelia. 'It helps me to sleep.'

'But Elira says that you consume it night and day. Atia thinks that that might be why the baby is drowsy.' He sounded angry now.

She stared daggers at the Illyrian, who was just behind him. Elira dropped her eyes. 'That's not true,' said Aurelia hotly, knowing he'd spoken the truth.

'What's not true?'

'Publius is fine,' she mumbled, lying. 'He's had a cold, and broken sleep because of the cough that came with it. That's why he has been lethargic of late.'

Lucius gazed at her long and hard. 'And you? Is it true that you're partaking of this stuff at all times?'

Shame filled Aurelia. She couldn't bring herself to tell another outright lie, but nor could she admit to what she'd been doing.

'Your silence proclaims your guilt. Well, you're to have no more of it. Learn how to fall asleep as the rest of us do – without any help.'

Fury replaced the shame. She scowled at Elira. 'Out! Close the door behind you.' When she and Lucius were alone, she hissed, 'If you had lost a father and a brother, you might know how I feel!'

At last his face softened. 'Sorrow is not unknown to me, wife. My mother was taken from us when I was only ten years old.'

She felt instant remorse. 'I remember.'

'That isn't to say that your loss has not been grievous.' After the slightest of hesitations, he went on, 'Or that my conduct has not been that of a husband towards you since the news of the defeat.'

Stunned, she looked up at him.

'I was greatly angered by your outburst, but that does not mean I could not have offered you comfort at the time of your greatest distress.' He reached out his hand.

This was as close to an apology as she would get, Aurelia realised. 'Thank you,' she whispered, clutching at his fingers as she would have if she'd been drowning. Now the tears came anew. When he sat beside her and put an arm around her shoulders, she leaned into his body and let her grief out, more glad of the human touch than she had ever been in her life. To his great credit, Lucius did not say a word. He just held her tightly, his physical presence giving her the reassurance that someone cared.

Lucius continued to spend time with her and the baby over the next couple of days and his presence helped to take Aurelia's mind off her sorrow a little. It certainly made having no papaverum easier to bear. Removing the flagon had been a good thing, she realised. Her cravings for it were far more intense than she'd expected. Aurelia dreaded to think what it would have been like if she had been consuming it for weeks rather than days. To her surprise, Lucius was also excellent with Publius, cuddling him, soothing him, walking around the courtyard as he talked to him. Aurelia began to reappraise her feelings towards her husband. Just because they were not made for each other did not mean that they could not get on. Perhaps this was the type of marriage that her mother had spoken of, she reflected. It wasn't what she had dreamed of, with Hanno, but it seemed to work. And *that* was better than living in utter misery.

Just over a week had passed since the news of the defeat had reached Capua and the city was still in a state of constant panic. Ominous signs were reported daily: south of the city, a heavy storm had rained stones upon the earth; the divination tablets at Caere had somehow grown smaller; threatening figures in the likeness of men, dressed in white, had seemingly appeared in innumerable locations in the countryside. The priests in the city's temples tried to issue explanations that offered some reassurance that the world was not about to end. According to Lucius, every soothsayer for a hundred miles had descended upon Capua to make the most of the population's desire to know the future.

Fresh rumours swept the streets every day. The Roman dead at Cannae had been mutilated beyond recognition; Hannibal had ordered the torture and execution of every single prisoner taken by his men; a bridge had been built over the River Aufidius made of Roman bodies; he was marching on Rome, on Capua, on both, burning the towns in his path; a Carthaginian fleet had landed thousands of soldiers and scores of elephants on Sicily, or on the southern coast of Italy itself; King Philip of Macedon was about to join the war on the side of Carthage. Aurelia knew better than to believe all of the stories, but it was difficult not to feel unsettled by them, or by the fact that the disquiet had also seen a severalfold increase in crime. Unaccompanied women were liable to be raped in broad daylight. Foreigners such as Egyptians or Phoenicians had been attacked. Civil disorder had also become common. On a number of occasions, the magistrates had been forced to deploy troops to prevent near-riots becoming the full-blown article. In consequence, Lucius had forbidden anyone to go out without his specific approval. When he ventured forth, it was with half a dozen slaves armed with sticks. Ignoring the law that banned bladed weapons within the city confines, he himself never went without a sword. Aurelia was beginning to feel claustrophobic within the confines of the house, yet she was not about to argue with her husband's decision.

Despite the social unrest and her confinement, her mood had achieved some degree of stability. Every moment of every day was still tinged with sorrow, but the routine of looking after the baby combined with Lucius' support was helping Aurelia to cope. The torrential outpourings of grief had become occasional rather than constant. Things had also been made easier by Atia's gentle insistence that they talk to each other. Aurelia had given in and, to her relief, their subsequent conversations – and shared tears – had helped their relationship, already made stronger by Aurelia's pregnancy and the subsequent arrival of the baby, to enter a new phase of intimacy. It was as Aurelia remembered her childhood, when she had shared everything with her mother.

Another visitor that day – a welcome surprise – had been Martialis. The old man had aged greatly. New lines etched his face; his hair was now altogether white. Tears had filled his eyes the instant he saw Aurelia; the same had happened to her. They had embraced like father and daughter. Martialis had had no news, but, like Aurelia, he assumed that Gaius had fallen at Cannae. Thus far, all news of the Roman and allied cavalry had been catastrophic. United in their grief, they had reminisced for a short time about those they had lost, but it hadn't taken long before their sorrow had killed the conversation. Unsurprisingly, it was the baby who had lifted the mood, gurgling with happiness as Martialis dandled him on his knee. When it was time for the old man to leave, he had done so with evident regret. Aware of how alone Martialis must have been feeling, Aurelia had insisted that he promise to call in again soon.

Later that day, Aurelia was dozing in a comfortable chair in the courtyard. Publius was asleep; her mother was in the kitchen, making arrangements for that evening's dinner. Lucius had retired to his office to write letters to his family's business partners in other cities. Aurelia was woken by a loud rap on the front door. Alarmed, she listened hard but heard no further sounds outside until the knock was repeated again, this time harder. Aurelia's heart beat a little faster. Was it Phanes? There had been no recent news of him, but that did not mean he would never cause trouble again. Calm yourself, she thought. A dozen men could not break down that door. Besides, there were always two armed slaves on duty there. Lucius appeared not to have heard the summons, so she indicated to Statilius that he should see who it was.

There was a strange look on his face when he returned a moment later. Aurelia rose as he approached. 'Statilius?'

'There is a soldier outside. He wants to speak to you.'

'What about?'

'He wouldn't say.'

She felt the faintest ray of hope. 'Is he a cavalryman? Or an allied infantryman?'

'No, a regular legionary. A hastatus, I think.'

Aurelia's hope died. She knew no citizen foot soldiers. What possible reason could one have to seek her out – other than to tell her something dreadful about the deaths of her father or brother? Dread took hold of her, but she batted it away. She felt a great compulsion to hear what the hastatus had to say. 'Let him in.'

'Do no such thing!' cried Lucius, emerging into the courtyard. 'We have no idea who he is.'

'Yet it is possible that he has news for me,' said Aurelia, heading towards the tablinum. 'At the very least, I want to see his face. I can do that without admitting him.'

To her relief, Lucius did not try to stop her. Grumbling, he followed. Statilius took up the rear, his expression the picture of worry.

The slaves detailed to guard the house's entrance were waiting by the door, clubs in hand. 'Open the viewing port,' she ordered. They eyed her warily, but when Lucius jerked his head, they rushed to obey. Swallowing her irritation that they had not done so at her command, Aurelia stepped up to the narrow rectangular opening. It was an unusual feature, but it meant the occupants could see whether it was safe to admit potential visitors. It took a moment for her eyes to adjust to the bright sunlight outside. A sturdy figure in a filthy, bloody tunic stood with his back to her. A battered helmet, missing its feathers, covered his head; a square plate protected the upper part of his torso front and back; she could see that he was armed with a sword. By the set of his slumped shoulders, he was exhausted.

'Well?' hissed Lucius.

'He's facing in the other direction.' Aurelia coughed to attract the soldier's attention.

He turned, and her mouth fell open. The unexpected uniform, the line of scabs on his jaw, the rings beneath his grey eyes, the layer of grime on every part of his exposed skin could not conceal who it was. 'Quintus!'

'Aurelia?' He covered the ground to the door in a heartbeat. 'Is that you?'

'Yes, yes, it is I!' Weeping with joy, she ripped at the bolts.

'It's your brother?' Lucius was by her side, helping.

'Yes. Thank all the gods, he's alive!'

Brother and sister fell into each other's arms the instant the door opened. They clung to one another with a fierceness and a joy that neither had ever felt before. Uncaring of who might see or hear, that Quintus stank of sweat and blood, that Lucius might disapprove, Aurelia sobbed her heart out. He shook with emotion, but shed no tears, instead transferring his feelings into their embrace.

'I thought you had joined the socii infantry,' said Aurelia eventually, remembering his letter.

'I only said that in case Father tried to find me.'

She laughed. 'What does it matter where you were? I cannot believe you are here. The news was so bad. It seemed impossible that you could have survived.'

He pulled back a little and gave her a sad smile. 'I damn near didn't.' She let out another laugh, but nervous this time, and his face grew even more serious. 'It was Corax, my centurion, who saved us. He kept the maniple together even when the units around us were collapsing and trying to flee. Rounded up a few more men. Spotted the weak point in the enemy line and smashed a hole in it wide enough for us to escape. If he hadn't done that, I wouldn't be here.'

'Thank all the gods! Have you seen Father, or heard any news of him? Or of Gaius?' Or Hanno? she wanted to add, even though he could have no way of knowing that.

'Gaius I have seen, but Father . . .' He shook his head sorrowfully. 'He wasn't among the few cavalrymen who joined up with us at Canusium after our retreat, nor with those who straggled in over the following couple of days. Word came that about fifty riders had escaped with the consul Varro to Venusia, so I went there as well. I had no joy.' A heavy sigh. 'I would have searched the battlefield, massive as it is, but the enemy camp is still close by. To venture anywhere near the place is to commit suicide.'

Aurelia's heart sank. 'You did what you could. We will pray that he reappears out of nowhere, like you and Gaius,' she said, determined to remain positive. 'If one miracle can happen, why not two?'

He nodded. 'Let us hope so.'

It was even possible that Hanno had not been killed, thought Aurelia. She did not feel traitorous for adding him to her prayers. 'Come in. Mother will be overjoyed to see you.'

His face lit up. 'Martialis said I would find her here too.' Entering, he offered his hand to Lucius. 'My pardon for not introducing myself immediately. I am Aurelia's brother, Quintus Fabricius. You must be Aurelia's husband.'

'Lucius Vibius Melito,' said Lucius, clasping Quintus' hand with his own. 'It's an honour to meet you.'

'Likewise. My congratulations on your union.' He saw Lucius staring at his garb. 'You're wondering why I am dressed as an ordinary hastatus?'

'It is . . . unusual,' Lucius replied, a little awkwardly.

'I never would have imagined you as an infantryman,' said Aurelia, smiling.

'It's a long story. I can tell you later.'

'This way.' Aurelia led the way, eager to find their mother. 'Have you been granted leave?'

A derisive snort. 'No one has been allowed that. Varro is gradually regrouping the army, but it will take weeks before order is restored. So many of the officers are dead; the majority of men have been separated from their units – if those units even exist any more. Basically, it's complete chaos. Corax told us that he wouldn't "notice" if any of his men wanted to go and visit their families, as long as we swore to return within a couple of weeks. He said that the consuls had' – here he threw an embarrassed look at Lucius – 'fucked up so much that we were entitled to it. Gaius has had no such luck. His commander is a complete martinet. I had to carry the good news of his survival to Martialis on his behalf.'

'Your centurion sounds like quite a man,' said Lucius thoughtfully.

A gurgling cry from Publius carried down the hallway. Quintus laughed. 'That must be your baby. Martialis spoke fondly of him.'

Aurelia beamed. 'It's our son, Publius. He was born a few weeks ago.'

'It is good to know that life is still entering the world.' The light in Quintus' eyes darkened for a moment, but he rallied himself. 'It's another reason to raise a toast.'

'Life goes on. Publius is part of the new generation,' said Aurelia, remembering with dread how she'd taunted the gods, and praying that nothing further came of it. 'Mother says that he looks a little like you at the same age.'

'Aha! I cannot wait to meet him.' Quintus grinned and for the first time, Aurelia really saw her brother again through the grime. On impulse, she entwined her arm with his.

'It is so wonderful to see you!'

'And you, sister. After what has happened, I did not think ever to see such a happy day again.'

Walking with Quintus and Lucius to find her son and Atia, Aurelia let her heart sing. Her grief for her father had not diminished, but she would return to it another time. For now, she would live in this moment. Rejoice that her remaining family had been reunited, and that Gaius had also come through the inferno of Cannae. Cherish in her heart the hope that, somewhere to the south, Hanno was alive too.

After the horror of the previous days, that seemed enough.

Author's Note

When the opportunity to write a set of novels about the Second Punic War (218–201 BC) came my way, I jumped at the chance. I have been fascinated by the time period since I was a boy, and I, like many, regard this as one of history's most hallowed episodes. The word 'epic' is overused today, but I feel that its use is justified with reference to this seventeen-year struggle, the balance of which was uncertain on so many occasions. If it had tipped but a fraction in the opposite direction during a number of those situations, life in Europe today would be very different. The Carthaginians were quite unlike the Romans, and not in all the bad ways 'history' would have us believe. They were intrepid explorers and inveterate traders, shrewd businessmen and brave soldiers. Where Rome's interests so often lay in conquest by war, theirs lay more in assuming power through controlling commerce and natural resources. It may be a small point, but my use of the word 'Carthaginian' rather than the Latin 'Punic' when referring to their language is quite deliberate. The Carthaginians would not have used the latter term.

Many readers will know the broad brush strokes of Hannibal's war with Rome; others will know less; a very few will be voracious readers of the ancient authors Livy and Polybius, the main sources for this period. For the record, I have done my best to stick to the historical details that have survived. In places, however, I have either changed events slightly to fit in with the story's development, or invented things. Such is the novelist's remit, as well as his/her bane. If I have made any errors, I apologise for them.

The term 'Italy' was in use in the third century BC as a geographical expression; it encompassed the entire peninsula south of Liguria and

Cisalpine Gaul. The term did not become a political one until Polybius' time (mid second century BC). I decided to use it anyway. It simplified matters, and avoided constant reference to the different parts of the Republic: Rome, Campania, Latium, Lucania, etc.

Describing Carthaginian soldiers, both native and non-native, is a whole minefield of its own. We have little historical information about the uniforms that Carthaginian citizens and the host of nationalities who fought for them wore, or the type of equipment and weapons that they carried. Without several textbooks and articles, which I'll name later, I would have been lost. A little more detail survives about the Roman army of the time, but it's still a case of having to make assumptions and logical leaps of faith. Another obstacle course to negotiate was Carthaginian names. Basically, there aren't very many, or at least not many that have survived the test of time. Most of the ones that have come down to us are unpronounceable, or sound awful. Some are both! Hillesbaal and Ithobaal don't exactly roll off the tongue. I could not stop myself from using Muttumbaal, however. There's a modern ring to the nickname 'Mutt'! There were a number of important historical characters named Hanno, but I desperately needed a good name for my hero, and they were in very short supply, hence the choice.

The novel begins soon after the first in the series, *Hannibal: Enemy of Rome*, ended. Not much is known of Hannibal's activities in the few months after his victory at the Trebbia. A town named Victumulae was sacked by his forces, however, and its population put to the sword. The terrible trek through the floodplain of the River Arno happened; in the process, Hannibal is known to have lost an eye. The stunning ambush at Lake Trasimene took place much as I've described. My attempt to produce words that sounded like the Gauls' carnyxes came about after listening repeatedly to John Kenny, a modern musician, playing a modern replica of this vertical trumpet. It sounds terrifying. Listen here: http://www.youtube.com/watch?v=NYM0xB5Jrc0.

In my opinion, the best detail about Trasimene is that you can still visit its exact location, a unique selling point when it comes to ancient battlefields. The sites of such clashes have almost always been lost. Not so Trasimene, because the natural features described by the ancient historians (the lakeshore, the pinch point etc.) are so unusual and because they can still be identified today. If you can, go there in late June one year, when Italian and Spanish re-enactors recreate the battle. It's an amazing sight, as well as a wonderful part of Italy.

However unlikely it is that an equestrian would have abandoned his exalted position to join up as a lowly veles, it wouldn't be the first time that a young man did something that makes no sense. Think *Beau Geste*! Besides, I had to come up with a way to take Quintus away from the cavalry. In my mind, he had to be a legionary at Cannae. The oath he took is very similar to the one made by soldiers to this day.

The re-equipping of Hannibal's Libyans with Roman armour is known to have happened. We don't know if they were also armed with enemy weapons and trained to fight differently, but it makes sense that they might have been. The dramatic ruse of the burning torches tied to the horns of cattle is recorded. So too are the details of the marriage ceremony. I have changed the wording of the marital vow, however. For the record – and I wish I'd made this clear in earlier books – it was *not* unusual for a girl of Aurelia's age to be wed. There are still places in the world today where it is normal for girls to marry this young, so let's not be surprised that it took place in Rome two thousand years ago! For those of you who find my use of the Fword/F-bomb objectionable or even 'incorrect', I say to you that the Romans were incredibly foulmouthed. Why not look up the Latin verb 'futuere' as well? It means 'to fuck'. That's enough evidence for me, and the end of my mini-rant.

It's also important to remember that women occupied a far lower station in life in ancient Rome than they do in our society today. Although they were not without power, their main role in life was to produce children and to oversee the running of a family home. Little is known of Roman midwifery, but I have used what information I could find. 'Kicking the enemy in the stomach' is a phrase that survives from this time. Minucius Flaccus was a fictitious character (in the first novel), but Minucius Rufus, his brother, was a real man who served as Master of the Horse under Fabius, the 'Delayer', who was also known as Verrucosus ('Warty').

Many of you had probably heard of Cannae before you read this book. It's no surprise that you had, and that the battle is still talked about nearly

2,200 years after it happened. For more than two millennia, it was one of, if not *the*, bloodiest day of combat ever to take place. It wasn't until the invention of the machine gun and the outbreak of the First World War that a greater number of casualties were caused by a single battle. On the morning of the battle, nearly 130,000 soldiers and around 16,000 horses were packed into an area of a few square kilometres. By the end of the day, in excess of 50,000 Roman troops were dead. Beside them on the field lay 8,000 or so of Hannibal's men. But it isn't just the scale of the casualties that makes Cannae so remarkable: it is the ingenuity of Hannibal's plan, and the discipline with which it was executed.

In ancient times, officers usually lost the power to control most of their men from the moment that battle commenced. There were no radios or walkie-talkies to communicate with, and it would have been impossible to see what was going on outside one's immediate surroundings. Battles were therefore often won by the side that led the best initial charge, say, or the side that achieved the first major advantage. Hannibal could not have been instructing his senior officers on the wings or among his cavalry during the fighting, which tells us that they knew in advance what he expected of them. What is more, they fulfilled their duty. It was relatively unsurprising that the Carthaginian heavy cavalry should succeed in driving off their Roman counterparts – they were a superior force in every way. However, for them to refrain from pursuing their fleeing enemies and to set about first one task – aiding the Numidians to attack the socii horsemen – and then another – falling upon the rear of the Roman bloc of legionaries – *was* truly remarkable. So too was the manner in which the Gaulish and Iberian infantry held against overwhelming enemy numbers. The fact that they were able to regroup and return to the fray *after* being broken is also incredible, this being unheard of in ancient warfare.

The battlefield of Cannae was farmland in 216 BC and it still is today, which means that a visit there is incredibly atmospheric. A hill rises conveniently close to the site, affording a bird's-eye view of the entire area. I urge you to visit it if you can. It lies a short distance to the west of the town of Barletta in Apulia, and only 50 kilometres north of Bari airport, which is serviced by budget airlines. I have been to Cannae three times now, and each visit brings a new appreciation of the place. I shot a short video piece there in November 2012, which can be seen at: http://www.youtube.com/watch?v=91-xrPJl0lg&feature=youtu.be.

After a defeat of the magnitude of Cannae, most ancient peoples would have surrendered. Yet the depths of Roman determination knew no bounds. Even though their standing army had all but been wiped off the face of the earth, they would not give in. Their strength of character in remaining defiant at such a time is amazing, and to be admired. Yet what might have happened if, in the immediate aftermath of Cannae, Hannibal had marched his army to Rome? It's one of history's great unanswered questions, and another potential minefield in which *everyone* tends to have a different opinion. All I'll say on the matter is that I like to think that the sight of Hannibal's victorious forces outside the walls would perhaps have been enough to make the Senate sue for peace. Would it have made any difference in the long run, though? I doubt it. Rome would have found a pretext for war, for revenge, as it did anyway, in 149 BC, when the third and final war against Carthage began.

But that's jumping over a lot of history, and most of the Second Punic War. Suffice it to say that Hannibal's war in Italy went on after Cannae, and so too did the struggle in Sicily and Iberia. The next volume of the series, working title *Hannibal: Clouds of War*, will continue the stories of Hanno, Quintus and Aurelia, on the island of Sicily. I hope that you feel the need to find out what happens to them next!

A bibliography of the textbooks I used while writing *Fields of Blood* would run to several pages, so I will mention only the most important, in alphabetical order by author: *The Punic Wars* by Nigel Bagnall, *The Punic Wars* by Brian Caven, *Greece and Rome at War* by Peter Connolly, *Hannibal* by Theodore A. Dodge, *The Fall of Carthage* and *Cannae*, both by Adrian Goldsworthy, *Love in Ancient Rome* by Pierre Grimal, *Armies of the Macedonian and Punic Wars* by Duncan Head, *Sexual Life in Ancient Rome* by Otto Kiefer, *Hannibal's War* by J. F. Lazenby, *Carthage Must Be Destroyed* by Richard Miles, *Daily Life in Carthage (at the Time of Hannibal)* by G. C. Picard, *The Life and Death of Carthage* by G. C. & C. Picard, *Love in Ancient Rome* by E. Royston Pike, *Roman Politics 220–150 BC* by H. H. Scullard, *Carthage and the Carthaginians* by Reginald B. Smith and *Warfare in the Classical World* by John Warry. I'm grateful to Osprey Publishing for numerous excellent volumes, to Oxford University Press for the outstanding *Oxford Classical Dictionary*, and to *Ancient Warfare* magazine for the superb article in Volume III, Issue 4: 'Forging a professional army: armies of the Barcids' by Alberto Perez and Paul McDonnell-Staff. Thanks, as always, to the members of romanarmytalk.com, whose rapid answers to my odd questions are so often of great use.

I owe gratitude too to a legion of people at my publishers, Random House. There's Selina Walker, my wonderful new editor; Katherine Murphy, my managing editor; latterly Rob Waddington, and more recently, Aslan Byrne, who worked and work to get my novels into every possible UK outlet; Jennifer Doyle, who organises some wonderfully inventive marketing; Richard Ogle who has designed my amazing new jackets; Amelia Harvell, who secures me all kinds of great publicity; Monique Corless and Caroline Sloan, who persuade so many foreign editors to buy my books; David Parrish, who makes sure that bookshops abroad do so too. My sincere thanks to you all. Your hard work is very much appreciated.

So many other people must be named: Charlie Viney, my agent, deserves my thanks as always. I'm appreciative of Richenda Todd, my copy editor, who provides highly incisive input; Claire Wheller, my first-class physio, who stops my body from falling to bits after spending too long at my PC; Arthur O'Connor, an old friend, who also supplies excellent criticism and improvements to my stories. Thanks also to you, my loyal readers. It's you who keep me in a job, for which I am endlessly grateful. Your emails from all over the world, and contacts on Facebook and Twitter, brighten up my days: please keep them coming! Last, but most definitely not least, I thank Sair, my wife, and Ferdia and Pippa, my children, for the huge amount of love and joy that they bring into my world.

Ways to contact me: email: ben@benkane.net

Twitter: @BenKaneAuthor

Facebook: facebook.com/benkanebooks

Glossary

acetum: vinegar, the most common disinfectant used by the Romans. Vinegar is excellent at killing bacteria, and its widespread use in western medicine continued until late in the nineteenth century.

aedile: a magistrate responsible for various civic duties in Rome.

Aesculapius: son of Apollo, the god of health and the protector of doctors. Revered by the Carthaginians as well as the Romans.

Agora: we have no idea what Carthaginians called the central meeting area in their city. I have used the Greek term to differentiate it from the main Forum in Rome. Without doubt, the Agora would have been the most important meeting place in Carthage.

Alps: In Latin, these mountains are called *Alpes*. Not used in the novel (unlike the Latin names for other geographical features) as it looks 'strange' to modern eyes.

amphora (pl. *amphorae*): a large, two-handled clay vessel with a narrow neck used to store wine, olive oil and other produce.

apodyterium: the room at the entrance to a Roman baths, where the customers undressed.

Apulia: a region of southeast Italy roughly equating to modern-day Puglia.

Ariminum: modern-day Rimini.

Arnus: the River Arno.

Arretium: modern-day Arezzo.

as (pl. *asses*): a small bronze coin.

atrium: the large chamber immediately beyond the entrance hall in a Roman house. Frequently built on a grand scale, this was the social and devotional centre of the home.

Aufidius: the River Ofanto.

Baal Hammon: the pre-eminent god at the time of the founding of Carthage. He was the protector of the city, the fertilising sun, the provider of wealth and the guarantor of success and happiness. The Tophet, or the sacred area where Baal Hammon was worshipped, is the site where the bones of children and babies have been found, giving rise to the controversial topic of child sacrifice. For those who are interested, there is an excellent discussion on the issue in Richard Miles's book, *Carthage Must Be Destroyed*. The term 'Baal' means 'Master' or 'Lord', and was used before the name of various gods.

Baal Saphon: the Carthaginian god of war.

Caere: modern-day Cerveteri.

caetrati (sing. *caetratus*): light Iberian infantry. They wore short-sleeved white tunics with a crimson border at the neck, hem and sleeves. Their only protection was a helmet of sinew or bronze, and a round buckler of leather and wicker, or wood, called a *caetra*. They were armed with *falcata* swords and daggers.

caldarium: an intensely hot room in Roman bath complexes. Used like a modern-day sauna, most also had a hot plunge pool. The *caldarium* was heated by hot air which flowed through hollow bricks in the walls and under the raised floor. The source of the piped heat was the *hypocaustum*, a furnace constantly kept hot by slaves.

caligae: heavy leather sandals worn by the Roman soldier. Sturdily constructed in three layers – a sole, insole and upper – *caligae* resembled an open-toed boot. The straps could be tightened to make them fit more closely. Dozens of metal studs on the sole gave the sandals good grip; these could also be replaced when necessary.

Campania: a fertile region of west central Italy.

Cannae: modern-day Canne della Battaglia, a site about 12 kilometres west of the town of Barletta, in Apulia.

Canusium: modern-day Canosa di Puglia.

Capua: modern-day Santa Maria Capua Vetere, near Naples, in Campania. In the third century BC, it was the second largest city in Italy and had not long been under the control of Rome.

carnyx (pl. carnyxes): a bronze trumpet, which was held vertically and topped by a bell shaped in the form of an animal, usually a boar.

Used by many Celtic peoples, it was ubiquitous in Gaul, and provided
a fearsome sound alone or in unison with other instruments. It was
often depicted on Roman coins, to denote victories over various
tribes.

Carthage: modern-day Tunis. It was reputedly founded in 814 BC,
although the earliest archaeological finds date from about sixty years
later.

cenaculae (sing. *cenacula*): the miserable multi-storey flats in which Roman
plebeians lived. Cramped, poorly lit, heated only by braziers, and often
dangerously constructed, the *cenaculae* had no running water or sanita-
tion. Access to the flats was via staircases built on the outside of the
building.

centurion (in Latin, *centurio*): disciplined career officer; centurions formed
the backbone of the Roman army. See also entry for maniple.

Ceres: the goddess of agriculture, grain crops and fertility.

Choma: the man-made quadrilateral area which lay to the south and
southeast of the main harbours in Carthage. It was probably constructed
to serve as a place to unload ships, to store goods, and to act as a pier
head protecting passing vessels from the worst of the wind.

Cisalpine Gaul: the northern area of modern-day Italy, comprising the Po
plain and its mountain borders from the Alps to the Apennines. In the
third century BC, it was not part of the Republic.

consul: one of two annually elected chief magistrates, appointed by the people
and ratified by the Senate. Effective rulers of Rome for twelve months,
they were in charge of civil and military matters and led the Republic's
armies into war. If in the field together, each man took charge of the
army on alternate days. In other circumstances, each could countermand
the other; both were supposed to heed the wishes of the Senate. No man
was meant to serve as consul more than once, although in practice this
was not the case.

contubernium (pl. *contubernia*): a group of eight legionaries who shared a
tent and who cooked and ate together.

crucifixion: contrary to popular belief, the Romans did not invent this awful
form of execution; in fact, the Carthaginians may well have done so.
The practice is first recorded during the Punic wars.

decurion: the cavalry officer in charge of ten men. In later times, the decurion commanded a *turma*, a unit of about thirty men

Diana: the goddess of the hunt, the moon and of childbirth.

dictator: in times of great crisis, the Senate could elect a dictator, a magistrate who, for six months, had supreme control over all other magistrates, and of the entire Republic. His second-in-command was called the Master of the Horse (a reference to cavalry).

didrachm: a silver coin, worth two drachmas, which was one of the main coins in third century BC Italy. Strangely, the Romans did not mint many coins of their own design until later on. The *denarius*, which was to become the main coin of the Republic, was not introduced until around 211 BC.

drachm: a silver coin of Greek denomination. See entry above.

equestrian: a Roman nobleman, ranking just below the class of senator. In the third century BC, men such as these provided the regular cavalry for the Roman army.

Eshmoun: the Carthaginian god of health and well-being, whose temple was the largest in Carthage.

Etruria: a region of central Italy, north of Rome and the homeland of the Etruscans, a people who had dominated much of northern Italy before the rise of Rome.

falcata sword: a lethal, slightly curved weapon with a sharp point used by light Iberian infantry. It was single-edged for the first half to two-thirds of its blade, but the remainder was double-edged. The hilt curved protectively around the hand and back towards the blade; it was often made in the shape of a horse's head. Apparently, the *caetrati* who used *falcata* swords were well able to fight legionaries.

Fides: the goddess of trust.

Fortuna: the goddess of luck and good fortune. Like all deities, she was notoriously fickle.

frigidarium: a room in Roman baths containing a cold plunge pool. It was often the last chamber in a bathing complex.

fugitivus: a runaway slave. The punishment branding the letter 'F' (for *fugitivus*) on the forehead is documented; so is the wearing of permanent neck chains, which had directions on how to return the slave to his or her owner.

Genua: modern-day Genoa.

Gerunium: an ancient town in Samnium, the modern-day location of which is not known. It lay close to Larinum (modern-day Larino).

gladius (pl. *gladii*): little information remains about the 'Spanish' sword of the Republican army, the *gladius hispaniensis*, with its waisted blade. It is not clear when it was adopted by the Romans, but it was probably after encountering the weapon during the First Punic War, when it was used by Celtiberian troops. The shaped hilt was made of bone and protected by a pommel and guard of wood. The *gladius* was worn on the right, except by centurions and other senior officers, who wore it on the left. It was actually quite easy to draw with the right hand, and was probably positioned like this to avoid entanglement with the *scutum* while being unsheathed.

gugga: In Plautus' comedy *Poenulus* one of the Roman characters refers to a Carthaginian trader as a 'gugga'. This insult can be translated as 'little rat'.

Hades: the underworld – hell. The god of the underworld was also called Hades.

hastati (sing. *hastatus*): experienced young soldiers who formed the first ranks in the Roman battle line in the third century BC. They were armed with mail or bronze breast and back plates, crested helmets, and *scuta*. They carried two *pila*, one light and one heavy, and a *gladius hispaniensis*.

Hercules (or, more correctly, Heracles): the greatest of Greek heroes, who completed twelve monumentally difficult labours.

Iberia: the modern-day Iberian Peninsula, encompassing Spain and Portugal.

Illyrian: someone from Illyricum (or Illyria): the Roman name for the lands that lay across the Adriatic Sea from Italy, including parts of modern-day Slovenia, Serbia, Croatia, Serbia, Bosnia and Montenegro.

Insubres: a tribe of Gauls.

Juno: sister and wife of Jupiter, she was the Roman goddess of marriage and women.

Jupiter: often referred to as Optimus Maximus – 'Greatest and Best'. Most powerful of the Roman gods, he was responsible for weather, especially storms.

lararium: a shrine found in Roman homes, where the household gods were worshipped.

Larinum: modern-day Larino.

latrones (sing. *latro*): thieves or brigands.

licium: linen loincloth worn by nobles. It is likely that all classes wore a variant of this.

Ligurians: natives of the coastal area that was bounded to the west by the River Rhône and to the east by the River Arno.

maniple: the main tactical unit of the Roman army in the third century BC. There were thirty maniples in a legion, and a total of about 4,200 men. Each maniple was commanded by two centurions, one more senior than the other. Maniples of *hastati* and *principes* were composed of two centuries of sixty legionaries; forty *velites* were also attached to each unit. A maniple of *triarii*, however, was smaller. It was composed of two centuries of thirty men each, and forty *velites*.

Mars: the Roman god of war.

Melqart: a Carthaginian god associated with the sea, and with Hercules. He was also the god most favoured by the Barca family. Hannibal notably made a pilgrimage to Melqart's shrine in southern Iberia before beginning his war on Rome.

Minerva: the Roman goddess of war and also of wisdom.

mollis: Latin word, meaning 'soft' or 'gentle', here used as a term of abuse for a homosexual.

Ocriculum: near modern-day Otricoli.

optiones (sing. *optio*): the officers who ranked immediately below centurions; an *optio* was the second-in-command of a century.

Oscans: ancient inhabitants of much of southern Italy, most especially Campania.

Padus: the River Po.

papaverum: the drug morphine. Made from the flowers of the opium plant, its use has been documented from at least 1,000 BC.

phalanx: the traditional tactical unit of Greek armies, and, it is thought, of the Libyan spearmen who fought for Carthage.

phalera (pl. *phalerae*): a sculpted disc-like decoration for bravery which was worn on a chest harness over a Roman soldier's armour. *Phalerae* were commonly made of bronze, but could be made of more precious metals as well.

Phoenicians: a seafaring, merchant people who lived mostly on the coastline of modern-day Lebanon. They were the founders of Carthage.

pilum (pl. *pila*): the Roman javelin. It consisted of a wooden shaft approximately 1.2 m (4 ft) long, joined to a thin iron shank approximately 0.6 m (2 ft) long, and was topped by a small pyramidal point. The javelin was heavy and, when launched, all of its weight was concentrated behind the head, giving it tremendous penetrative force. It could strike through a shield to injure the man carrying it, or lodge in the shield, making it impossible for the man to continue using it. The range of the *pilum* was about 30 m (100 ft), although the effective range was probably about half this distance.

Placentia: modern-day Piacenza.

porta decumana: one of the four entrances to a marching camp. It was found on one of the two short sides of the camp (which was roughly rectangular) opposite the *porta praetoria*, which lay close to the commanders' quarters. The *via praetoria* linked these two gates, and the *via principalis* the other two.

porta praetoria: see entry above.

principes (sing. *princeps*): these soldiers – described as family men in their prime – formed the second rank of the Roman battle line in the third century BC. They were similar to the *hastati*, and as such were armed and dressed in much the same manner.

proconsul: a magistrate who operated outside Rome in place of a consul. His position lay outside the normal annual magistracy and was usually used for military purposes, i.e. to conduct a war on Rome's behalf.

pteryges: also spelt *pteruges*. These were a twin layer of stiffened linen strips that protected the waist and groin of the wearer. They either came attached to a cuirass of the same material, or as a detachable piece of equipment to be used below a bronze breastplate. Although *pteryges* were designed by the Greeks, many nations used them, including the Romans and Carthaginians.

Rhodanus: the River Rhône.

Saguntum: modern-day Sagunto. In the late third century BC, it was populated by Greeks and had allied itself to Rome in an effort to resist Carthaginian influence. When Hannibal attacked it in the spring of 219 BC, he did so in the knowledge that it would provoke a war with Rome.

Samnium: a confederated area in the central southern Apennines. It fought three wars against Rome in the fourth and third centuries BC, losing the final one. The Samnites did not rest easily under Roman rule, however. They backed both Pyrrhus of Epirus and Hannibal in their wars against the Republic.

scutarii (sing. *scutarius*): heavy Iberian infantry, Celtiberians who carried round shields, or ones very similar to those of the Roman legionaries. Richer individuals may have had mail shirts; others may have worn leather cuirasses. Many *scutarii* wore greaves. Their bronze helmets were very similar to the Gallic Montefortino style. They were armed with straight-edged swords that were slightly shorter than the Gaulish equivalent, and known for their excellent quality.

scutum (pl. *scuta*): an elongated oval Roman army shield, about 1.2 m (4 ft) tall and 0.75 m (2 ft 6 in) wide. It was made from two or three layers of wood, the pieces laid at right angles to each other; it was then covered with linen or canvas, and leather. The *scutum* was heavy, weighing between 6 and 10 kg (13–22 lbs). A large metal boss decorated its centre, with the horizontal grip placed behind this. Decorative designs were often painted on the front, and a wooden spine ran down the front of it. A leather cover was used to protect the shield when not in use, e.g. while marching. Some of the Iberian and Gaulish warriors used very similar shields.

Senate: a body of three hundred senators who were prominent Roman noblemen. The Senate met in the Curia in central Rome, and its function was to advise the magistrates – the consuls, praetors, quaestors etc. – on domestic and foreign policy, religion and finance.

Seres: the Roman name for the Chinese people.

Sibylline Books: ancient texts stored in the temple of Jupiter in Rome, and reputed to have been written by the Sibyls, mythical oracles.

signifer (pl. *signiferi*): a standard-bearer and junior officer. This was a position of high esteem, with one for every century in a legion.

socii: allies of Rome. By the time of the Punic wars, all the non-Roman peoples of Italy had been forced into military alliances with Rome. In theory, these peoples were still independent, but in practice they were subjects, who were obliged to send quotas of troops to fight for the Republic whenever it was demanded.

strigil: a small, curved iron tool used to clean the skin after bathing. First perfumed oil was rubbed in, and then the *strigil* was used to scrape off the combination of sweat, dirt and oil.

tablinum: the office or reception area beyond the *atrium*. The *tablinum* usually opened on to an enclosed colonnaded garden, the peristyle.

Tanit: along with Baal Hammon, the pre-eminent deity in Carthage. She was regarded as a mother goddess, and as the patroness and protector of the city.

Telamon: modern-day Talamone, in Tuscany. In 225 BC, it was the site of an enormous battle between the Romans and an army of invading Gauls, which was heading south for Rome.

tesserae: pieces of stone or marble which were cut into roughly cubic shape and fitted closely on to a bed of mortar to form a mosaic. This practice was introduced in the third century BC.

tepidarium: the largest area in a Roman baths and often where bathers met and talked. Containing a large, warm pool, it was a place to linger.

Ticinus: the River Ticino.

Trasimene: the modern-day Lago Trasimeno, in north-central Italy, close to Perugia and Siena.

Trebia: the River Trebbia.

triarii (sing. *triarius*): the oldest, most experienced soldiers in a legion of the third century BC. These men were often held back until the most desperate of situations in a battle. The fantastic Roman expression 'Matters have come down to the *triarii*' makes this clear. They wore bronze crested helmets, mail shirts and a greave on their leading (left) legs. They each carried a *scutum*, and were armed with a *gladius hispaniensis* and a long, thrusting spear.

tribune: senior staff officer within a legion; also one of ten political positions in Rome, where they served as 'tribunes of the people', defending the rights of the plebeians. The tribunes could also veto measures taken by the Senate or consuls, except in times of war. To assault a tribune was a crime of the highest order.

triplex acies: the standard deployment of a legion for battle. Three lines were formed some distance apart, with four cohorts in the front line and three in the middle and rear lines.

triumph: the procession to the temple of Jupiter on the Capitoline Hill of a Roman general who had won a large-scale military victory.

turma (pl. *turmae*): a cavalry unit of thirty men.

velites (sing. *veles*): light skirmishers of the third century BC who were recruited from the poorest social class. They were young men whose only protection was a small, round shield and, in some cases, a simple bronze helmet. They carried a sword, but their primary weapons were 1.2-m (4-ft) javelins. They also wore wolf-skin headdresses of some kind. It's unclear if the *velites* had any officers.

Venusia: modern-day Venosa.

Vestal Virgins: the only female priesthood in Rome, who served Vesta, the goddess of the hearth.

Via Appia: the main road from Rome to Brundisium (modern-day Brindisi) in the far south of Italy.

Via Latina: in the third century BC, this road ran south from Rome, through the country of the Latins and into Campania.

via praetoria: see entry under *porta decumana*.

via principalis: see entry under *porta decumana*.

Victumulae: a town in the vicinity of Placentia (modern-day Piacenza) in northern Italy. Its exact location is unknown.

Volturnus: the River Volturno.

Vulcan (or Vulcanus): a Roman god of destructive fire, who was often worshipped to prevent – fire!

About Ben Kane

When I was a boy, we had no TV at home, which is perhaps the reason I became an avid reader. I read just about any genre, but especially military and historical fiction. Yet my love of animals won out when it came to leaving school, and I trained as a veterinary surgeon. After spells of working in Ireland and the UK, my itchy feet took me abroad in 1997. The travelling bug bit me hard. For three and a half years, I returned only to earn enough money to travel again. It was during this time that I first had thoughts of writing historical military fiction.

I came back to the UK in early 2001 as the terrible foot-and-mouth disease outbreak began. I volunteered immediately and spent nearly a year working in Northumberland. Supervising the slaughter of livestock was truly awful, but I was able to visit the Roman sites along Hadrian's Wall as well. My imagination ran riot in every place I visited, wondering what the Italian legionaries first posted there must have thought. It was then that my determination to become a writer of historical fiction took firm root. What started as a hobby became an obsession, and by 2006, I was writing *The Forgotten Legion*.

Landing a book deal in 2007 changed my life. After about 18 months, I was able to switch careers and become a fulltime writer and now I buy textbooks and military/civilian replica Roman items as part of my job! I also travel to the places that I write about; I see and feel and breathe them for myself. Over the last two years, I've followed Spartacus' trail across Italy; I've stood at Cannae, and pictured Hannibal's army meeting the massed legions of Rome; I've watched the sea lapping against the fortifications of Syracuse, where the Romans besieged the city for close to two years.

Writing about Roman history has become my world, as evidenced by the walk I did in April 2013 along Hadrian's Wall in full Roman military kit, raising money for the charities Combat Stress and Medecins sans Frontieres. You can find out more about my books, my research and the walk on my website.

Ben Kane, May 2013

CONNECT WITH
BEN KANE ONLINE

Be the first to hear Ben's news, find out all about his latest book releases and join the discussion at:

www.benkane.net

Become a fan on Facebook:

 www.facebook.com/benkanebooks

Follow Ben on Twitter:

@BenKaneAuthor